DOVER · THRIFT · EDITIONS

3 by Shakespeare

A Midsummer Night's Dream (Comedy)
Romeo and Juliet (Tragedy)
Richard III (History)

WILLIAM SHAKESPEARE

DOVER PUBLICATIONS, INC.
Mineola, New York

DOVER THRIFT EDITIONS

General Editor: Mary Carolyn Waldrep

Editor of This Volume: Jim Miller

Bibliographical Note

This Dover edition, first published in 2006, is a new collection and contains the unabridged texts of three plays: *A Midsummer Night's Dream* as published in Volume III of *The Caxton Edition of the Complete Works of William Shakespeare*, Caxton Publishing Company, London, n.d., and reprinted as a Dover Thrift Edition in 1992; *Romeo and Juliet* as published in Volume VI of the second edition of *The Works of William Shakespeare*, Macmillan and Co., London, 1892, and reprinted as a Dover Thrift Edition in 1993; and *Richard III* as published in Volume X of *The Caxton Edition of the Complete Works of William Shakespeare* and reprinted as a Dover Thrift Edition in 1995. Introductory notes were written, and footnotes revised or written anew, specially for the Dover editions.

Library of Congress Cataloging-in-Publication Data

Shakespeare, William, 1564–1616.
[Plays. Selections]
3 by Shakespeare / William Shakespeare.
p. cm. — (Dover thrift editions)
Contents: A midsummer night's dream (comedy) — Romeo and Juliet (tragedy) — Richard III (history).
ISBN 0-486-44721-9 (pbk.)
1. Romeo (Fictitious character)—Drama. 2. Juliet (Fictitious character)—Drama. 3. Richard III, King of England, 1452–1485—Drama. 4. Great Britain—History—Richard III, 1483–1485—Drama. 5. Athens (Greece)—Drama. 6. Verona (Italy)—Drama. 7. Courtship—Drama. I. Title: Three by Shakespeare. II. Shakespeare, William, 1564–1616, Midsummer night's dream. III. Shakespeare, William, 1564–1616. Romeo and Juliet. IV. Shakespeare, William, 1564–1616. King Richard III. V. Title. VI. Series.

PR2759 2006
822.3'3—dc22

2005052172

Manufactured in the United States of America
Dover Publications, Inc., 31 East 2nd Street, Mineola, N.Y. 11501

Contents

A Midsummer Night's Dream

Note

WILLIAM SHAKESPEARE (1564–1616) probably wrote *A Midsummer Night's Dream* between 1594 and 1595. In several respects the play heralds a movement away from the conventionality of the early toward the subtleties and ambiguities of the mature comedies. It demonstrates both Shakespeare's great facility for a wide range of verse forms and rhyme schemes, and his ability to bring together in a single work plots and characters derived from diverse literary sources. The story of the marriage of Theseus, Duke of Athens, and Hippolyta, Queen of the Amazons, was available to Shakespeare in two forms: in Chaucer's *Knight's Tale* and in Thomas North's *Lives of the noble Grecians and Romanes* (1579), a translation of Plutarch. The story of the crossed lovers Lysander, Hermia and Demetrius is also in Chaucer's work, though Shakespeare complicates things by introducing a second woman, Helena, and by playing on the vagaries of love. Bottom and his troupe of Athenian laborers provide an often hilarious depiction of the theatrical world of Elizabethan England. Their play-within-the-play, *Pyramus and Thisbe*, is derived from Arthur Golding's translation of Ovid's *Metamorphoses*. As for Bottom's transformation into an ass, Shakespeare's most likely source was Apuleius' *Golden Ass*, translated by William Adlington in 1566. English folklore and popular literature contained ample material on the "puck," Robin Goodfellow, whereas Oberon and Titania, King and Queen of the Fairies, appear in various literary works, both English and French. Of course, in *A Midsummer Night's Dream* these preexisting literary creations take on a new, inimitably Shakespearean, life.

The play is in part about the potentially tragic conflict between social order and the freedom of the imagination embodied in the young lovers. The experience of love unfolds as a journey away from the city, and the parental and political authority that governs there, into a sylvan realm of fantasy, dream and delusion. Marriage comes to symbolize the reconciliation of forces that in another context would remain in tragic opposition to one another. But, in a typically Shakespearean manner, the play turns upon the metaphor of the theater itself, questioning, sometimes mockingly, sometimes reverently, the nature of art and imagination, and their relationship to the world they reflect and transform.

Dramatis Personae

THESEUS, Duke of Athens.
EGEUS, father to Hermia.
LYSANDER, } in love with Hermia.
DEMETRIUS, }
PHILOSTRATE, master of the revels to Theseus.
QUINCE, a carpenter.
SNUG, a joiner.
BOTTOM, a weaver.
FLUTE, a bellows-mender.
SNOUT, a tinker.
STARVELING, a tailor.

HIPPOLYTA, Queen of the Amazons, betrothed to Theseus.
HERMIA, daughter to Egeus, in love with Lysander.
HELENA, in love with Demetrius.

OBERON, King of the Fairies.
TITANIA, Queen of the Fairies.
PUCK, or Robin Goodfellow.
PEASEBLOSSOM, }
COBWEB, } fairies.
MOTH, }
MUSTARDSEED, }

Other fairies attending their King and Queen. Attendants on Theseus and Hippolyta.

SCENE—*Athens, and a wood near it*

Act I—Scene I—Athens

THE PALACE OF THESEUS

Enter THESEUS, HIPPOLYTA, PHILOSTRATE, *and* Attendants.

THE. Now, fair Hippolyta, our nuptial hour
Draws on apace; four happy days bring in
Another moon: but, O, methinks, how slow
This old moon wanes! she lingers[1] my desires,
Like to a step-dame, or a dowager,
Long withering out a young man's revenue.

HIP. Four days will quickly steep themselves in night;
Four nights will quickly dream away the time,
And then the moon, like to a silver bow
New-bent in heaven, shall behold the night
Of our solemnities.[2]

THE. Go, Philostrate,
Stir up the Athenian youth to merriments;
Awake the pert[3] and nimble spirit of mirth:
Turn melancholy forth to funerals;
The pale companion is not for our pomp. [*Exit* PHILOSTRATE.
Hippolyta, I woo'd thee with my sword,
And won thy love, doing thee injuries;
But I will wed thee in another key,
With pomp, with triumph[4] and with revelling.

Enter EGEUS, HERMIA, LYSANDER, *and* DEMETRIUS.

1 *lingers*] prolongs.
2 *solemnities*] celebration (of the wedding).
3 *pert*] lively.
4 *triumph*] public festivity.

EGE. Happy be Theseus, our renownèd duke!
THE. Thanks, good Egeus: what's the news with thee?
EGE. Full of vexation come I, with complaint
Against my child, my daughter Hermia.
Stand forth, Demetrius. My noble lord,
This man hath my consent to marry her.
Stand forth, Lysander: and, my gracious duke,
This man hath bewitch'd the bosom[5] of my child:
Thou, thou, Lysander, thou hast given her rhymes,
And interchanged love-tokens with my child:
Thou hast by moonlight at her window sung,
With feigning[6] voice, verses of feigning love;
And stolen the impression of her fantasy[7]
With bracelets of thy hair, rings, gawds, conceits,[8]
Knacks,[9] trifles, nosegays, sweetmeats, messengers
Of strong prevailment[10] in unharden'd[11] youth:
With cunning hast thou filch'd my daughter's heart;
Turn'd her obedience, which is due to me,
To stubborn harshness: and, my gracious duke,
Be it so she will not here before your Grace
Consent to marry with Demetrius,
I beg the ancient privilege of Athens,
As she is mine, I may dispose of her:
Which shall be either to this gentleman
Or to her death, according to our law
Immediately[12] provided in that case.
THE. What say you, Hermia? be advised, fair maid:
To you your father should be as a god;
One that composed your beauties; yea, and one
To whom you are but as a form in wax
By him imprinted and within his power
To leave the figure or disfigure it.
Demetrius is a worthy gentleman.
HER. So is Lysander.

[5] *bosom*] heart.
[6] *feigning*] soft.
[7] *stolen . . . fantasy*] captured her imagination and love.
[8] *gawds, conceits*] baubles, fanciful presents.
[9] *Knacks*] knickknacks.
[10] *prevailment*] influence.
[11] *unharden'd*] impressionable.
[12] *Immediately*] expressly.

THE. In himself he is;
But in this kind, wanting your father's voice,[13]
The other must be held the worthier.
HER. I would my father look'd but with my eyes.
THE. Rather your eyes must with his judgement look.
HER. I do entreat your Grace to pardon me.
I know not by what power I am made bold,
Nor how it may concern[14] my modesty,
In such a presence here to plead my thoughts;
But I beseech your Grace that I may know
The worst that may befall me in this case,
If I refuse to wed Demetrius.
THE. Either to die the death, or to abjure
For ever the society of men.
Therefore, fair Hermia, question your desires;
Know of your youth, examine well your blood,
Whether, if you yield not to your father's choice,
You can endure the livery of a nun;
For aye[15] to be in shady cloister mew'd,[16]
To live a barren sister all your life,
Chanting faint hymns to the cold fruitless moon.
Thrice-blessed they that master so their blood,
To undergo such maiden pilgrimage;
But earthlier happy is the rose distill'd,[17]
Than that which, withering on the virgin thorn,
Grows, lives, and dies in single blessedness.
HER. So will I grow, so live, so die, my lord,
Ere I will yield my virgin patent[18] up
Unto his lordship, whose unwished yoke
My soul consents not to give sovereignty.
THE. Take time to pause; and, by the next new moon,—
The sealing-day betwixt my love and me,
For everlasting bond of fellowship,—
Upon that day either prepare to die
For disobedience to your father's will,

[13] *in this kind . . . voice*] in business of this nature, lacking your father's approval.
[14] *concern*] befit.
[15] *aye*] ever.
[16] *mew'd*] confined.
[17] *earthlier . . . distill'd*] i.e., happier on earth is the one who will live on after death through his or her child.
[18] *virgin patent*] privilege of remaining a virgin.

Or else to wed Demetrius, as he would;
Or on Diana's altar to protest[19]
For aye austerity and single life.

DEM. Relent, sweet Hermia: and, Lysander, yield
Thy crazed title[20] to my certain right.

LYS. You have her father's love, Demetrius;
Let me have Hermia's: do you marry him.

EGE. Scornful Lysander! true, he hath my love,
And what is mine my love shall render him.
And she is mine, and all my right of her
I do estate unto Demetrius.

LYS. I am, my lord, as well derived[21] as he,
As well possess'd;[22] my love is more than his;
My fortunes every way as fairly rank'd,
If not with vantage,[23] as Demetrius';
And, which is more than all these boasts can be,
I am beloved of beauteous Hermia:
Why should not I then prosecute my right?
Demetrius, I'll avouch it to his head,[24]
Made love to Nedar's daughter, Helena,
And won her soul; and she, sweet lady, dotes,
Devoutly dotes, dotes in idolatry,
Upon this spotted[25] and inconstant man.

THE. I must confess that I have heard so much,
And with Demetrius thought to have spoke thereof;
But, being over-full of self-affairs,
My mind did lose it. But, Demetrius, come;
And come, Egeus; you shall go with me,
I have some private schooling[26] for you both.
For you, fair Hermia, look you arm yourself
To fit your fancies[27] to your father's will;
Or else the law of Athens yields you up,—
Which by no means we may extenuate,—[28]

[19] *protest*] vow.
[20] *crazed title*] invalid claim.
[21] *well derived*] nobly born.
[22] *well possess'd*] wealthy.
[23] *vantage*] superiority.
[24] *avouch it to his head*] declare it in his presence.
[25] *spotted*] guilty.
[26] *schooling*] admonition.
[27] *fancies*] thoughts of love.
[28] *extenuate*] mitigate.

To death, or to a vow of single life.
Come, my Hippolyta: what cheer, my love?
Demetrius and Egeus, go along:
I must employ you in some business
Against[29] our nuptial, and confer with you
Of something nearly that concerns yourselves.

EGE. With duty and desire we follow you.

[*Exeunt all but* LYSANDER *and* HERMIA.

LYS. How now, my love! why is your cheek so pale?
How chance the roses there do fade so fast?

HER. Belike for want of rain, which I could well
Beteem[30] them from the tempest of my eyes.

LYS. Ay me! for aught that I could ever read,
Could ever hear by tale or history,
The course of true love never did run smooth;
But, either it was different in blood,—

HER. O cross![31] too high to be enthrall'd to low.

LYS. Or else misgraffed in respect of years,—

HER. O spite! too old to be engaged to young.

LYS. Or else it stood upon the choice of friends,—

HER. O hell! to choose love by another's eyes.

LYS. Or, if there were a sympathy in choice,
War, death, or sickness did lay siege to it,
Making it momentany as a sound,
Swift as a shadow, short as any dream;
Brief as the lightning in the collied[32] night,
That, in a spleen,[33] unfolds both heaven and earth,
And ere a man hath power to say "Behold!"
The jaws of darkness do devour it up:
So quick bright things come to confusion.[34]

HER. If then true lovers have been ever cross'd,[35]
It stands as an edict in destiny:
Then let us teach our trial patience,
Because it is a customary cross,

[29] *against*] in preparation for.
[30] *Beteem*] grant.
[31] *cross*] The cross symbolizes here that which thwarts or hinders.
[32] *collied*] dark.
[33] *spleen*] fit of passion.
[34] *confusion*] ruin.
[35] *ever cross'd*] always thwarted.

As due to love as thoughts and dreams and sighs,
Wishes and tears, poor fancy's followers.

LYS. A good persuasion:[36] therefore, hear me, Hermia.
I have a widow aunt, a dowager
Of great revenue, and she hath no child:
From Athens is her house remote seven leagues;
And she respects me as[37] her only son.
There, gentle Hermia, may I marry thee;
And to that place the sharp Athenian law
Cannot pursue us. If thou lovest me, then,
Steal forth thy father's house to-morrow night;
And in the wood, a league without the town,
Where I did meet thee once with Helena,
To do observance to a morn of May,[38]
There will I stay for thee.

HER. My good Lysander!
I swear to thee, by Cupid's strongest bow,
By his best arrow with the golden head,
By the simplicity of Venus' doves,
By that which knitteth souls and prospers loves,
And by that fire which burn'd the Carthage queen,
When the false Troyan[39] under sail was seen,
By all the vows that ever men have broke,
In number more than ever women spoke,
In that same place thou hast appointed me,
To-morrow truly will I meet with thee.

LYS. Keep promise, love. Look, here comes Helena.

Enter HELENA.

HER. God speed fair Helena! whither away?

HEL. Call you me fair? that fair again unsay.
Demetrius loves your fair: O happy fair!
Your eyes are lode-stars;[40] and your tongue's sweet air
More tuneable[41] than lark to shepherd's ear,
When wheat is green, when hawthorn buds appear.
Sickness is catching: O, were favour so,

[36] *persuasion*] opinion.
[37] *respects me as*] thinks of me as.
[38] *do observance to a morn of May*] celebrate May Day.
[39] *false Troyan*] Aeneas, who abandoned his lover Dido, Queen of Carthage.
[40] *lode-stars*] stars that guide and attract.
[41] *tuneable*] harmonious.

Yours would I catch, fair Hermia, ere I go;
My ear should catch your voice, my eye your eye,
My tongue should catch your tongue's sweet melody.
Were the world mine, Demetrius being bated,[42]
The rest I'ld give to be to you translated.[43]
O, teach me how you look; and with what art
You sway the motion[44] of Demetrius' heart!

HER. I frown upon him, yet he loves me still.

HEL. O that your frowns would teach my smiles such skill!

HER. I give him curses, yet he gives me love.

HEL. O that my prayers could such affection move![45]

HER. The more I hate, the more he follows me.

HEL. The more I love, the more he hateth me.

HER. His folly, Helena, is no fault of mine.

HEL. None, but your beauty: would that fault were mine!

HER. Take comfort: he no more shall see my face;
Lysander and myself will fly this place.
Before the time I did Lysander see,
Seem'd Athens as a paradise to me:
O, then, what graces in my love do dwell,
That he hath turn'd a heaven unto a hell!

LYS. Helen, to you our minds we will unfold:
To-morrow night, when Phoebe[46] doth behold
Her silver visage in the watery glass,[47]
Decking with liquid pearl the bladed grass,
A time that lovers' flights doth still conceal,
Through Athens' gates have we devised to steal.

HER. And in the wood, where often you and I
Upon faint[48] primrose-beds were wont to lie,
Emptying our bosoms of their counsel sweet,
There my Lysander and myself shall meet;
And thence from Athens turn away our eyes,
To seek new friends and stranger companies.
Farewell, sweet playfellow: pray thou for us;
And good luck grant thee thy Demetrius!

[42] *bated*] excepted.
[43] *to you translated*] transformed into you.
[44] *sway the motion*] control the impulse.
[45] *such affection move*] arouse such passion.
[46] *Phoebe*] the goddess of the moon.
[47] *glass*] mirror.
[48] *faint*] pale.

Keep word, Lysander: we must starve our sight
From lovers' food till morrow deep midnight.

LYS. I will, my Hermia. [*Exit* HERMIA.
Helena, adieu:
As you on him, Demetrius dote on you! [*Exit*.

HEL. How happy some o'er other some can be!
Through Athens I am thought as fair as she.
But what of that? Demetrius thinks not so;
He will not know what all but he do know:
And as he errs, doting on Hermia's eyes,
So I, admiring of his qualities:
Things base and vile, holding no quantity,[49]
Love can transpose to form and dignity:
Love looks not with the eyes, but with the mind;
And therefore is wing'd Cupid painted blind:
Nor hath Love's mind of any judgement taste;
Wings, and no eyes, figure[50] unheedy haste:
And therefore is Love said to be a child,
Because in choice he is so oft beguiled.
As waggish boys in game themselves forswear,
So the boy Love is perjured everywhere:
For ere Demetrius look'd on Hermia's eyne,[51]
He hail'd down oaths that he was only mine;
And when this hail some heat from Hermia felt,
So he dissolved, and showers of oaths did melt.
I will go tell him of fair Hermia's flight:
Then to the wood will he to-morrow night
Pursue her; and for this intelligence
If I have thanks, it is a dear expense:
But herein mean I to enrich my pain,
To have his sight thither and back again. [*Exit*.

[49] *holding no quantity*] not having the value given them.
[50] *figure*] symbolize.
[51] *eyne*] eyes.

Scene II—The same

QUINCE'S HOUSE

Enter QUINCE, SNUG, BOTTOM, FLUTE, SNOUT, *and* STARVELING.

QUIN. Is all our company here?

BOT. You were best to call them generally,[1] man by man, according to the scrip.[2]

QUIN. Here is the scroll of every man's name, which is thought fit, through all Athens, to play in our interlude[3] before the duke and the duchess, on his wedding-day at night.

BOT. First, good Peter Quince, say what the play treats on; then read the names of the actors; and so grow to a point.[4]

QUIN. Marry, our play is, The most lamentable comedy, and most cruel death of Pyramus and Thisbe.

BOT. A very good piece of work, I assure you, and a merry. Now, good Peter Quince, call forth your actors by the scroll. Masters, spread yourselves.

QUIN. Answer as I call you. Nick Bottom, the weaver.

BOT. Ready. Name what part I am for, and proceed.

QUIN. You, Nick Bottom, are set down for Pyramus.

BOT. What is Pyramus? a lover, or a tyrant?

QUIN. A lover, that kills himself most gallant for love.

BOT. That will ask some tears in the true performing of it: if I do it, let the audience look to their eyes; I will move storms, I will condole[5] in some measure. To the rest: yet my chief humour[6] is for a tyrant: I could play Ercles[7] rarely, or a part to tear a cat in, to make all split.[8]

The raging rocks
And shivering shocks
Shall break the locks
Of prison-gates;

[1] *generally*] Bottom's malapropism for "severally" (one by one).
[2] *scrip*] written list.
[3] *interlude*] short play.
[4] *grow to a point*] get to the end.
[5] *condole*] show signs of lamentation.
[6] *humour*] inclination.
[7] *Ercles*] Hercules.
[8] *a part . . . split*] a dramatic role that allows for ranting and extravagant gestures.

And Phibbus' car[9]
Shall shine from far,
And make and mar
The foolish Fates.

This was lofty! Now name the rest of the players. This is Ercles' vein, a tyrant's vein; a lover is more condoling.

QUIN. Francis Flute, the bellows-mender.

FLU. Here, Peter Quince.

QUIN. Flute, you must take Thisbe on you.

FLU. What is Thisbe? a wandering knight?[10]

QUIN. It is the lady that Pyramus must love.

FLU. Nay, faith, let not me play a woman; I have a beard coming.

QUIN. That's all one: you shall play it in a mask, and you may speak as small[11] as you will.

BOT. An[12] I may hide my face, let me play Thisbe too, I'll speak in a monstrous little voice, "Thisne, Thisne;" "Ah Pyramus, my lover dear! thy Thisbe dear, and lady dear!"

QUIN. No, no; you must play Pyramus: and, Flute, you Thisbe.

BOT. Well, proceed.

QUIN. Robin Starveling, the tailor.

STAR. Here, Peter Quince.

QUIN. Robin Starveling, you must play Thisbe's mother. Tom Snout, the tinker.

SNOUT. Here, Peter Quince.

QUIN. You, Pyramus' father: myself, Thisbe's father: Snug, the joiner; you, the lion's part: and, I hope, here is a play fitted.

SNUG. Have you the lion's part written? pray you, if it be, give it me, for I am slow of study.

QUIN. You may do it extempore, for it is nothing but roaring.

BOT. Let me play the lion too: I will roar, that I will do any man's heart good to hear me; I will roar, that I will make the duke say, "Let him roar again, let him roar again."

QUIN. An you should do it too terribly, you would fright the duchess and the ladies, that they would shriek; and that were enough to hang us all.

ALL. That would hang us, every mother's son.

[9] *Phibbus' car*] Phoebus Apollo's chariot, the sun.
[10] *wandering knight*] knight-errant.
[11] *as small*] in as clear and high-pitched a voice.
[12] *An*] if.

BOT. I grant you, friends, if you should fright the ladies out of their wits, they would have no more discretion but to hang us: but I will aggravate[13] my voice so, that I will roar you as gently as any sucking dove; I will roar you an't were any nightingale.

QUIN. You can play no part but Pyramus; for Pyramus is a sweet-faced man; a proper[14] man, as one shall see in a summer's day; a most lovely, gentleman-like man: therefore you must needs play Pyramus.

BOT. Well, I will undertake it. What beard were I best to play it in?

QUIN. Why, what you will.

BOT. I will discharge[15] it in either your straw colour beard, your orange-tawny beard, your purple-in-grain[16] beard, or your French crown[17] colour beard, your perfect yellow.

QUIN. Some of your French crowns[18] have no hair at all, and then you will play barefaced. But, masters, here are your parts: and I am to entreat you, request you, and desire you, to con[19] them by tomorrow night; and meet me in the palace wood, a mile without the town, by moonlight; there will we rehearse, for if we meet in the city, we shall be dogged with company, and our devices known. In the mean time I will draw a bill of properties, such as our play wants. I pray you, fail me not.

BOT. We will meet; and there we may rehearse most obscenely[20] and courageously. Take pains; be perfect:[21] adieu.

QUIN. At the duke's oak we meet.

BOT. Enough; hold or cut bow-strings.[22]

[*Exeunt*.

[13] *aggravate*] Bottom's malapropism for "diminish" (tone down).

[14] *proper*] handsome.

[15] *discharge*] perform.

[16] *purple-in-grain*] scarlet or crimson.

[17] *crown*] coin.

[18] *crowns*] heads, bald as a result of syphilis.

[19] *con*] memorize.

[20] *obscenely*] Bottom's error for "seemly."

[21] *perfect*] word-perfect.

[22] *hold . . . bow-strings*] i.e., be there or give up the play altogether.

Act II—Scene I—A wood near Athens

Enter, from opposite sides, a FAIRY *and* PUCK.

PUCK. How now, spirit! whither wander you?
FAI. Over hill, over dale,
Thorough[1] bush, thorough brier,
Over park, over pale,
Thorough flood, thorough fire,
I do wander every where,
Swifter than the moon's sphere;
And I serve the fairy queen,
To dew her orbs upon the green.[2]
The cowslips tall her pensioners[3] be:
In their gold coats spots you see;
Those be rubies, fairy favours,
In those freckles live their savours:[4]
I must go seek some dewdrops here,
And hang a pearl in every cowslip's ear.
Farewell, thou lob of[5] spirits; I'll be gone:
Our queen and all her elves come here anon.
PUCK. The king doth keep his revels here to-night:
Take heed the queen come not within his sight;
For Oberon is passing fell and wrath,[6]
Because that she as her attendant hath

[1] *Thorough*] through.
[2] *To dew her orbs upon the green*] to sprinkle with dew the fairy rings on the village green.
[3] *pensioners*] bodyguards.
[4] *their savours*] the cowslips' fragrance.
[5] *lob of*] country bumpkin among.
[6] *passing fell and wrath*] exceedingly fierce and angry.

A lovely boy, stolen from an Indian king;
She never had so sweet a changeling:[7]
And jealous Oberon would have the child
Knight of his train, to trace[8] the forests wild;
But she perforce[9] withholds the loved boy,
Crowns him with flowers, and makes him all her joy:
And now they never meet in grove or green,
By fountain clear, or spangled starlight sheen,
But they do square,[10] that all their elves for fear
Creep into acorn cups and hide them there.

FAI. Either I mistake your shape and making quite,
Or else you are that shrewd[11] and knavish sprite
Call'd Robin Goodfellow:[12] are not you he
That frights the maidens of the villagery;
Skim milk, and sometimes labour in the quern,[13]
And bootless[14] make the breathless housewife churn;
And sometime make the drink to bear no barm;[15]
Mislead night-wanderers, laughing at their harm?
Those that Hobgoblin call you, and sweet Puck,
You do their work, and they shall have good luck:
Are not you he?

PUCK. Thou speak'st aright;
I am that merry wanderer of the night.
I jest to Oberon, and make him smile,
When I a fat and bean-fed horse beguile,
Neighing in likeness of a filly foal:
And sometimes lurk I in a gossip's bowl,[16]
In very likeness of a roasted crab;[17]
And when she drinks, against her lips I bob
And on her withered dewlap[18] pour the ale.

[7] *changeling*] "Changeling" is normally the name for the frail fairy child left in place of a stolen child. In this instance, however, the changeling is the stolen child.
[8] *trace*] range.
[9] *perforce*] by means of force.
[10] *square*] quarrel.
[11] *shrewd*] mischievous.
[12] *Robin Goodfellow*] a mischievous sprite in English folklore.
[13] *quern*] hand mill for grinding grain.
[14] *bootless*] in vain.
[15] *barm*] yeast or froth.
[16] *a gossip's bowl*] a gossiping old woman's drink of spiced ale with crab apples.
[17] *crab*] crab apple.
[18] *dewlap*] wrinkled skin on the neck.

The wisest aunt,[19] telling the saddest tale,
Sometime for three-foot stool mistaketh me;
Then slip I from her bum, down topples she,
And "tailor" cries, and falls into a cough;
And then the whole quire[20] hold their hips and laugh;
And waxen in their mirth, and neeze,[21] and swear
A merrier hour was never wasted there.
But, room, fairy! here comes Oberon.

FAI. And here my mistress. Would that he were gone!

Enter, from one side, OBERON, *with his train; from the other,* TITANIA, *with hers.*

OBE. Ill met by moonlight, proud Titania.

TITA. What, jealous Oberon! Fairies, skip hence:
I have forsworn his bed and company.

OBE. Tarry, rash wanton: am not I thy lord?

TITA. Then I must be thy lady: but I know
When thou hast stolen away from fairy land,
And in the shape of Corin sat all day,
Playing on pipes of corn, and versing love
To amorous Phillida.[22] Why art thou here,
Come from the farthest steep of India?
But that, forsooth, the bouncing Amazon,
Your buskin'd[23] mistress and your warrior love,
To Theseus must be wedded, and you come
To give their bed joy and prosperity.

OBE. How canst thou thus for shame, Titania,
Glance at[24] my credit with Hippolyta,
Knowing I know thy love to Theseus?
Didst thou not lead him through the glimmering night
From Perigenia, whom he ravished?
And make him with fair Aegle break his faith,
With Ariadne and Antiopa?

TITA. These are the forgeries of jealousy:
And never, since the middle summer's spring,[25]

[19] *aunt*] old gossip.
[20] *quire*] company.
[21] *neeze*] sneeze.
[22] *Corin . . . Phillida*] traditional names for pastoral lovers.
[23] *buskin'd*] wearing buskins (laced boots reaching halfway to the knee).
[24] *Glance at*] hint at, censure.
[25] *middle summer's spring*] beginning of midsummer.

Met we on hill, in dale, forest, or mead,
By paved fountain or by rushy brook,
Or in[26] the beached margent[27] of the sea,
To dance our ringlets[28] to the whistling wind,
But with thy brawls thou hast disturb'd our sport.
Therefore the winds, piping to us in vain,
As in revenge, have suck'd up from the sea
Contagious fogs; which, falling in the land,
Have every pelting[29] river made so proud,
That they have overborne their continents:[30]
The ox hath therefore stretch'd his yoke in vain,
The ploughman lost his sweat; and the green corn
Hath rotted ere his youth attain'd a beard:
The fold stands empty in the drowned field,
And crows are fatted with the murrion[31] flock;
The nine men's morris[32] is fill'd up with mud;
And the quaint mazes in the wanton green,[33]
For lack of tread, are undistinguishable:
The human mortals want their winter here;[34]
No night is now with hymn or carol blest:
Therefore the moon, the governess of floods,
Pale in her anger, washes all the air,
That rheumatic diseases do abound:
And thorough this distemperature we see
The seasons alter: hoary-headed frosts
Fall in the fresh lap of the crimson rose;
And on old Hiems'[35] thin and icy crown
An odorous chaplet[36] of sweet summer buds
Is, as in mockery, set: the spring, the summer,
The childing[37] autumn, angry winter, change

[26] *in*] on.
[27] *margent*] edge.
[28] *ringlets*] circular dances.
[29] *pelting*] paltry.
[30] *continents*] banks.
[31] *murrion*] diseased.
[32] *nine men's morris*] a game played with nine counters on the village green.
[33] *quaint mazes in the wanton green*] labyrinthine figures made on the lush village green.
[34] *want . . . here*] lack their usual winter mood.
[35] *Hiems'*] Hiems is the personification of winter.
[36] *chaplet*] garland.
[37] *childing*] fruitful.

Their wonted liveries; and the mazed[38] world,
By their increase, now knows not which is which:
And this same progeny of evils comes
From our debate, from our dissension;
We are their parents and original.[39]

OBE. Do you amend it, then; it lies in you:
Why should Titania cross her Oberon?
I do but beg a little changeling boy,
To be my henchman.[40]

TITA. Set your heart at rest:
The fairy land buys not the child of me.
His mother was a votaress of my order:
And, in the spiced Indian air, by night,
Full often hath she gossip'd by my side;
And sat with me on Neptune's yellow sands,
Marking the embarked traders on the flood;
When we have laugh'd to see the sails conceive
And grow big-bellied with the wanton wind;
Which she, with pretty and with swimming gait[41]
Following,—her womb then rich with my young squire,—
Would imitate, and sail upon the land,
To fetch me trifles, and return again,
As from a voyage, rich with merchandise.
But she, being mortal, of that boy did die;
And for her sake do I rear up her boy;
And for her sake I will not part with him.

OBE. How long within this wood intend you stay?

TITA. Perchance till after Theseus' wedding-day.
If you will patiently dance in our round,
And see our moonlight revels, go with us;
If not, shun me, and I will spare your haunts.

OBE. Give me that boy, and I will go with thee.

TITA. Not for thy fairy kingdom. Fairies, away!
We shall chide downright, if I longer stay.
[*Exit* TITANIA *with her train.*

OBE. Well, go thy way: thou shalt not from this grove
Till I torment thee for this injury.

[38] *mazed*] perplexed.
[39] *original*] source.
[40] *henchman*] page boy.
[41] *swimming gait*] gliding step.

My gentle Puck, come hither. Thou rememberest
Since once I sat upon a promontory,
And heard a mermaid, on a dolphin's back,
Uttering such dulcet and harmonious breath,[42]
That the rude sea grew civil at her song,
And certain stars shot madly from their spheres,
To hear the sea-maid's music.

PUCK. I remember.

OBE. That very time I saw, but thou couldst not,
Flying between the cold moon and the earth,
Cupid all arm'd: a certain aim he took
At a fair vestal throned by the west,
And loosed his love-shaft smartly from his bow,
As it should pierce a hundred thousand hearts:
But I might see young Cupid's fiery shaft
Quench'd in the chaste beams of the watery moon,
And the imperial votaress passed on,
In maiden meditation, fancy-free.[43]
Yet mark'd I where the bolt of Cupid fell:
It fell upon a little western flower,
Before milk-white, now purple with love's wound,
And maidens call it love-in-idleness.[44]
Fetch me that flower; the herb I shew'd thee once:
The juice of it on sleeping eye-lids laid
Will make or man or woman madly dote
Upon the next live creature that it sees.
Fetch me this herb; and be thou here again
Ere the leviathan[45] can swim a league.

PUCK. I'll put a girdle round about the earth
In forty minutes. [*Exit.*

OBE. Having once this juice,
I'll watch Titania when she is asleep,
And drop the liquor of it in her eyes.
The next thing then she waking looks upon,
Be it on lion, bear, or wolf, or bull,
On meddling monkey, or on busy ape,
She shall pursue it with the soul of love:

42 *breath*] notes, words.
43 *fancy-free*] free from love.
44 *love-in-idleness*] a popular name for the pansy.
45 *leviathan*] sea monster.

And ere I take this charm from off her sight,
As I can take it with another herb,
I'll make her render up her page to me.
But who comes here? I am invisible;
And I will overhear their conference.

Enter DEMETRIUS, HELENA *following him.*

DEM. I love thee not, therefore pursue me not.
Where is Lysander and fair Hermia?
The one I'll slay, the other slayeth me.
Thou told'st me they were stolen unto this wood;
And here am I, and wode[46] within this wood;
Because I cannot meet my Hermia.
Hence, get thee gone, and follow me no more.
HEL. You draw me, you hard-hearted adamant;[47]
But yet you draw not iron, for my heart
Is true as steel: leave you[48] your power to draw,
And I shall have no power to follow you.
DEM. Do I entice you? do I speak you fair?[49]
Or, rather, do I not in plainest truth
Tell you, I do not nor I cannot love you?
HEL. And even for that do I love you the more.
I am your spaniel; and, Demetrius,
The more you beat me, I will fawn on you:
Use me but as your spaniel, spurn me, strike me,
Neglect me, lose me; only give me leave,
Unworthy as I am, to follow you.
What worser place can I beg in your love,—
And yet a place of high respect with me,—
Than to be used as you use your dog?
DEM. Tempt not too much the hatred of my spirit;
For I am sick when I do look on thee.
HEL. And I am sick when I look not on you.
DEM. You do impeach your modesty too much,
To leave the city, and commit yourself
Into the hands of one that loves you not;
To trust the opportunity of night

[46] *wode*] mad, frantic. The normal Shakespearean form of "wode" is "wood."
[47] *adamant*] lodestone.
[48] *leave you*] abandon.
[49] *fair*] kindly.

And the ill counsel of a desert place
With the rich worth of your virginity.
HEL. Your virtue is my privilege:[50] for that[51]
It is not night when I do see your face,
Therefore I think I am not in the night;
Nor doth this wood lack worlds of company,
For you in my respect[52] are all the world:
Then how can it be said I am alone,
When all the world is here to look on me?
DEM. I'll run from thee and hide me in the brakes,[53]
And leave thee to the mercy of wild beasts.
HEL. The wildest hath not such a heart as you.
Run when you will, the story shall be changed:
Apollo flies, and Daphne holds the chase;[54]
The dove pursues the griffin;[55] the mild hind
Makes speed to catch the tiger; bootless speed,
When cowardice pursues, and valour flies.
DEM. I will not stay thy questions;[56] let me go:
Or, if thou follow me, do not believe
But I shall do thee mischief in the wood.
HEL. Ay, in the temple, in the town, the field,
You do me mischief. Fie, Demetrius!
Your wrongs do set a scandal on my sex:
We cannot fight for love, as men may do;
We should be woo'd, and were not made to woo. [*Exit* DEM.
I'll follow thee, and make a heaven of hell,
To die upon[57] the hand I love so well. [*Exit*.
OBE. Fare thee well, nymph: ere he do leave this grove,
Thou shalt fly him, and he shall seek thy love.

Re-enter PUCK.

Hast thou the flower there? Welcome, wanderer.
PUCK. Ay, there it is.

[50] *privilege*] safeguard.
[51] *for that*] since.
[52] *in my respect*] in my opinion.
[53] *brakes*] thickets.
[54] *Apollo . . . chase*] an allusion to the myth in which the amorous god Apollo pursues Daphne.
[55] *griffin*] a mythical beast with the head of an eagle and the body of a lion.
[56] *stay thy questions*] wait around for your arguments.
[57] *upon*] by.

OBE. I pray thee, give it me.
I know a bank where the wild thyme blows,
Where oxlips and the nodding violet grows;
Quite over-canopied with luscious woodbine,
With sweet musk-roses, and with eglantine:
There sleeps Titania sometime of the night,
Lull'd in these flowers with dances and delight;
And there the snake throws her enamell'd skin,
Weed[58] wide enough to wrap a fairy in:
And with the juice of this I'll streak[59] her eyes,
And make her full of hateful fantasies.
Take thou some of it, and seek through this grove:
A sweet Athenian lady is in love
With a disdainful youth: anoint his eyes;
But do it when the next thing he espies
May be the lady: thou shalt know the man
By the Athenian garments he hath on.
Effect it with some care that he may prove
More fond on her than she upon her love:
And look thou meet me ere the first cock crow.

PUCK. Fear not, my lord, your servant shall do so. [*Exeunt*.

Scene II—Another part of the wood

Enter TITANIA, *with her train.*

TITA. Come, now a roundel[1] and a fairy song;
Then, for the third part of a minute, hence;
Some to kill cankers[2] in the musk-rose buds;
Some war with rere-mice[3] for their leathern wings,
To make my small elves coats; and some keep back
The clamorous owl, that nightly hoots and wonders
At our quaint spirits. Sing me now asleep;
Then to your offices, and let me rest.

[58] *Weed*] garment.
[59] *streak*] anoint.

[1] *roundel*] dance in a circle.
[2] *cankers*] caterpillars.
[3] *rere-mice*] bats.

SONG

FIRST FAI. You spotted snakes with double tongue,
Thorny hedgehogs, be not seen;
Newts[4] and blind-worms, do no wrong,
Come not near our fairy queen.

CHORUS

Philomel,[5] with melody
Sing in our sweet lullaby;
Lulla, lulla, lullaby, lulla, lulla, lullaby:
Never harm,
Nor spell, nor charm,
Come our lovely lady nigh;
So, good night, with lullaby.

FIRST FAI. Weaving spiders, come not here;
Hence, you long-legg'd spinners, hence!
Beetles black, approach not near;
Worm nor snail, do no offence.

CHORUS

Philomel, with melody, &c.

SEC. FAI. Hence, away! now all is well:
One aloof stand sentinel. [*Exeunt* Fairies. TITANIA *sleeps.*

Enter OBERON, *and squeezes the flower on* TITANIA'S *eyelids.*

OBE. What thou seest when thou dost wake,
Do it for thy true-love take;
Love and languish for his sake:
Be it ounce,[6] or cat, or bear,
Pard,[7] or boar with bristled hair,
In thy eye that shall appear
When thou wakest, it is thy dear:
Wake when some vile thing is near. [*Exit.*

Enter LYSANDER *and* HERMIA.

[4] *Newts*] small lizards.
[5] *Philomel*] nightingale.
[6] *ounce*] lynx.
[7] *Pard*] leopard.

LYS. Fair love, you faint with wandering in the wood;
And to speak troth,[8] I have forgot our way:
We'll rest us, Hermia, if you think it good,
And tarry for the comfort of the day.
HER. Be it so, Lysander: find you out a bed;
For I upon this bank will rest my head.
LYS. One turf shall serve as pillow for us both;
One heart, one bed, two bosoms, and one troth.
HER. Nay, good Lysander; for my sake, my dear,
Lie further off yet, do not lie so near.
LYS. O, take the sense,[9] sweet, of my innocence!
Love takes the meaning in love's conference.
I mean, that my heart unto yours is knit,
So that but one heart we can make of it:
Two bosoms interchained with an oath;
So then two bosoms and a single troth.
Then by your side no bed-room me deny;
For lying so, Hermia, I do not lie.
HER. Lysander riddles very prettily:
Now much beshrew[10] my manners and my pride,
If Hermia meant to say Lysander lied.
But, gentle friend, for love and courtesy
Lie further off; in human[11] modesty,
Such separation as may well be said
Becomes a virtuous bachelor and a maid,
So far be distant; and, good night, sweet friend:
Thy love ne'er alter till thy sweet life end!
LYS. Amen, amen, to that fair prayer, say I;
And then end life when I end loyalty!
Here is my bed: sleep give thee all his rest!
HER. With half that wish the wisher's eyes be press'd! [*They sleep.*

Enter PUCK.

PUCK. Through the forest have I gone,
But Athenian found I none,
On whose eyes I might approve[12]
This flower's force in stirring love.

[8] *troth*] truth.
[9] *take the sense*] consider the significance.
[10] *much beshrew*] a curse on.
[11] *human*] benevolent.
[12] *approve*] test.

Night and silence.—Who is here?
Weeds of Athens he doth wear:
This is he, my master said,
Despised the Athenian maid;
And here the maiden, sleeping sound,
On the dank and dirty ground.
Pretty soul! she durst not lie
Near this lack-love, this kill-courtesy.
Churl, upon thy eyes I throw
All the power this charm doth owe.[13]
When thou wakest, let love forbid
Sleep his seat on thy eyelid:
So awake when I am gone;
For I must now to Oberon. [*Exit.*

Enter DEMETRIUS *and* HELENA, *running.*

HEL. Stay, though thou kill me, sweet Demetrius.
DEM. I charge thee, hence, and do not haunt me thus.
HEL. O, wilt thou darkling[14] leave me? do not so.
DEM. Stay, on thy peril: I alone will go. [*Exit.*
HEL. O, I am out of breath in this fond[15] chase!
The more my prayer, the lesser is my grace.[16]
Happy is Hermia, wheresoe'er she lies;
For she hath blessed and attractive eyes.
How came her eyes so bright? Not with salt tears:
If so, my eyes are oftener wash'd than hers.
No, no, I am as ugly as a bear;
For beasts that meet me run away for fear:
Therefore no marvel though Demetrius
Do, as a monster, fly my presence thus.
What wicked and dissembling glass[17] of mine
Made me compare with Hermia's sphery eyne?[18]
But who is here? Lysander! on the ground!
Dead? or asleep? I see no blood, no wound.
Lysander, if you live, good sir, awake.

[13] *owe*] possess.
[14] *darkling*] in the dark.
[15] *fond*] both doting and foolish.
[16] *my grace*] the favor I receive.
[17] *glass*] mirror.
[18] *sphery eyne*] starlike eyes.

LYS. [*Awaking*] And run through fire I will for thy sweet sake.
Transparent Helena! Nature shews art,
That through thy bosom makes me see thy heart.
Where is Demetrius? O, how fit a word
Is that vile name to perish on my sword!

HEL. Do not say so, Lysander; say not so.
What though he love your Hermia? Lord, what though?
Yet Hermia still loves you: then be content.

LYS. Content with Hermia! No; I do repent
The tedious minutes I with her have spent.
Not Hermia but Helena I love:
Who will not change a raven for a dove?
The will of man is by his reason sway'd
And reason says you are the worthier maid.
Things growing are not ripe until their season:
So I, being young, till now ripe not to reason;
And touching now the point of human skill,
Reason becomes the marshal to my will,
And leads me to your eyes; where I o'erlook
Love's stories, written in love's richest book.

HEL. Wherefore was I to this keen[19] mockery born?
When at your hands did I deserve this scorn?
Is't not enough, is't not enough, young man,
That I did never, no, nor never can,
Deserve a sweet look from Demetrius' eye,
But you must flout my insufficiency?
Good troth, you do me wrong, good sooth, you do,
In such disdainful manner me to woo.
But fare you well: perforce I must confess
I thought you lord of more true gentleness.
O, that a lady, of[20] one man refused,
Should of another therefore be abused! [*Exit*.

LYS. She sees not Hermia. Hermia, sleep thou there:
And never mayst thou come Lysander near!
For as a surfeit of the sweetest things
The deepest loathing to the stomach brings,
Or as the heresies that men do leave
Are hated most of those they did deceive,
So thou, my surfeit and my heresy,

[19] *keen*] bitter.
[20] *of*] by.

Of all be hated, but the most of me!
And, all my powers, address[21] your love and might
To honour Helen and to be her knight! [*Exit.*

HER. [*Awaking*] Help me, Lysander, help me! do thy best
To pluck this crawling serpent from my breast!
Ay me, for pity! what a dream was here!
Lysander, look how I do quake with fear:
Methought a serpent eat my heart away,
And you sat smiling at his cruel prey.[22]
Lysander! what, removed? Lysander! lord!
What, out of hearing? gone? no sound, no word?
Alack, where are you? speak, an if you hear:
Speak, of all loves![23] I swoon almost with fear.
No? then I well perceive you are not nigh:
Either death or you I'll find immediately. [*Exit.*

[21] *address*] direct.
[22] *prey*] act of preying.
[23] *of all loves*] in the the name of all loves.

Act III—Scene I—The wood

TITANIA LYING ASLEEP

Enter QUINCE, SNUG, BOTTOM, FLUTE, SNOUT, *and* STARVELING.

BOT. Are we all met?

QUIN. Pat, pat; and here's a marvellous convenient place for our rehearsal. This green plot shall be our stage, this hawthorn-brake our tiring-house;[1] and we will do it in action as we will do it before the duke.

BOT. Peter Quince,—

QUIN. What sayest thou, bully[2] Bottom?

BOT. There are things in this comedy of Pyramus and Thisbe that will never please. First, Pyramus must draw a sword to kill himself; which the ladies cannot abide. How answer you that?

SNOUT. By'r lakin,[3] a parlous[4] fear.

STAR. I believe we must leave the killing out, when all is done.

BOT. Not a whit: I have a device to make all well. Write me a prologue; and let the prologue seem to say, we will do no harm with our swords, and that Pyramus is not killed indeed; and, for the more better assurance, tell them that I Pyramus am not Pyramus, but Bottom the weaver: this will put them out of fear.

QUIN. Well, we will have such a prologue; and it shall be written in eight and six.[5]

BOT. No, make it two more; let it be written in eight and eight.

SNOUT. Will not the ladies be afeard of the lion?

[1] *tiring-house*] dressing room.
[2] *bully*] good fellow.
[3] *By'r lakin*] by our ladykin (the Virgin Mary).
[4] *parlous*] perilous.
[5] *eight and six*] alternate lines of eight and six syllables, a common ballad meter.

STAR. I fear it, I promise you.

BOT. Masters, you ought to consider with yourselves: to bring in,—God shield us!—a lion among ladies, is a most dreadful thing; for there is not a more fearful[6] wild-fowl than your lion living: and we ought to look to't.

SNOUT. Therefore another prologue must tell he is not a lion.

BOT. Nay, you must name his name, and half his face must be seen through the lion's neck; and he himself must speak through, saying thus, or to the same defect,[7]—"Ladies,"—or, "Fair ladies,—I would wish you," —or, "I would request you,"—or, "I would entreat you,—not to fear, not to tremble: my life for yours. If you think I come hither as a lion, it were pity of my life: no, I am no such thing; I am a man as other men are:" and there indeed let him name his name, and tell them plainly, he is Snug the joiner.

QUIN. Well, it shall be so. But there is two hard things; that is, to bring the moonlight into a chamber; for, you know, Pyramus and Thisbe meet by moonlight.

SNOUT. Doth the moon shine that night we play our play?

BOT. A calendar, a calendar! look in the almanac; find out moonshine, find out moonshine.

QUIN. Yes, it doth shine that night.

BOT. Why, then may you leave a casement of the great chamber window, where we play, open, and the moon may shine in at the casement.

QUIN. Ay; or else one must come in with a bush of thorns[8] and a lantern, and say he comes to disfigure,[9] or to present,[10] the person of moonshine. Then, there is another thing: we must have a wall in the great chamber; for Pyramus and Thisbe, says the story, did talk through the chink of a wall.

SNOUT. You can never bring in a wall. What say you, Bottom?

BOT. Some man or other must present Wall: and let him have some plaster, or some loam, or some rough-cast[11] about him, to signify "wall"; and let him hold his fingers thus, and through that cranny shall Pyramus and Thisbe whisper.

QUIN. If that may be, then all is well. Come, sit down, every mother's

[6] *fearful*] terrifying.

[7] *defect*] Bottom's malapropism for "effect."

[8] *bush of thorns*] The man in the moon was said to have been exiled there for collecting firewood on Sundays.

[9] *disfigure*] Quince's malapropism for "figure."

[10] *present*] represent.

[11] *rough-cast*] plaster mixed with pebbles.

son, and rehearse your parts. Pyramus, you begin: when you have spoken your speech, enter into that brake: and so every one according to his cue.

Enter PUCK *behind.*

PUCK. What hempen home-spuns[12] have we swaggering here,
So near the cradle of the fairy queen?
What, a play toward![13] I'll be an auditor;
An actor too perhaps, if I see cause.

QUIN. Speak, Pyramus. Thisbe, stand forth.

BOT. Thisbe, the flowers of odious savours sweet,—

QUIN. Odours, odours.

BOT. ——odours savours sweet:
So hath thy breath, my dearest Thisbe dear.
But hark, a voice! stay thou but here awhile,
And by and by I will to thee appear. [*Exit.*

PUCK. A stranger Pyramus than e'er play'd here. [*Exit.*

FLU. Must I speak now?

QUIN. Ay, marry, must you; for you must understand he goes but to see a noise that he heard, and is to come again.

FLU. Most radiant Pyramus, most lily-white of hue,
Of colour like the red rose on triumphant brier,
Most brisky juvenal,[14] and eke most lovely Jew,[15]
As true as truest horse, that yet would never tire,
I'll meet thee, Pyramus, at Ninny's[16] tomb.

QUIN. "Ninus' tomb," man: why, you must not speak that yet; that you answer to Pyramus: you speak all your part at once, cues and all. Pyramus enter: your cue is past; it is, "never tire."

FLU. O,—As true as truest horse, that yet would never tire.

Re-enter PUCK, *and* BOTTOM *with an ass's head.*

BOT. If I were fair, Thisbe, I were only thine.

QUIN. O monstrous! O strange! we are haunted. Pray, masters! fly, masters! Help!

[*Exeunt* QUINCE, SNUG, FLUTE, SNOUT, *and* STARVELING.

PUCK. I'll follow you, I'll lead you about a round,
Through bog, through bush, through brake, through brier:

[12] *hempen home-spuns*] rustics, wearing homespun clothes of hemp.
[13] *toward*] in rehearsal.
[14] *brisky juvenal*] nimble youth.
[15] *Jew*] youth (a play on the first syllable of "juvenal").
[16] *Ninny's*] Ninus, the legendary founder of Babylon.

Sometime a horse I'll be, sometime a hound,
A hog, a headless bear, sometime a fire;
And neigh, and bark, and grunt, and roar, and burn,
Like horse, hound, hog, bear, fire, at every turn. [*Exit.*

BOT. Why do they run away? this is a knavery of them to make me afeard.

Re-enter SNOUT.

SNOUT. O Bottom, thou art changed! what do I see on thee?

BOT. What do you see? you see an ass-head of your own, do you? [*Exit* SNOUT.

Re-enter QUINCE.

QUIN. Bless thee, Bottom! bless thee! thou art translated.[17] [*Exit.*

BOT. I see their knavery: this is to make an ass of me; to fright me, if they could. But I will not stir from this place, do what they can: I will walk up and down here, and I will sing, that they shall hear I am not afraid. [*Sings.*

The ousel[18] cock so black of hue,
With orange-tawny bill,
The throstle[19] with his note so true,
The wren with little quill;[20]

TITA. [*Awaking*] What angel wakes me from my flowery bed?

BOT. [*Sings*]

The finch, the sparrow, and the lark,
The plain-song cuckoo gray,
Whose note full many a man doth mark,
And dares not answer nay;—

for, indeed, who would set his wit to[21] so foolish a bird? who would give a bird the lie, though he cry "cuckoo" never so?

TITA. I pray thee, gentle mortal, sing again:
Mine ear is much enamour'd of thy note;
So is mine eye enthralled to thy shape;
And thy fair virtue's force perforce doth move me

[17] *translated*] transformed.

[18] *ousel*] blackbird.

[19] *throstle*] thrush.

[20] *quill*] musical pipe.

[21] *set his wit to*] match his wit against.

On the first view to say, to swear, I love thee.

BOT. Methinks, mistress, you should have little reason for that: and yet, to say the truth, reason and love keep little company together now-a-days; the more the pity, that some honest neighbours will not make them friends. Nay, I can gleek[22] upon occasion.

TITA. Thou art as wise as thou art beautiful.

BOT. Not so, neither: but if I had wit enough to get out of this wood, I have enough to serve mine own turn.

TITA. Out of this wood do not desire to go:
Thou shalt remain here, whether thou wilt or no.
I am a spirit of no common rate:[23]
The summer still doth tend[24] upon my state;
And I do love thee: therefore, go with me;
I'll give thee fairies to attend on thee;
And they shall fetch thee jewels from the deep,
And sing, while thou on pressed flowers dost sleep:
And I will purge thy mortal grossness so,
That thou shalt like an airy spirit go.
Peaseblossom! Cobweb! Moth! and Mustardseed!

Enter PEASEBLOSSOM, COBWEB, MOTH, *and* MUSTARDSEED.

FIRST FAI. Ready.
SEC. FAI. And I.
THIRD FAI. And I.
FOURTH FAI. And I.
ALL. Where shall we go?

TITA. Be kind and courteous to this gentleman;
Hop in his walks, and gambol in his eyes;
Feed him with apricocks and dewberries,
With purple grapes, green figs, and mulberries;
The honey-bags steal from the humble-bees,
And for night-tapers crop their waxen thighs,
And light them at the fiery glow-worm's eyes,
To have my love to bed and to arise;
And pluck the wings from painted butterflies,
To fan the moonbeams from his sleeping eyes:
Nod to him, elves, and do him courtesies.

FIRST FAI. Hail, mortal!

SEC. FAI. Hail!

[22] *gleek*] joke, scoff.
[23] *rate*] rank.
[24] *still doth tend*] always attends.

THIRD FAI. Hail!

FOURTH FAI. Hail!

BOT. I cry your worships mercy, heartily: I beseech your worship's name.

COB. Cobweb.

BOT. I shall desire you of more acquaintance, good Master Cobweb: if I cut my finger, I shall make bold with you. Your name, honest gentleman?

PEAS. Peaseblossom.

BOT. I pray you, commend me to Mistress Squash,[26] your mother, and to Master Peascod, your father. Good Master Peaseblossom, I shall desire you of more acquaintance too. Your name, I beseech you, sir?

MUS. Mustardseed.

BOT. Good Master Mustardseed, I know your patience[27] well: that same cowardly, giant-like ox-beef hath devoured many a gentleman of your house: I promise you your kindred hath made my eyes water ere now. I desire your more acquaintance, good Master Mustardseed.

TITA. Come, wait upon him; lead him to my bower.
The moon methinks looks with a watery eye;
And when she weeps, weeps every little flower,
Lamenting some enforced[28] chastity.
Tie up my love's tongue, bring him silently. [*Exeunt*

Scene II—Another part of the wood

Enter OBERON.

OBE. I wonder if Titania be awaked;
Then, what it was that next came in her eye,
Which she must dote on in extremity.

Enter PUCK.

Here comes my messenger.
How now, mad spirit!
What night-rule[1] now about this haunted grove?

PUCK. My mistress with a monster is in love.
Near to her close and consecrated bower,

[26] *Squash*] unripe pea pod.
[27] *patience*] endurance in adversity.
[28] *enforced*] violated.

[1] *night-rule*] nighttime revelry.

While she was in her dull and sleeping hour,
A crew of patches, rude mechanicals,[2]
That work for bread upon Athenian stalls,
Were met together to rehearse a play,
Intended for great Theseus' nuptial-day.
The shallowest thick-skin of that barren sort,[3]
Who Pyramus presented, in their sport
Forsook his scene, and enter'd in a brake:
When I did him at this advantage take,
An ass's nole[4] I fixed on his head:
Anon his Thisbe must be answered,
And forth my mimic[5] comes. When they him spy,
As wild geese that the creeping fowler eye,
Or russet-pated choughs,[6] many in sort,
Rising and cawing at the gun's report,
Sever themselves and madly sweep the sky,
So, at his sight, away his fellows fly;
And, at our stamp,[7] here o'er and o'er one falls;
He murder cries, and help from Athens calls.
Their sense thus weak, lost with their fears thus strong,
Made senseless things begin to do them wrong;
For briers and thorns at their apparel snatch;
Some sleeves, some hats, from yielders all things catch.
I led them on in this distracted fear,
And left sweet Pyramus translated there:
When in that moment, so it came to pass,
Titania waked, and straightway loved an ass.

OBE. This falls out better than I could devise.
But hast thou yet latch'd[8] the Athenian's eyes
With the love-juice, as I did bid thee do?

PUCK. I took him sleeping,—that is finish'd too,—
And the Athenian woman by his side;
That, when he waked, of force[9] she must be eyed.

Enter HERMIA *and* DEMETRIUS.

[2] *patches, rude mechanicals*] clowns, uncivilized workingmen.
[3] *The shallowest . . . sort*] the stupidest blockhead of that brainless company.
[4] *nole*] head.
[5] *mimic*] actor.
[6] *russet-pated choughs*] red-headed jackdaws.
[7] *at our stamp*] on hearing our footsteps.
[8] *latch'd*] moistened.
[9] *of force*] necessarily.

OBE. Stand close: this is the same Athenian.
PUCK. This is the woman, but not this the man.
DEM. Oh, why rebuke you him that loves you so?
Lay breath so bitter on your bitter foe.
HER. Now I but chide; but I should use[10] thee worse,
For thou, I fear, hast given me cause to curse.
If thou hast slain Lysander in his sleep,
Being o'er shoes in blood, plunge in the deep,
And kill me too.
The sun was not so true unto the day
As he to me: would he have stolen away
From sleeping Hermia? I'll believe as soon
This whole earth may be bored, and that the moon
May through the centre creep, and so displease
Her brother's noontide with the Antipodes.
It cannot be but thou hast murder'd him;
So should a murderer look, so dead,[11] so grim.
DEM. So should the murder'd look; and so should I,
Pierced through the heart with your stern cruelty:
Yet you, the murderer, look as bright, as clear,
As yonder Venus in her glimmering sphere.
HER. What's this to my Lysander? where is he?
Ah, good Demetrius, wilt thou give him me?
DEM. I had rather give his carcass to my hounds.
HER. Out, dog! out, cur! thou drivest me past the bounds
Of maiden's patience. Hast thou slain him, then?
Henceforth be never number'd among men!
O, once tell true, tell true, even for my sake!
Durst thou have look'd upon him being awake,
And hast thou kill'd him sleeping? O brave touch!
Could not a worm,[12] an adder, do so much?
An adder did it; for with doubler[13] tongue
Than thine, thou serpent, never adder stung.
DEM. You spend your passion on a misprised mood:[14]
I am not guilty of Lysander's blood;
Nor is he dead, for aught that I can tell.

[10] *use*] treat.
[11] *dead*] deadly.
[12] *worm*] serpent.
[13] *doubler*] more forked and more deceitful.
[14] *a misprised mood*] a fit of anger caused by a mistake.

HER. I pray thee, tell me then that he is well.
DEM. An if I could, what should I get therefore?
HER. A privilege, never to see me more.
And from thy hated presence part I so:
See me no more, whether he be dead or no. [*Exit*.
DEM. There is no following her in this fierce vein:
Here therefore for a while I will remain.
So sorrow's heaviness doth heavier grow
For debt that bankrupt sleep doth sorrow owe;
Which now in some slight measure it will pay,
If for his tender[15] here I make some stay. [*Lies down and sleeps.*
OBE. What hast thou done? thou hast mistaken quite,
And laid the love-juice on some true-love's sight:
Of thy misprision must perforce ensue
Some true love turn'd, and not a false turn'd true.
PUCK. Then fate o'er-rules, that, one man holding troth,
A million fail, confounding oath on oath.[16]
OBE. About the wood go swifter than the wind,
And Helena of Athens look thou find:
All fancy-sick[17] she is and pale of cheer,[18]
With sighs of love, that costs the fresh blood dear:
By some illusion see thou bring her here:
I'll charm his eyes against[19] she do appear.
PUCK. I go, I go; look how I go,
Swifter than arrow from the Tartar's bow. [*Exit*.
OBE. Flower of this purple dye,
Hit with Cupid's archery,
Sink in apple of his eye.
When his love he doth espy,
Let her shine as gloriously
As the Venus of the sky.
When thou wakest, if she be by,
Beg of her for remedy.

Re-enter PUCK.

PUCK. Captain of our fairy band,
Helena is here at hand;

[15] *his tender*] sleep's offering of itself.
[16] *confounding oath on oath*] subverting one oath by another.
[17] *fancy-sick*] lovesick.
[18] *cheer*] countenance.
[19] *against*] in provision for the time when.

And the youth, mistook by me,
Pleading for a lover's fee.
Shall we their fond pageant[20] see?
Lord, what fools these mortals be!

OBE. Stand aside: the noise they make
Will cause Demetrius to awake.

PUCK. Then will two at once woo one;
That must needs be sport alone;
And those things do best please me
That befal preposterously.[21]

Enter LYSANDER *and* HELENA.

LYS. Why should you think that I should woo in scorn?
Scorn and derision never come in tears:
Look, when I vow, I weep; and vows so born,
In their nativity all truth appears.
How can these things in me seem scorn to you,
Bearing the badge of faith, to prove them true?

HEL. You do advance your cunning more and more.
When truth kills truth, O devilish-holy fray!
These vows are Hermia's: will you give her o'er?
Weigh oath with oath, and you will nothing weigh:
Your vows to her and me, put in two scales,
Will even weigh; and both as light as tales.

LYS. I had no judgement when to her I swore.

HEL. Nor none, in my mind,[22] now you give her o'er.

LYS. Demetrius loves her, and he loves not you.

DEM. [*Awaking*] O Helen, goddess, nymph, perfect, divine!
To what, my love, shall I compare thine eyne?
Crystal is muddy. O, how ripe in show
Thy lips, those kissing cherries, tempting grow!
That pure congealed white, high Taurus'[23] snow,
Fann'd with the eastern wind, turns to a crow
When thou hold'st up thy hand: O, let me kiss
This princess of pure white, this seal of bliss!

HEL. O spite! O hell! I see you all are bent
To set against me for your merriment:
If you were civil and knew courtesy,

[20] *fond pageant*] foolish spectacle.
[21] *preposterously*] contrary to the natural order of things.
[22] *mind*] opinion.
[23] *Taurus'*] Taurus is a mountain range in southern Turkey.

You would not do me thus much injury.
Can you not hate me, as I know you do,
But you must join in souls to mock me too?
If you were men, as men you are in show,
You would not use a gentle lady so;
To vow, and swear, and superpraise my parts,[24]
When I am sure you hate me with your hearts.
You both are rivals, and love Hermia;
And now both rivals, to mock Helena:
A trim[25] exploit, a manly enterprise,
To conjure tears up in a poor maid's eyes
With your derision! none of noble sort
Would so offend a virgin, and extort
A poor soul's patience, all to make you sport.

LYS. You are unkind, Demetrius; be not so;
For you love Hermia; this you know I know:
And here, with all good will, with all my heart,
In Hermia's love I yield you up my part;
And yours of Helena to me bequeath,
Whom I do love, and will do till my death.

HEL. Never did mockers waste more idle breath.

DEM. Lysander, keep thy Hermia; I will none:[26]
If e'er I loved her, all that love is gone.
My heart to her but as guest-wise sojourn'd,
And now to Helen is it home return'd,
There to remain.

LYS. Helen, it is not so.

DEM. Disparage not the faith thou dost not know,
Lest, to thy peril, thou aby[27] it dear.
Look, where thy love comes; yonder is thy dear.

Re-enter HERMIA.

HER. Dark night, that from the eye his function takes,
The ear more quick of apprehension makes;
Wherein it doth impair the seeing sense,
It pays the hearing double recompense.
Thou art not by mine eye, Lysander, found;

[24] *superpraise my parts*] overpraise my qualities.
[25] *trim*] fine.
[26] *I will none*] I want nothing to do with her.
[27] *aby*] pay for.

Mine ear, I thank it, brought me to thy sound.
But why unkindly didst thou leave me so?
LYS. Why should he stay, whom love doth press to go?
HER. What love could press Lysander from my side?
LYS. Lysander's love, that would not let him bide,
Fair Helena, who more engilds the night
Than all yon fiery oes[28] and eyes of light.
Why seek'st thou me? could not this make thee know,
The hate I bare thee made me leave thee so?
HER. You speak not as you think: it cannot be.
HEL. Lo, she is one of this confederacy!
Now I perceive they have conjoin'd all three
To fashion this false sport, in spite of[29] me.
Injurious Hermia! most ungrateful maid!
Have you conspired, have you with these contrived
To bait me with this foul derision?
Is all the counsel that we two have shared,
The sisters' vows, the hours that we have spent,
When we have chid[30] the hasty-footed time
For parting us,—O, is all forgot?
All school-days' friendship, childhood innocence?
We, Hermia, like two artificial[31] gods,
Have with our needles created both one flower,
Both on one sampler, sitting on one cushion,
Both warbling of one song, both in one key;
As if our hands, our sides, voices, and minds,
Had been incorporate.[32] So we grew together,
Like to a double cherry, seeming parted,
But yet an union in partition;
Two lovely berries moulded on one stem;
So, with two seeming bodies, but one heart;
Two of the first, like coats in heraldry,
Due but to one, and crowned with one crest.[33]
And will you rent[34] our ancient love asunder,

[28] *fiery oes*] circles of fire, stars.
[29] *in spite of*] out of spite for.
[30] *chid*] scolded.
[31] *artificial*] artistically creative.
[32] *incorporate*] of one body.
[33] *Two of the first, . . . crest*] Our two bodies resemble two coats of arms in heraldry, which belong to a single person, and are surrounded by a single crest.
[34] *rent*] rend, tear.

To join with men in scorning your poor friend?
It is not friendly, 't is not maidenly:
Our sex, as well as I, may chide you for it,
Though I alone do feel the injury.

HER. I am amazed at your passionate words.
I scorn you not: it seems that you scorn me.

HEL. Have you not set Lysander, as in scorn,
To follow me and praise my eyes and face?
And made your other love, Demetrius,
Who even but now did spurn me with his foot,
To call me goddess, nymph, divine and rare,
Precious, celestial? Wherefore speaks he this
To her he hates? and wherefore doth Lysander
Deny your love, so rich within his soul,
And tender[35] me, forsooth, affection,
But by your setting on,[36] by your consent?
What though I be not so in grace as you,
So hung upon with love, so fortunate,
But miserable most, to love unloved?
This you should pity rather than despise.

HER. I understand not what you mean by this.

HEL. Ay, do, persever,[37] counterfeit sad[38] looks,
Make mouths upon[39] me when I turn my back;
Wink each at other; hold the sweet jest up:
This sport, well carried, shall be chronicled.
If you have any pity, grace, or manners,
You would not make me such an argument.[40]
But fare ye well: 't is partly my own fault;
Which death or absence soon shall remedy.

LYS. Stay, gentle Helena; hear my excuse:
My love, my life, my soul, fair Helena!

HEL. O excellent!

HER. Sweet, do not scorn her so.

DEM. If she cannot entreat, I can compel.

LYS. Thou canst compel no more than she entreat:
Thy threats have no more strength than her weak prayers.

[35] *tender*] offer.
[36] *setting on*] instigation.
[37] *persever*] persevere.
[38] *sad*] serious.
[39] *Make mouths upon*] make faces at.
[40] *make me such an argument*] ridicule me so.

Helen, I love thee; by my life, I do:
I swear by that which I will lose for thee,
To prove him false that says I love thee not.
DEM. I say I love thee more than he can do.
LYS. If thou say so, withdraw, and prove it too.
DEM. Quick, come!
HER. Lysander, whereto tends all this?
LYS. Away, you Ethiope![41]
DEM. No, no; he'll . . .[42]
Seem to break loose; take on as you would follow,
But yet come not: you are a tame man, go!
LYS. Hang off,[43] thou cat, thou burr![44] vile thing, let loose,
Or I will shake thee from me like a serpent!
HER. Why are you grown so rude? what change is this?
Sweet love,—
LYS. Thy love! out, tawny Tartar, out!
Out, loathed medicine! hated potion, hence!
HER. Do you not jest?
HEL. Yes, sooth; and so do you.
LYS. Demetrius, I will keep my word with thee.
DEM. I would I had your bond, for I perceive
A weak bond holds you: I'll not trust your word.
LYS. What, should I hurt her, strike her, kill her dead?
Although I hate her, I'll not harm her so.
HER. What, can you do me greater harm than hate?
Hate me! wherefore? O me! what news,[45] my love!
Am not I Hermia? are not you Lysander?
I am as fair now as I was erewhile.[46]
Since night you loved me; yet since night you left me:
Why, then you left me,—O, the gods forbid!—
In earnest, shall I say?
LYS. Ay, by my life;
And never did desire to see thee more.
Therefore be out of hope, of question, of doubt;
Be certain, nothing truer; 't is no jest
That I do hate thee, and love Helena.

[41] *Ethiope*] sneering allusion to Hermia's brunette complexion.
[42] *No, no; he'll . . .*] The text seems to be corrupt here.
[43] *Hang off*] let go.
[44] *burr*] the prickly envelope of the fruit on a burdock.
[45] *what news*] What is the matter?
[46] *erewhile*] up to this time.

HER. O me! you juggler! you canker-blossom!
You thief of love! what, have you come by night
And stolen my love's heart from him?
HEL. Fine, i' faith!
Have you no modesty, no maiden shame,
No touch of bashfulness? What, will you tear
Impatient answers from my gentle tongue?
Fie, fie! you counterfeit, you puppet,[47] you!
HER. Puppet? why so? ay, that way goes the game.
Now I perceive that she hath made compare
Between our statures; she hath urged[48] her height;
And with her personage, her tall personage,
Her height, forsooth, she hath prevail'd with him.
And are you grown so high in his esteem,
Because I am so dwarfish and so low?
How low am I, thou painted maypole? speak;
How low am I? I am not yet so low
But that my nails can reach unto thine eyes.
HEL. I pray you, though you mock me, gentlemen,
Let her not hurt me: I was never curst;[49]
I have no gift at all in shrewishness;
I am a right[50] maid for my cowardice:
Let her not strike me. You perhaps may think,
Because she is something lower[51] than myself,
That I can match her.
HER. Lower! hark, again.
HEL. Good Hermia, do not be so bitter with me.
I evermore did love you, Hermia,
Did ever keep your counsels, never wrong'd you;
Save that, in love unto Demetrius,
I told him of your stealth[52] unto this wood.
He follow'd you; for love I follow'd him;
But he hath chid me hence, and threaten'd me
To strike me, spurn me, nay, to kill me too:
And now, so[53] you will let me quiet go,

[47] *puppet*] someone of short stature.
[48] *urged*] asserted.
[49] *curst*] shrewish.
[50] *right*] proper.
[51] *something lower*] somewhat shorter.
[52] *stealth*] secret flight.
[53] *so*] if.

To Athens will I bear my folly back,
And follow you no further: let me go:
You see how simple and how fond[54] I am.
HER. Why, get you gone: who is't that hinders you?
HEL. A foolish heart, that I leave here behind.
HER. What, with Lysander?
HEL. With Demetrius.
LYS. Be not afraid; she shall not harm thee, Helena.
DEM. No, sir, she shall not, though you take her part.
HEL. O, when she's angry, she is keen and shrewd!
She was a vixen when she went to school;
And though she be but little, she is fierce.
HER. Little again! nothing but low and little!
Why will you suffer her to flout me thus?
Let me come to her.
LYS. Get you gone, you dwarf;
You minimus,[55] of hindering knot-grass[56] made;
You bead, you acorn.
DEM. You are too officious
In her behalf that scorns your services.
Let her alone: speak not of Helena;
Take not her part; for, if thou dost intend
Never so little show of love to her,
Thou shalt aby it.
LYS. Now she holds me not;
Now follow, if thou darest, to try whose right,
Of thine or mine, is most in Helena.
DEM. Follow! nay, I'll go with thee, cheek by jole.[57]
[*Exeunt* LYSANDER *and* DEMETRIUS.
HER. You, mistress, all this coil is 'long of you:[58]
Nay, go not back.
HEL. I will not trust you, I,
Nor longer stay in your curst company.
Your hands than mine are quicker for a fray,
My legs are longer though, to run away. [*Exit*.
HER. I am amazed, and know not what to say. [*Exit*.
OBE. This is thy negligence: still thou mistakest,

[54] *fond*] foolish.
[55] *minimus*] tiny creature.
[56] *knot-grass*] a weed that, when eaten by a child, was thought to impede growth.
[57] *cheek by jole*] cheek to cheek.
[58] *this coil is 'long of you*] this confusion is on account of you.

Or else committ'st thy knaveries wilfully.
PUCK. Believe me, king of shadows, I mistook.
Did not you tell me I should know the man
By the Athenian garments he had on?
And so far blameless proves my enterprise,
That I have 'nointed an Athenian's eyes;
And so far am I glad it so did sort,[59]
As this their jangling I esteem a sport.
OBE. Thou see'st these lovers seek a place to fight:
Hie therefore, Robin, overcast the night;
The starry welkin[60] cover thou anon
With drooping fog, as black as Acheron;[61]
And lead these testy rivals so astray,
As one come not within another's way.
Like to Lysander sometime frame thy tongue,
Then stir Demetrius up with bitter wrong;
And sometime rail thou like Demetrius;
And from each other look thou lead them thus,
Till o'er their brows death-counterfeiting sleep
With leaden legs and batty wings doth creep:
Then crush this herb into Lysander's eye;
Whose liquor hath this virtuous property,
To take from thence all error with his might,
And make his eyeballs roll with wonted[62] sight.
When they next wake, all this derision
Shall seem a dream and fruitless vision;
And back to Athens shall the lovers wend,
With league whose date[63] till death shall never end.
Whiles I in this affair do thee employ,
I'll to my queen and beg her Indian boy;
And then I will her charmed eye release
From monster's view, and all things shall be peace.
PUCK. My fairy lord, this must be done with haste,
For night's swift dragons[64] cut the clouds full fast,
And yonder shines Aurora's harbinger;[65]

59 *sort*] turn out.
60 *welkin*] sky.
61 *Acheron*] a river in Hades, the water of which was black.
62 *wonted*] normal.
63 *date*] duration.
64 *dragons*] the dragons drawing the chariot of night.
65 *Aurora's harbinger*] Venus, the morning star.

At whose approach, ghosts, wandering here and there,
Troop home to churchyards: damned spirits all,
That in crossways and floods have burial,[66]
Already to their wormy beds are gone;
For fear lest day should look their shames upon,
They wilfully themselves exile from light,
And must for aye consort with black-brow'd night.

OBE. But we are spirits of another sort:
I with the morning's love[67] have oft made sport;
And, like a forester, the groves may tread,
Even till the eastern gate, all fiery-red,
Opening on Neptune with fair blessed beams,
Turns into yellow gold his salt green streams.
But, notwithstanding, haste; make no delay:
We may effect this business yet ere day. [*Exit.*

PUCK. Up and down, up and down,
I will lead them up and down:
I am fear'd in field and town:
Goblin, lead them up and down.
Here comes one.

Re-enter LYSANDER.

LYS. Where art thou, proud Demetrius? speak thou now.

PUCK. Here, villain; drawn[68] and ready. Where art thou?

LYS. I will be with thee straight.[69]

PUCK. Follow me, then,
To plainer ground. [*Exit* LYSANDER, *as following the voice.*

Re-enter DEMETRIUS.

DEM. Lysander! speak again:
Thou runaway, thou coward, art thou fled?
Speak! In some bush? Where dost thou hide thy head?

PUCK. Thou coward, art thou bragging to the stars,
Telling the bushes that thou look'st for wars,
And wilt not come? Come, recreant;[70] come, thou child;
I'll whip thee with a rod: he is defiled
That draws a sword on thee.

[66] *That . . . burial*] those who have committed suicide or have drowned.

[67] *the morning's love*] Cephalus, a youthful huntsman loved by Aurora, goddess of the morning.

[68] *drawn*] sword drawn.

[69] *straight*] immediately.

[70] *recreant*] coward, deserter.

DEM. Yea, art thou there?
PUCK. Follow my voice: we'll try no manhood here. [*Exeunt.*

Re-enter LYSANDER.

LYS. He goes before me and still dares me on:
When I come where he calls, then he is gone.
The villain is much lighter-heel'd than I:
I follow'd fast, but faster he did fly;
That fallen am I in dark uneven way,
And here will rest me. [*Lies down.*] Come, thou gentle day!
For if but once thou show me thy grey light,
I'll find Demetrius, and revenge this spite. [*Sleeps.*

Re-enter PUCK *and* DEMETRIUS.

PUCK. Ho, ho, ho! Coward, why comest thou not?
DEM. Abide me, if thou darest; for well I wot[71]
Thou runn'st before me, shifting every place,
And darest not stand, nor look me in the face.
Where art thou now?
PUCK. Come hither: I am here.
DEM. Nay, then, thou mock'st me. Thou shalt buy this dear,
If ever I thy face by daylight see:
Now, go thy way. Faintness constraineth me
To measure out my length on this cold bed.
By day's approach look to be visited. [*Lies down and sleeps.*

Re-enter HELENA.

HEL. O weary night, O long and tedious night,
Abate[72] thy hours! Shine comforts from the east,
That I may back to Athens by daylight,
From these that my poor company detest:
And sleep, that sometimes shuts up sorrow's eye,
Steal me awhile from mine own company.
[*Lies down and sleeps.*

PUCK. Yet but three? Come one more;
Two of both kinds makes up four.
Here she comes, curst and sad:
Cupid is a knavish lad,
Thus to make poor females mad.

[71] *wot*] know.
[72] *Abate*] shorten.

Re-enter HERMIA.

HER. Never so weary, never so in woe;
Bedabbled with the dew, and torn with briers;
I can no further crawl, no further go;
My legs can keep no pace with my desires.
Here will I rest me till the break of day.
Heavens shield Lysander, if they mean a fray!
[*Lies down and sleeps.*

PUCK. On the ground
Sleep sound:
I'll apply
To your eye,
Gentle lover, remedy.
[*Squeezing the juice on* LYSANDER's *eye.*
When thou wakest
Thou takest
True delight
In the sight
Of thy former lady's eye:
And the country proverb known,
That every man should take his own,
In your waking shall be shown:
Jack shall have Jill;
Nought shall go ill;
The man shall have his mare again, and all shall be well. [*Exit.*

Act IV—Scene I—The same

LYSANDER, DEMETRIUS, HELENA, AND HERMIA, LYING ASLEEP

Enter TITANIA *and* BOTTOM; PEASEBLOSSOM, COBWEB, MOTH, MUSTARDSEED, *and other* Fairies *attending;* OBERON *behind unseen.*

TITA. Come, sit thee down upon this flowery bed,
While I thy amiable cheeks do coy,[1]
And stick musk-roses in thy sleek smooth head,
And kiss thy fair large ears, my gentle joy.

BOT. Where's Peaseblossom?

PEAS. Ready.

BOT. Scratch my head, Peaseblossom. Where's Mounsieur Cobweb?

COB. Ready.

BOT. Mounsieur Cobweb, good mounsieur, get you your weapons in your hand, and kill me a red-hipped humble-bee on the top of a thistle; and, good mounsieur, bring me the honey-bag. Do not fret yourself too much in the action, mounsieur; and, good mounsieur, have a care the honey-bag break not; I would be loth to have you overflown with a honey-bag, signior. Where's Mounsieur Mustardseed?

MUS. Ready.

BOT. Give me your neaf,[2] Mounsieur Mustardseed. Pray you, leave your courtesy, good mounsieur.

MUS. What's your will?

BOT. Nothing, good mounsieur, but to help Cavalery[3] Cobweb to scratch. I must to the barber's, mounsieur; for methinks I am

[1] *amiable cheeks do coy*] caress your lovely cheeks.
[2] *neaf*] fist.
[3] *Cavalery*] gentleman.

marvellous hairy about the face; and I am such a tender ass, if my hair do but tickle me, I must scratch.

TITA. What, wilt thou hear some music, my sweet love?

BOT. I have a reasonable good ear in music. Let's have the tongs and the bones.[4]

TITA. Or say, sweet love, what thou desirest to eat.

BOT. Truly, a peck of provender: I could munch your good dry oats. Methinks I have a great desire to a bottle[5] of hay: good hay, sweet hay, hath no fellow.[6]

TITA. I have a venturous fairy that shall seek
The squirrel's hoard, and fetch thee new nuts.

BOT. I had rather have a handful or two of dried peas. But, I pray you, let none of your people stir me: I have an exposition[7] of sleep come upon me.

TITA. Sleep thou, and I will wind thee in my arms.
Fairies, be gone, and be all ways away.[8] [*Exeunt* Fairies.
So doth the woodbine the sweet honeysuckle
Gently entwist; the female ivy so
Enrings the barky fingers of the elm.
O, how I love thee! how I dote on thee! [*They sleep.*

Enter PUCK.

OBE. [*Advancing*] Welcome, good Robin. See'st thou this sweet sight?
Her dotage now I do begin to pity:
For, meeting her of late behind the wood,
Seeking sweet favours for this hateful fool,
I did upbraid her, and fall out with her;
For she his hairy temples then had rounded
With coronet of fresh and fragrant flowers;
And that same dew, which sometime on the buds
Was wont to swell, like round and orient[9] pearls,
Stood now within the pretty flowerets' eyes,
Like tears, that did their own disgrace bewail.
When I had at my pleasure taunted her,
And she in mild terms begg'd my patience,

[4] *the tongs and the bones*] rustic musical instruments.
[5] *bottle*] bundle.
[6] *fellow*] equal.
[7] *exposition*] Bottom's malapropism for "disposition."
[8] *be all ways away*] disperse in all directions.
[9] *orient*] from the East and, thereby, of the finest quality.

I then did ask of her her changeling child;
Which straight she gave me, and her fairy sent
To bear him to my bower in fairy land.
And now I have the boy, I will undo
This hateful imperfection of her eyes:
And, gentle Puck, take this transformed scalp
From off the head of this Athenian swain;[10]
That, he awaking when the other[11] do,
May all to Athens back again repair,
And think no more of this night's accidents
But as the fierce vexation of a dream.
But first I will release the fairy queen.
Be as thou wast wont to be;
See as thou wast wont to see:
Dian's bud[12] o'er Cupid's flower[13]
Hath such force and blessed power.
Now, my Titania; wake you, my sweet queen.

TITA. My Oberon! what visions have I seen!
Methought I was enamour'd of an ass.

OBE. There lies your love.

TITA. How came these things to pass?
O, how mine eyes do loathe his visage now!

OBE. Silence awhile. Robin, take off this head.
Titania, music call; and strike more dead
Than common sleep of all these five the sense.

TITA. Music, ho! music, such as charmeth sleep! [*Music, still.*

PUCK. Now, when thou wakest, with thine own fool's eyes peep.

OBE. Sound, music! Come, my queen, take hands with me,
And rock the ground whereon these sleepers be.
Now thou and I are new in amity,
And will to-morrow midnight solemnly
Dance in Duke Theseus' house triumphantly,
And bless it to all fair prosperity:
There shall the pairs of faithful lovers be
Wedded, with Theseus, all in jollity.

PUCK. Fairy king, attend, and mark:
I do hear the morning lark.

[10] *swain*] peasant.
[11] *other*] others.
[12] *Dian's bud*] *Agnus castus* (or the chaste tree).
[13] *Cupid's flower*] the pansy.

OBE. Then, my queen, in silence sad,[14]
Trip we after night's shade:
We the globe can compass soon,
Swifter than the wandering moon.
TITA. Come, my lord; and in our flight,
Tell me how it came this night,
That I sleeping here was found
With these mortals on the ground. *[Exeunt.*
[Horns winded within.

Enter THESEUS, HIPPOLYTA, EGEUS, *and train.*

THE. Go, one of you, find out the forester;
For now our observation[15] is perform'd;
And since we have the vaward[16] of the day,
My love shall hear the music of my hounds.
Uncouple in the western valley; let them go:
Dispatch, I say, and find the forester. *[Exit an attendant.*
We will, fair queen, up to the mountain's top,
And mark the musical confusion
Of hounds and echo in conjunction.
HIP. I was with Hercules and Cadmus once,
When in a wood of Crete they bay'd[17] the bear
With hounds of Sparta: never did I hear
Such gallant chiding; for, besides the groves,
The skies, the fountains, every region near
Seem'd all one mutual cry: I never heard
So musical a discord, such sweet thunder.
THE. My hounds are bred out of the Spartan kind,
So flew'd,[18] so sanded;[19] and their heads are hung
With ears that sweep away the morning dew;
Crook-knee'd, and dew-lapp'd like Thessalian bulls;
Slow in pursuit, but match'd in mouth[20] like bells,
Each under each.[21] A cry[22] more tuneable

[14] *sad*] serious, solemn.
[15] *observation*] celebration (of the rites of May Day).
[16] *vaward*] vanguard, earliest part.
[17] *bay'd*] pursued with barking dogs.
[18] *flew'd*] with large, hanging chaps.
[19] *sanded*] sandy in color.
[20] *mouth*] voice.
[21] *Each under each*] in various notes.
[22] *cry*] pack of hounds.

Was never holla'd to, nor cheer'd with horn,
In Crete, in Sparta, nor in Thessaly:
Judge when you hear. But, soft! what nymphs are these?

EGE. My lord, this is my daughter here asleep;
And this, Lysander; this Demetrius is;
This Helena, old Nedar's Helena:
I wonder of their being here together.

THE. No doubt they rose up early to observe
The rite of May; and, hearing our intent,
Came here in grace of our solemnity.[23]
But speak, Egeus; is not this the day
That Hermia should give answer of her choice?

EGE. It is, my lord.

THE. Go, bid the huntsmen wake them with their horns.

[*Horns and shout within.* LYS., DEM., HEL., *and* HER., *wake and start up.*

Good morrow, friends. Saint Valentine[24] is past:
Begin these wood-birds but to couple now?

LYS. Pardon, my lord.

THE. I pray you all, stand up.
I know you two are rival enemies:
How comes this gentle concord in the world,
That hatred is so far from jealousy,
To sleep by hate, and fear no enmity?

LYS. My lord, I shall reply amazedly,
Half sleep, half waking: but as yet, I swear,
I cannot truly say how I came here;
But, as I think,—for truly would I speak,
And now I do bethink me, so it is,—
I came with Hermia hither: our intent
Was to be gone from Athens, where[25] we might,
Without[26] the peril of the Athenian law.

EGE. Enough, enough, my lord; you have enough:
I beg the law, the law, upon his head.
They would have stolen away; they would, Demetrius,
Thereby to have defeated you and me,
You of your wife and me of my consent,
Of my consent that she should be your wife.

[23] *in grace of our solemnity*] in honor of our marriage.

[24] *Saint Valentine*] Birds were said to choose their mates on St. Valentine's Day.

[25] *where*] wherever.

[26] *Without*] beyond.

DEM. My lord, fair Helen told me of their stealth,
Of this their purpose hither to this wood;
And I in fury hither follow'd them,
Fair Helena in fancy[27] following me.
But, my good lord, I wot not by what power,—
But by some power it is,—my love to Hermia,
Melted as the snow, seems to me now
As the remembrance of an idle gaud,[28]
Which in my childhood I did dote upon;
And all the faith, the virtue of my heart,
The object and the pleasure of mine eye,
Is only Helena. To her, my lord,
Was I betroth'd ere I saw Hermia:
But, like in sickness, did I loathe this food;
But, as in health, come to my natural taste,
Now I do wish it, love it, long for it,
And will for evermore be true to it.
THE. Fair lovers, you are fortunately met:
Of this discourse we more will hear anon.
Egeus, I will overbear[29] your will;
For in the temple, by and by, with us
These couples shall eternally be knit:
And, for the morning now is something[30] worn,
Our purposed hunting shall be set aside.
Away with us to Athens! three and three,
We'll hold a feast in great solemnity.
Come, Hippolyta. [*Exeunt* THE., HIP., EGE., *and train.*
DEM. These things seem small and undistinguishable,
Like far-off mountains turned into clouds.
HER. Methinks I see these things with parted eye,[31]
When every thing seems double.
HEL. So methinks:
And I have found Demetrius like a jewel,[32]
Mine own, and not mine own.
DEM. Are you sure
That we are awake? It seems to me

[27] *fancy*] love.
[28] *idle gaud*] useless bauble.
[29] *overbear*] overrule.
[30] *something*] somewhat.
[31] *with parted eye*] with eye out of focus.
[32] *like a jewel*] just like one who finds and possesses a jewel not his own.

That yet we sleep, we dream. Do not you think
The Duke was here, and bid us follow him?

HER. Yea; and my father.

HEL. And Hippolyta.

LYS. And he did bid us follow to the temple.

DEM. Why, then, we are awake: let's follow him;
And by[33] the way let us recount our dreams. [*Exeunt.*

BOT. [*Awaking*] When my cue comes, call me, and I will answer: my next is, "Most fair Pyramus." Heigh-ho! Peter Quince! Flute, the bellows-mender! Snout, the tinker! Starveling! God's my life, stolen hence, and left me asleep! I have had a most rare vision. I have had a dream, past the wit of man to say what dream it was: man is but an ass, if he go about to expound this dream. Methought I was—there is no man can tell what. Methought I was,—and methought I had,—but man is but a patched[34] fool, if he will offer to say what methought I had. The eye of man hath not heard, the ear of man hath not seen, man's hand is not able to taste, his tongue to conceive, nor his heart to report, what my dream was. I will get Peter Quince to write a ballad of this dream: it shall be called Bottom's Dream, because it hath no bottom; and I will sing it in the latter end of a play, before the Duke: peradventure, to make it the more gracious, I shall sing it at her death.[35] [*Exit.*

Scene II—Athens

QUINCE'S HOUSE

Enter QUINCE, FLUTE, SNOUT, *and* STARVELING.

QUIN. Have you sent to Bottom's house? is he come home yet?

STAR. He cannot be heard of. Out of doubt he is transported.[1]

FLU. If he come not, then the play is marred: it goes not forward, doth it?

[33] *by*] along.
[34] *patched*] dressed in motley.
[35] *her death*] Thisbe's death in the play.

---

[1] *transported*] carried off or transformed.

QUIN. It is not possible: you have not a man in all Athens able to discharge[2] Pyramus but he.

FLU. No, he hath simply the best wit of any handicraft man in Athens.

QUIN. Yea, and the best person too; and he is a very paramour for a sweet voice.

FLU. You must say "paragon": a paramour is, God bless us, a thing of naught.[3]

Enter SNUG.

SNUG. Masters, the Duke is coming from the temple, and there is two or three lords and ladies more married: if our sport had gone forward, we had all been made men.

FLU. O sweet bully Bottom! Thus hath he lost sixpence a day[4] during his life; he could not have scaped sixpence a day: an the Duke had not given him sixpence a day for playing Pyramus, I'll be hanged; he would have deserved it: sixpence a day in Pyramus, or nothing.

Enter BOTTOM.

BOT. Where are these lads? where are these hearts?

QUIN. Bottom! O most courageous day! O most happy hour!

BOT. Masters, I am to discourse wonders: but ask me not what; for if I tell you, I am no true Athenian. I will tell you every thing, right as it fell out.

QUIN. Let us hear, sweet Bottom.

BOT. Not a word of me. All that I will tell you is, that the Duke hath dined. Get your apparel together, good strings to your beards, new ribbons to your pumps;[5] meet presently at the palace; every man look o'er his part; for the short and the long is, our play is preferred.[6] In any case, let Thisbe have clean linen; and let not him that plays the lion pare his nails, for they shall hang out for the lion's claws. And, most dear actors, eat no onions nor garlic, for we are to utter sweet breath; and I do not doubt but to hear them say, it is a sweet comedy. No more words: away! go, away! [*Exeunt.*

[2] *discharge*] play the part of.

[3] *a thing of naught*] something shameful, wicked.

[4] *sixpence a day*] i.e., a royal pension.

[5] *pumps*] light shoes.

[6] *preferred*] chosen for consideration.

Act V—Scene I—Athens

THE PALACE OF THESEUS

Enter THESEUS, HIPPOLYTA, PHILOSTRATE, Lords, *and* Attendants.

HIP. 'T is strange, my Theseus, that these lovers speak of.
THE. More strange than true: I never may believe
These antique[1] fables, nor these fairy toys.[2]
Lovers and madmen have such seething brains,
Such shaping fantasies, that apprehend
More than cool reason ever comprehends.
The lunatic, the lover and the poet
Are of imagination all compact:[3]
One sees more devils than vast hell can hold,
That is, the madman: the lover, all as frantic,
Sees Helen's beauty in a brow of Egypt:[4]
The poet's eye, in a fine frenzy rolling,
Doth glance from heaven to earth, from earth to heaven;
And as imagination bodies forth
The forms of things unknown, the poet's pen
Turns them to shapes, and gives to airy nothing
A local habitation and a name.
Such tricks hath strong imagination,
That, if it would but apprehend some joy,
It comprehends some bringer of that joy;
Or in the night, imagining some fear,[5]
How easy is a bush supposed a bear!

[1] *antique*] strange.
[2] *toys*] trifles.
[3] *all compact*] entirely constituted.
[4] *Sees . . . Egypt*] sees Helen of Troy's beauty in the face of a Gypsy.
[5] *some fear*] something inducing fear.

HIP. But all the story of the night told over,
And all their minds transfigured so together,
More witnesseth than fancy's images,
And grows to something of great constancy;[6]
But, howsoever, strange and admirable.
THE. Here come the lovers, full of joy and mirth.

Enter LYSANDER, DEMETRIUS, HERMIA, *and* HELENA.

Joy, gentle friends! joy and fresh days of love
Accompany your hearts!
LYS. More than to us
Wait in your royal walks, your board, your bed!
THE. Come now; what masques, what dances shall we have,
To wear away this long age of three hours
Between our after-supper and bed-time?
Where is our usual manager of mirth?
What revels are in hand? Is there no play,
To ease the anguish of a torturing hour?
Call Philostrate.
PHIL. Here, mighty Theseus.
THE. Say, what abridgement[7] have you for this evening?
What masque? what music? How shall we beguile
The lazy time, if not with some delight?
PHIL. There is a brief how many sports are ripe:[8]
Make choice of which your highness will see first.
[*Giving a paper.*
THE. [*reads*] The battle with the Centaurs, to be sung
By an Athenian eunuch to the harp.
We'll none of that: that have I told my love,
In glory of my kinsman Hercules.
[*Reads*] The riot of the tipsy Bacchanals,
Tearing the Thracian singer[9] in their rage.
That is an old device;[10] and it was play'd
When I from Thebes came last a conqueror.
[*Reads*] The thrice three Muses mourning for the death
Of Learning, late deceased in beggary.

[6] *constancy*] consistency.
[7] *abridgement*] pastime, entertainment.
[8] *a brief . . . ripe*] a written statement of how many entertainments are ready to be performed.
[9] *the Thracian singer*] Orpheus, the legendary poet.
[10] *device*] dramatic piece.

That is some satire, keen and critical,
Not sorting with[11] a nuptial ceremony.
[*Reads*] A tedious brief scene of young Pyramus
And his love Thisbe; very tragical mirth.
Merry and tragical! tedious and brief!
That is, hot ice and wondrous strange snow.
How shall we find the concord of this discord?

PHIL. A play there is, my lord, some ten words long,
Which is as brief as I have known a play;
But by ten words, my lord, it is too long,
Which makes it tedious; for in all the play
There is not one word apt, one player fitted:
And tragical, my noble lord, it is;
For Pyramus therein doth kill himself.
Which, when I saw rehearsed, I must confess,
Made mine eyes water; but more merry tears
The passion of loud laughter never shed.

THE. What are they that do play it?

PHIL. Hard-handed men, that work in Athens here,
Which never labour'd in their minds till now;
And now have toil'd their unbreathed[12] memories
With this same play, against[13] your nuptial.

THE. And we will hear it.

PHIL. No, my noble lord;
It is not for you: I have heard it over,
And it is nothing, nothing in the world;
Unless you can find sport in their intents,
Extremely stretch'd and conn'd with cruel pain,
To do you service.

THE. I will hear that play;
For never any thing can be amiss,
When simpleness and duty tender it.
Go, bring them in: and take your places, ladies.
[*Exit* PHILOSTRATE.

HIP. I love not to see wretchedness o'ercharged,
And duty in his service perishing.

THE. Why, gentle sweet, you shall see no such thing.

HIP. He says they can do nothing in this kind.

[11] *sorting with*] befitting.
[12] *unbreathed*] unexercised.
[13] *against*] in expectation of.

THE. The kinder we, to give them thanks for nothing.
Our sport shall be to take what they mistake:
And what poor duty cannot do, noble respect
Takes it in might, not merit.[14]
Where I have come, great clerks[15] have purposed
To greet me with premeditated welcomes;
Where I have seen them shiver and look pale,
Make periods in the midst of sentences,
Throttle their practised accent in their fears,
And, in conclusion, dumbly have broke off,
Not paying me a welcome. Trust me, sweet,
Out of this silence yet I picked a welcome;
And in the modesty of fearful duty
I read as much as from the rattling tongue
Of saucy and audacious eloquence.
Love, therefore, and tongue-tied simplicity
In least speak most, to my capacity.[16]

Re-enter PHILOSTRATE.

PHIL. So please your Grace, the Prologue is address'd.[17]
THE. Let him approach. [*Flourish of trumpets.*

Enter QUINCE *for the* Prologue.

PRO. If we offend, it is with our good will.
That you should think, we come not to offend,
But with good will. To show our simple skill,
That is the true beginning of our end.
Consider, then, we come but in despite.
We do not come, as minding to content you,
Our true intent is. All for your delight,
We are not here. That you should here repent you,
The actors are at hand; and, by their show,
You shall know all, that you are like to know.[18]
THE. This fellow doth not stand upon points.[19]
LYS. He hath rid his prologue like a rough colt; he knows not the stop.

[14] *Takes . . . merit*] values it for the intention rather than for its intrinsic merit.
[15] *clerks*] scholars.
[16] *to my capacity*] as I understand it.
[17] *the Prologue is address'd*] the actor who will speak the Prologue is ready.
[18] *If . . . to know*] The mispunctuation of the Prologue reverses its intended meaning.
[19] *does not stand upon points*] (1) is not respectful; (2) does not follow the correct punctuation.

A good moral, my lord: it is not enough to speak, but to speak true.

HIP. Indeed he hath played on his prologue like a child on a recorder; a sound, but not in government.[20]

THE. His speech was like a tangled chain; nothing impaired, but all disordered. Who is next?

Enter PYRAMUS *and* THISBE, WALL, MOONSHINE, *and* LION.

PRO. Gentles, perchance you wonder at this show;
But wonder on, till truth make all things plain.
This man is Pyramus, if you would know;
This beauteous lady Thisbe is certain.
This man, with lime and rough-cast, doth present
Wall, that vile Wall which did these lovers sunder;
And through Wall's chink, poor souls, they are content
To whisper. At the which let no man wonder.
This man, with lanthorn, dog, and bush of thorn,
Presenteth Moonshine; for, if you will know,
By moonshine did these lovers think no scorn
To meet at Ninus' tomb, there, there to woo.
This grisly beast, which Lion hight[21] by name,
The trusty Thisbe, coming first by night,
Did scare away, or rather did affright;
And, as she fled, her mantle she did fall,[22]
Which Lion vile with bloody mouth did stain.
Anon comes Pyramus, sweet youth and tall,[23]
And finds his trusty Thisbe's mantle slain:
Whereat, with blade, with bloody blameful blade,
He bravely broach'd his boiling bloody breast;
And Thisbe, tarrying in mulberry shade,
His dagger drew, and died. For all the rest,
Let Lion, Moonshine, Wall, and lovers twain
At large[24] discourse, while here they do remain.

[*Exeunt* Prologue, PYRAMUS, THISBE, LION, *and* MOONSHINE.

THE. I wonder if the lion be to speak.

DEM. No wonder, my lord: one lion may, when many asses do.

[20] *in government*] controlled.
[21] *hight*] is called.
[22] *did fall*] dropped.
[23] *tall*] spirited.
[24] *At large*] in detail.

WALL. In this same interlude it doth befall
That I, one Snout by name, present a wall;
And such a wall, as I would have you think,
That had in it a crannied hole or chink,
Through which the lovers, Pyramus and Thisbe,
Did whisper often very secretly.
This loam, this rough-cast, and this stone, doth show
That I am that same wall; the truth is so:
And this the cranny is, right and sinister,[25]
Through which the fearful lovers are to whisper.

THE. Would you desire lime and hair to speak better?

DEM. It is the wittiest partition that ever I heard discourse, my lord.

THE. Pyramus draws near the wall: silence!

Re-enter PYRAMUS.

PYR. O grim-look'd night! O night with hue so black!
O night, which ever art when day is not!
O night, O night! alack, alack, alack,
I fear my Thisbe's promise is forgot!
And thou, O wall, O sweet, O lovely wall,
That stand'st between her father's ground and mine!
Thou wall, O wall, O sweet and lovely wall,
Show me thy chink, to blink through with mine eyne!
[WALL *holds up his fingers.*
Thanks, courteous wall: Jove shield thee well for this!
But what see I? No Thisbe do I see.
O wicked wall, through whom I see no bliss!
Cursed be thy stones for thus deceiving me!

THE. The wall, methinks, being sensible,[26] should curse again.

PYR. No, in truth, sir, he should not. "Deceiving me" is Thisbe's cue: she is to enter now, and I am to spy her through the wall. You shall see, it will fall pat as I told you. Yonder she comes.

Re-enter THISBE.

THIS. O wall, full often hast thou heard my moans,
For parting my fair Pyramus and me!
My cherry lips have often kiss'd thy stones,
Thy stones with lime and hair knit up in thee.

[25] *sinister*] left.
[26] *sensible*] endowed with feeling.

PYR. I see a voice: now will I to the chink,
To spy an I can hear my Thisbe's face.
Thisbe!
THIS. My love thou art, my love I think.
PYR. Think what thou wilt, I am thy lover's grace;
And, like Limander, am I trusty still.
THIS. And I like Helen,[27] till the Fates me kill.
PYR. Not Shafalus to Procrus[28] was so true.
THIS. As Shafalus to Procrus, I to you.
PYR. O, kiss me through the hole of this vile wall!
THIS. I kiss the wall's hole, not your lips at all.
PYR. Wilt thou at Ninny's tomb meet me straightway?
THIS. 'Tide life, 'tide death,[29] I come without delay.
[*Exeunt* PYRAMUS *and* THISBE.
WALL. Thus have I, wall, my part discharged so;
And, being done, thus wall away doth go.

THE. Now is the mural down between the two neighbours.

DEM. No remedy, my lord, when walls are so wilful to hear without warning.

HIP. This is the silliest stuff that ever I heard.

THE. The best in this kind are but shadows;[30] and the worst are no worse, if imagination amend them.

HIP. It must be your imagination then, and not theirs.

THE. If we imagine no worse of them than they of themselves, they may pass for excellent men. Here come two noble beasts in, a man and a lion.

Re-enter LION *and* MOONSHINE.

LION. You, ladies, you, whose gentle hearts do fear
The smallest monstrous mouse that creeps on floor,
May now perchance both quake and tremble here,
When lion rough in wildest rage doth roar.
Then know that I, one Snug the joiner, am
A lion-fell,[31] nor else no lion's dam;
For, if I should as lion come in strife
Into this place, 't were pity on my life.

THE. A very gentle beast, and of a good conscience.

[27] *Limander ... Helen*] the actors' blunders for "Leander" and "Hero," two legendary doomed lovers.

[28] *Shafalus to Procrus*] a blunder for Cephalus and Procris, two legendary lovers.

[29] *'Tide life, 'tide death*] whether I live or die.

[30] *shadows*] images, representations.

[31] *A lion-fell*] both a fierce lion and merely a lion's skin.

DEM. The very best at a beast, my lord, that e'er I saw.

LYS. This lion is a very fox for his valour.

THE. True; and a goose for his discretion.[32]

DEM. Not so, my lord; for his valour cannot carry his discretion; and the fox carries the goose.

THE. His discretion, I am sure, cannot carry his valour; for the goose carries not the fox. It is well: leave it to his discretion, and let us listen to the moon.

MOON. This lanthorn doth the horned moon present;—

DEM. He should have worn the horns on his head.[33]

THE. He is no crescent, and his horns are invisible within the circumference.

MOON. This lanthorn doth the horned moon present;
Myself the man i' the moon do seem to be.

THE. This is the greatest error of all the rest: the man should be put into the lantern. How is it else the man i' the moon?

DEM. He dares not come there for the candle; for, you see, it is already in snuff.[34]

HIP. I am aweary of this moon: would he would change!

THE. It appears, by his small light of discretion, that he is in the wane; but yet, in courtesy, in all reason, we must stay the time.

LYS. Proceed, Moon.

MOON. All that I have to say, is, to tell you that the lanthorn is the moon; I, the man i' the moon; this thorn-bush, my thorn-bush; and this dog, my dog.

DEM. Why, all these should be in the lantern; for all these are in the moon. But, silence! here comes Thisbe.

Re-enter THISBE.

THIS. This is old Ninny's tomb. Where is my love?

LION. [*Roaring*] Oh———— [THISBE *runs off.*

DEM. Well roared, Lion.

THE. Well run, Thisbe.

HIP. Well shone, Moon. Truly, the moon shines with a good grace.
[*The* LION *shakes* THISBE's *mantle, and exit.*

THE. Well moused, Lion.

DEM. And then came Pyramus.

LYS. And so the lion vanished.

Re-enter PYRAMUS.

[32] *discretion*] good sense.

[33] *horns on his head*] i.e., as the sign of a cuckold.

[34] *in snuff*] (1) needing to be snuffed; (2) offended.

PYR. Sweet Moon, I thank thee for thy sunny beams;
I thank thee, Moon, for shining now so bright;
For, by thy gracious, golden, glittering gleams,
I trust to take of truest Thisbe sight.
But stay, O spite!
But mark, poor knight,
What dreadful dole[35] is here!
Eyes, do you see?
How can it be?
O dainty duck! O dear!
Thy mantle good,
What, stain'd with blood!
Approach, ye Furies fell!
O Fates, come, come,
Cut thread and thrum;[36]
Quail,[37] crush, conclude, and quell![38]

THE. This passion, and the death of a dear friend, would go near to make a man look sad.

HIP. Beshrew my heart, but I pity the man.

PYR. O wherefore, Nature, didst thou lions frame?[39]
Since lion vile hath here deflower'd my dear:
Which is—no, no—which was the fairest dame
That lived, that loved, that liked, that look'd with cheer.[40]
Come, tears, confound;
Out, sword, and wound
The pap[41] of Pyramus;
Ay, that left pap,
Where heart doth hop: [*Stabs himself.*
Thus die I, thus, thus, thus.
Now am I dead,
Now am I fled;
My soul is in the sky:
Tongue, lose thy light;
Moon, take thy flight: [*Exit* MOONSHINE.
Now die, die, die, die, die. [*Dies.*

DEM. No die, but an ace,[42] for him; for he is but one.

[35] *dole*] grief.
[36] *thrum*] the tufted end of weavers' thread.
[37] *Quail*] overpower.
[38] *quell*] destroy.
[39] *frame*] form, produce.
[40] *cheer*] face.
[41] *pap*] breast.
[42] *No die, but an ace*] a play on die-casting terms. The "ace" is the side of a die showing only one spot. In Shakespearean London, "ace" was pronounced so as to be scarcely distinguishable from "ass" (idiot).

LYS. Less than an ace, man; for he is dead; he is nothing.

THE. With the help of a surgeon he might yet recover, and prove an ass.

HIP. How chance Moonshine is gone before Thisbe comes back and finds her lover?

THE. She will find him by starlight. Here she comes; and her passion ends the play.

Re-enter THISBE.

HIP. Methinks she should not use a long one for such a Pyramus: I hope she will be brief.

DEM. A mote will turn the balance, which Pyramus, which Thisbe, is the better; he for a man, God warrant us; she for a woman, God bless us.

LYS. She hath spied him already with those sweet eyes.

DEM. And thus she means,[43] videlicet:—

THIS.
Asleep, my love?
What, dead, my dove?
O Pyramus, arise!
Speak, speak. Quite dumb?
Dead, dead? A tomb
Must cover thy sweet eyes.
These lily lips,
This cherry nose,
These yellow cowslip cheeks,
Are gone, are gone:
Lovers, make moan:
His eyes were green as leeks.
O Sisters Three,[44]
Come, come to me,
With hands as pale as milk:
Lay them in gore,
Since you have shore[45]
With shears his thread of silk.[46]
Tongue, not a word:
Come, trusty sword;
Come, blade, my breast imbrue:[47] [*Stabs herself.*

[43] *means*] laments.

[44] *Sisters Three*] the three beings in Greek mythology who determine human and divine fate.

[45] *shore*] shorn.

[46] *thread of silk*] the thread symbolizing his life.

[47] *imbrue*] shed the blood of.

And, farewell, friends;
Thus Thisbe ends:
Adieu, adieu, adieu. [*Dies.*

THE. Moonshine and Lion are left to bury the dead.

DEM. Ay, and Wall too.

BOT. [*Starting up*] No, I assure you; the wall is down that parted their fathers. Will it please you to see the epilogue, or to hear a Bergomask dance[48] between two of our company?

THE. No epilogue, I pray you; for your play needs no excuse. Never excuse; for when the players are all dead, there need none to be blamed. Marry, if he that writ it had played Pyramus and hanged himself in Thisbe's garter, it would have been a fine tragedy: and so it is, truly; and very notably discharged. But, come, your Bergomask: let your epilogue alone. [A *dance.*

The iron tongue of midnight hath told[49] twelve:
Lovers, to bed; 't is almost fairy time.
I fear we shall out-sleep the coming morn,
As much as we this night have overwatch'd.
This palpable-gross[50] play hath well beguiled
The heavy gait of night. Sweet friends, to bed.
A fortnight hold we this solemnity,
In nightly revels and new jollity. [*Exeunt.*

Enter PUCK.

PUCK. Now the hungry lion roars,
And the wolf behowls the moon;
Whilst the heavy ploughman snores,
All with weary task fordone.[51]
Now the wasted brands do glow,
Whilst the screech-owl, screeching loud,
Puts the wretch that lies in woe
In remembrance of a shroud.
Now it is the time of night,
That the graves, all gaping wide,
Every one lets forth his sprite,
In the church-way paths to glide:

48 *Bergomask dance*] a dance named after the Italian commune of Bergamo, noted for the rusticity of its populace.

49 *told*] counted.

50 *palpable-gross*] palpably stupid.

51 *fordone*] exhausted.

And we fairies, that do run
By the triple Hecate's[52] team,
From the presence of the sun,
Following darkness like a dream,
Now are frolic:[53] not a mouse
Shall disturb this hallow'd house:
I am sent with broom before,
To sweep the dust behind the door.

Enter OBERON *and* TITANIA *with their train.*

OBE. Through the house give glimmering light,
By the dead and drowsy fire:
Every elf and fairy sprite
Hop as light as bird from brier;
And this ditty, after me,
Sing, and dance it trippingly.[54]
TITA. First, rehearse your song by rote,
To each word a warbling note:
Hand in hand, with fairy grace,
Will we sing, and bless this place. [*Song and dance.*
OBE. Now, until the break of day,
Through this house each fairy stray.
To the best bride-bed will we,
Which by us shall blessed be;
And the issue there create[55]
Ever shall be fortunate.
So shall all the couples three
Ever true in loving be;
And the blots of Nature's hand
Shall not in their issue stand;
Never mole, hare lip, nor scar,
Nor mark prodigious,[56] such as are
Despised in nativity,
Shall upon their children be.

[52] *triple Hecate's*] The goddess Hecate has three roles in classical mythology: as Luna in heaven, as Diana on earth and as Proserpina in hell. Her chariot was drawn by a "triple . . . team" of dragons.

[53] *frolic*] merry.

[54] *trippingly*] nimbly.

[55] *create*] created.

[56] *prodigious*] portentous.

With this field-dew consecrate,[57]
Every fairy take his gait;[58]
And each several[59] chamber bless,
Through this palace, with sweet peace,
Ever shall in safety rest,
And the owner of it blest.
Trip away; make no stay;
Meet me all by break of day.

[*Exeunt* OBERON, TITANIA, *and train.*

PUCK. If we shadows have offended,
Think but this, and all is mended,
That you have but slumber'd here,
While these visions did appear.
And this weak and idle theme,
No more yielding but a dream,
Gentles, do not reprehend:
If you pardon, we will mend.
And, as I am an honest Puck,
If we have unearned luck
Now to scape the serpent's tongue,[60]
We will make amends ere long;
Else the Puck a liar call:
So, good night unto you all.
Give me your hands,[61] if we be friends,
And Robin shall restore amends. [*Exit.*

57 *consecrate*] consecrated.
58 *take his gait*] make his way.
59 *several*] separate.
60 *the serpent's tongue*] hissing (of the audience).
61 *hands*] applause.

Romeo and Juliet

Note

WILLIAM SHAKESPEARE (1564–1616) is thought to have written *Romeo and Juliet* in the mid-1590s. The play, a tragedy of young love become sacrificial in an adverse environment of family feuds and mischance, is one of Shakespeare's earliest efforts in the tragic genre and bears many of the traits of the lyric poetry and romantic comedies with which it is contemporaneous. The immediate source for the play was Arthur Brooke's narrative poem *The Tragical History of Romeus and Juliet* (1562), which was in turn derived from a late fifteenth-century Italian novella. With its rich Petrarchan strains, its stock characters and the breadth of poetic forms it employs, *Romeo and Juliet* reveals a Shakespeare still coming to terms with his own technical virtuosity and originality. Yet one's critical reservations tend to be swept aside by the play's moments of comic vitality and its winning vision of innocent love doomed to an untimely end.

Dramatis Personae

ESCALUS, Prince of Verona.
PARIS, a young nobleman, kinsman to the Prince.
MONTAGUE, CAPULET, heads of two houses at variance with each other.
An old man, of the Capulet family.
ROMEO, son to Montague.
MERCUTIO, kinsman to the Prince, and friend to Romeo.
BENVOLIO, nephew to Montague, and friend to Romeo.
TYBALT, nephew to Lady Capulet.
FRIAR LAURENCE, a Franciscan.
FRIAR JOHN, of the same order.
BALTHASAR, servant to Romeo.
SAMPSON, GREGORY, servants to Capulet.
PETER, servant to Juliet's nurse.
ABRAHAM, servant to Montague.
An Apothecary.
Three Musicians.
Page to Paris; another Page; an Officer.

LADY MONTAGUE, wife to Montague.
LADY CAPULET, wife to Capulet.
JULIET, daughter to Capulet.
Nurse to Juliet.

Citizens of Verona; kinsfolk of both houses; Maskers, Guards, Watchmen, and Attendants.

Chorus.

SCENE: *Verona; Mantua.*

PROLOGUE.

Enter Chorus.

CHOR. Two households, both alike in dignity,
In fair Verona, where we lay our scene,
From ancient grudge break to new mutiny,
Where civil blood makes civil hands unclean.
From forth the fatal loins of these two foes
A pair of star-cross'd lovers take their life;
Whose misadventured piteous overthrows
Do with their death bury their parents' strife.
The fearful passage of their death mark'd love,
And the continuance of their parents' rage,
Which, but their children's end, nought could remove,
Is now the two hours' traffic of our stage;
The which if you with patient ears attend,
What here shall miss, our toil shall strive to mend.

ACT I.

SCENE I. *Verona. A public place.*

Enter SAMPSON *and* GREGORY, *of the house of Capulet, with swords and bucklers.*

SAM. Gregory, on my word, we'll not carry coals.[1]

GRE. No, for then we should be colliers.

SAM. I mean, an we be in choler, we'll draw.

GRE. Ay, while you live, draw your neck out o' the collar.[2]

SAM. I strike quickly, being moved.

GRE. But thou art not quickly moved to strike.

SAM. A dog of the house of Montague moves me.

GRE. To move is to stir, and to be valiant is to stand: therefore, if thou art moved, thou runn'st away.

SAM. A dog of that house shall move me to stand: I will take the wall[3] of any man or maid of Montague's.

GRE. That shows thee a weak slave; for the weakest goes to the wall.

SAM. 'Tis true; and therefore women, being the weaker vessels, are ever thrust to the wall: therefore I will push Montague's men from the wall and thrust his maids to the wall.

GRE. The quarrel is between our masters and us their men.

SAM. 'Tis all one, I will show myself a tyrant: when I have fought with the men, I will be civil with the maids; I will cut off their heads.

GRE. The heads of the maids?

SAM. Ay, the heads of the maids, or their maidenheads; take it in what sense thou wilt.

GRE. They must take it in sense that feel it.

[1] *carry coals*] tolerate insults.

[2] *collar*] hangman's noose.

[3] *take the wall*] walk on the side of the street nearest the wall; thus, insult.

SAM. Me they shall feel while I am able to stand: and 'tis known I am a pretty piece of flesh.

GRE. 'Tis well thou art not fish; if thou hadst, thou hadst been poor John.[4] Draw thy tool; here comes two of the house of Montagues.

Enter ABRAHAM *and* BALTHASAR.

SAM. My naked weapon is out: quarrel; I will back thee.

GRE. How! turn thy back and run?

SAM. Fear me not.

GRE. No, marry: I fear thee!

SAM. Let us take the law of our sides; let them begin.

GRE. I will frown as I pass by, and let them take it as they list.

SAM. Nay, as they dare. I will bite my thumb at them; which is a disgrace to them, if they bear it.

ABR. Do you bite your thumb at us, sir?

SAM. I do bite my thumb, sir.

ABR. Do you bite your thumb at us, sir?

SAM. [*Aside to* GRE.] Is the law of our side, if I say ay?

GRE. No.

SAM. No, sir, I do not bite my thumb at you, sir; but I bite my thumb, sir.

GRE. Do you quarrel, sir?

ABR. Quarrel, sir! no, sir.

SAM. But if you do, sir, I am for you: I serve as good a man as you.

ABR. No better.

SAM. Well, sir.

Enter BENVOLIO.

GRE. [*Aside to* SAM.] Say 'better': here comes one of my master's kinsmen.

SAM. Yes, better, sir.

ABR. You lie.

SAM. Draw, if you be men. Gregory, remember thy swashing[5] blow. [*They fight.*

BEN. Part, fools! [*Beating down their weapons.*
Put up your swords; you know not what you do.

[4] *poor John*] salted and dried hake, a coarse kind of fish.

[5] *swashing*] smashing.

Enter TYBALT.

TYB. What, art thou drawn among these heartless hinds?[6]
Turn thee, Benvolio, look upon thy death.
BEN. I do but keep the peace: put up thy sword,
Or manage it to part these men with me.
TYB. What, drawn, and talk of peace! I hate the word,
As I hate hell, all Montagues, and thee:
Have at thee, coward! [*They fight.*

Enter several of both houses, who join the fray; then enter Citizens *and* Peace-officers, *with clubs.*

FIRST OFF. Clubs, bills,[7] and partisans! strike! beat them down!
Down with the Capulets! down with the Montagues!

Enter old CAPULET *in his gown, and* LADY CAPULET.

CAP. What noise is this? Give me my long sword, ho!
LA. CAP. A crutch, a crutch! why call you for a sword?
CAP. My sword, I say! Old Montague is come,
And flourishes his blade in spite of me.

Enter old MONTAGUE *and* LADY MONTAGUE.

MON. Thou villain Capulet!—Hold me not, let me go.
LA. MON. Thou shalt not stir one foot to seek a foe.

Enter PRINCE ESCALUS, *with his train.*

PRIN. Rebellious subjects, enemies to peace,
Profaners of this neighbour-stained steel,—
Will they not hear? What, ho! you men, you beasts,
That quench the fire of your pernicious rage
With purple fountains issuing from your veins,
On pain of torture, from those bloody hands
Throw your mistemper'd weapons to the ground,
And hear the sentence of your moved prince.
Three civil brawls, bred of an airy word,
By thee, old Capulet, and Montague,
Have thrice disturb'd the quiet of our streets,
And made Verona's ancient citizens

[6] *heartless hinds*] (1) cowardly menials; (2) female deer unprotected by a hart.
[7] *bills*] a kind of pike or halberd.

Cast by their grave beseeming ornaments,
To wield old partisans, in hands as old,
Canker'd with peace, to part your canker'd hate:
If ever you disturb our streets again,
Your lives shall pay the forfeit of the peace.
For this time, all the rest depart away:
You, Capulet, shall go along with me;
And, Montague, come you this afternoon,
To know our farther pleasure in this case,
To old Free-town, our common judgement-place.
Once more, on pain of death, all men depart.

[*Exeunt all but* MONTAGUE, LADY MONTAGUE, *and* BENVOLIO.

MON. Who set this ancient quarrel new abroach?
Speak, nephew, were you by when it began?
BEN. Here were the servants of your adversary
And yours close fighting ere I did approach:
I drew to part them: in the instant came
The fiery Tybalt, with his sword prepared;
Which, as he breathed defiance to my ears,
He swung about his head, and cut the winds,
Who, nothing hurt withal, hiss'd him in scorn:
While we were interchanging thrusts and blows,
Came more and more, and fought on part and part,[8]
Till the Prince came, who parted either part.
LA. MON. O, where is Romeo? saw you him to-day?
Right glad I am he was not at this fray.
BEN. Madam, an hour before the worshipp'd sun
Peer'd forth the golden window of the east,
A troubled mind drave me to walk abroad;
Where, underneath the grove of sycamore
That westward rooteth from the city's side,
So early walking did I see your son:
Towards him I made; but he was ware of me,
And stole into the covert of the wood:
I, measuring his affections[9] by my own,
Which then most sought where most might not be found,
Being one too many by my weary self,

[8] *on part and part*] on one side and the other.
[9] *affections*] wishes, inclination.

Pursued my humour, not pursuing his,
And gladly shunn'd who gladly fled from me.

MON. Many a morning hath he there been seen,
With tears augmenting the fresh morning's dew,
Adding to clouds more clouds with his deep sighs:
But all so soon as the all-cheering sun
Should in the farthest east begin to draw
The shady curtains from Aurora's bed,
Away from light steals home my heavy son,
And private in his chamber pens himself,
Shuts up his windows, locks fair daylight out,
And makes himself an artificial night:
Black and portentous must this humour prove,
Unless good counsel may the cause remove.

BEN. My noble uncle, do you know the cause?

MON. I neither know it nor can learn of him.

BEN. Have you importuned him by any means?

MON. Both by myself and many other friends:
But he, his own affections' counsellor,
Is to himself—I will not say how true—
But to himself so secret and so close,
So far from sounding and discovery,
As is the bud bit with an envious worm,
Ere he can spread his sweet leaves to the air,
Or dedicate his beauty to the sun.
Could we but learn from whence his sorrows grow,
We would as willingly give cure as know.

Enter ROMEO.

BEN. See, where he comes: so please you step aside;
I'll know his grievance, or be much denied.

MON. I would thou wert so happy by thy stay,
To hear true shrift. Come, madam, let's away.

[*Exeunt* MONTAGUE *and* LADY.

BEN. Good morrow, cousin.

ROM. Is the day so young?

BEN. But new struck nine.

ROM. Ay me! sad hours seem long.
Was that my father that went hence so fast?

BEN. It was. What sadness lengthens Romeo's hours?

ROM. Not having that which, having, makes them short.

BEN. In love?

ROM. Out—
BEN. Of love?
ROM. Out of her favour, where I am in love.
BEN. Alas, that love, so gentle in his view,
Should be so tyrannous and rough in proof![10]
ROM. Alas, that love, whose view is muffled still,
Should without eyes see pathways to his will!
Where shall we dine? O me! What fray was here?
Yet tell me not, for I have heard it all.
Here's much to do with hate, but more with love:
Why, then, O brawling love! O loving hate!
O any thing, of nothing first create!
O heavy lightness! serious vanity!
Mis-shapen chaos of well-seeming forms!
Feather of lead, bright smoke, cold fire, sick health!
Still-waking sleep, that is not what it is!
This love feel I, that feel no love in this.
Dost thou not laugh?
BEN. No, coz, I rather weep.
ROM. Good heart, at what?
BEN. At thy good heart's oppression.
ROM. Why, such is love's transgression.
Griefs of mine own lie heavy in my breast;
Which thou wilt propagate,[11] to have it prest
With more of thine: this love that thou hast shown
Doth add more grief to too much of mine own.
Love is a smoke raised with the fume of sighs;
Being purged, a fire sparkling in lovers' eyes;
Being vex'd, a sea nourish'd with lovers' tears:
What is it else? a madness most discreet,
A choking gall and a preserving sweet.
Farewell, my coz.
BEN. Soft! I will go along:
An if you leave me so, you do me wrong.
ROM. Tut, I have lost myself; I am not here;
This is not Romeo, he's some other where.
BEN. Tell me in sadness,[12] who is that you love?
ROM. What, shall I groan and tell thee?

[10] *proof*] experience.
[11] *propagate*] increase.
[12] *sadness*] seriousness.

BEN. Groan! why, no;
But sadly tell me who.
ROM. Bid a sick man in sadness make his will:
Ah, word ill urged to one that is so ill!
In sadness, cousin, I do love a woman.
BEN. I aim'd so near when I supposed you loved.
ROM. A right good mark-man! And she's fair I love.
BEN. A right fair mark, fair coz, is soonest hit.
ROM. Well, in that hit you miss: she'll not be hit
With Cupid's arrow; she hath Dian's wit,
And in strong proof[13] of chastity well arm'd,
From love's weak childish bow she lives unharm'd.
She will not stay[14] the siege of loving terms,
Nor bide the encounter of assailing eyes,
Nor ope her lap to saint-seducing gold:
O, she is rich in beauty, only poor
That, when she dies, with beauty dies her store.
BEN. Then she hath sworn that she will still[15] live chaste?
ROM. She hath, and in that sparing makes huge waste;
For beauty, starved with her severity,
Cuts beauty off from all posterity.
She is too fair, too wise, wisely too fair,
To merit bliss by making me despair:
She hath forsworn to love; and in that vow
Do I live dead, that live to tell it now.
BEN. Be ruled by me, forget to think of her.
ROM. O, teach me how I should forget to think.
BEN. By giving liberty unto thine eyes;
Examine other beauties.
ROM. 'Tis the way
To call hers, exquisite, in question more:[16]
These happy masks that kiss fair ladies' brows,
Being black, put us in mind they hide the fair;
He that is strucken blind cannot forget
The precious treasure of his eyesight lost:
Show me a mistress that is passing[17] fair,

[13] *proof*] impenetrable armor.
[14] *stay*] undergo, endure.
[15] *still*] always.
[16] *in question more*] even more strongly to mind.
[17] *passing*] exceedingly.

What doth her beauty serve but as a note
Where I may read who pass'd that passing fair?
Farewell: thou canst not teach me to forget.
BEN. I'll pay that doctrine,[18] or else die in debt. [*Exeunt.*

SCENE II. *A street.*

Enter CAPULET, PARIS, *and* Servant.

CAP. But Montague is bound as well as I,
In penalty alike; and 'tis not hard, I think,
For men so old as we to keep the peace.
PAR. Of honourable reckoning[1] are you both;
And pity 'tis you lived at odds so long.
But now, my lord, what say you to my suit?
CAP. But saying o'er what I have said before:
My child is yet a stranger in the world;
She hath not seen the change of fourteen years:
Let two more summers wither in their pride
Ere we may think her ripe to be a bride.
PAR. Younger than she are happy mothers made.
CAP. And too soon marr'd are those so early made.
The earth hath swallow'd all my hopes but she,
She is the hopeful lady of my earth:[2]
But woo her, gentle Paris, get her heart;
My will to her consent is but a part;
An she agree, within her scope of choice
Lies my consent and fair according voice:
This night I hold an old accustom'd feast,
Whereto I have invited many a guest,
Such as I love; and you among the store,
One more, most welcome, makes my number more.
At my poor house look to behold this night
Earth-treading stars that make dark heaven light:
Such comfort as do lusty young men feel
When well-apparell'd April on the heel

[18] *pay that doctrine*] give that instruction.

[1] *reckoning*] repute.
[2] *hopeful . . . earth*] heir of my property and line.

Of limping winter treads, even such delight
Among fresh female buds shall you this night
Inherit at my house; hear all, all see,
And like her most whose merit most shall be:
Which on more view, of many mine being one
May stand in number, though in reckoning none.
Come, go with me. [*To* Servant] Go, sirrah, trudge about
Through fair Verona; find those persons out
Whose names are written there, and to them say,
My house and welcome on their pleasure stay.

[*Exeunt* CAPULET *and* PARIS.

SERV. Find them out whose names are written here! It is written that the shoemaker should meddle with his yard and the tailor with his last,[3] the fisher with his pencil and the painter with his nets; but I am sent to find those persons whose names are here writ, and can never find what names the writing person hath here writ. I must to the learned. In good time.

Enter BENVOLIO *and* ROMEO.

BEN. Tut, man, one fire burns out another's burning.
One pain is lessen'd by another's anguish;
Turn giddy, and be holp by backward turning;
One desperate grief cures with another's languish:
Take thou some new infection to thy eye,
And the rank poison of the old will die.

ROM. Your plantain-leaf is excellent for that.

BEN. For what, I pray thee?

ROM. For your broken shin.

BEN. Why, Romeo, art thou mad?

ROM. Not mad, but bound more than a madman is;
Shut up in prison, kept without my food,
Whipt and tormented and— God-den,[4] good fellow.

SERV. God gi' god-den. I pray, sir, can you read?

ROM. Ay, mine own fortune in my misery.

SERV. Perhaps you have learned it without book: but, I pray, can you read any thing you see?

ROM. Ay, if I know the letters and the language.

SERV. Ye say honestly: rest you merry!

ROM. Stay, fellow; I can read. [*Reads.*

[3] *last*] the mold on which shoes are made.

[4] *God-den*] Good evening.

'Signior Martino and his wife and daughters; County Anselme and his beauteous sisters; the lady widow of Vitruvio; Signior Placentio and his lovely nieces; Mercutio and his brother Valentine; mine uncle Capulet, his wife, and daughters; my fair niece Rosaline; Livia; Signior Valentio and his cousin Tybalt; Lucio and the lively Helena.'

A fair assembly: whither should they come?
SERV. Up.[5]
ROM. Whither? to supper?
SERV. To our house.
ROM. Whose house?
SERV. My master's.
ROM. Indeed, I should have ask'd you that before.
SERV. Now I'll tell you without asking: my master is the great rich Capulet; and if you be not of the house of Montagues, I pray, come and crush a cup of wine. Rest you merry! [*Exit.*
BEN. At this same ancient feast of Capulet's
Sups the fair Rosaline whom thou so lovest,
With all the admired beauties of Verona:
Go thither, and with unattainted[6] eye
Compare her face with some that I shall show,
And I will make thee think thy swan a crow.
ROM. When the devout religion of mine eye
Maintains such falsehood, then turn tears to fires;
And these, who, often drown'd, could never die,
Transparent heretics, be burnt for liars!
One fairer than my love! the all-seeing sun
Ne'er saw her match since first the world begun.
BEN. Tut, you saw her fair, none else being by,
Herself poised with herself in either eye:
But in that crystal scales let there be weigh'd
Your lady's love against some other maid,
That I will show you shining at this feast,
And she shall scant show well that now seems best.
ROM. I'll go along, no such sight to be shown,
But to rejoice in splendour of mine own. [*Exeunt.*

[5] *come . . . Up*] The servant is quibbling, "come up" being a vulgar phrase.
[6] *unattainted*] not infected, impartial.

SCENE III. *A room in Capulet's house.*

Enter LADY CAPULET *and* NURSE.

LA. CAP. Nurse, where's my daughter? call her forth to me.
NURSE. Now, by my maidenhead at twelve year old,
I bade her come. What, lamb! what, lady-bird!
God forbid!—Where's this girl? What, Juliet!

Enter JULIET.

JUL. How now! who calls?
NURSE. Your mother.
JUL. Madam, I am here. What is your will?
LA. CAP. This is the matter. Nurse, give leave awhile,
We must talk in secret:—Nurse, come back again;
I have remember'd me, thou's[1] hear our counsel.
Thou know'st my daughter's of a pretty age.
NURSE. Faith, I can tell her age unto an hour.
LA. CAP. She's not fourteen.
NURSE. I'll lay fourteen of my teeth,—
And yet, to my teen[2] be it spoken, I have but four,—
She is not fourteen. How long is it now
To Lammas-tide?
LA. CAP. A fortnight and odd days.
NURSE. Even or odd, of all days in the year,
Come Lammas-eve at night shall she be fourteen.
Susan and she—God rest all Christian souls!—
Were of an age: well, Susan is with God;
She was too good for me:—but, as I said,
On Lammas-eve at night shall she be fourteen;
That shall she, marry; I remember it well.
'Tis since the earthquake now eleven years;
And she was wean'd,—I never shall forget it—
Of all the days of the year, upon that day:
For I had then laid wormwood[3] to my dug,
Sitting in the sun under the dove-house wall;

[1] *thou's*] thou shalt.
[2] *teen*] grief, pain.
[3] *wormwood*] *Artemisia absinthium*, proverbial for its bitterness and medicinal properties.

My lord and you were then at Mantua:—
Nay, I do bear a brain:—but, as I said,
When it did taste the wormwood on the nipple
Of my dug, and felt it bitter, pretty fool,
To see it tetchy, and fall out with the dug!
Shake, quoth the dove-house: 'twas no need, I trow,
To bid me trudge.
And since that time it is eleven years;
For then she could stand high-lone;[4] nay, by the rood,
She could have run and waddled all about;
For even the day before, she broke her brow:[5]
And then my husband,—God be with his soul!
A' was a merry man—took up the child:
'Yea,' quoth he, 'dost thou fall upon thy face?
Thou wilt fall backward when thou hast more wit;
Wilt thou not, Jule?' and, by my holidame,[6]
The pretty wretch left crying, and said 'Ay.'
To see now how a jest shall come about!
I warrant, an I should live a thousand years,
I never should forget it: 'Wilt thou not, Jule?' quoth he;
And, pretty fool, it stinted,[7] and said 'Ay.'

LA. CAP. Enough of this; I pray thee, hold thy peace.

NURSE. Yes, madam: yet I cannot choose but laugh,
To think it should leave crying, and say 'Ay':
And yet, I warrant, it had upon it brow
A bump as big as a young cockerel's stone;[8]
A perilous knock; and it cried bitterly:
'Yea,' quoth my husband, 'fall'st upon thy face?
Thou wilt fall backward when thou comest to age;
Wilt thou not, Jule?' It stinted, and said 'Ay.'

JUL. And stint thou too, I pray thee, Nurse, say I.

NURSE. Peace, I have done. God mark thee to his grace!
Thou wast the prettiest babe that e'er I nursed:
An I might live to see thee married once,[9]
I have my wish.

LA. CAP. Marry, that 'marry' is the very theme

[4] *high-lone*] on her own feet, unsupported.
[5] *broke her brow*] (fell and) cut her head.
[6] *holidame*] halidom, salvation.
[7] *stinted*] ceased.
[8] *stone*] testicle.
[9] *once*] ever, at some time.

I came to talk of. Tell me, daughter Juliet,
How stands your disposition to be married?
JUL. It is an honour that I dream not of.
NURSE. An honour! were not I thine only nurse,
I would say thou hadst suck'd wisdom from thy teat.
LA. CAP. Well, think of marriage now; younger than you
Here in Verona, ladies of esteem,
Are made already mothers. By my count,
I was your mother much upon these years
That you are now a maid. Thus then in brief;
The valiant Paris seeks you for his love.
NURSE. A man, young lady! lady, such a man
As all the world—why, he's a man of wax.[10]
LA. CAP. Verona's summer hath not such a flower.
NURSE. Nay, he's a flower; in faith, a very flower.
LA. CAP. What say you? can you love the gentleman?
This night you shall behold him at our feast:
Read o'er the volume of young Paris' face,
And find delight writ there with beauty's pen;
Examine every married[11] lineament,
And see how one another lends content;
And what obscured in this fair volume lies
Find written in the margent of his eyes.
This precious book of love, this unbound lover,
To beautify him, only lacks a cover:
The fish lives in the sea; and 'tis much pride
For fair without the fair within to hide:
That book in many's eyes doth share the glory,
That in gold clasps locks in the golden story:
So shall you share all that he doth possess,
By having him making yourself no less.
NURSE. No less! nay, bigger: women grow by men.
LA. CAP. Speak briefly, can you like of Paris' love?
JUL. I'll look to like, if looking liking move:
But no more deep will I endart mine eye
Than your consent gives strength to make it fly.

Enter a Servingman.

[10] *a man of wax*] as handsome as if modeled in wax.
[11] *married*] proportioned.

SERV. Madam, the guests are come, supper served up, you called, my young lady asked for, the Nurse cursed in the pantry, and every thing in extremity. I must hence to wait; I beseech you, follow straight.

LA. CAP. We follow thee. [*Exit* Servingman.] Juliet, the County stays.

NURSE. Go, girl, seek happy nights to happy days. [*Exeunt.*

SCENE IV. *A street.*

Enter ROMEO, MERCUTIO, BENVOLIO, *with five or six other* Maskers, *and* Torch-bearers.

ROM. What, shall this speech be spoke for our excuse?
Or shall we on without apology?
BEN. The date is out of such prolixity:
We'll have no Cupid hoodwink'd[1] with a scarf,
Bearing a Tartar's painted bow of lath,
Scaring the ladies like a crow-keeper;[2]
Nor no without-book prologue, faintly spoke
After the prompter, for our entrance:
But, let them measure us by what they will,
We'll measure them a measure,[3] and be gone.
ROM. Give me a torch: I am not for this ambling;[4]
Being but heavy, I will bear the light.
MER. Nay, gentle Romeo, we must have you dance.
ROM. Not I, believe me: you have dancing shoes
With nimble soles: I have a soul of lead
So stakes me to the ground, I cannot move.
MER. You are a lover; borrow Cupid's wings,
And soar with them above a common bound.
ROM. I am too sore enpierced with his shaft
To soar with his light feathers, and so bound,
I cannot bound a pitch[5] above dull woe:
Under love's heavy burthen do I sink.

[1] *hoodwink'd*] blindfolded.
[2] *crow-keeper*] scarecrow.
[3] *measure them a measure*] dance.
[4] *ambling*] affected movement, as in a dance.
[5] *pitch*] height to which the falcon soars before swooping down for the kill.

MER. And, to sink in it, should you burthen love;
Too great oppression for a tender thing.
ROM. Is love a tender thing? it is too rough,
Too rude, too boisterous, and it pricks like thorn.
MER. If love be rough with you, be rough with love;
Prick love for pricking, and you beat love down.
Give me a case[6] to put my visage in:
A visor for a visor! what care I
What curious eye doth quote[7] deformities?
Here are the beetle-brows shall blush for me.
BEN. Come, knock and enter, and no sooner in
But every man betake him to his legs.
ROM. A torch for me: let wantons light of heart
Tickle the senseless rushes with their heels;
For I am proverb'd with a grandsire phrase;
I'll be a candle-holder, and look on.
The game was ne'er so fair, and I am done.
MER. Tut, dun's the mouse,[8] the constable's own word:
If thou art dun, we'll draw thee from the mire
Of this sir-reverence[9] love, wherein thou stick'st
Up to the ears. Come, we burn daylight, ho.
ROM. Nay, that's not so.
MER. I mean, sir, in delay
We waste our lights in vain, like lamps by day.
Take our good[10] meaning, for our judgement sits
Five times in that ere once in our five wits.
ROM. And we mean well, in going to this mask;
But 'tis no wit to go.
MER. Why, may one ask?
ROM. I dreamt a dream to-night.
MER. And so did I.
ROM. Well, what was yours?
MER. That dreamers often lie.
ROM. In bed asleep, while they do dream things true.
MER. O, then, I see Queen Mab hath been with you.
She is the fairies' midwife, and she comes
In shape no bigger than an agate-stone

[6] *case*] mask.
[7] *quote*] perceive.
[8] *dun's the mouse*] a proverbial expression meaning "stay still."
[9] *sir-reverence*] a corruption of "save your reverence," a form of apology.
[10] *good*] intended.

On the fore-finger of an alderman,
Drawn with a team of little atomies[11]
Athwart men's noses as they lie asleep:
Her waggon-spokes made of long spinners' legs;
The cover, of the wings of grasshoppers;
Her traces, of the smallest spider's web;
Her collars, of the moonshine's watery beams;
Her whip, of cricket's bone; the lash, of film;[12]
Her waggoner, a small grey-coated gnat,
Not half so big as a round little worm
Prick'd from the lazy finger of a maid:
Her chariot is an empty hazel-nut,
Made by the joiner squirrel or old grub,
Time out o' mind the fairies' coachmakers.
And in this state she gallops night by night
Through lovers' brains, and then they dream of love;
O'er courtiers' knees, that dream on court'sies straight;[13]
O'er lawyers' fingers, who straight dream on fees;
O'er ladies' lips, who straight on kisses dream,
Which oft the angry Mab with blisters plagues,
Because their breaths with sweetmeats tainted are:
Sometime she gallops o'er a courtier's nose,
And then dreams he of smelling out a suit;
And sometime comes she with a tithe-pig's tail
Tickling a parson's nose as a' lies asleep,
Then dreams he of another benefice:
Sometime she driveth o'er a soldier's neck,
And then dreams he of cutting foreign throats,
Of breaches, ambuscadoes, Spanish blades,
Of healths five fathom deep; and then anon
Drums in his ear, at which he starts and wakes,
And being thus frighted swears a prayer or two,
And sleeps again. This is that very Mab
That plats the manes of horses in the night,
And bakes the elf-locks[14] in foul sluttish hairs,
Which once untangled much misfortune bodes:
This is the hag, when maids lie on their backs,
That presses them and learns them first to bear,

[11] *atomies*] tiny creatures.
[12] *film*] gossamer.
[13] *straight*] immediately.
[14] *elf-locks*] tangles.

Making them women of good carriage:
This is she—
ROM. Peace, peace, Mercutio, peace!
Thou talk'st of nothing.
MER. True, I talk of dreams;
Which are the children of an idle brain,
Begot of nothing but vain fantasy,
Which is as thin of substance as the air,
And more inconstant than the wind, who wooes
Even now the frozen bosom of the north,
And, being anger'd, puffs away from thence,
Turning his face to the dew-dropping south.
BEN. This wind you talk of blows us from ourselves;
Supper is done, and we shall come too late.
ROM. I fear, too early: for my mind misgives
Some consequence, yet hanging in the stars,
Shall bitterly begin his fearful date[15]
With this night's revels, and expire the term
Of a despised life closed in my breast,
By some vile forfeit of untimely death:
But He, that hath the steerage of my course,
Direct my sail! On, lusty gentlemen.
BEN. Strike, drum. [*Exeunt.*

SCENE V. *A hall in Capulet's house.*

Musicians *waiting. Enter* Servingmen, *with napkins.*

FIRST SERV. Where's Potpan, that he helps not to take away? he shift a trencher![1] he scrape a trencher!

SEC. SERV. When good manners shall lie all in one or two men's hands, and they unwashed too, 'tis a foul thing.

FIRST SERV. Away with the joint-stools,[2] remove the court-cupboard,[3] look to the plate. Good thou, save me a piece of marchpane;[4] and, as thou lovest me, let the porter let in Susan Grindstone and Nell. Antony, and Potpan!

[15] *date*] time, duration.

---

[1] *trencher*] plate.
[2] *joint-stools*] wooden stools.
[3] *court-cupboard*] movable buffet or closet.
[4] *marchpane*] sweet biscuit made of sugar and almonds.

SEC. SERV. Ay, boy, ready.

FIRST SERV. You are looked for and called for, asked for and sought for, in the great chamber.

THIRD SERV. We cannot be here and there too. Cheerly, boys; be brisk a while, and the longer liver take all. [*They retire behind.*

Enter CAPULET, *with* JULIET *and others of his house, meeting the* Guests *and* Maskers.

CAP. Welcome, gentlemen! ladies that have their toes
Unplagued with corns will have a bout with you:
Ah ha, my mistresses! which of you all
Will now deny to dance? she that makes dainty,
She, I'll swear, hath corns; am I come near ye now?
Welcome, gentlemen! I have seen the day
That I have worn a visor, and could tell
A whispering tale in a fair lady's ear,
Such as would please: 'tis gone, 'tis gone, 'tis gone:
You are welcome, gentlemen! Come, musicians, play.
A hall, a hall! give room! and foot it, girls.
[*Music plays, and they dance.*
More light, you knaves; and turn the tables up,
And quench the fire, the room is grown too hot.
Ah, sirrah, this unlook'd-for sport comes well.
Nay, sit, nay, sit, good cousin Capulet;
For you and I are past our dancing days:
How long is't now since last yourself and I
Were in a mask?

SEC. CAP. By'r lady, thirty years.

CAP. What, man! 'tis not so much, 'tis not so much:
'Tis since the nuptial of Lucentio,
Come Pentecost as quickly as it will,
Some five and twenty years; and then we mask'd.

SEC. CAP. 'Tis more, 'tis more: his son is elder, sir;
His son is thirty.

CAP. Will you tell me that?
His son was but a ward two years ago.

ROM. [*To a* Servingman] What lady's that, which doth enrich the hand
Of yonder knight?

SERV. I know not, sir.

ROM. O, she doth teach the torches to burn bright!
It seems she hangs upon the cheek of night

Like a rich jewel in an Ethiop's ear;
Beauty too rich for use, for earth too dear!
So shows a snowy dove trooping with crows,
As yonder lady o'er her fellows shows.
The measure done, I'll watch her place of stand,
And, touching hers, make blessed my rude hand.
Did my heart love till now? forswear it, sight!
For I ne'er saw true beauty till this night.

TYB. This, by his voice, should be a Montague.
Fetch me my rapier, boy. What dares the slave
Come hither, cover'd with an antic face,[5]
To fleer[6] and scorn at our solemnity?
Now, by the stock and honour of my kin,
To strike him dead I hold it not a sin.

CAP. Why, how now, kinsman! wherefore storm you so?

TYB. Uncle, this is a Montague, our foe;
A villain, that is hither come in spite,
To scorn at our solemnity this night.

CAP. Young Romeo is it?

TYB. 'Tis he, that villain Romeo.

CAP. Content thee, gentle coz, let him alone,
He bears him like a portly[7] gentleman;
And, to say truth, Verona brags of him
To be a virtuous and well-govern'd youth:
I would not for the wealth of all this town
Here in my house do him disparagement:
Therefore be patient, take no note of him:
It is my will, the which if thou respect,
Show a fair presence and put off these frowns,
An ill-beseeming semblance for a feast.

TYB. It fits, when such a villain is a guest:
I'll not endure him.

CAP. He shall be endured:
What, goodman[8] boy! I say, he shall: go to;
Am I the master here, or you? go to.
You'll not endure him! God shall mend my soul,

[5] *antic face*] odd-looking mask.
[6] *fleer*] grin mockingly.
[7] *portly*] well-bred, dignified.
[8] *goodman*] below the rank of gentleman.

You'll make a mutiny among my guests!
You will set cock-a-hoop![9] you'll be the man!
TYB. Why, uncle, 'tis a shame.
CAP. Go to, go to;
You are a saucy boy: is't so, indeed?
This trick may chance to scathe you, I know what:
You must contrary me! marry, 'tis time.
Well said, my hearts! You are a princox; go:
Be quiet, or— More light, more light! For shame!
I'll make you quiet. What, cheerly, my hearts!
TYB. Patience perforce with wilful choler meeting
Makes my flesh tremble in their different greeting.
I will withdraw: but this intrusion shall,
Now seeming sweet, convert to bitterest gall. [*Exit.*
ROM. [*To* JULIET] If I profane with my unworthiest hand
This holy shrine, the gentle fine is this,
My lips, two blushing pilgrims, ready stand
To smooth that rough touch with a tender kiss.
JUL. Good pilgrim, you do wrong your hand too much,
Which mannerly devotion shows in this;
For saints have hands that pilgrims' hands do touch,
And palm to palm is holy palmers' kiss.
ROM. Have not saints lips, and holy palmers too?
JUL. Ay, pilgrim, lips that they must use in prayer.
ROM. O, then, dear saint, let lips do what hands do;
They pray, grant thou, lest faith turn to despair.
JUL. Saints do not move, though grant for prayers' sake.
ROM. Then move not, while my prayer's effect I take.
Thus from my lips by thine my sin is purged. [*Kissing her.*
JUL. Then have my lips the sin that they have took.
ROM. Sin from my lips? O trespass sweetly urged!
Give me my sin again.
JUL. You kiss by the book.
NURSE. Madam, your mother craves a word with you.
ROM. What is her mother?
NURSE. Marry, bachelor,
Her mother is the lady of the house,
And a good lady, and a wise and virtuous:
I nursed her daughter, that you talk'd withal;

[9] *set cock-a-hoop*] pick a quarrel.

I tell you, he that can lay hold of her
Shall have the chinks.[10]
ROM. Is she a Capulet?
O dear account! my life is my foe's debt.
BEN. Away, be gone; the sport is at the best.
ROM. Ay, so I fear; the more is my unrest.
CAP. Nay, gentlemen, prepare not to be gone;
We have a trifling foolish[11] banquet towards.[12]
Is it e'en so? why, then, I thank you all;
I thank you, honest gentlemen; good night.
More torches here! Come on then, let's to bed.
Ah, sirrah, by my fay, it waxes late:
I'll to my rest. [*Exeunt all but* JULIET *and* NURSE.
JUL. Come hither, Nurse. What is yond gentleman?
NURSE. The son and heir of old Tiberio.
JUL. What's he that now is going out of door?
NURSE. Marry, that, I think, be young Petruchio.
JUL. What's he that follows there, that would not dance?
NURSE. I know not.
JUL. Go ask his name. If he be married,
My grave is like to be my wedding bed.
NURSE. His name is Romeo, and a Montague,
The only son of your great enemy.
JUL. My only love sprung from my only hate!
Too early seen unknown, and known too late!
Prodigious birth of love it is to me,
That I must love a loathed enemy.
NURSE. What's this? what's this?
JUL. A rhyme I learn'd even now
Of one I danced withal. [*One calls within 'Juliet.'*
NURSE. Anon, anon!
Come, let's away; the strangers all are gone. [*Exeunt.*

[10] *have the chinks*] acquire a financial fortune.
[11] *foolish*] small-scale.
[12] *towards*] in preparation.

ACT II.

PROLOGUE.

Enter Chorus.

CHOR. Now old desire doth in his death-bed lie,
And young affection gapes to be his heir;
That fair for which love groan'd for and would die,
With tender Juliet match'd, is now not fair.
Now Romeo is beloved and loves again,
Alike bewitched by the charm of looks,
But to his foe supposed he must complain,
And she steal love's sweet bait from fearful hooks:
Being held a foe, he may not have access
To breathe such vows as lovers use to swear;
And she as much in love, her means much less
To meet her new beloved any where:
But passion lends them power, time means, to meet,
Tempering extremities with extreme sweet. [*Exit.*

SCENE I. *A lane by the wall of Capulet's orchard.*

Enter ROMEO, *alone.*

ROM. Can I go forward when my heart is here?
Turn back, dull earth, and find thy centre out.
[*He climbs the wall, and leaps down within it.*

Enter BENVOLIO *with* MERCUTIO.

BEN. Romeo! my cousin Romeo!
MER. He is wise;

And, on my life, hath stol'n him home to bed.
BEN. He ran this way, and leap'd this orchard wall:
Call, good Mercutio.
MER. Nay, I'll conjure too.
Romeo! humours! madman! passion! lover!
Appear thou in the likeness of a sigh:
Speak but one rhyme, and I am satisfied;
Cry but 'ay me!' pronounce but 'love' and 'dove';
Speak to my gossip Venus one fair word,
One nick-name for her purblind son and heir,
Young Adam Cupid, he that shot so trim
When King Cophetua[1] loved the beggar-maid!
He heareth not, he stirreth not, he moveth not;
The ape[2] is dead, and I must conjure him.
I conjure thee by Rosaline's bright eyes,
By her high forehead and her scarlet lip,
By her fine foot, straight leg and quivering thigh,
And the demesnes that there adjacent lie,
That in thy likeness thou appear to us!
BEN. An if he hear thee, thou wilt anger him.
MER. This cannot anger him: 'twould anger him
To raise a spirit in his mistress' circle
Of some strange[3] nature, letting it there stand
Till she had laid it and conjured it down;
That were some spite: my invocation
Is fair and honest, and in his mistress' name
I conjure only but to raise up him.
BEN. Come, he hath hid himself among these trees,
To be consorted[4] with the humorous[5] night:
Blind is his love, and best befits the dark.
MER. If love be blind, love cannot hit the mark.
Now will he sit under a medlar-tree,
And wish his mistress were that kind of fruit
As maids call medlars when they laugh alone.
O, Romeo, that she were, O, that she were
An open et cetera, thou a poperin pear![6]

[1] *King Cophetua*] a legendary figure who married a beggar.
[2] *ape*] a term of endearment.
[3] *strange*] other person's.
[4] *consorted*] associated.
[5] *humorous*] damp and inducing strange moods.
[6] *medlars . . . poperin pear*] the fruits are euphemisms for sexual organs.

Romeo, good night: I'll to my truckle-bed;[7]
This field-bed is too cold for me to sleep:
Come, shall we go?

BEN. Go then, for 'tis in vain.
To seek him here that means not to be found. [*Exeunt.*

SCENE II. *Capulet's orchard.*

Enter ROMEO.

ROM. He jests at scars that never felt a wound.
[JULIET *appears above at a window.*
But, soft! what light through yonder window breaks?
It is the east, and Juliet is the sun!
Arise, fair sun, and kill the envious moon,
Who is already sick and pale with grief,
That thou her maid art far more fair than she:
Be not her maid, since she is envious;
Her vestal livery is but sick and green,
And none but fools do wear it; cast it off.
It is my lady; O, it is my love!
O, that she knew she were!
She speaks, yet she says nothing: what of that?
Her eye discourses, I will answer it.
I am too bold, 'tis not to me she speaks:
Two of the fairest stars in all the heaven,
Having some business, do intreat her eyes
To twinkle in their spheres till they return.
What if her eyes were there, they in her head?
The brightness of her cheek would shame those stars,
As daylight doth a lamp; her eyes in heaven
Would through the airy region stream so bright
That birds would sing and think it were not night.
See, how she leans her cheek upon her hand!
O, that I were a glove upon that hand,
That I might touch that cheek!

JUL. Ay me!

ROM. She speaks:

[7] *truckle-bed*] a bed on casters that could be pushed under another bed.

O, speak again, bright angel! for thou art
As glorious to this night, being o'er my head,
As is a winged messenger of heaven
Unto the white-upturned wondering eyes
Of mortals that fall back to gaze on him,
When he bestrides the lazy-pacing clouds
And sails upon the bosom of the air.
JUL. O Romeo, Romeo! wherefore art thou Romeo?
Deny thy father and refuse thy name;
Or, if thou wilt not, be but sworn my love,
And I'll no longer be a Capulet.
ROM. [*Aside*] Shall I hear more, or shall I speak at this?
JUL. 'Tis but thy name that is my enemy;
Thou art thyself, though not a Montague.
What's Montague? it is nor hand, nor foot,
Nor arm, nor face, nor any other part
Belonging to a man. O, be some other name!
What's in a name? that which we call a rose
By any other name would smell as sweet;
So Romeo would, were he not Romeo call'd,
Retain that dear perfection which he owes[1]
Without that title. Romeo, doff thy name,
And for thy name, which is no part of thee,
Take all myself.
ROM. I take thee at thy word:
Call me but love, and I'll be new baptized;
Henceforth I never will be Romeo.
JUL. What man art thou, that, thus bescreen'd in night,
So stumblest on my counsel?
ROM. By a name
I know not how to tell thee who I am:
My name, dear saint, is hateful to myself,
Because it is an enemy to thee;
Had I it written, I would tear the word.
JUL. My ears have yet not drunk a hundred words
Of thy tongue's uttering, yet I know the sound:
Art thou not Romeo, and a Montague?
ROM. Neither, fair maid, if either thee dislike.
JUL. How camest thou hither, tell me, and wherefore?

[1] *owes*] possesses.

The orchard walls are high and hard to climb,
And the place death, considering who thou art,
If any of my kinsmen find thee here.

ROM. With love's light wings did I o'er-perch these walls,
For stony limits cannot hold love out:
And what love can do, that dares love attempt;
Therefore thy kinsmen are no let[2] to me.

JUL. If they do see thee, they will murder thee.

ROM. Alack, there lies more peril in thine eye
Than twenty of their swords: look thou but sweet,
And I am proof against their enmity.

JUL. I would not for the world they saw thee here.

ROM. I have night's cloak to hide me from their eyes;
And but thou love me, let them find me here:
My life were better ended by their hate,
Than death prorogued,[3] wanting of thy love.

JUL. By whose direction found'st thou out this place?

ROM. By love, that first did prompt me to inquire;
He lent me counsel, and I lent him eyes.
I am no pilot; yet, wert thou as far
As that vast shore wash'd with the farthest sea,
I would adventure for such merchandise.

JUL. Thou know'st the mask of night is on my face,
Else would a maiden blush bepaint my cheek
For that which thou hast heard me speak to-night.
Fain would I dwell on form, fain, fain deny
What I have spoke: but farewell compliment![4]
Dost thou love me? I know thou wilt say 'Ay,'
And I will take thy word: yet, if thou swear'st,
Thou mayst prove false: at lovers' perjuries,
They say, Jove laughs. O gentle Romeo,
If thou dost love, pronounce it faithfully:
Or if thou think'st I am too quickly won,
I'll frown and be perverse and say thee nay,
So thou wilt woo; but else, not for the world.
In truth, fair Montague, I am too fond;[5]

[2] *let*] hindrance.
[3] *prorogued*] postponed.
[4] *compliment*] formality.
[5] *fond*] foolish.

And therefore thou mayst think my 'havior light:
But trust me, gentleman, I'll prove more true
Than those that have more cunning to be strange.[6]
I should have been more strange, I must confess,
But that thou overheard'st, ere I was ware,
My true love's passion: therefore pardon me,
And not impute this yielding to light love,
Which the dark night hath so discovered.

ROM. Lady, by yonder blessed moon I swear,
That tips with silver all these fruit-tree tops,—

JUL. O, swear not by the moon, th' inconstant moon,
That monthly changes in her circled orb,
Lest that thy love prove likewise variable.

ROM. What shall I swear by?

JUL. Do not swear at all;
Or, if thou wilt, swear by thy gracious self,
Which is the god of my idolatry,
And I'll believe thee.

ROM. If my heart's dear love—

JUL. Well, do not swear: although I joy in thee,
I have no joy of this contract to-night:
It is too rash, too unadvised, too sudden,
Too like the lightning, which doth cease to be
Ere one can say 'It lightens.' Sweet, good night!
This bud of love, by summer's ripening breath,
May prove a beauteous flower when next we meet.
Good night, good night! as sweet repose and rest
Come to thy heart as that within my breast!

ROM. O, wilt thou leave me so unsatisfied?

JUL. What satisfaction canst thou have to-night?

ROM. The exchange of thy love's faithful vow for mine.

JUL. I gave thee mine before thou didst request it:
And yet I would it were to give again.

ROM. Wouldst thou withdraw it? for what purpose, love?

JUL. But to be frank,[7] and give it thee again.
And yet I wish but for the thing I have:
My bounty is as boundless as the sea,
My love as deep; the more I give to thee,

[6] *strange*] reserved, distant.
[7] *frank*] bountiful.

The more I have, for both are infinite.
I hear some noise within; dear love, adieu! [NURSE *calls within.*
Anon, good Nurse! Sweet Montague, be true.
Stay but a little, I will come again. [*Exit.*

ROM. O blessed, blessed night! I am afeard,
Being in night, all this is but a dream,
Too flattering-sweet to be substantial.

Re-enter JULIET, *above.*

JUL. Three words, dear Romeo, and good night indeed.
If that thy bent of love be honourable,
Thy purpose marriage, send me word to-morrow,
By one that I'll procure to come to thee,
Where and what time thou wilt perform the rite,
And all my fortunes at thy foot I'll lay,
And follow thee my lord throughout the world.

NURSE. [*Within*] Madam!

JUL. I come, anon.—But if thou mean'st not well,
I do beseech thee—

NURSE. [*Within*] Madam!

JUL. By and by, I come:—
To cease thy suit, and leave me to my grief:
To-morrow will I send.

ROM. So thrive my soul,—

JUL. A thousand times good night! [*Exit.*

ROM. A thousand times the worse, to want thy light.
Love goes toward love, as schoolboys from their books,
But love from love, toward school with heavy looks. [*Retiring slowly.*

Re-enter JULIET, *above.*

JUL. Hist! Romeo, hist!—O, for a falconer's voice,
To lure this tassel-gentle[8] back again!
Bondage is hoarse, and may not speak aloud;
Else would I tear the cave where Echo lies,
And make her airy tongue more hoarse than mine,
With repetition of my Romeo's name.
Romeo!

ROM. It is my soul that calls upon my name:
How silver-sweet sound lovers' tongues by night,
Like softest music to attending ears!

[8] *tassel-gentle*] male goshawk.

JUL. Romeo!
ROM. My dear?
JUL. At what o'clock to-morrow
Shall I send to thee?
ROM. At the hour of nine.
JUL. I will not fail: 'tis twenty years till then.
I have forgot why I did call thee back.
ROM. Let me stand here till thou remember it.
JUL. I shall forget, to have thee still stand there,
Remembering how I love thy company.
ROM. And I'll still stay, to have thee still forget,
Forgetting any other home but this.
JUL. 'Tis almost morning; I would have thee gone:
And yet no farther than a wanton's bird,
Who lets it hop a little from her hand,
Like a poor prisoner in his twisted gyves,
And with a silk thread plucks it back again,
So loving-jealous of his liberty.
ROM. I would I were thy bird.
JUL. Sweet, so would I:
Yet I should kill thee with much cherishing.
Good night, good night! parting is such sweet sorrow
That I shall say good night till it be morrow. [*Exit.*
ROM. Sleep dwell upon thine eyes, peace in thy breast!
Would I were sleep and peace, so sweet to rest!
Hence will I to my ghostly[9] father's cell,
His help to crave and my dear hap[10] to tell. [*Exit.*

SCENE III. *Friar Laurence's cell.*

Enter FRIAR LAURENCE, *with a basket.*

FRI. L. The grey-eyed morn smiles on the frowning night,
Chequering the eastern clouds with streaks of light;
And flecked darkness like a drunkard reels
From forth day's path and Titan's[1] fiery wheels:
Now, ere the sun advance his burning eye,

[9] *ghostly*] spiritual.
[10] *hap*] fortune.

[1] *Titan's*] the Titan Helios, god of the sun.

The day to cheer and night's dank dew to dry,
I must up-fill this osier cage of ours
With baleful weeds and precious-juiced flowers.
The earth that's nature's mother is her tomb;
What is her burying grave, that is her womb:
And from her womb children of divers kind
We sucking on her natural bosom find,
Many for many virtues excellent,
None but for some, and yet all different.
O, mickle[2] is the powerful grace that lies
In herbs, plants, stones, and their true qualities:
For nought so vile that on the earth doth live,
But to the earth some special good doth give;
Nor aught so good, but, strain'd from that fair use,
Revolts from true birth, stumbling on abuse:
Virtue itself turns vice, being misapplied,
And vice sometime 's by action dignified.
Within the infant rind of this small flower
Poison hath residence, and medicine power:
For this, being smelt, with that part cheers each part,
Being tasted, slays all senses with the heart.
Two such opposed kings encamp them still
In man as well as herbs, grace and rude will;
And where the worser is predominant,
Full soon the canker death eats up that plant.

Enter ROMEO.

ROM. Good morrow, father.
FRI. L. Benedicite!
What early tongue so sweet saluteth me?
Young son, it argues a distemper'd head
So soon to bid good morrow to thy bed:
Care keeps his watch in every old man's eye,
And where care lodges, sleep will never lie;
But where unbruised youth with unstuff'd brain
Doth couch his limbs, there golden sleep doth reign:
Therefore thy earliness doth me assure
Thou art up-roused by some distemperature;
Or if not so, then here I hit it right,
Our Romeo hath not been in bed to-night.

[2] *mickle*] great.

ROM. That last is true; the sweeter rest was mine.
FRI. L. God pardon sin! wast thou with Rosaline?
ROM. With Rosaline, my ghostly father? no;
I have forgot that name and that name's woe.
FRI. L. That's my good son: but where hast thou been then?
ROM. I'll tell thee ere thou ask it me again.
I have been feasting with mine enemy;
Where on a sudden one hath wounded me,
That's by me wounded: both our remedies
Within thy help and holy physic lies:
I bear no hatred, blessed man, for, lo,
My intercession likewise steads[3] my foe.
FRI. L. Be plain, good son, and homely in thy drift;
Riddling confession finds but riddling shrift.
ROM. Then plainly know my heart's dear love is set
On the fair daughter of rich Capulet:
As mine on hers, so hers is set on mine;
And all combined, save what thou must combine
By holy marriage: when, and where, and how,
We met, we woo'd and made exchange of vow,
I'll tell thee as we pass; but this I pray,
That thou consent to marry us to-day.
FRI. L. Holy Saint Francis, what a change is here!
Is Rosaline, that thou didst love so dear,
So soon forsaken? young men's love then lies
Not truly in their hearts, but in their eyes.
Jesu Maria, what a deal of brine
Hath wash'd thy sallow cheeks for Rosaline!
How much salt water thrown away in waste,
To season love, that of it doth not taste!
The sun not yet thy sighs from heaven clears,
Thy old groans ring yet in mine ancient ears;
Lo, here upon thy cheek the stain doth sit
Of an old tear that is not wash'd off yet:
If e'er thou wast thyself and these woes thine,
Thou and these woes were all for Rosaline:
And art thou changed? pronounce this sentence then:
Women may fall when there's no strength in men.
ROM. Thou chid'st me oft for loving Rosaline.

[3] *steads*] benefits.

FRI. L. For doting, not for loving, pupil mine.
ROM. And bad'st me bury love.
FRI. L. Not in a grave,
To lay one in, another out to have.
ROM. I pray thee, chide not: she whom I love now
Doth grace for grace and love for love allow;
The other did not so.
FRI. L. O, she knew well
Thy love did read by rote and could not spell.
But come, young waverer, come, go with me,
In one respect I'll thy assistant be;
For this alliance may so happy prove,
To turn your households' rancour to pure love.
ROM. O, let us hence; I stand on sudden haste.
FRI. L. Wisely and slow; they stumble that run fast. [*Exeunt*.

SCENE IV. *A street.*

Enter BENVOLIO *and* MERCUTIO.

MER. Where the devil should this Romeo be? Came he not home to-night?
BEN. Not to his father's; I spoke with his man.
MER. Ah, that same pale hard-hearted wench, that Rosaline,
Torments him so that he will sure run mad.
BEN. Tybalt, the kinsman to old Capulet,
Hath sent a letter to his father's house.
MER. A challenge, on my life.
BEN. Romeo will answer it.
MER. Any man that can write may answer a letter.
BEN. Nay, he will answer the letter's master, how he dares, being dared.
MER. Alas, poor Romeo, he is already dead! stabbed with a white wench's black eye; shot thorough[1] the ear with a love-song; the very pin[2] of his heart cleft with the blind bow-boy's butt-shaft:[3] and is he a man to encounter Tybalt?
BEN. Why, what is Tybalt?

[1] *thorough*] through.
[2] *pin*] center, middle of a target.
[3] *butt-shaft*] barbless arrow.

MER. More than prince of cats,[4] I can tell you. O, he's the courageous captain of compliments.[5] He fights as you sing prick-song,[6] keeps time, distance and proportion;[7] rests me his minim rest, one, two, and the third in your bosom: the very butcher of a silk button, a duellist, a duellist; a gentleman of the very first house,[8] of the first and second cause:[9] ah, the immortal passado! the punto reverso! the hai![10]

BEN. The what?

MER. The pox of such antic, lisping, affecting fantasticoes;[11] these new tuners of accents! 'By Jesu, a very good blade! a very tall[12] man! a very good whore!' Why, is not this a lamentable thing, grandsire, that we should be thus afflicted with these strange flies,[13] these fashion-mongers, these perdona-mi's, who stand so much on the new form that they cannot sit at ease on the old bench? O, their bones,[14] their bones!

Enter ROMEO.

BEN. Here comes Romeo, here comes Romeo.

MER. Without his roe, like a dried herring: O flesh, flesh, how art thou fishified! Now is he for the numbers that Petrarch flowed in: Laura to his lady was but a kitchen-wench; marry, she had a better love to be-rhyme her; Dido, a dowdy; Cleopatra, a gipsy; Helen and Hero, hildings[15] and harlots; Thisbe, a grey eye or so, but not to the purpose. Signior Romeo, bon jour! there's a French salutation to your French slop.[16] You gave us the counterfeit fairly last night.

ROM. Good morrow to you both. What counterfeit did I give you?

MER. The slip,[17] sir, the slip; can you not conceive?

ROM. Pardon, good Mercutio, my business was great; and in such a case as mine a man may strain courtesy.

[4] *prince of cats*] The prince of cats in *Reynard the Fox* is named Tybert.

[5] *captain of compliments*] master of ceremony.

[6] *prick-song*] sheet music.

[7] *proportion*] rhythm.

[8] *house*] rank, fencing school.

[9] *cause*] i.e., to take up a quarrel.

[10] *passado . . . punto reverso . . . hai*] fencing terms: forward thrust; backhanded stroke; home thrust.

[11] *fantasticoes*] coxcombs.

[12] *tall*] valiant.

[13] *strange flies*] parasites.

[14] *bones*] French *bon* pronounced to create an English pun.

[15] *hildings*] wretches.

[16] *slop*] large trousers.

[17] *slip*] a counterfeit coin.

MER. That's as much as to say, Such a case as yours constrains a man to bow in the hams.

ROM. Meaning, to court'sy.

MER. Thou hast most kindly hit it.

ROM. A most courteous exposition.

MER. Nay, I am the very pink of courtesy.

ROM. Pink for flower.

MER. Right.

ROM. Why, then is my pump[18] well flowered.

MER. Well said: follow me this jest now, till thou hast worn out thy pump, that, when the single sole of it is worn, the jest may remain, after the wearing, solely singular.

ROM. O single-soled jest, solely singular for the singleness![19]

MER. Come between us, good Benvolio; my wits faint.

ROM. Switch and spurs, switch and spurs; or I'll cry a match.[20]

MER. Nay, if thy wits run the wild-goose chase,[21] I have done; for thou hast more of the wild-goose in one of thy wits than, I am sure, I have in my whole five: was I with you there for the goose?

ROM. Thou wast never with me for any thing when thou wast not there for the goose.[22]

MER. I will bite thee by the ear for that jest.

ROM. Nay, good goose, bite not.

MER. Thy wit is a very bitter sweeting;[23] it is a most sharp sauce.

ROM. And is it not well served in to a sweet goose?

MER. O, here's a wit of cheveril,[24] that stretches from an inch narrow to an ell broad!

ROM. I stretch it out for that word 'broad'; which added to the goose, proves thee far and wide a broad goose.

MER. Why, is not this better now than groaning for love? now art thou sociable, now art thou Romeo; now art thou what thou art, by art as well as by nature: for this drivelling love is like a great natural,[25] that runs lolling up and down to hide his bauble[26] in a hole.

BEN. Stop there, stop there.

[18] *pump*] a light shoe (often decorated with ribbons shaped as flowers).

[19] *singleness*] silliness.

[20] *cry a match*] claim victory.

[21] *wild-goose chase*] a horse race in which the leader chooses whatever course he wishes.

[22] *goose*] prostitute.

[23] *sweeting*] apple sauce.

[24] *cheveril*] kid leather.

[25] *natural*] idiot, fool.

[26] *bauble*] the fool's club, here with a bawdy quibble.

MER. Thou desirest me to stop in my tale against the hair.[27]

BEN. Thou wouldst else have made thy tale large.

MER. O, thou art deceived; I would have made it short: for I was come to the whole depth of my tale, and meant indeed to occupy the argument no longer.

ROM. Here's goodly gear!

Enter NURSE *and* PETER.

MER. A sail, a sail!

BEN. Two, two; a shirt and a smock.[28]

NURSE. Peter!

PETER. Anon.

NURSE. My fan, Peter.

MER. Good Peter, to hide her face; for her fan's the fairer of the two.

NURSE. God ye good morrow, gentlemen.

MER. God ye good den, fair gentlewoman.

NURSE. Is it good den?

MER. 'Tis no less, I tell you; for the bawdy hand of the dial is now upon the prick of noon.

NURSE. Out upon you! what a man[29] are you?

ROM. One, gentlewoman, that God hath made himself to mar.

NURSE. By my troth, it is well said; 'for himself to mar,' quoth a'? Gentlemen, can any of you tell me where I may find the young Romeo?

ROM. I can tell you; but young Romeo will be older when you have found him than he was when you sought him: I am the youngest of that name, for fault of a worse.

NURSE. You say well.

MER. Yea, is the worst well? very well took, i' faith; wisely, wisely.

NURSE. If you be he, sir, I desire some confidence[30] with you.

BEN. She will indite[31] him to some supper.

MER. A bawd, a bawd, a bawd! So ho!

ROM. What hast thou found?

MER. No hare, sir; unless a hare, sir, in a lenten pie, that is something stale and hoar[32] ere it be spent. [*Sings.*

[27] *against the hair*] against the grain, with quibbling.

[28] *a shirt . . . smock*] i.e., a man and a woman.

[29] *what a man*] what sort of a man.

[30] *confidence*] the Nurse's malapropism for "conference."

[31] *indite*] a deliberate malapropism for "invite."

[32] *hoar*] moldy, punning on "whore."

An old hare hoar,
And an old hare hoar,
Is very good meat in lent:
But a hare that is hoar,
Is too much for a score,
When it hoars ere it be spent.

Romeo, will you come to your father's? we'll to dinner thither.

ROM. I will follow you.

MER. Farewell, ancient lady; farewell, [*singing*] 'lady, lady, lady.'

[*Exeunt* MERCUTIO *and* BENVOLIO.

NURSE. Marry, farewell! I pray you, sir, what saucy merchant[33] was this, that was so full of his ropery?[34]

ROM. A gentleman, nurse, that loves to hear himself talk, and will speak more in a minute than he will stand to in a month.

NURSE. An a' speak any thing against me, I'll take him down, an a' were lustier than he is, and twenty such Jacks;[35] and if I cannot, I'll find those that shall. Scurvy knave! I am none of his flirt-gills;[36] I am none of his skains-mates.[37] [*Turning to* PETER] And thou must stand by too, and suffer every knave to use me at his pleasure?

PETER. I saw no man use you at his pleasure; if I had, my weapon should quickly have been out, I warrant you: I dare draw as soon as another man, if I see occasion in a good quarrel and the law on my side.

NURSE. Now, afore God, I am so vexed that every part about me quivers. Scurvy knave! Pray you, sir, a word: and as I told you, my young lady bade me inquire you out; what she bade me say, I will keep to myself: but first let me tell ye, if ye should lead her into a fool's paradise, as they say, it were a very gross kind of behaviour, as they say: for the gentlewoman is young, and therefore, if you should deal double with her, truly it were an ill thing to be offered to any gentlewoman, and very weak[38] dealing.

ROM. Nurse, commend me to thy lady and mistress. I protest unto thee—

[33] *merchant*] fellow.

[34] *ropery*] malapropism for "roguery."

[35] *Jacks*] term of contempt for an impudent fellow.

[36] *flirt-gills*] loose women.

[37] *skains-mates*] cutthroats.

[38] *weak*] contemptible.

NURSE. Good heart, and, i' faith, I will tell her as much: Lord, Lord, she will be a joyful woman.

ROM. What wilt thou tell her, Nurse? thou dost not mark me.

NURSE. I will tell her, sir, that you do protest; which, as I take it, is a gentlemanlike offer.

ROM. Bid her devise
Some means to come to shrift this afternoon;
And there she shall at Friar Laurence' cell
Be shrived and married. Here is for thy pains.

NURSE. No, truly, sir; not a penny.

ROM. Go to; I say you shall.

NURSE. This afternoon, sir? well, she shall be there.

ROM. And stay, good nurse, behind the abbey-wall:
Within this hour my man shall be with thee,
And bring thee cords made like a tackled stair;[39]
Which to the high top-gallant of my joy
Must be my convoy in the secret night.
Farewell; be trusty, and I'll quit[40] thy pains:
Farewell; commend me to thy mistress.

NURSE. Now God in heaven bless thee! Hark you, sir.

ROM. What say'st thou, my dear nurse?

NURSE. Is your man secret? Did you ne'er hear say,
Two may keep counsel, putting one away?

ROM. I warrant thee, my man's as true as steel.

NURSE. Well, sir; my mistress is the sweetest lady—Lord, Lord! when 'twas a little prating thing—O, there is a nobleman in town, one Paris, that would fain lay knife aboard; but she, good soul, had as lieve see a toad, a very toad, as see him. I anger her sometimes, and tell her that Paris is the properer man; but, I'll warrant you, when I say so, she looks as pale as any clout[41] in the versal[42] world. Doth not rosemary and Romeo begin both with a[43] letter?

ROM. Ay, nurse; what of that? both with an R.

NURSE. Ah, mocker! that's the dog's name; R is for the—No; I know it begins with some other letter—and she hath the prettiest sententious[44] of it, of you and rosemary, that it would do you good to hear it.

[39] *tackled stair*] rope ladder.
[40] *quit*] reward.
[41] *clout*] piece of cloth.
[42] *versal*] universal, whole.
[43] *a*] one and the same.
[44] *sententious*] a malapropism, probably for "sentence," pithy saying.

ROM. Commend me to thy lady.
NURSE. Ay, a thousand times. [*Exit* ROMEO.] Peter!
PET. Anon.
NURSE. Peter, take my fan, and go before, and apace. [*Exeunt.*

SCENE V. *Capulet's orchard.*

Enter JULIET.

JUL. The clock struck nine when I did send the Nurse;
In half an hour she promised to return.
Perchance she cannot meet him: that's not so.
O, she is lame! love's heralds should be thoughts,
Which ten times faster glide than the sun's beams,
Driving back shadows over louring hills:
Therefore do nimble-pinion'd doves draw love,[1]
And therefore hath the wind-swift Cupid wings.
Now is the sun upon the highmost hill
Of this day's journey, and from nine till twelve
Is three long hours; yet she is not come.
Had she affections and warm youthful blood,
She would be as swift in motion as a ball;
My words would bandy[2] her to my sweet love,
And his to me:
But old folks, many feign as they were dead;
Unwieldy, slow, heavy and pale as lead.

Enter NURSE, *with* PETER.

O God, she comes! O honey Nurse, what news?
Hast thou met with him? Send thy man away.
NURSE. Peter, stay at the gate. [*Exit* PETER.
JUL. Now, good sweet Nurse,—O Lord, why look'st thou sad?
Though news be sad, yet tell them merrily;
If good, thou shamest the music of sweet news
By playing it to me with so sour a face.
NURSE. I am a-weary; give me leave a while.
Fie how my bones ache! what a jaunce[3] have I had!

[1] *love*] Venus, goddess of love, whose chariot was drawn by doves.
[2] *bandy*] strike (as a ball).
[3] *jaunce*] hard journey.

JUL. I would thou hadst my bones and I thy news:
Nay, come, I pray thee, speak; good, good Nurse, speak.
NURSE. Jesu, what haste? can you not stay a while?
Do you not see that I am out of breath?
JUL. How art thou out of breath, when thou hast breath
To say to me that thou art out of breath?
The excuse that thou dost make in this delay
Is longer than the tale thou dost excuse.
Is thy news good, or bad? answer to that;
Say either, and I'll stay the circumstance:[4]
Let me be satisfied, is't good or bad?
NURSE. Well, you have made a simple choice; you know not how to choose a man: Romeo! no, not he; though his face be better than any man's, yet his leg excels all men's; and for a hand, and a foot, and a body, though they be not to be talked on, yet they are past compare: he is not the flower of courtesy, but, I'll warrant him, as gentle as a lamb. Go thy ways, wench; serve God. What, have you dined at home?
JUL. No, no: but all this did I know before.
What says he of our marriage? what of that?
NURSE. Lord, how my head aches! what a head have I!
It beats as it would fall in twenty pieces.
My back o' t' other side,—ah, my back, my back!
Beshrew your heart for sending me about,
To catch my death with jauncing up and down!
JUL. I' faith, I am sorry that thou art not well.
Sweet, sweet, sweet Nurse, tell me, what says my love?
NURSE. Your love says, like an honest gentleman, and a courteous, and a kind, and a handsome, and, I warrant, a virtuous,—Where is your mother?
JUL. Where is my mother! why, she is within;
Where should she be? How oddly thou repliest!
'Your love says, like an honest gentleman,
Where is your mother?'
NURSE. O God's lady dear!
Are you so hot? marry, come up, I trow;
Is this the poultice for my aching bones?
Henceforward do your messages yourself.

[4] *stay the circumstance*] wait until later for the details.

JUL. Here's such a coil![5] come, what says Romeo?
NURSE. Have you got leave to go to shrift to-day?
JUL. I have.
NURSE. Then hie you hence to Friar Laurence' cell,
There stays a husband to make you a wife:
Now comes the wanton blood up in your cheeks,
They'll be in scarlet straight at any news.
Hie you to church; I must another way,
To fetch a ladder, by the which your love
Must climb a bird's nest soon when it is dark;
I am the drudge, and toil in your delight;
But you shall bear the burthen soon at night.
Go; I'll to dinner; hie you to the cell.
JUL. Hie to high fortune! Honest Nurse, farewell. [*Exeunt.*

SCENE VI. *Friar Laurence's cell.*

Enter FRIAR LAURENCE *and* ROMEO.

FRI. L. So smile the heavens upon this holy act
That after-hours with sorrow chide us not!
ROM. Amen, amen! but come what sorrow can,
It cannot countervail[1] the exchange of joy
That one short minute gives me in her sight:
Do thou but close our hands with holy words,
Then love-devouring death do what he dare,
It is enough I may but call her mine.
FRI. L. These violent delights have violent ends,
And in their triumph die; like fire and powder
Which as they kiss consume: the sweetest honey
Is loathsome in his own deliciousness,
And in the taste confounds[2] the appetite:
Therefore, love moderately; long love doth so;
Too swift arrives as tardy as too slow.

Enter JULIET.

[5] *coil*] turmoil, confusion.

---

[1] *countervail*] equal.
[2] *confounds*] destroys, does away with.

Here comes the lady. O, so light a foot
Will ne'er wear out the everlasting flint.
A lover may bestride the gossamer
That idles in the wanton summer air,
And yet not fall; so light is vanity.

JUL. Good even to my ghostly confessor.

FRI. L. Romeo shall thank thee, daughter, for us both.

JUL. As much to him, else is his thanks too much.

ROM. Ah, Juliet, if the measure of thy joy
Be heap'd like mine, and that thy skill be more
To blazon it, then sweeten with thy breath
This neighbour air, and let rich music's tongue
Unfold the imagined happiness that both
Receive in either by this dear encounter.

JUL. Conceit,[3] more rich in matter than in words,
Brags of his substance, not of ornament:
They are but beggars that can count their worth;
But my true love is grown to such excess,
I cannot sum up sum of half my wealth.

FRI. L. Come, come with me, and we will make short work;
For, by your leaves, you shall not stay alone
Till holy church incorporate two in one. [*Exeunt.*

[3] *Conceit*] Imagination.

ACT III.

SCENE I. *A public place.*

Enter MERCUTIO, BENVOLIO, Page, *and* Servants.

BEN. I pray thee, good Mercutio, let's retire:
The day is hot, the Capulets abroad,
And, if we meet, we shall not 'scape a brawl;
For now these hot days is the mad blood stirring.

MER. Thou art like one of those fellows that when he enters the confines of a tavern claps me his sword upon the table, and says 'God send me no need of thee!' and by the operation of the second cup draws it on the drawer,[1] when indeed there is no need.

BEN. Am I like such a fellow?

MER. Come, come, thou art as hot a Jack in thy mood as any in Italy, and as soon moved to be moody,[2] and as soon moody to be moved.

BEN. And what to?

MER. Nay, an there were two such, we should have none shortly, for one would kill the other. Thou! why, thou wilt quarrel with a man that hath a hair more, or a hair less, in his beard than thou hast: thou wilt quarrel with a man for cracking nuts, having no other reason but because thou hast hazel eyes; what eye, but such an eye, would spy out such a quarrel? thy head is as full of quarrels as an egg is full of meat, and yet thy head hath been beaten as addle as an egg for quarrelling: thou hast quarrelled with a man for coughing in the street, because he hath wakened thy dog that hath lain asleep in the sun: didst thou not fall out with a tailor for wearing his new doublet before Easter? with another, for tying his new shoes with old riband? and yet thou wilt tutor me from quarrelling!

[1] *drawer*] waiter.
[2] *moody*] angry.

BEN. An I were so apt to quarrel as thou art, any man should buy the fee-simple of my life for an hour and a quarter.

MER. The fee-simple! O simple!

Enter TYBALT *and others.*

BEN. By my head, here come the Capulets.

MER. By my heel, I care not.

TYB. Follow me close, for I will speak to them.
Gentlemen, good den: a word with one of you.

MER. And but one word with one of us? couple it with something; make it a word and a blow.

TYB. You shall find me apt enough to that, sir, an you will give me occasion.

MER. Could you not take some occasion without giving?

TYB. Mercutio, thou consort'st with Romeo,—

MER. Consort! what, dost thou make us minstrels? an thou make minstrels of us, look to hear nothing but discords: here's my fiddlestick; here's that shall make you dance. 'Zounds, consort!

BEN. We talk here in the public haunt of men:
Either withdraw unto some private place,
Or reason coldly of your grievances,
Or else depart; here all eyes gaze on us.

MER. Men's eyes were made to look, and let them gaze;
I will not budge for no man's pleasure, I.

Enter ROMEO.

TYB. Well, peace be with you, sir: here comes my man.

MER. But I'll be hang'd, sir, if he wear your livery:
Marry, go before to field, he'll be your follower;
Your worship in that sense may call him man.

TYB. Romeo, the love I bear thee can afford
No better term than this,—thou art a villain.

ROM. Tybalt, the reason that I have to love thee
Doth much excuse the appertaining rage
To such a greeting: villain am I none;
Therefore farewell; I see thou know'st me not.

TYB. Boy, this shall not excuse the injuries
That thou hast done me; therefore turn and draw.

ROM. I do protest, I never injured thee,
But love thee better than thou canst devise
Till thou shalt know the reason of my love:

And so, good Capulet,—which name I tender
As dearly as mine own,—be satisfied.

MER. O calm, dishonourable, vile submission!
Alla stoccata[3] carries it away. [*Draws.*
Tybalt, you rat-catcher, will you walk?

TYB. What wouldst thou have with me?

MER. Good king of cats, nothing but one of your nine lives, that I mean to make bold withal, and, as you shall use me hereafter, dry-beat[4] the rest of the eight. Will you pluck your sword out of his pilcher[5] by the ears? make haste, lest mine be about your ears ere it be out.

TYB. I am for you. [*Drawing.*

ROM. Gentle Mercutio, put thy rapier up.

MER. Come, sir, your passado. [*They fight.*

ROM. Draw, Benvolio; beat down their weapons.
Gentlemen, for shame, forbear this outrage!
Tybalt, Mercutio, the prince expressly hath
Forbid this bandying in Verona streets:
Hold, Tybalt! good Mercutio!
[TYBALT *under* ROMEO'S *arm stabs* MERCUTIO *and flies with his followers.*

MER. I am hurt;
A plague o' both your houses! I am sped:[6]
Is he gone, and hath nothing?

BEN. What, art thou hurt?

MER. Ay, ay, a scratch, a scratch; marry, 'tis enough.
Where is my page? Go, villain, fetch a surgeon. [*Exit* Page.

ROM. Courage, man; the hurt cannot be much.

MER. No, 'tis not so deep as a well, nor so wide as a church-door; but 'tis enough, 'twill serve: ask for me to-morrow, and you shall find me a grave man. I am peppered, I warrant, for this world. A plague o' both your houses! 'Zounds, a dog, a rat, a mouse, a cat, to scratch a man to death! a braggart, a rogue, a villain, that fights by the book of arithmetic![7] Why the devil came you between us? I was hurt under your arm.

ROM. I thought all for the best.

[3] *Alla stoccata*] a technical term for a fencing thrust.
[4] *dry-beat*] cudgel.
[5] *pilcher*] scabbard.
[6] *sped*] done for.
[7] *book of arithmetic*] fencing manual.

MER. Help me into some house, Benvolio,
Or I shall faint. A plague o' both your houses!
They have made worms' meat of me: I have it,
And soundly too: your houses!

[*Exeunt* MERCUTIO *and* BENVOLIO.

ROM. This gentleman, the Prince's near ally,[8]
My very friend, hath got this mortal hurt
In my behalf; my reputation stain'd
With Tybalt's slander,—Tybalt, that an hour
Hath been my kinsman: O sweet Juliet,
Thy beauty hath made me effeminate,
And in my temper soften'd valour's steel!

Re-enter BENVOLIO.

BEN. O Romeo, Romeo, brave Mercutio's dead!
That gallant spirit hath aspired the clouds,
Which too untimely here did scorn the earth.
ROM. This day's black fate on more days doth depend;
This but begins the woe others must end.

Re-enter TYBALT.

BEN. Here comes the furious Tybalt back again.
ROM. Alive, in triumph! and Mercutio slain!
Away to heaven, respective lenity,[9]
And fire-eyed fury be my conduct[10] now!
Now, Tybalt, take the 'villain' back again
That late thou gavest me; for Mercutio's soul
Is but a little way above our heads,
Staying for thine to keep him company:
Either thou, or I, or both, must go with him.
TYB. Thou, wretched boy, that didst consort him here,
Shalt with him hence.
Rom. This shall determine that.

[*They fight*; TYBALT *falls.*

BEN. Romeo, away, be gone!
The citizens are up, and Tybalt slain:
Stand not amazed: the Prince will doom thee death
If thou art taken: hence, be gone, away!

[8] *ally*] relative.
[9] *respective lenity*] concern for mildness.
[10] *conduct*] guide.

ROM. O, I am fortune's fool!
BEN. Why dost thou stay? [*Exit* ROMEO.

Enter Citizens, &c.

FIRST CIT. Which way ran he that kill'd Mercutio?
Tybalt, that murderer, which way ran he?
BEN. There lies that Tybalt.
FIRST CIT. Up, sir, go with me;
I charge thee in the Prince's name, obey.

Enter PRINCE, *attended*; MONTAGUE, CAPULET, *their* Wives, *and others.*

PRIN. Where are the vile beginners of this fray?
BEN. O noble Prince, I can discover[11] all
The unlucky manage of this fatal brawl:
There lies the man, slain by young Romeo,
That slew thy kinsman, brave Mercutio.
LA. CAP. Tybalt, my cousin! O my brother's child!
O Prince! O cousin! husband! O, the blood is spilt
Of my dear kinsman! Prince, as thou art true,
For blood of ours, shed blood of Montague.
O cousin, cousin!
PRIN. Benvolio, who began this bloody fray?
BEN. Tybalt, here slain, whom Romeo's hand did slay,
Romeo that spoke him fair, bid him bethink
How nice[12] the quarrel was, and urged withal
Your high displeasure: all this uttered
With gentle breath, calm look, knees humbly bow'd,
Could not take truce with the unruly spleen[13]
Of Tybalt deaf to peace, but that he tilts
With piercing steel at bold Mercutio's breast;
Who, all as hot, turns deadly point to point,
And, with a martial scorn, with one hand beats
Cold death aside, and with the other sends
It back to Tybalt, whose dexterity
Retorts it: Romeo he cries aloud,
'Hold, friends! friends, part!' and, swifter than his tongue,
His agile arm beats down their fatal points,

[11] *discover*] reveal.
[12] *nice*] trivial.
[13] *take . . . spleen*] make peace with the uncontrollable rage.

And 'twixt them rushes; underneath whose arm
An envious thrust from Tybalt hit the life
Of stout Mercutio, and then Tybalt fled:
But by and by comes back to Romeo,
Who had but newly entertain'd revenge,
And to't they go like lightning: for, ere I
Could draw to part them, was stout Tybalt slain;
And, as he fell, did Romeo turn and fly;
This is the truth, or let Benvolio die.

LA. CAP. He is a kinsman to the Montague,
Affection makes him false, he speaks not true:
Some twenty of them fought in this black strife,
And all those twenty could but kill one life.
I beg for justice, which thou, Prince, must give;
Romeo slew Tybalt, Romeo must not live.

PRIN. Romeo slew him, he slew Mercutio;
Who now the price of his dear blood doth owe?

MON. Not Romeo, Prince, he was Mercutio's friend;
His fault concludes but what the law should end,
The life of Tybalt.

PRIN. And for that offence
Immediately we do exile him hence:
I have an interest in your hate's proceeding,
My blood for your rude brawls doth lie a-bleeding;
But I'll amerce[14] you with so strong a fine,
That you shall all repent the loss of mine:
I will be deaf to pleading and excuses;
Nor tears nor prayers shall purchase out abuses:[1]
Therefore use none: let Romeo hence in haste,
Else, when he's found, that hour is his last.
Bear hence this body, and attend our will:
Mercy but murders, pardoning those that kill. [*Exeunt.*

[14] *amerce*] punish by imposing a fine.
[15] *purchase out abuses*] buy off the fine for misdeeds.

SCENE II. *Capulet's orchard.*

Enter JULIET.

JUL. Gallop apace, you fiery-footed steeds,
Towards Phoebus' lodging: such a waggoner
As Phaethon would whip you to the west,
And bring in cloudy night immediately.
Spread thy close curtain, love-performing night,
That runaways' eyes may wink, and Romeo
Leap to these arms, untalk'd of and unseen.
Lovers can see to do their amorous rites
By their own beauties; or, if love be blind,
It best agrees with night. Come, civil night,
Thou sober-suited matron, all in black,
And learn me how to lose a winning match,
Play'd for a pair of stainless maidenhoods:
Hood my unmann'd[1] blood bating in my cheeks
With thy black mantle, till strange love grown bold
Think true love acted simple modesty.
Come, night, come, Romeo, come, thou day in night;
For thou wilt lie upon the wings of night
Whiter than new snow on a raven's back.
Come, gentle night, come, loving, black-brow'd night,
Give me my Romeo; and, when he shall die,
Take him and cut him out in little stars,
And he will make the face of heaven so fine,
That all the world will be in love with night,
And pay no worship to the garish sun.
O, I have bought the mansion of a love,
But not possess'd it, and, though I am sold,
Not yet enjoy'd; so tedious is this day
As is the night before some festival
To an impatient child that hath new robes
And may not wear them. O, here comes my Nurse,
And she brings news, and every tongue that speaks
But Romeo's name speaks heavenly eloquence.

[1] *unmann'd*] (1) untrained; (2) still without husband.

Enter NURSE, *with cords.*

Now, Nurse, what news? What hast thou there? the cords
That Romeo bid thee fetch?
NURSE. Ay, ay, the cords. [*Throws them down.*
JUL. Ay me! what news? why dost thou wring thy hands?
NURSE. Ah, well-a-day! he's dead, he's dead, he's dead.
We are undone, lady, we are undone.
Alack the day! he's gone, he's kill'd, he's dead.
JUL. Can heaven be so envious?
NURSE. Romeo can,
Though heaven cannot. O Romeo, Romeo!
Who ever would have thought it? Romeo!
JUL. What devil art thou that dost torment me thus?
This torture should be roar'd in dismal hell.
Hath Romeo slain himself? say thou but 'I,'[2]
And that bare vowel 'I' shall poison more
Than the death-darting eye of cockatrice:
I am not I, if there be such an I,
Or those eyes shut, that make thee answer 'I.'
If he be slain, say 'I'; or if not, no:
Brief sounds determine of my weal or woe.
NURSE. I saw the wound, I saw it with mine eyes—
God save the mark!—here on his manly breast:
A piteous corse, a bloody piteous corse;
Pale, pale as ashes, all bedaub'd in blood,
All in gore[3] blood: I swounded at the sight.
JUL. O, break, my heart! poor bankrupt, break at once!
To prison, eyes, ne'er look on liberty!
Vile earth, to earth resign, end motion here,
And thou and Romeo press one heavy bier!
NURSE. O Tybalt, Tybalt, the best friend I had!
O courteous Tybalt! honest gentleman!
That ever I should live to see thee dead!
JUL. What storm is this that blows so contrary?
Is Romeo slaughter'd, and is Tybalt dead?
My dear-loved cousin, and my dearer lord?
Then, dreadful trumpet, sound the general doom!
For who is living, if those two are gone?

[2] *'I'*] ay, yes.
[3] *gore*] clotted.

NURSE. Tybalt is gone, and Romeo banished;
Romeo that kill'd him, he is banished.
JUL. O God! did Romeo's hand shed Tybalt's blood?
NURSE. It did, it did; alas the day, it did!
JUL. O serpent heart, hid with a flowering face!
Did ever dragon keep so fair a cave?
Beautiful tyrant! fiend angelical!
Dove-feather'd raven! wolvish-ravening lamb!
Despised substance of divinest show!
Just opposite to what thou justly seem'st,
A damned saint, an honourable villain!
O nature, what hadst thou to do in hell,
When thou didst bower the spirit of a fiend
In mortal paradise of such sweet flesh?
Was ever book containing such vile matter
So fairly bound? O, that deceit should dwell
In such a gorgeous palace!
NURSE. There's no trust,
No faith, no honesty in men; all perjured,
All forsworn, all naught,[4] all dissemblers.
Ah, where's my man? give me some aqua vitae:
These griefs, these woes, these sorrows make me old.
Shame come to Romeo!
JUL. Blister'd be thy tongue
For such a wish! he was not born to shame:
Upon his brow shame is ashamed to sit;
For 'tis a throne where honour may be crown'd
Sole monarch of the universal earth.
O, what a beast was I to chide at him!
NURSE. Will you speak well of him that kill'd your cousin?
JUL. Shall I speak ill of him that is my husband?
Ah, poor my lord, what tongue shall smooth thy name,
When I, thy three-hours wife, have mangled it?
But wherefore, villain, didst thou kill my cousin?
That villain cousin would have kill'd my husband:
Back, foolish tears, back to your native spring;
Your tributary drops belong to woe,
Which you mistaking offer up to joy.
My husband lives, that Tybalt would have slain;

[4] *naught*] worthless, wicked.

And Tybalt's dead, that would have slain my husband:
All this is comfort; wherefore weep I then?
Some word there was, worser than Tybalt's death,
That murder'd me: I would forget it fain;
But, O, it presses to my memory,
Like damned guilty deeds to sinners' minds:
'Tybalt is dead, and Romeo banished';
That 'banished,' that one word 'banished,'
Hath slain ten thousand Tybalts. Tybalt's death
Was woe enough, if it had ended there:
Or, if sour woe delights in fellowship,
And needly[5] will be rank'd with other griefs,
Why follow'd not, when she said 'Tybalt's dead,'
Thy father, or thy mother, nay, or both,
Which modern[6] lamentation might have moved?
But with a rear-ward[7] following Tybalt's death,
'Romeo is banished': to speak that word,
Is father, mother, Tybalt, Romeo, Juliet,
All slain, all dead. 'Romeo is banished.'
There is no end, no limit, measure, bound,
In that word's death; no words can that woe sound.
Where is my father, and my mother, Nurse?

NURSE. Weeping and wailing over Tybalt's corse:
Will you go to them? I will bring you thither.

JUL. Wash they his wounds with tears: mine shall be spent,
When theirs are dry, for Romeo's banishment.
Take up those cords: poor ropes, you are beguiled,
Both you and I; for Romeo is exiled:
He made you for a highway to my bed;
But I, a maid, die maiden-widowed.
Come, cords; come, Nurse; I'll to my wedding-bed;
And death, not Romeo, take my maidenhead!

NURSE. Hie to your chamber: I'll find Romeo
To comfort you: I wot[8] well where he is.
Hark ye, your Romeo will be here at night:
I'll to him; he is hid at Laurence' cell.

JUL. O, find him! give this ring to my true knight,
And bid him come to take his last farewell. [*Exeunt*.

[5] *needly*] necessarily.

[6] *modern*] commonplace, ordinary.

[7] *rear-ward*] rear guard.

[8] *wot*] know.

SCENE III. *Friar Laurence's cell.*

Enter FRIAR LAURENCE.

FRI. L. Romeo, come forth; come forth, thou fearful man:
Affliction is enamour'd of thy parts,
And thou art wedded to calamity.

Enter ROMEO.

ROM. Father, what news? what is the Prince's doom?
What sorrow craves acquaintance at my hand,
That I yet know not?
FRI. L. Too familiar
Is my dear son with such sour company:
I bring thee tidings of the Prince's doom.
ROM. What less than dooms-day is the Prince's doom?
FRI. L. A gentler judgement vanish'd[1] from his lips,
Not body's death, but body's banishment.
ROM. Ha, banishment! be merciful, say 'death';
For exile hath more terror in his look,
Much more than death: do not say 'banishment.'
FRI. L. Here from Verona art thou banished:
Be patient, for the world is broad and wide.
ROM. There is no world without Verona walls,
But purgatory, torture, hell itself.
Hence banished is banish'd from the world,
And world's exile is death: then 'banished'
Is death mis-term'd: calling death 'banished,'
Thou cut'st my head off with a golden axe,
And smilest upon the stroke that murders me.
FRI. L. O deadly sin! O rude unthankfulness!
Thy fault our law calls death; but the kind Prince,
Taking thy part, hath rush'd[2] aside the law,
And turn'd that black word death to banishment:
This is dear mercy, and thou seest it not.
ROM. 'Tis torture, and not mercy: heaven is here,
Where Juliet lives; and every cat and dog

[1] *vanish'd*] issued.
[2] *rush'd*] violently thrust.

And little mouse, every unworthy thing,
Live here in heaven and may look on her,
But Romeo may not: more validity,[3]
More honourable state,[4] more courtship[5] lives
In carrion-flies than Romeo: they may seize
On the white wonder of dear Juliet's hand,
And steal immortal blessing from her lips;
Who, even in pure and vestal modesty,
Still blush, as thinking their own kisses sin;
But Romeo may not; he is banished:
This may flies do, but I from this must fly:
They are free men, but I am banished:
And say'st thou yet, that exile is not death?
Hadst thou no poison mix'd, no sharp-ground knife,
No sudden mean of death, though ne'er so mean,
But 'banished' to kill me?—'Banished'?
O Friar, the damned use that word in hell;
Howling attends it: how hast thou the heart,
Being a divine, a ghostly confessor,
A sin-absolver, and my friend profess'd,
To mangle me with that word 'banished'?

FRI. L. Thou fond mad man, hear me but speak a word.

ROM. O, thou wilt speak again of banishment.

FRI. L. I'll give thee armour to keep off that word;
Adversity's sweet milk, philosophy,
To comfort thee, though thou art banished.

ROM. Yet 'banished'? Hang up philosophy!
Unless philosophy can make a Juliet,
Displant a town, reverse a prince's doom,
It helps not, it prevails not: talk no more.

FRI. L. O, then I see that madmen have no ears.

ROM. How should they, when that wise men have no eyes?

FRI. L. Let me dispute with thee of thy estate.[6]

ROM. Thou canst not speak of that thou dost not feel:
Wert thou as young as I, Juliet thy love,
An hour but married, Tybalt murdered,
Doting like me, and like me banished,

[3] *validity*] value.

[4] *state*] rank.

[5] *courtship*] (1) civility befitting a courtier; (2) wooing.

[6] *dispute . . . estate*] discuss your situation with you.

Then mightst thou speak, then mightst thou tear thy hair,
And fall upon the ground, as I do now,
Taking the measure of an unmade grave. [*Knocking within.*

FRI. L. Arise; one knocks; good Romeo, hide thyself.

ROM. Not I; unless the breath of heart-sick groans
Mist-like infold me from the search of eyes. [*Knocking.*

FRI. L. Hark, how they knock! Who's there? Romeo, arise;
Thou wilt be taken.—Stay awhile!—Stand up; [*Knocking.*
Run to my study.—By and by!—God's will,
What simpleness is this!—I come, I come! [*Knocking.*
Who knocks so hard? whence come you? what's your will?

NURSE. [*Within*] Let me come in, and you shall know my errand;
I come from Lady Juliet.

FRI. L. Welcome, then.

Enter NURSE.

NURSE. O holy Friar, O, tell me, holy Friar,
Where is my lady's lord, where's Romeo?

FRI. L. There on the ground, with his own tears made drunk.

NURSE. O, he is even in my mistress' case,
Just in her case!

FRI. L. O woeful sympathy!
Piteous predicament!

NURSE. Even so lies she,
Blubbering and weeping, weeping and blubbering.
Stand up, stand up; stand, an you be a man:
For Juliet's sake, for her sake, rise and stand;
Why should you fall into so deep an O?

ROM. Nurse!

NURSE. Ah sir! ah sir! Well, death's the end of all.

ROM. Spakest thou of Juliet? how is it with her?
Doth she not think me an old murderer,
Now I have stain'd the childhood of our joy
With blood removed but little from her own?
Where is she? and how doth she? and what says
My conceal'd lady to our cancell'd love?

NURSE. O, she says nothing, sir, but weeps and weeps;
And now falls on her bed; and then starts up,
And Tybalt calls; and then on Romeo cries,
And then down falls again.

ROM. As if that name,

Shot from the deadly level[7] of a gun,
Did murder her, as that name's cursed hand
Murder'd her kinsman. O, tell me, Friar, tell me,
In what vile part of this anatomy
Doth my name lodge? tell me, that I may sack
The hateful mansion. [*Drawing his sword.*

FRI. L. Hold thy desperate hand:
Art thou a man? thy form cries out thou art:
Thy tears are womanish; thy wild acts denote
The unreasonable fury of a beast:
Unseemly woman in a seeming man!
Or ill-beseeming beast in seeming both!
Thou hast amazed me: by my holy order,
I thought thy disposition better temper'd.
Hast thou slain Tybalt? wilt thou slay thyself?
And slay thy lady that in thy life lives,
By doing damned hate upon thyself?
Why rail'st thou on thy birth, the heaven and earth?
Since birth and heaven and earth, all three do meet
In thee at once, which thou at once wouldst lose.
Fie, fie, thou shamest thy shape, thy love, thy wit;
Which, like a usurer, abound'st in all,
And usest none in that true use indeed
Which should bedeck thy shape, thy love, thy wit:
Thy noble shape is but a form of wax,
Digressing from the valour of a man;
Thy dear love sworn, but hollow perjury,
Killing that love which thou hast vow'd to cherish;
Thy wit, that ornament to shape and love,
Mis-shapen in the conduct of them both,
Like powder in a skilless soldier's flask,
Is set a-fire by thine own ignorance,
And thou dismember'd with thine own defence.
What, rouse thee, man! thy Juliet is alive,
For whose dear sake thou wast but lately dead;
There art thou happy: Tybalt would kill thee,
But thou slew'st Tybalt; there art thou happy too:
The law, that threaten'd death, becomes thy friend,
And turns it to exile; there art thou happy:

[7] *level*] aim.

A pack of blessings lights upon thy back;
Happiness courts thee in her best array;
But, like a misbehaved and sullen wench,
Thou pout'st upon thy fortune and thy love:
Take heed, take heed, for such die miserable.
Go, get thee to thy love, as was decreed,
Ascend her chamber, hence and comfort her:
But look thou stay not till the watch be set,
For then thou canst not pass to Mantua;
Where thou shalt live till we can find a time
To blaze[8] your marriage, reconcile your friends,
Beg pardon of the Prince, and call thee back
With twenty hundred thousand times more joy
Than thou went'st forth in lamentation.
Go before, Nurse: commend me to thy lady,
And bid her hasten all the house to bed,
Which heavy sorrow makes them apt unto:
Romeo is coming.

NURSE. O Lord, I could have stay'd here all the night
To hear good counsel: O, what learning is!
My lord, I'll tell my lady you will come.

ROM. Do so, and bid my sweet prepare to chide.

NURSE. Here, sir, a ring she bid me give you, sir:
Hie you, make haste, for it grows very late. [*Exit.*

ROM. How well my comfort is revived by this!

FRI. L. Go hence; good night; and here stands all your state:
Either be gone before the watch be set,
Or by the break of day disguised from hence:
Sojourn in Mantua; I'll find out your man,
And he shall signify from time to time
Every good hap to you that chances here:
Give me thy hand; 'tis late: farewell; good night.

ROM. But that a joy past joy calls out on me,
It were a grief, so brief to part with thee:
Farewell. [*Exeunt.*

[8] *blaze*] make public.

SCENE IV. *A room in Capulet's house.*

Enter CAPULET, LADY CAPULET, *and* PARIS.

CAP. Things have fall'n out, sir, so unluckily,
That we have had no time to move our daughter.
Look you, she loved her kinsman Tybalt dearly,
And so did I. Well, we were born to die.
'Tis very late; she'll not come down to-night:
I promise you, but for your company,
I would have been a-bed an hour ago.
PAR. These times of woe afford no time to woo.
Madam, good night: commend me to your daughter.
LA. CAP. I will, and know her mind early to-morrow;
To-night she's mew'd up to her heaviness.
CAP. Sir Paris, I will make a desperate tender[1]
Of my child's love: I think she will be ruled
In all respects by me; nay more, I doubt it not.
Wife, go you to her ere you go to bed;
Acquaint her here of my son Paris' love;
And bid her, mark you me, on Wednesday next—
But, soft! what day is this?
PAR. Monday, my lord.
CAP. Monday! ha, ha! Well, Wednesday is too soon;
O' Thursday let it be: o' Thursday, tell her,
She shall be married to this noble earl.
Will you be ready? do you like this haste?
We'll keep no great ado; a friend or two;
For, hark you, Tybalt being slain so late,
It may be thought we held him carelessly,
Being our kinsman, if we revel much:
Therefore we'll have some half-a-dozen friends,
And there an end. But what say you to Thursday?
PAR. My lord, I would that Thursday were to-morrow.
CAP. Well, get you gone: o' Thursday be it then.
Go you to Juliet ere you go to bed,

[1] *desperate tender*] reckless offer.

Prepare her, wife, against this wedding-day.
Farewell, my lord. Light to my chamber, ho!
Afore me,[2] it is so very very late,
That we may call it early by and by:
Good night. [*Exeunt*.

SCENE V. *Capulet's orchard.*

Enter ROMEO *and* JULIET, *above, at the window.*

JUL. Wilt thou be gone? it is not yet near day:
It was the nightingale, and not the lark,
That pierced the fearful hollow of thine ear;
Nightly she sings on yond pomegranate-tree:
Believe me, love, it was the nightingale.
ROM. It was the lark, the herald of the morn,
No nightingale: look, love, what envious streaks
Do lace the severing clouds in yonder east:
Night's candles are burnt out, and jocund day
Stands tiptoe on the misty mountain tops:
I must be gone and live, or stay and die.
JUL. Yond light is not day-light, I know it, I:
It is some meteor that the sun exhales,
To be to thee this night a torch-bearer,
And light thee on thy way to Mantua:
Therefore stay yet; thou need'st not to be gone.
ROM. Let me be ta'en, let me be put to death;
I am content, so thou wilt have it so.
I'll say yon grey is not the morning's eye,
'Tis but the pale reflex of Cynthia's[1] brow;
Nor that is not the lark, whose notes do beat
The vaulty heaven so high above our heads:
I have more care to stay than will to go:
Come, death, and welcome! Juliet wills it so.
How is't, my soul? let's talk: it is not day.
JUL. It is, it is: hie hence, be gone, away!
It is the lark that sings so out of tune,
Straining harsh discords and unpleasing sharps.

[2] *Afore me*] by my life.

[1] *Cynthia's*] the moon's.

Some say the lark makes sweet division;[2]
This doth not so, for she divideth us:
Some say the lark and loathed toad change eyes;
O, now I would they had changed voices too!
Since arm from arm that voice doth us affray,[3]
Hunting thee hence with hunts-up[4] to the day.
O, now be gone; more light and light it grows.

ROM. More light and light: more dark and dark our woes!

Enter NURSE, *to the chamber.*

NURSE. Madam!
JUL. Nurse?
NURSE. Your lady mother is coming to your chamber:
The day is broke; be wary, look about. [*Exit.*
JUL. Then, window, let day in, and let life out.
ROM. Farewell, farewell! one kiss, and I'll descend. [*Descends.*
JUL. Art thou gone so? my lord, my love, my friend!
I must hear from thee every day in the hour,
For in a minute there are many days:
O, by this count I shall be much in years
Ere I again behold my Romeo!
ROM. Farewell!
I will omit no opportunity
That may convey my greetings, love, to thee.
JUL. O, think'st thou we shall ever meet again?
ROM. I doubt it not; and all these woes shall serve
For sweet discourses in our time to come.
JUL. O God! I have an ill-divining soul.
Methinks I see thee, now thou art below,
As one dead in the bottom of a tomb:
Either my eyesight fails or thou look'st pale.
ROM. And trust me, love, in my eye so do you:
Dry sorrow drinks our blood. Adieu, adieu! [*Exit.*
JUL. O fortune, fortune! all men call thee fickle:
If thou art fickle, what dost thou with him
That is renown'd for faith? Be fickle, fortune;
For then, I hope, thou wilt not keep him long,
But send him back.

[2] *division*] melodic variation.
[3] *affray*] frighten.
[4] *hunts-up*] a tune played to awaken huntsmen.

LA. CAP. [*Within*] Ho, daughter! are you up?
JUL. Who is't that calls? it is my lady mother!
Is she not down[5] so late, or up so early?
What unaccustom'd cause procures her hither?

Enter LADY CAPULET.

LA. CAP. Why, how now, Juliet!
JUL. Madam, I am not well.
LA. CAP. Evermore weeping for your cousin's death?
What, wilt thou wash him from his grave with tears?
An if thou couldst, thou couldst not make him live;
Therefore have done: some grief shows much of love,
But much of grief shows still some want of wit.
JUL. Yet let me weep for such a feeling loss.
LA. CAP. So shall you feel the loss, but not the friend
Which you weep for.
JUL. Feeling so the loss,
I cannot choose but ever weep the friend.
LA. CAP. Well, girl, thou weep'st not so much for his death
As that the villain lives which slaughter'd him.
JUL. What villain, madam?
LA. CAP. That same villain, Romeo.
JUL. [*Aside*] Villain and he be many miles asunder.
God pardon him! I do, with all my heart;
And yet no man like he doth grieve my heart.
LA. CAP. That is because the traitor murderer lives.
JUL. Ay, madam, from the reach of these my hands:
Would none but I might venge my cousin's death!
LA. CAP. We will have vengeance for it, fear thou not:
Then weep no more. I'll send to one in Mantua,
Where that same banish'd runagate doth live,
Shall give him such an unaccustom'd dram
That he shall soon keep Tybalt company:
And then, I hope, thou wilt be satisfied.
JUL. Indeed, I never shall be satisfied
With Romeo, till I behold him—dead—
Is my poor heart so for a kinsman vex'd.
Madam, if you could find out but a man
To bear a poison, I would temper it,

[5] *down*] in bed.

That Romeo should, upon receipt thereof,
Soon sleep in quiet. O, how my heart abhors
To hear him named, and cannot come to him,
To wreak the love I bore my cousin
Upon his body that hath slaughter'd him!

LA. CAP. Find thou the means, and I'll find such a man.
But now I'll tell thee joyful tidings, girl.

JUL. And joy comes well in such a needy time:
What are they, I beseech your ladyship?

LA. CAP. Well, well, thou hast a careful[6] father, child;
One who, to put thee from thy heaviness,
Hath sorted out a sudden day of joy,
That thou expect'st not, nor I look'd not for.

JUL. Madam, in happy time, what day is that?

LA. CAP. Marry, my child, early next Thursday morn,
The gallant, young, and noble gentleman,
The County Paris, at Saint Peter's Church,
Shall happily make thee there a joyful bride.

JUL. Now, by Saint Peter's Church, and Peter too,
He shall not make me there a joyful bride.
I wonder at this haste; that I must wed
Ere he that should be husband comes to woo.
I pray you, tell my lord and father, madam,
I will not marry yet; and, when I do, I swear,
It shall be Romeo, whom you know I hate,
Rather than Paris. These are news indeed!

LA. CAP. Here comes your father; tell him so yourself,
And see how he will take it at your hands.

Enter CAPULET *and* NURSE.

CAP. When the sun sets, the air doth drizzle dew;
But for the sunset of my brother's son
It rains downright.
How now! a conduit,[7] girl? what, still in tears?
Evermore showering? In one little body
Thou counterfeit'st a bark, a sea, a wind:
For still thy eyes, which I may call the sea,
Do ebb and flow with tears; the bark thy body is,

[6] *careful*] provident, attentive.
[7] *conduit*] water pipe.

Sailing in this salt flood; the winds, thy sighs;
Who raging with thy tears, and they with them,
Without a sudden calm will overset
Thy tempest-tossed body. How now, wife!
Have you deliver'd to her our decree?

LA. CAP. Ay, sir; but she will none, she gives you thanks.
I would the fool were married to her grave!

CAP. Soft! take me with you,[8] take me with you, wife.
How! will she none? doth she not give us thanks?
Is she not proud? doth she not count her blest,
Unworthy as she is, that we have wrought
So worthy a gentleman to be her bridegroom?

JUL. Not proud, you have, but thankful that you have:
Proud can I never be of what I hate;
But thankful even for hate that is meant love.

CAP. How, how! how, how! chop-logic! What is this?
'Proud,' and 'I thank you,' and 'I thank you not';
And yet 'not proud': mistress minion,[9] you,
Thank me no thankings, nor proud me no prouds,
But fettle[10] your fine joints 'gainst Thursday next,
To go with Paris to Saint Peter's Church,
Or I will drag thee on a hurdle[11] thither.
Out, you green-sickness[12] carrion! out, you baggage!
You tallow-face!

LA. CAP. Fie, fie! what, are you mad?

JUL. Good father, I beseech you on my knees,
Hear me with patience but to speak a word.

CAP. Hang thee, young baggage! disobedient wretch!
I tell thee what: get thee to church o' Thursday,
Or never after look me in the face:
Speak not, reply not, do not answer me;
My fingers itch. Wife, we scarce thought us blest
That God had lent us but this only child;
But now I see this one is one too much,
And that we have a curse in having her:

[8] *take me with you*] let me understand you.
[9] *minion*] spoiled minx.
[10] *fettle*] prepare.
[11] *hurdle*] a conveyance on which criminals were taken to the place of execution.
[12] *green-sickness*] anemic. Anemia was considered a young woman's ailment. Thus here the implication is "immature," "foolish."

Out on her, hilding!
NURSE. God in heaven bless her!
You are to blame, my lord, to rate[13] her so.
CAP. And why, my lady wisdom? hold your tongue,
Good prudence; smatter[14] with your gossips, go.
NURSE. I speak no treason.
CAP. O, God ye god-den.
NURSE. May not one speak?
CAP. Peace, you mumbling fool!
Utter your gravity[15] o'er a gossip's bowl;
For here we need it not.
LA. CAP. You are too hot.
CAP. God's bread! it makes me mad:
Day, night, hour, tide, time, work, play,
Alone, in company, still my care hath been
To have her match'd: and having now provided
A gentleman of noble parentage,
Of fair demesnes, youthful, and nobly train'd,
Stuff'd, as they say, with honourable parts,
Proportion'd as one's thought would wish a man;
And then to have a wretched puling fool,
A whining mammet,[16] in her fortune's tender,
To answer 'I'll not wed; I cannot love,
I am too young; I pray you, pardon me.'
But, an you will not wed, I'll pardon you:
Graze where you will, you shall not house with me:
Look to't, think on't, I do not use to jest.
Thursday is near; lay hand on heart, advise:
An you be mine, I'll give you to my friend;
An you be not, hang, beg, starve, die in the streets,
For, by my soul, I'll ne'er acknowledge thee,
Nor what is mine shall never do thee good:
Trust to't, bethink you; I'll not be forsworn. [*Exit.*
JUL. Is there no pity sitting in the clouds,
That sees into the bottom of my grief?
O, sweet my mother, cast me not away!
Delay this marriage for a month, a week;

[13] *rate*] berate, scold.
[14] *smatter*] chatter, prattle.
[15] *gravity*] wisdom.
[16] *mammet*] doll, puppet.

Or, if you do not, make the bridal bed
In that dim monument where Tybalt lies.
LA. CAP. Talk not to me, for I'll not speak a word:
Do as thou wilt, for I have done with thee. [*Exit.*
JUL. O God!—O Nurse, how shall this be prevented?
My husband is on earth, my faith in heaven;
How shall that faith return again to earth,
Unless that husband send it me from heaven
By leaving earth? comfort me, counsel me.
Alack, alack, that heaven should practise stratagems
Upon so soft a subject as myself!
What say'st thou? hast thou not a word of joy?
Some comfort, Nurse.
NURSE. Faith, here it is.
Romeo is banish'd, and all the world to nothing,[17]
That he dares ne'er come back to challenge you;
Or, if he do, it needs must be by stealth.
Then, since the case so stands as now it doth,
I think it best you married with the County.
O, he's a lovely gentleman!
Romeo's a dishclout to him: an eagle, madam,
Hath not so green, so quick, so fair an eye
As Paris hath. Beshrew my very heart,
I think you are happy in this second match,
For it excels your first: or if it did not,
Your first is dead, or 'twere as good he were
As living here and you no use of him.
JUL. Speakest thou from thy heart?
NURSE. And from my soul too; else beshrew them both.
JUL. Amen!
NURSE. What?
JUL. Well, thou hast comforted me marvellous much.
Go in, and tell my lady I am gone,
Having displeased my father, to Laurence' cell,
To make confession and to be absolved.
NURSE. Marry, I will, and this is wisely done. [*Exit.*
JUL. Ancient damnation![18] O most wicked fiend!
Is it more sin to wish me thus forsworn,

[17] *all the world to nothing*] the odds are overwhelmingly against you.
[18] *Ancient damnation*] evil old woman.

Or to dispraise my lord with that same tongue
Which she hath praised him with above compare
So many thousand times? Go, counsellor;
Thou and my bosom henceforth shall be twain.
I'll to the Friar, to know his remedy:
If all else fail, myself have power to die. [*Exit*.

ACT IV.

SCENE I. *Friar Laurence's cell.*

Enter FRIAR LAURENCE *and* PARIS.

FRI. L. On Thursday, sir? the time is very short.
PAR. My father Capulet will have it so;
And I am nothing slow to slack his haste.
FRI. L. You say you do not know the lady's mind:
Uneven is the course; I like it not.
PAR. Immoderately she weeps for Tybalt's death,
And therefore have I little talk'd of love,
For Venus smiles not in a house of tears.
Now, sir, her father counts it dangerous
That she doth give her sorrow so much sway,
And in his wisdom hastes our marriage,
To stop the inundation of her tears,
Which, too much minded by herself alone,
May be put from her by society:
Now do you know the reason of this haste.
FRI. L. [*Aside*] I would I knew not why it should be slow'd.
Look, sir, here comes the lady toward my cell.

Enter JULIET.

PAR. Happily met, my lady and my wife!
JUL. That may be, sir, when I may be a wife.
PAR. That may be must be, love, on Thursday next.
JUL. What must be shall be.
FRI. L. That's a certain text.
PAR. Come you to make confession to this father?

JUL. To answer that, I should confess to you.
PAR. Do not deny to him that you love me.
JUL. I will confess to you that I love him.
PAR. So will ye, I am sure, that you love me.
JUL. If I do so, it will be of more price,
Being spoke behind your back, than to your face.
PAR. Poor soul, thy face is much abused with tears.
JUL. The tears have got small victory by that;
For it was bad enough before their spite.
PAR. Thou wrong'st it more than tears with that report.
JUL. That is no slander, sir, which is a truth,
And what I spake, I spake it to my face.
PAR. Thy face is mine, and thou hast slander'd it.
JUL. It may be so, for it is not mine own.
Are you at leisure, holy father, now;
Or shall I come to you at evening mass?
FRI. L. My leisure serves me, pensive daughter, now.
My lord, we must entreat the time alone.
PAR. God shield I should disturb devotion!
Juliet, on Thursday early will I rouse ye:
Till then, adieu, and keep this holy kiss. [*Exit.*
JUL. O, shut the door, and when thou hast done so,
Come weep with me; past hope, past cure, past help!
FRI. L. Ah, Juliet, I already know thy grief;
It strains me past the compass of my wits:
I hear thou must, and nothing may prorogue it,
On Thursday next be married to this County.
JUL. Tell me not, Friar, that thou hear'st of this,
Unless thou tell me how I may prevent it:
If in thy wisdom thou canst give no help,
Do thou but call my resolution wise,
And with this knife I'll help it presently.[1]
God join'd my heart and Romeo's, thou our hands;
And ere this hand, by thee to Romeo's seal'd,
Shall be the label to another deed,
Or my true heart with treacherous revolt
Turn to another, this shall slay them both:
Therefore, out of thy long-experienced time,
Give me some present counsel; or, behold,

[1] *presently*] instantly.

'Twixt my extremes[2] and me this bloody knife
Shall play the umpire, arbitrating that
Which the commission of[3] thy years and art
Could to no issue of true honour bring.
Be not so long to speak; I long to die,
If what thou speak'st speak not of remedy.

FRI. L. Hold, daughter: I do spy a kind of hope,
Which craves as desperate an execution
As that is desperate which we would prevent.
If, rather than to marry County Paris,
Thou hast the strength of will to slay thyself,
Then is it likely thou wilt undertake
A thing like death to chide away this shame,
That copest[4] with death himself to 'scape from it;
And, if thou darest, I'll give thee remedy.

JUL. O, bid me leap, rather than marry Paris,
From off the battlements of yonder tower;
Or walk in thievish ways; or bid me lurk
Where serpents are; chain me with roaring bears;
Or shut me nightly in a charnel-house,
O'er-cover'd quite with dead men's rattling bones,
With reeky shanks and yellow chapless[5] skulls;
Or bid me go into a new-made grave,
And hide me with a dead man in his shroud;
Things that to hear them told, have made me tremble;
And I will do it without fear or doubt,
To live an unstain'd wife to my sweet love.

FRI. L. Hold, then; go home, be merry, give consent
To marry Paris: Wednesday is to-morrow;
To-morrow night look that thou lie alone,
Let not thy nurse lie with thee in thy chamber:
Take thou this vial, being then in bed,
And this distilled liquor drink thou off:
When presently through all thy veins shall run
A cold and drowsy humour; for no pulse
Shall keep his native progress, but surcease:
No warmth, no breath, shall testify thou livest;

[2] *extremes*] extreme difficulties.
[3] *commission of*] authority deriving from.
[4] *copest*] associates.
[5] *chapless*] without the lower jaw.

The roses in thy lips and cheeks shall fade
To paly ashes; thy eyes' windows fall,
Like death, when he shuts up the day of life;
Each part, deprived of supple government,
Shall, stiff and stark and cold, appear like death:
And in this borrow'd likeness of shrunk death
Thou shalt continue two and forty hours,
And then awake as from a pleasant sleep.
Now, when the bridegroom in the morning comes
To rouse thee from thy bed, there art thou dead:
Then, as the manner of our country is,
In thy best robes uncover'd on the bier
Thou shalt be borne to that same ancient vault
Where all the kindred of the Capulets lie.
In the mean time, against thou shalt awake,
Shall Romeo by my letters know our drift;
And hither shall he come: and he and I
Will watch thy waking, and that very night
Shall Romeo bear thee hence to Mantua.
And this shall free thee from this present shame,
If no inconstant toy[6] nor womanish fear
Abate thy valour in the acting it.

JUL. Give me, give me! O, tell not me of fear!

FRI. L. Hold; get you gone, be strong and prosperous
In this resolve: I'll send a friar with speed
To Mantua, with my letters to thy lord.

JUL. Love give me strength! and strength shall help afford.
Farewell, dear father! [*Exeunt.*

SCENE II. *Hall in Capulet's house.*

Enter CAPULET, LADY CAPULET, NURSE, *and two* Servingmen.

CAP. So many guests invite as here are writ. [*Exit* First Servant.
Sirrah, go hire me twenty cunning cooks.

SEC. SERV. You shall have none ill, sir, for I'll try if they can lick their fingers.

CAP. How canst thou try them so?

[6] *toy*] whim, idle fancy.

SEC. SERV. Marry, sir, 'tis an ill cook that cannot lick his own fingers: therefore he that cannot lick his fingers goes not with me.
CAP. Go, be gone. [*Exit* Sec. Servant.
We shall be much unfurnish'd[1] for this time.
What, is my daughter gone to Friar Laurence?
NURSE. Ay, forsooth.
CAP. Well, he may chance to do some good on her:
A peevish self-will'd harlotry[2] it is.

Enter JULIET.

NURSE. See where she comes from shrift with merry look.
CAP. How now, my headstrong! where have you been gadding?
JUL. Where I have learn'd me to repent the sin
Of disobedient opposition
To you and your behests, and am enjoin'd
By holy Laurence to fall prostrate here,
To beg your pardon: pardon, I beseech you!
Henceforward I am ever ruled by you.
CAP. Send for the County; go tell him of this:
I'll have this knot knit up to-morrow morning.
JUL. I met the youthful lord at Laurence' cell,
And gave him what becomed[3] love I might,
Not stepping o'er the bounds of modesty.
CAP. Why, I am glad on 't; this is well: stand up:
This is as 't should be. Let me see the County;
Ay, marry, go, I say, and fetch him hither.
Now, afore God, this reverend holy Friar,
All our whole city is much bound to him.
JUL. Nurse, will you go with me into my closet,[4]
To help me sort such needful ornaments
As you think fit to furnish me to-morrow?
LA. CAP. No, not till Thursday; there is time enough.
CAP. Go, Nurse, go with her: we'll to church to-morrow.
[*Exeunt* JULIET *and* NURSE.
LA. CAP. We shall be short in our provision:
'Tis now near night.
CAP. Tush, I will stir about,

[1] *unfurnish'd*] unprepared.
[2] *harlotry*] good-for-nothing.
[3] *becomed*] becoming, befitting.
[4] *closet*] private room.

And all things shall be well, I warrant thee, wife:
Go thou to Juliet, help to deck up her;
I'll not to bed to-night; let me alone;
I'll play the housewife for this once. What, ho!
They are all forth: well, I will walk myself
To County Paris, to prepare him up
Against to-morrow: my heart is wondrous light,
Since this same wayward girl is so reclaim'd. [*Exeunt*.

SCENE III. *Juliet's chamber.*

Enter JULIET *and* NURSE.

JUL. Ay, those attires are best: but, gentle Nurse,
I pray thee, leave me to myself to-night;
For I have need of many orisons
To move the heavens to smile upon my state,
Which, well thou know'st, is cross[1] and full of sin.

Enter LADY CAPULET.

LA. CAP. What, are you busy, ho? need you my help?
JUL. No, madam; we have cull'd such necessaries
As are behoveful for our state to-morrow:
So please you, let me now be left alone,
And let the Nurse this night sit up with you,
For I am sure you have your hands full all
In this so sudden business.
LA. CAP. Good night:
Get thee to bed and rest, for thou hast need.
[*Exeunt* LADY CAPULET *and* NURSE.
JUL. Farewell! God knows when we shall meet again.
I have a faint cold fear thrills through my veins,
That almost freezes up the heat of life:
I'll call them back again to comfort me.
Nurse!—What should she do here?
My dismal scene I needs must act alone.
Come, vial.
What if this mixture do not work at all?

[1] *cross*] perverse.

Shall I be married then to-morrow morning?
No, no: this shall forbid it. Lie thou there. [*Laying down a dagger.*
What if it be a poison, which the Friar
Subtly hath minister'd to have me dead,
Lest in this marriage he should be dishonour'd,
Because he married me before to Romeo?
I fear it is: and yet, methinks, it should not,
For he hath still been tried a holy man.
How if, when I am laid into the tomb,
I wake before the time that Romeo
Come to redeem me? there's a fearful point.
Shall I not then be stifled in the vault,
To whose foul mouth no healthsome air breathes in,
And there die strangled ere my Romeo comes?
Or, if I live, is it not very like,
The horrible conceit of death and night,
Together with the terror of the place,
As in a vault, an ancient receptacle,
Where for this many hundred years the bones
Of all my buried ancestors are pack'd;
Where bloody Tybalt, yet but green in earth,
Lies festering in his shroud; where, as they say,
At some hours in the night spirits resort;
Alack, alack, is it not like that I
So early waking, what with loathsome smells
And shrieks like mandrakes' torn out of the earth,
That living mortals hearing them run mad:
O, if I wake, shall I not be distraught,
Environed with all these hideous fears?
And madly play with my forefathers' joints?
And pluck the mangled Tybalt from his shroud?
And, in this rage,[2] with some great kinsman's bone,
As with a club, dash out my desperate brains?
O, look! methinks I see my cousin's ghost
Seeking out Romeo, that did spit his body
Upon a rapier's point: stay, Tybalt, stay!
Romeo, I come! this do I drink to thee.
[*She falls upon her bed, within the curtains.*

[2] *rage*] madness.

SCENE IV. *Hall in Capulet's house.*

Enter LADY CAPULET *and* NURSE.

LA. CAP. Hold, take these keys, and fetch more spices, Nurse.
NURSE. They call for dates and quinces in the pastry.[1]

Enter CAPULET.

CAP. Come, stir, stir, stir! the second cock hath crow'd,
The curfew-bell hath rung, 'tis three o'clock:
Look to the baked meats, good Angelica:
Spare not for cost.
NURSE. Go, you cot-quean,[2] go,
Get you to bed; faith, you'll be sick to-morrow
For this night's watching.
CAP. No, not a whit: what! I have watch'd ere now
All night for lesser cause, and ne'er been sick.
LA. CAP. Ay, you have been a mouse-hunt[3] in your time;
But I will watch you from such watching now.
[*Exeunt* LADY CAPULET *and* NURSE.
CAP. A jealous-hood,[4] a jealous-hood!
Enter three or four Servingmen, *with spits, and logs, and baskets.*

Now, fellow,
What's there?
FIRST SERV. Things for the cook, sir, but I know not what.
CAP. Make haste, make haste. [*Exit* First Serv.] Sirrah, fetch drier logs:
Call Peter, he will show thee where they are.
SEC. SERV. I have a head, sir, that will find out logs,
And never trouble Peter for the matter.
CAP. Mass, and well said; a merry whoreson, ha!
Thou shalt be logger-head.[5] [*Exit* Sec. Serv.] Good faith, 'tis day:
The County will be here with music straight,

[1] *pastry*] room in which pies were made.
[2] *cot-quean*] a man who plays the housewife.
[3] *mouse-hunt*] woman chaser.
[4] *jealous-hood*] jealousy.
[5] *logger-head*] blockhead.

For so he said he would. [*Music within.*] I hear him near.
Nurse! Wife! What, ho! What, Nurse, I say!

Re-enter NURSE.

Go waken Juliet, go and trim her up;
I'll go and chat with Paris: hie, make haste,
Make haste: the bridegroom he is come already:
Make haste, I say. [*Exeunt.*

SCENE V. *Juliet's chamber.*

Enter NURSE.

NURSE. Mistress! what, mistress! Juliet! fast,[1] I warrant her, she:
Why, lamb! why, lady! fie, you slug-a-bed!
Why, love, I say! madam! sweet-heart! why, bride!
What, not a word? you take your pennyworths[2] now;
Sleep for a week; for the next night, I warrant,
The County Paris hath set up his rest[3]
That you shall rest but little. God forgive me,
Marry, and amen, how sound is she asleep!
I needs must wake her. Madam, madam, madam!
Ay, let the County take you in your bed;
He'll fright you up, i' faith. Will it not be? [*Undraws the curtains.*
What, dress'd! and in your clothes! and down again!
I must needs wake you. Lady! lady! lady!
Alas, alas! Help, help! my lady's dead!
O, well-a-day, that ever I was born!
Some aqua-vitae, ho! My lord! my lady!

Enter LADY CAPULET.

LA. CAP. What noise is here?
NURSE. O lamentable day!
LA. CAP. What is the matter?
NURSE. Look, look! O heavy day!
LA. CAP. O me, O me! My child, my only life,
Revive, look up, or I will die with thee.

[1] *fast*] fast asleep.
[2] *pennyworths*] small quantities (of sleep).
[3] *set up his rest*] determined, with a bawdy innuendo of couching the lance for the charge.

Help, help! call help.

Enter CAPULET.

CAP. For shame, bring Juliet forth; her lord is come.
NURSE. She's dead, deceased, she's dead; alack the day!
LA. CAP. Alack the day, she's dead, she's dead, she's dead!
CAP. Ha! let me see her. Out, alas! she's cold;
Her blood is settled and her joints are stiff;
Life and these lips have long been separated.
Death lies on her like an untimely frost
Upon the sweetest flower of all the field.
NURSE. O lamentable day!
LA. CAP. O woeful time!
CAP. Death, that hath ta'en her hence to make me wail,
Ties up my tongue and will not let me speak.

Enter FRIAR LAURENCE *and* PARIS, *with* Musicians.

FRI. L. Come, is the bride ready to go to church?
CAP. Ready to go, but never to return.
O son, the night before thy wedding-day
Hath Death lain with thy wife: see, there she lies,
Flower as she was, deflowered by him.
Death is my son-in-law, Death is my heir;
My daughter he hath wedded: I will die,
And leave him all; life, living, all is Death's.
PAR. Have I thought long to see this morning's face,
And doth it give me such a sight as this?
LA. CAP. Accurst, unhappy, wretched, hateful day!
Most miserable hour that e'er time saw
In lasting labour of his pilgrimage!
But one, poor one, one poor and loving child,
But one thing to rejoice and solace in,
And cruel death hath catch'd it from my sight!
NURSE. O woe! O woeful, woeful, woeful day!
Most lamentable day, most woeful day,
That ever, ever, I did yet behold!
O day! O day! O day! O hateful day!
Never was seen so black a day as this:
O woeful day, O woeful day!
PAR. Beguiled, divorced, wronged, spited, slain!
Most detestable death, by thee beguiled,

By cruel cruel thee quite overthrown!
O love! O life! not life, but love in death!
CAP. Despised, distressed, hated, martyr'd, kill'd!
Uncomfortable[4] time, why camest thou now
To murder, murder our solemnity?[5]
O child! O child! my soul, and not my child!
Dead art thou! Alack, my child is dead;
And with my child my joys are buried!
FRI. L. Peace, ho, for shame! confusion's[6] cure lives not
In these confusions. Heaven and yourself
Had part in this fair maid; now heaven hath all,
And all the better is it for the maid:
Your part in her you could not keep from death;
But heaven keeps his part in eternal life.
The most you sought was her promotion,
For 'twas your heaven she should be advanced:
And weep ye now, seeing she is advanced
Above the clouds, as high as heaven itself?
O, in this love, you love your child so ill,
That you run mad, seeing that she is well:
She's not well married that lives married long,
But she's best married that dies married young.
Dry up your tears, and stick your rosemary
On this fair corse, and, as the custom is,
In all her best array bear her to church:
For though fond nature bids us all lament,
Yet nature's tears are reason's merriment.
CAP. All things that we ordained festival,
Turn from their office to black funeral:
Our instruments to melancholy bells;
Our wedding cheer to a sad burial feast;
Our solemn hymns to sullen dirges change;
Our bridal flowers serve for a buried corse,
And all things change them to the contrary.
FRI. L. Sir, go you in; and, madam, go with him;
And go, Sir Paris; every one prepare
To follow this fair corse unto her grave:

[4] *Uncomfortable*] joyless.
[5] *solemnity*] celebration, ceremony.
[6] *confusion's*] calamity's.

The heavens do lour upon you for some ill;
Move them no more by crossing their high will.
[*Exeunt* CAPULET, LADY CAPULET, PARIS, *and* FRIAR.

FIRST MUS. Faith, we may put up our pipes, and be gone.

NURSE. Honest good fellows, ah, put up, put up;
For, well you know, this is a pitiful case. [*Exit.*

FIRST MUS. Ay, by my troth, the case may be amended.

Enter PETER.

PET. Musicians, O, musicians, 'Heart's ease,[7] Heart's ease': O, an you will have me live, play 'Heart's ease.'

FIRST MUS. Why 'Heart's ease'?

PET. O, musicians, because my heart itself plays 'My heart is full of woe': O, play me some merry dump,[8] to comfort me.

FIRST MUS. Not a dump we; 'tis no time to play now.

PET. You will not then?

FIRST MUS. No.

PET. I will then give it you soundly.

FIRST MUS. What will you give us?

PET. No money, on my faith, but the gleek;[9] I will give you the minstrel.

FIRST MUS. Then will I give you the serving-creature.

PET. Then will I lay the serving-creature's dagger on your pate. I will carry no crotchets:[10] I'll re you, I'll fa you; do you note me?

FIRST MUS. An you re us and fa us, you note us.

SEC. MUS. Pray you, put up your dagger, and put out[11] your wit.

PET. Then have at you with my wit! I will dry-beat you with an iron wit, and put up my iron dagger. Answer me like men:

'When griping grief the heart doth wound
And doleful dumps the mind oppress,
Then music with her silver sound'—

why 'silver sound'? why 'music with her silver sound'?—What say you, Simon Catling?[12]

[7] *'Heart's ease'*] a popular tune of the time.
[8] *dump*] melancholy tune.
[9] *gleek*] gesture of scorn.
[10] *carry no crotchets*] endure none of your whims (with the musical pun).
[11] *put out*] display.
[12] *Catling*] a lute string.

FIRST MUS. Marry, sir, because silver hath a sweet sound.

PET. Pretty! What say you, Hugh Rebeck?[13]

SEC. MUS. I say, 'silver sound,' because musicians sound for silver.

PET. Pretty too! What say you, James Soundpost?

THIRD MUS. Faith, I know not what to say.

PET. O, I cry you mercy; you are the singer: I will say for you. It is 'music with her silver sound,' because musicians have no gold for sounding:

'Then music with her silver sound
With speedy help doth lend redress.' [*Exit.*

FIRST MUS. What a pestilent knave is this same!

SEC. MUS. Hang him, Jack! Come, we'll in here; tarry for the mourners, and stay dinner. [*Exeunt.*

[13] *Rebeck*] a three-stringed fiddle.

ACT V.

SCENE I. *Mantua. A street.*

Enter ROMEO.

ROM. If I may trust the flattering truth of sleep,
My dreams presage some joyful news at hand:
My bosom's lord sits lightly in his throne,
And all this day an unaccustom'd spirit
Lifts me above the ground with cheerful thoughts.
I dreamt my lady came and found me dead—
Strange dream, that gives a dead man leave to think!—
And breathed such life with kisses in my lips,
That I revived and was an emperor.
Ah me! how sweet is love itself possess'd,
When but love's shadows are so rich in joy!

Enter BALTHASAR, *booted*.

News from Verona! How now, Balthasar!
Dost thou not bring me letters from the Friar?
How doth my lady? Is my father well?
How fares my Juliet? that I ask again;
For nothing can be ill, if she be well.
BAL. Then she is well, and nothing can be ill:
Her body sleeps in Capels' monument,
And her immortal part with angels lives.
I saw her laid low in her kindred's vault,
And presently took post to tell it you:
O, pardon me for bringing these ill news,
Since you did leave it for my office, sir.
ROM. Is it e'en so? then I defy you, stars!

Thou know'st my lodging: get me ink and paper,
And hire post-horses; I will hence to-night.
BAL. I do beseech you, sir, have patience:
Your looks are pale and wild, and do import
Some misadventure.
ROM. Tush, thou art deceived:
Leave me, and do the thing I bid thee do.
Hast thou no letters to me from the Friar?
BAL. No, my good lord.
ROM. No matter: get thee gone,
And hire those horses; I'll be with thee straight. [*Exit* BALTHASAR.
Well, Juliet, I will lie with thee to-night.
Let's see for means:—O mischief, thou art swift
To enter in the thoughts of desperate men!
I do remember an apothecary,
And hereabouts a' dwells, which late I noted
In tatter'd weeds, with overwhelming[1] brows,
Culling of simples;[2] meagre were his looks;
Sharp misery had worn him to the bones:
And in his needy shop a tortoise hung,
An alligator stuff'd and other skins
Of ill-shaped fishes; and about his shelves
A beggarly account of empty boxes,
Green earthen pots, bladders and musty seeds,
Remnants of packthread and old cakes of roses,[3]
Were thinly scatter'd, to make up a show.
Noting this penury, to myself I said,
An if a man did need a poison now,
Whose sale is present death in Mantua,
Here lives a caitiff wretch would sell it him.
O, this same thought did but forerun my need,
And this same needy man must sell it me.
As I remember, this should be the house:
Being holiday, the beggar's shop is shut.
What, ho! apothecary!

Enter Apothecary.

[1] *overwhelming*] jutting out, overhanging.
[2] *Culling of simples*] gathering medicinal herbs.
[3] *cakes of roses*] rose petals compressed into cakes to be used as perfume.

AP. Who calls so loud?
ROM. Come hither, man. I see that thou art poor;
Hold, there is forty ducats: let me have
A dram of poison; such soon-speeding gear
As will disperse itself through all the veins,
That the life-weary taker may fall dead,
And that the trunk may be discharged of breath
As violently as hasty powder fired
Doth hurry from the fatal cannon's womb.
AP. Such mortal drugs I have; but Mantua's law
Is death to any he that utters[4] them.
ROM. Art thou so bare and full of wretchedness,
And fear'st to die? famine is in thy cheeks,
Need and oppression starveth in thy eyes,
Contempt and beggary hangs upon thy back,
The world is not thy friend, nor the world's law:
The world affords no law to make thee rich;
Then be not poor, but break it, and take this.
AP. My poverty, but not my will, consents.
ROM. I pay thy poverty and not thy will.
AP. Put this in any liquid thing you will,
And drink it off; and, if you had the strength
Of twenty men, it would dispatch you straight.
ROM. There is thy gold, worse poison to men's souls,
Doing more murder in this loathsome world,
Than these poor compounds that thou mayst not sell:
I sell thee poison, thou hast sold me none.
Farewell: buy food, and get thyself in flesh.
Come, cordial and not poison, go with me
To Juliet's grave; for there must I use thee. [*Exeunt*.

[4] *utters*] dispenses.

SCENE II. *Friar Laurence's cell.*

Enter FRIAR JOHN.

FRI. J. Holy Franciscan friar! brother, ho!

Enter FRIAR LAURENCE.

FRI. L. This same should be the voice of Friar John.
Welcome from Mantua: what says Romeo?
Or, if his mind be writ, give me his letter.
FRI. J. Going to find a bare-foot brother out,
One of our order, to associate[1] me,
Here in this city visiting the sick,
And finding him, the searchers of the town,[2]
Suspecting that we both were in a house
Where the infectious pestilence did reign,
Seal'd up the doors and would not let us forth;
So that my speed to Mantua there was stay'd.
FRI. L. Who bare my letter then to Romeo?
FRI. J. I could not send it,—here it is again,—
Nor get a messenger to bring it thee,
So fearful were they of infection.
FRI. L. Unhappy fortune! by my brotherhood,
The letter was not nice,[3] but full of charge
Of dear import, and the neglecting it
May do much danger. Friar John, go hence;
Get me an iron crow[4] and bring it straight
Unto my cell.
FRI. J. Brother, I'll go and bring it thee. [*Exit.*
FRI. L. Now must I to the monument alone;
Within this three hours will fair Juliet wake:
She will beshrew me much that Romeo
Hath had no notice of these accidents;
But I will write again to Mantua,

[1] *associate*] accompany.
[2] *searchers of the town*] officers of the town responsible for public health during a plague.
[3] *nice*] trivial.
[4] *crow*] crowbar.

And keep her at my cell till Romeo come:
Poor living corse, closed in a dead man's tomb! [*Exit*.

SCENE III. *A churchyard; in it a monument belonging to the Capulets.*

Enter PARIS *and his* Page, *bearing flowers and a torch*.

PAR. Give me thy torch, boy: hence, and stand aloof:
Yet put it out, for I would not be seen.
Under yond yew-trees lay thee all along,[1]
Holding thine ear close to the hollow ground;
So shall no foot upon the churchyard tread,
Being loose, unfirm, with digging up of graves,
But thou shalt hear it: whistle then to me,
As signal that thou hear'st something approach.
Give me those flowers. Do as I bid thee, go.
PAGE. [*Aside*] I am almost afraid to stand alone
Here in the churchyard; yet I will adventure. [*Retires*.
PAR. Sweet flower, with flowers thy bridal bed I strew,—
O woe! thy canopy is dust and stones;—
Which with sweet water nightly I will dew,
Or, wanting that, with tears distill'd by moans:
The obsequies that I for thee will keep
Nightly shall be to strew thy grave and weep. [*The* Page *whistles*.
The boy gives warning something doth approach.
What cursed foot wanders this way to-night,
To cross my obsequies and true love's rite?
What, with a torch! Muffle me, night, a while. [*Retires*.

Enter ROMEO *and* BALTHASAR, *with a torch, mattock, &c*.

ROM. Give me that mattock and the wrenching iron.
Hold, take this letter; early in the morning
See thou deliver it to my lord and father.
Give me the light: upon thy life, I charge thee,
Whate'er thou hear'st or seest, stand all aloof,
And do not interrupt me in my course.
Why I descend into this bed of death
Is partly to behold my lady's face,
But chiefly to take thence from her dead finger

[1] *all along*] at full length.

A precious ring, a ring that I must use
In dear employment: therefore hence, be gone:
But if thou, jealous,[2] dost return to pry
In what I farther shall intend to do,
By heaven, I will tear thee joint by joint
And strew this hungry churchyard with thy limbs:
The time and my intents are savage-wild,
More fierce and more inexorable far
Than empty tigers or the roaring sea.

BAL. I will be gone, sir, and not trouble you.

ROM. So shalt thou show me friendship. Take thou that:
Live, and be prosperous: and farewell, good fellow.

BAL. [*Aside*] For all this same, I'll hide me hereabout:
His looks I fear, and his intents I doubt. [*Retires.*

ROM. Thou detestable maw, thou womb of death,
Gorged with the dearest morsel of the earth,
Thus I enforce thy rotten jaws to open,
And in despite I'll cram thee with more food. [*Opens the tomb.*

PAR. This is that banish'd haughty Montague
That murder'd my love's cousin, with which grief,
It is supposed, the fair creature died,
And here is come to do some villanous shame
To the dead bodies: I will apprehend him. [*Comes forward.*
Stop thy unhallow'd toil, vile Montague!
Can vengeance be pursued further than death?
Condemned villain, I do apprehend thee:
Obey, and go with me; for thou must die.

ROM. I must indeed, and therefore came I hither.
Good gentle youth, tempt not a desperate man;
Fly hence and leave me: think upon these gone;
Let them affright thee. I beseech thee, youth,
Put not another sin upon my head,
By urging me to fury: O, be gone!
By heaven, I love thee better than myself,
For I come hither arm'd against myself:
Stay not, be gone: live, and hereafter say,
A madman's mercy bid thee run away.

PAR. I do defy thy conjurations[3]
And apprehend thee for a felon here.

[2] *jealous*] suspicious.
[3] *conjurations*] solemn appeals.

ROM. Wilt thou provoke me? then have at thee, boy! [*They fight.*
PAGE. O Lord, they fight! I will go call the watch. [*Exit.*
PAR. O, I am slain! [*Falls.*] If thou be merciful,
Open the tomb, lay me with Juliet. [*Dies.*
ROM. In faith, I will. Let me peruse this face:
Mercutio's kinsman, noble County Paris!
What said my man, when my betossed soul
Did not attend him as we rode? I think
He told me Paris should have married Juliet:
Said he not so? or did I dream it so?
Or am I mad, hearing him talk of Juliet,
To think it was so? O, give me thy hand,
One writ with me in sour misfortune's book!
I'll bury thee in a triumphant grave;
A grave? O, no, a lantern,[4] slaughter'd youth;
For here lies Juliet, and her beauty makes
This vault a feasting presence[5] full of light.
Death, lie thou there, by a dead man interr'd.
[*Laying* PARIS *in the monument.*
How oft when men are at the point of death
Have they been merry! which their keepers call
A lightning before death: O, how may I
Call this a lightning? O my love! my wife!
Death, that hath suck'd the honey of thy breath,
Hath had no power yet upon thy beauty:
Thou art not conquer'd; beauty's ensign yet
Is crimson in thy lips and in thy cheeks,
And death's pale flag is not advanced there.
Tybalt, liest thou there in thy bloody sheet?
O, what more favour can I do to thee
Than with that hand that cut thy youth in twain
To sunder his that was thine enemy?
Forgive me, cousin! Ah, dear Juliet,
Why art thou yet so fair? shall I believe
That unsubstantial death is amorous,
And that the lean abhorred monster keeps
Thee here in dark to be his paramour?
For fear of that, I still will stay with thee,

[4] *lantern*] turret full of windows.
[5] *presence*] presence chamber.

And never from this palace of dim night
Depart again: here, here will I remain
With worms that are thy chamber-maids; O, here
Will I set up my everlasting rest,
And shake the yoke of inauspicious stars
From this world-wearied flesh. Eyes, look your last!
Arms, take your last embrace! and, lips, O you
The doors of breath, seal with a righteous kiss
A dateless[6] bargain to engrossing death!
Come, bitter conduct, come, unsavoury guide!
Thou desperate pilot, now at once run on
The dashing rocks thy sea-sick weary bark.
Here's to my love! [*Drinks.*] O true apothecary!
Thy drugs are quick. Thus with a kiss I die. [*Dies.*

Enter, at the other end of the churchyard, FRIAR LAURENCE, *with a lantern, crow, and spade.*

FRI. L. Saint Francis be my speed![7] how oft to-night
Have my old feet stumbled at graves! Who's there?
BAL. Here's one, a friend, and one that knows you well.
FRI. L. Bliss be upon you! Tell me, good my friend,
What torch is yond that vainly lends his light
To grubs and eyeless skulls? as I discern,
It burneth in the Capels' monument.
BAL. It doth so, holy sir; and there's my master,
One that you love.
FRI. L. Who is it?
BAL. Romeo.
FRI. L. How long hath he been there?
BAL. Full half an hour.
FRI. L. Go with me to the vault.
BAL. I dare not, sir:
My master knows not but I am gone hence;
And fearfully did menace me with death,
If I did stay to look on his intents.
FRI. L. Stay, then; I'll go alone: fear comes upon me;
O, much I fear some ill unlucky thing.
BAL. As I did sleep under this yew-tree here,

[6] *dateless*] eternal.
[7] *speed*] protecting and assisting power.

I dreamt my master and another fought,
And that my master slew him.
FRI. L. Romeo! [*Advances.*
Alack, alack, what blood is this, which stains
The stony entrance of this sepulchre?
What mean these masterless and gory swords
To lie discolour'd by this place of peace? [*Enters the tomb.*
Romeo! O, pale! Who else? what, Paris too?
And steep'd in blood? Ah, what an unkind hour
Is guilty of this lamentable chance!
The lady stirs. [JULIET *wakes.*
JUL. O comfortable Friar! where is my lord?
I do remember well where I should be,
And there I am: where is my Romeo? [*Noise within.*
FRI. L. I hear some noise. Lady, come from that nest
Of death, contagion and unnatural sleep:
A greater power than we can contradict
Hath thwarted our intents: come, come away:
Thy husband in thy bosom there lies dead;
And Paris too: come, I'll dispose of thee
Among a sisterhood of holy nuns:
Stay not to question, for the watch is coming;
Come, go, good Juliet; I dare no longer stay.
JUL. Go, get thee hence, for I will not away. [*Exit* FRI. L.
What's here? a cup, closed in my true love's hand?
Poison, I see, hath been his timeless end:
O churl! drunk all, and left no friendly drop
To help me after? I will kiss thy lips;
Haply some poison yet doth hang on them,
To make me die with a restorative. [*Kisses him.*
Thy lips are warm.
FIRST WATCH. [*Within*] Lead, boy: which way?
JUL. Yea, noise? then I'll be brief. O happy dagger!
[*Snatching* ROMEO'S *dagger.*
This is thy sheath [*Stabs herself*]; there rust, and let me die.
[*Falls on* ROMEO'S *body, and dies.*

Enter Watch, *with the* Page *of* PARIS.

PAGE. This is the place; there, where the torch doth burn.
FIRST WATCH. The ground is bloody; search about the churchyard:

Go, some of you, whoe'er you find attach.[8]
Pitiful sight! here lies the County slain;
And Juliet bleeding, warm, and newly dead,
Who here hath lain this two days buried.
Go, tell the Prince: run to the Capulets:
Raise up the Montagues: some others search:
We see the ground whereon these woes do lie;
But the true ground of all these piteous woes
We cannot without circumstance[9] descry.

Re-enter some of the Watch, *with* BALTHASAR.

SEC. WATCH. Here's Romeo's man; we found him in the churchyard.
FIRST WATCH. Hold him in safety, till the Prince come hither.

Re-enter FRIAR LAURENCE, *and another* Watchman.

THIRD WATCH. Here is a friar, that trembles, sighs and weeps:
We took this mattock and this spade from him,
As he was coming from this churchyard's side.
FIRST WATCH. A great suspicion: stay the friar too.

Enter the PRINCE *and* Attendants.

PRINCE. What misadventure is so early up,
That calls our person from our morning rest?

Enter CAPULET, LADY CAPULET, *and others.*

CAP. What should it be that they so shriek abroad?
LA. CAP. The people in the street cry Romeo,
Some Juliet, and some Paris, and all run
With open outcry toward our monument.
PRINCE. What fear is this which startles in our ears?
FIRST WATCH. Sovereign, here lies the County Paris slain;
And Romeo dead; and Juliet, dead before,
Warm and new kill'd.
PRINCE. Search, seek, and know how this foul murder comes.
FIRST WATCH. Here is a friar, and slaughter'd Romeo's man,
With instruments upon them fit to open
These dead men's tombs.
CAP. O heavens! O wife, look how our daughter bleeds!

[8] *attach*] arrest.
[9] *circumstance*] detailed information.

This dagger hath mista'en, for, lo, his house
Is empty on the back of Montague,
And it mis-sheathed in my daughter's bosom!
LA. CAP. O me! this sight of death is as a bell
That warns my old age to a sepulchre.

Enter MONTAGUE *and others.*

PRINCE. Come, Montague; for thou art early up,
To see thy son and heir more early down.
MON. Alas, my liege, my wife is dead to-night;
Grief of my son's exile hath stopp'd her breath:
What further woe conspires against mine age?
PRINCE. Look, and thou shalt see.
MON. O thou untaught! what manners is in this,
To press before thy father to a grave?
PRINCE. Seal up the mouth of outrage[10] for a while,
Till we can clear these ambiguities,
And know their spring, their head, their true descent;
And then will I be general of your woes,
And lead you even to death: meantime forbear,
And let mischance be slave to patience.
Bring forth the parties of suspicion.
FRI. L. I am the greatest, able to do least,
Yet most suspected, as the time and place
Doth make against me, of this direful murder;
And here I stand, both to impeach and purge
Myself condemned and myself excused.
PRINCE. Then say at once what thou dost know in this.
FRI. L. I will be brief, for my short date of breath
Is not so long as is a tedious tale.
Romeo, there dead, was husband to that Juliet;
And she, there dead, that Romeo's faithful wife:
I married them; and their stol'n marriage-day
Was Tybalt's dooms-day, whose untimely death
Banish'd the new-made bridegroom from this city;
For whom, and not for Tybalt, Juliet pined.
You, to remove that siege of grief from her,
Betroth'd and would have married her perforce
To County Paris: then comes she to me,

[10] *outrage*] outcry.

And with wild looks bid me devise some mean
To rid her from this second marriage,
Or in my cell there would she kill herself.
Then gave I her, so tutor'd by my art,
A sleeping potion; which so took effect
As I intended, for it wrought on her
The form of death: meantime I writ to Romeo,
That he should hither come as this dire night,
To help to take her from her borrow'd grave,
Being the time the potion's force should cease.
But he which bore my letter, Friar John,
Was stay'd by accident, and yesternight
Return'd my letter back. Then all alone
At the prefixed hour of her waking
Came I to take her from her kindred's vault,
Meaning to keep her closely[11] at my cell
Till I conveniently could send to Romeo:
But when I came, some minute ere the time
Of her awaking, here untimely lay
The noble Paris and true Romeo dead.
She wakes, and I entreated her come forth,
And bear this work of heaven with patience:
But then a noise did scare me from the tomb,
And she too desperate would not go with me,
But, as it seems, did violence on herself.
All this I know; and to the marriage
Her nurse is privy: and, if aught in this
Miscarried by my fault, let my old life
Be sacrificed some hour before his time
Unto the rigour of severest law.

PRINCE. We still[12] have known thee for a holy man.
Where's Romeo's man? what can he say in this?

BAL. I brought my master news of Juliet's death,
And then in post he came from Mantua
To this same place, to this same monument.
This letter he early bid me give his father,
And threaten'd me with death, going in the vault,
If I departed not and left him there.

[11] *closely*] in secret.
[12] *still*] always.

PRINCE. Give me the letter; I will look on it.
Where is the County's page, that raised the watch?
Sirrah, what made your master in this place?
PAGE. He came with flowers to strew his lady's grave;
And bid me stand aloof, and so I did:
Anon comes one with light to ope the tomb;
And by and by my master drew on him;
And then I ran away to call the watch.
PRINCE. This letter doth make good the Friar's words,
Their course of love, the tidings of her death:
And here he writes that he did buy a poison
Of a poor 'pothecary, and therewithal
Came to this vault to die and lie with Juliet.
Where be these enemies? Capulet! Montague!
See, what a scourge is laid upon your hate,
That heaven finds means to kill your joys with love!
And I, for winking at your discords too,
Have lost a brace of kinsmen: all are punish'd.
CAP. O brother Montague, give me thy hand:
This is my daughter's jointure,[13] for no more
Can I demand.
MON. But I can give thee more:
For I will raise her statue in pure gold;
That whiles Verona by that name is known,
There shall no figure at such rate[14] be set
As that of true and faithful Juliet.
CAP. As rich shall Romeo's by his lady's lie;
Poor sacrifices of our enmity!
PRINCE. A glooming peace this morning with it brings;
The sun for sorrow will not show his head:
Go hence, to have more talk of these sad things;
Some shall be pardon'd and some punished:
For never was a story of more woe
Than this of Juliet and her Romeo. [*Exeunt*.

[13] *jointure*] the marriage portion supplied by the bridegroom.
[14] *rate*] value.

Richard III

Note

Richard III was probably written between 1592 and 1593, soon after Shakespeare completed the three Henry VI plays. Shakespeare's primary source for the play's historical events was the 1587 edition of Raphael Holinshed's *Chronicles of England, Scotland and Ireland*, and the basis of his information on Richard was Sir Thomas More's *The Life of Richard III* (1513). More's portrayal of a villainous, deformed Richard is hardly surprising. Henry VIII, whom More served, was the son of Henry Tudor, the Lancastrian claimant to the crown who defeated Richard at the Battle of Bosworth Field and assumed the throne as Henry VII. (Henry's accession effectively ended the long and bloody dynastic civil wars known as the Wars of the Roses [1455–85].)

Despite the character's basis in sixteenth-century propaganda, Shakespeare's fictional Richard is better known than the historical figure. Ruthless and ambitious, the hunchbacked king vies with Iago in his depravity. Richard's political machinations exceed even those of Machiavelli, whom, as he boasts in 3 *Henry VI*, he will "set . . . to school" (III. ii. 193). Richard's deformed soul is matched by his deformed physiognomy—he is a "poisonous bunch-backed toad," an "elvish-mark'd, abortive rooting hog," "hell's black intelligencer." But Richard flaunts his physical appearance as readily as his malevolence. Since, as he says in his opening soliloquy, he is not "made to court an amorous looking-glass," he is "determined to prove a villain," a royal deceiver, a plotter extraordinaire. He becomes all this and more—one of Shakespeare's most memorable villains.

Dramatis Personæ

KING EDWARD the Fourth.

EDWARD, Prince of Wales, afterwards King Edward V, } sons to
RICHARD, Duke of York. } the King.

GEORGE, Duke of Clarence, } brothers to the King.
RICHARD, Duke of Gloucester, afterwards King Richard III. } brothers to the King.

A young son of Clarence.

HENRY, Earl of Richmond, afterwards King Henry VII.

CARDINAL BOURCHIER, Archbishop of Canterbury.

THOMAS ROTHERHAM, Archbishop of York.

JOHN MORTON, Bishop of Ely.

DUKE OF BUCKINGHAM.

DUKE OF NORFOLK.

EARL OF SURREY, his son.

EARL RIVERS, brother to Elizabeth.

MARQUIS OF DORSET and LORD GREY, sons to Elizabeth.

EARL OF OXFORD.

LORD HASTINGS.

LORD STANLEY, called also EARL OF DERBY.

LORD LOVEL.

SIR THOMAS VAUGHAN.

SIR RICHARD RATCLIFF.

SIR WILLIAM CATESBY.

SIR JAMES TYRREL.

SIR JAMES BLOUNT.

SIR WALTER HERBERT.

SIR ROBERT BRAKENBURY, Lieutenant of the Tower.

SIR WILLIAM BRANDON.

CHRISTOPHER URSWICK, a priest.

Another Priest.

TRESSEL and BERKELEY, gentlemen attending on the Lady Anne.
Lord Mayor of London.
Sheriff of Wiltshire.

ELIZABETH, queen to King Edward IV.
MARGARET, widow of King Henry VI.
DUCHESS OF YORK, mother to King Edward IV.
LADY ANNE, widow of Edward Prince of Wales, son to King Henry VI; afterwards married to Richard.
A young daughter of Clarence (MARGARET PLANTAGENET).

Ghosts of those murdered by Richard III, Lords and other Attendants; a Pursuivant, Scrivener, Citizens, Murderers, Messengers, Soldiers, &c.

SCENE: *England*

ACT I.

SCENE I. *London. A Street.*

Enter RICHARD, DUKE OF GLOUCESTER, *solus*

GLOU. Now is the winter of our discontent
Made glorious summer by this sun of York;[1]
And all the clouds that lour'd upon our house
In the deep bosom of the ocean buried.
Now are our brows bound with victorious wreaths;
Our bruised arms hung up for monuments;
Our stern alarums changed to merry meetings,
Our dreadful marches to delightful measures.
Grim-visaged war hath smooth'd his wrinkled front;
And now, instead of mounting barbed[2] steeds
To fright the souls of fearful adversaries,
He capers nimbly in a lady's chamber
To the lascivious pleasing of a lute.
But I, that am not shaped for sportive tricks,
Nor made to court an amorous looking-glass;
I, that am rudely stamp'd, and want love's majesty
To strut before a wanton ambling nymph;
I, that am curtail'd of this fair proportion,[3]
Cheated of feature by dissembling nature,[4]
Deform'd, unfinish'd, sent before my time
Into this breathing world, scarce half made up,
And that so lamely and unfashionable
That dogs bark at me as I halt by them;

1. *this sun of York*] a punning reference to the badge of the "blazing sun" adopted by Edward IV.
2. *barbed*] caparisoned with warlike trappings.
3. *this fair proportion*] the fair shape (which "serves love's majesty," two lines above).
4. *Cheated . . . nature*] robbed of attractive figure by distorting nature.

Why, I, in this weak piping time of peace,[5]
Have no delight to pass away the time,
Unless to spy my shadow in the sun,
And descant on mine own deformity:
And therefore, since I cannot prove a lover,
To entertain these fair well-spoken days,[6]
I am determined to prove a villain,
And hate the idle pleasures of these days.
Plots have I laid, inductions[7] dangerous,
By drunken prophecies, libels and dreams,
To set my brother Clarence and the king
In deadly hate the one against the other:
And if King Edward be as true and just
As I am subtle, false and treacherous,
This day should Clarence closely be mew'd up,[8]
About a prophecy, which says that G
Of Edward's heirs the murderer shall be.
Dive, thoughts, down to my soul: here Clarence comes.[9]

Enter CLARENCE, *guarded, and* BRAKENBURY

Brother, good day: what means this armed guard
That waits upon your grace?
CLAR. His majesty,
Tendering[10] my person's safety, hath appointed
This conduct[11] to convey me to the Tower.
GLOU. Upon what cause?
CLAR. Because my name is George.
GLOU. Alack, my lord, that fault is none of yours;
He should, for that, commit your godfathers:
O, belike his majesty hath some intent
That you shall be new-christen'd in the Tower.
But what's the matter, Clarence? may I know?
CLAR. Yea, Richard, when I know; for I protest
As yet I do not: but, as I can learn,
He hearkens after prophecies and dreams;

5. *piping time of peace*] The pipe and tabor were usual emblems of peace, as the drum and fife were of war.
6. *these fair . . . days*] these happy, prosperous days.
7. *inductions*] preparatory steps, groundwork.
8. *mew'd up*] confined.
9. *a prophecy . . . comes*] G is the initial of Clarence's Christian name George (under which he is listed in the *Dramatis Personae*). King Edward purportedly was greatly disturbed by a prophecy that Edward would be succeeded by someone whose name began with "G."
10. *Tendering*] having tender regard for.
11. *conduct*] escort.

And from the cross-row[12] plucks the letter G,
And says a wizard told him that by G
His issue disinherited should be;
And, for my name of George begins with G,
It follows in his thought that I am he.
These, as I learn, and such like toys as these
Have moved his highness to commit me now.

GLOU. Why, this it is, when men are ruled by women:
'Tis not the king that sends you to the Tower;
My Lady Grey his wife, Clarence, 'tis she
That tempers[13] him to this extremity.
Was it not she and that good man of worship,
Anthony Woodville, her brother there,
That made him send Lord Hastings to the Tower,
From whence this present day he is deliver'd?
We are not safe, Clarence; we are not safe.

CLAR. By heaven, I think there's no man is secure,
But the queen's kindred and night-walking heralds,
That trudge betwixt the king and Mistress Shore.
Heard ye not what an humble suppliant
Lord Hastings was to her for his delivery?

GLOU. Humbly complaining to her deity
Got my lord chamberlain his liberty.
I'll tell you what; I think it is our way,
If we will keep in favour with the king,
To be her men and wear her livery:
The jealous o'erworn widow and herself,[14]
Since that our brother dubb'd them gentlewomen,
Are mighty gossips in this monarchy.

BRAK. I beseech your graces both to pardon me;
His majesty hath straitly given in charge
That no man shall have private conference,
Of what degree soever, with his brother.

GLOU. Even so; an 't please your worship, Brakenbury,
You may partake of any thing we say:
We speak no treason, man: we say the king
Is wise and virtuous, and his noble queen
Well struck in years, fair, and not jealous;

---

12. *cross-row*] alphabet; more frequently called "criss-cross-row." "Criss-cross" is a corruption of "Christ's cross," the prayer "Christ's cross be my speed" commonly standing at the head of the alphabet as printed in the elementary school books of the day.
13. *tempers*] frames or disposes.
14. *o'erworn widow and herself*] Edward IV's Queen and Jane Shore, his mistress. Though the latter was influential for a time, after Edward's death she was imprisoned for witchcraft and later died in poverty.

We say that Shore's wife hath a pretty foot,
A cherry lip, a bonny eye, a passing pleasing tongue;
And that the queen's kindred are made gentle-folks:
How say you, sir? can you deny all this?
BRAK. With this, my lord, myself have nought to do.
GLOU. Naught to do with Mistress Shore! I tell thee, fellow,
He that doth naught[15] with her, excepting one,
Were best he do it secretly alone.
BRAK. What one, my lord?
GLOU. Her husband, knave: wouldst thou betray me?
BRAK. I beseech your grace to pardon me, and withal
Forbear your conference with the noble duke.
CLAR. We know thy charge, Brakenbury, and will obey.
GLOU. We are the queen's abjects,[16] and must obey.
Brother, farewell: I will unto the king;
And whatsoever you will employ me in,
Were it to call King Edward's widow sister,
I will perform it to enfranchise you.
Meantime, this deep disgrace in brotherhood
Touches me deeper than you can imagine.
CLAR. I know it pleaseth neither of us well.
GLOU. Well, your imprisonment shall not be long;
I will deliver you, or else lie for you:[17]
Meantime, have patience.
CLAR. I must perforce. Farewell.

[*Exeunt* CLARENCE, BRAKENBURY, *and* Guard.]

GLOU. Go tread the path that thou shalt ne'er return,
Simple, plain Clarence! I do love thee so,
That I will shortly send thy soul to heaven,
If heaven will take the present at our hands.
But who comes here? the new-deliver'd Hastings?

Enter LORD HASTINGS

HAST. Good time of day unto my gracious lord!
GLOU. As much unto my good lord chamberlain!
Well are you welcome to the open air.
How hath your lordship brook'd imprisonment?
HAST. With patience, noble lord, as prisoners must:
But I shall live, my lord, to give them thanks
That were the cause of my imprisonment.

---

15. *Naught . . . naught*] a quibble between "nought," i.e., nothing, and "naught," i.e., naughtily.
16. *abjects*] base slaves, the scum of the people.
17. *lie for you*] lie imprisoned in your stead.

GLOU. No doubt, no doubt; and so shall Clarence too;
For they that were your enemies are his,
And have prevail'd as much on him[18] as you.
HAST. More pity that the eagle should be mew'd,[19]
While kites and buzzards prey at liberty.
GLOU. What news abroad?
HAST. No news so bad abroad as this at home;
The king is sickly, weak and melancholy,
And his physicians fear him[20] mightily.
GLOU. Now, by Saint Paul, this news is bad indeed.
O, he hath kept an evil diet long,
And overmuch consumed his royal person:
'Tis very grievous to be thought upon.
What, is he in his bed?
HAST. He is.
GLOU. Go you before, and I will follow you. [*Exit* HASTINGS.]
He cannot live, I hope; and must not die,
Till George be pack'd with post-horse up to heaven.
I'll in, to urge his hatred more to Clarence,
With lies well steel'd with weighty arguments;
And, if I fail not in my deep intent,
Clarence hath not another day to live:
Which done, God take King Edward to his mercy,
And leave the world for me to bustle in!
For then I'll marry Warwick's youngest daughter.[21]
What though I kill'd her husband and her father?
The readiest way to make the wench amends
Is to become her husband and her father:
The which will I, not all so much for love,
As for another secret close intent,
By marrying her which I must reach unto.
But yet I run before my horse to market:
Clarence still breathes; Edward still lives and reigns:
When they are gone, then must I count my gains. [*Exit.*]

18. *on him*] against him.
19. *mew'd*] hawks were "mewed" or kept in confinement while moulting.
20. *fear him*] fear for, are anxious about, him.
21. *Warwick's youngest daughter*] Anne, younger daughter of the Earl of Warwick, had been affianced (rather than actually married) to Queen Margaret and Henry VI's son, Edward, Prince of Wales, who was slain at the battle of Tewkesbury, May 4, 1471.

SCENE II. *The Same. Another Street*

Enter the corpse of KING HENRY THE SIXTH, Gentlemen *with halberds*[1] *to guard it;* LADY ANNE *being the mourner*

ANNE. Set down, set down your honourable load—
If honour may be shrouded in a hearse—
Whilst I awhile obsequiously lament
The untimely fall of virtuous Lancaster.
Poor key-cold[2] figure of a holy king!
Pale ashes of the house of Lancaster!
Thou bloodless remnant of that royal blood!
Be it lawful that I invocate thy ghost,
To hear the lamentations of poor Anne,
Wife to thy Edward, to thy slaughtered son,
Stabb'd by the selfsame hand that made these wounds!
Lo, in these windows that let forth thy life
I pour the helpless balm of my poor eyes.
Cursed be the hand that made these fatal holes!
Cursed be the heart that had the heart to do it!
Cursed the blood that let this blood from hence!
More direful hap[3] betide that hated wretch,
That makes us wretched by the death of thee,
Than I can wish to adders, spiders, toads,
Or any creeping venom'd thing that lives!
If ever he have child, abortive be it,
Prodigious,[4] and untimely brought to light,
Whose ugly and unnatural aspect
May fright the hopeful mother at the view;
And that be heir to his unhappiness!
If ever he have wife, let her be made
As miserable by the death of him,
As I am made by my poor lord and thee!
Come, now towards Chertsey[5] with your holy load,
Taken from Paul's[6] to be interred there;
And still, as you are weary of the weight,

1. *halberds*] battle-axes fitted to long poles.
2. *key-cold*] cold as a key; in common use as an intensive of "cold."
3. *hap*] fortune.
4. *Prodigious*] like a prodigy or monster.
5. *Chertsey*] a monastery near London.
6. *Paul's*] St. Paul's Church, the principal cathedral in London.

Rest you, whiles I lament King Henry's corse.[7]

Enter GLOUCESTER

GLOU. Stay, you that bear the corse, and set it down.
ANNE. What black magician conjures up this fiend,
To stop devoted charitable deeds?
GLOU. Villains, set down the corse; or, by Saint Paul,
I'll make a corse of him that disobeys.
GENT. My lord, stand back, and let the coffin pass.
GLOU. Unmanner'd dog! stand thou, when I command:
Advance thy halberd higher than my breast,
Or, by Saint Paul, I'll strike thee to my foot,
And spurn upon thee, beggar, for thy boldness.
ANNE. What, do you tremble? are you all afraid?
Alas, I blame you not; for you are mortal,
And mortal eyes cannot endure the devil.
Avaunt, thou dreadful minister of hell!
Thou hadst but power over his mortal body,
His soul thou canst not have; therefore, be gone.
GLOU. Sweet saint, for charity, be not so curst.
ANNE. Foul devil, for God's sake, hence, and trouble us not;
For thou hast made the happy earth thy hell,
Fill'd it with cursing cries and deep exclaims.
If thou delight to view thy heinous deeds,
Behold this pattern of thy butcheries.
O, gentlemen, see, see! dead Henry's wounds
Open their congeal'd mouths and bleed afresh.
Blush, blush, thou lump of foul deformity;
For 'tis thy presence that exhales[8] this blood
From cold and empty veins, where no blood dwells;
Thy deed, inhuman and unnatural,
Provokes this deluge most unnatural.
O God, which this blood madest, revenge his death!
O earth, which this blood drink'st, revenge his death!
Either heaven with lightning strike the murderer dead,
Or earth, gape open wide and eat him quick,[9]
As thou dost swallow up this good king's blood,
Which his hell-govern'd arm hath butchered!
GLOU. Lady, you know no rules of charity,
Which renders good for bad, blessings for curses.

---

7. *corse*] corpse.
8. *exhales*] draws forth. It was a popular notion that a murdered corpse bled in presence of the murderer.
9. *quick*] alive.

ANNE. Villain, thou know'st no law of God nor man:
No beast so fierce but knows some touch of pity.
GLOU. But I know none, and therefore am no beast.
ANNE. O wonderful, when devils tell the truth!
GLOU. More wonderful, when angels are so angry.
Vouchsafe, divine perfection of a woman,
Of these supposed evils, to give me leave,
By circumstance,[10] but to acquit myself.
ANNE. Vouchsafe, defused[11] infection of a man,
For these known evils, but to give me leave,
By circumstance, to curse thy cursed self.
GLOU. Fairer than tongue can name thee, let me have
Some patient leisure to excuse myself.
ANNE. Fouler than heart can think thee, thou canst make
No excuse current,[12] but to hang thyself.
GLOU. By such despair, I should accuse myself.
ANNE. And, by despairing, shouldst thou stand excused
For doing worthy vengeance on thyself,
Which didst unworthy slaughter upon others.
GLOU. Say that I slew them not?
ANNE. Why, then they are not dead:
But dead they are, and, devilish slave, by thee.
GLOU. I did not kill your husband.
ANNE. Why, then he is alive.
GLOU. Nay, he is dead; and slain by Edward's hand.
ANNE. In thy foul throat thou liest: Queen Margaret saw
Thy murderous falchion[13] smoking in his blood;
The which thou once didst bend against her breast,
But that thy brothers beat aside the point.
GLOU. I was provoked by her slanderous tongue,
Which laid their guilt upon my guiltless shoulders.
ANNE. Thou wast provoked by thy bloody mind,
Which never dreamt on aught but butcheries:
Didst thou not kill this king?
GLOU. I grant ye.
ANNE. Dost grant me, hedgehog? then, God grant me too
Thou mayst be damned for that wicked deed!
O, he was gentle, mild, and virtuous!
GLOU. The fitter for the King of heaven, that hath him.
ANNE. He is in heaven, where thou shalt never come.

10. *circumstance*] circumstantial detail.
11. *defused*] uncouthly spread, shapeless.
12. *current*] having currency, worth.
13. *falchion*] scimitar.

GLOU. Let him thank me, that holp to send him thither;
For he was fitter for that place than earth.
ANNE. And thou unfit for any place but hell.
GLOU. Yes, one place else, if you will hear me name it.
ANNE. Some dungeon.
GLOU. Your bed-chamber.
ANNE. Ill rest betide the chamber where thou liest!
GLOU. So will it, madam, till I lie with you.
ANNE. I hope so.
GLOU. I know so. But, gentle Lady Anne,
To leave this keen encounter of our wits,
And fall somewhat into a slower method,
Is not the causer of the timeless[14] deaths
Of these Plantagenets, Henry and Edward,
As blameful as the executioner?
ANNE. Thou art the cause, and most accursed effect.[15]
GLOU. Your beauty was the cause of that effect;
Your beauty, which did haunt me in my sleep
To undertake the death of all the world,
So I might live one hour in your sweet bosom.
ANNE. If I thought that, I tell thee, homicide,
These nails should rend that beauty from my cheeks.
GLOU. These eyes could never endure sweet beauty's wreck;
You should not blemish it, if I stood by:
As all the world is cheered by the sun,
So I by that; it is my day, my life.
ANNE. Black night o'ershade thy day, and death thy life!
GLOU. Curse not thyself, fair creature; thou art both.
ANNE. I would I were, to be revenged on thee.
GLOU. It is a quarrel most unnatural,
To be revenged on him that loveth you.
ANNE. It is a quarrel just and reasonable,
To be revenged on him that slew my husband.
GLOU. He that bereft thee, lady, of thy husband,
Did it to help thee to a better husband.
ANNE. His better doth not breathe upon the earth.
GLOU. He lives that loves you better than he could.
ANNE. Name him.
GLOU. Plantagenet.
ANNE. Why, that was he.
GLOU. The selfsame name, but one of better nature.

14. *timeless*] untimely.
15. *effect*] effecter, doer, executioner. The act is put for the agent. In the next line "effect" is employed in the ordinary manner, and means "the deaths of these Plantagenets."

ANNE. Where is he?
GLOU. Here. [*She spitteth at him.*] Why dost thou spit at me?
ANNE. Would it were mortal poison, for thy sake!
GLOU. Never came poison from so sweet a place.
ANNE. Never hung poison on a fouler toad.
Out of my sight! thou dost infect my eyes.
GLOU. Thine eyes, sweet lady, have infected mine.
ANNE. Would they were basilisks,[16] to strike thee dead!
GLOU. I would they were, that I might die at once;
For now they kill me with a living death.
Those eyes of thine from mine have drawn salt tears,
Shamed their aspect with store of childish drops:
These eyes, which never shed remorseful tear,
No, when my father York and Edward wept,
To hear the piteous moan that Rutland made
When black-faced Clifford shook his sword at him;
Nor when thy warlike father, like a child,
Told the sad story of my father's death,
And twenty times made pause to sob and weep,
That all the standers-by had wet their cheeks,
Like trees bedash'd with rain: in that sad time
My manly eyes did scorn an humble tear;
And what these sorrows could not thence exhale,[17]
Thy beauty hath, and made them blind with weeping.
I never sued to friend nor enemy;
My tongue could never learn sweet smoothing words;
But, now thy beauty is proposed my fee,
My proud heart sues, and prompts my tongue to speak.
[*She looks scornfully at him.*]
Teach not thy lips such scorn, for they were made
For kissing, lady, not for such contempt.
If thy revengeful heart cannot forgive,
Lo, here I lend thee this sharp-pointed sword;
Which if thou please to hide in this true bosom,
And let the soul forth that adoreth thee,
I lay it naked to the deadly stroke,
And humbly beg the death upon my knee.
[*He lays his breast open: she offers at it with his sword.*]
Nay, do not pause; for I did kill King Henry,
But 'twas thy beauty that provoked me.
Nay, now dispatch; 'twas I that stabb'd young Edward,
But 'twas thy heavenly face that set me on.

16. *basilisks*] fabulous reptiles who could kill with a look.
17. *exhale*] draw forth.

[*Here she lets fall the sword.*]

Take up the sword again, or take up me.
ANNE. Arise, dissembler: though I wish thy death,
I will not be the executioner.
GLOU. Then bid me kill myself, and I will do it.
ANNE. I have already.
GLOU. Tush, that was in thy rage:
Speak it again, and, even with the word,
That hand, which, for thy love, did kill thy love,
Shall, for thy love, kill a far truer love;
To both their deaths shalt thou be accessary.
ANNE. I would I knew thy heart.
GLOU. 'Tis figured in my tongue.
ANNE. I fear me both are false.
GLOU. Then never man was true.
ANNE. Well, well, put up your sword.
GLOU. Say, then, my peace is made.
ANNE. That shall you know hereafter.
GLOU. But shall I live in hope?
ANNE. All men, I hope, live so.
GLOU. Vouchsafe to wear this ring.
ANNE. To take is not to give.
GLOU. Look, how this ring encompasseth thy finger,
Even so thy breast encloseth my poor heart;
Wear both of them, for both of them are thine.
And if thy poor devoted suppliant may
But beg one favour at thy gracious hand,
Thou dost confirm his happiness for ever.
ANNE. What is it?
GLOU. That it would please thee leave these sad designs
To him that hath more cause to be a mourner,
And presently repair to Crosby Place;[18]
Where, after I have solemnly interr'd
At Chertsey monastery this noble king,
And wet his grave with my repentant tears,
I will with all expedient[19] duty see you:
For divers unknown reasons, I beseech you,
Grant me this boon.
ANNE. With all my heart; and much it joys me too,

18. *Crosby Place*] a fine house of timber and stone in Bishopsgate Street, London, built a few years before by Sir John Crosby, a prominent citizen of London. Richard occupied it while he was Protector. The building, after undergoing successive renovations, was demolished in January, 1908.

19. *expedient*] expeditious.

To see you are become so penitent.
Tressel and Berkeley, go along with me.
GLOU. Bid me farewell.
ANNE. 'Tis more than you deserve;
But since you teach me how to flatter you,
Imagine I have said farewell already.
[*Exeunt* LADY ANNE, TRESSEL, *and* BERKELEY.]
GLOU. Sirs, take up the corse.
GENT. Towards Chertsey, noble lord?
GLOU. No, to White-Friars;[20] there attend my coming.
[*Exeunt all but* GLOUCESTER.]
Was ever woman in this humour woo'd?
Was ever woman in this humour won?
I'll have her; but I will not keep her long.
What! I, that kill'd her husband and his father,
To take[21] her in her heart's extremest hate,
With curses in her mouth, tears in her eyes,
The bleeding witness of her hatred by;
Having God, her conscience, and these bars against me,
And I nothing to back my suit at all,
But the plain devil and dissembling looks,
And yet to win her, all the world to nothing![22]
Ha!
Hath she forgot already that brave prince,
Edward, her lord, whom I, some three months since,
Stabb'd in my angry mood at Tewksbury?
A sweeter and a lovelier gentleman,
Framed in the prodigality of nature,
Young, valiant, wise, and, no doubt, right royal,
The spacious world cannot again afford:
And will she yet debase her eyes on me,
That cropp'd the golden prime of this sweet prince,
And made her widow to a woful bed?
On me, whose all not equals Edward's moiety?[23]
On me, that halt and am unshapen thus?
My dukedom to a beggarly denier,[24]

---

20. *White-Friars*] According to the 1587 edition of Holinshed's *Chronicles*, one of Shakespeare's major sources for his English history plays, the corpse was taken to the religious house of the Dominicans, in the city of London, known as Blackfriars, and not to White-Friars, a neighbouring house of the Carmelites or white friars. Districts in the city of London are still familiarly known as Blackfriars and Whitefriars.
21. *take*] capture, captivate.
22. *all the world to nothing*] the odds against me being all the world to nothing.
23. *moiety*] one of two equal parts, a half.
24. *denier*] a coin of very small value; from the Latin *denarius*.

I do mistake my person all this while:
Upon my life, she finds, although I cannot,
Myself to be a marvellous proper man.
I'll be at charges[25] for a looking-glass,
And entertain[26] some score or two of tailors,
To study fashions to adorn my body:
Since I am crept in favour with myself,
I will maintain it with some little cost.
But first I'll turn yon fellow in his grave;
And then return lamenting to my love.
Shine out, fair sun, till I have bought a glass,
That I may see my shadow as I pass. [*Exit.*]

SCENE III. *The Palace.*

Enter QUEEN ELIZABETH, LORD RIVERS, *and* LORD GREY

RIV. Have patience, madam: there's no doubt his majesty
Will soon recover his accustom'd health.
GREY. In that you brook[1] it ill, it makes him worse:
Therefore, for God's sake, entertain good comfort,
And cheer his grace with quick and merry words.
Q. ELIZ. If he were dead, what would betide of me?
RIV. No other harm but loss of such a lord.
Q. ELIZ. The loss of such a lord includes all harm.
GREY. The heavens have bless'd you with a goodly son,
To be your comforter when he is gone.
Q. ELIZ. Oh, he is young, and his minority
Is put unto the trust of Richard Gloucester,
A man that loves not me, nor none of you.
RIV. Is it concluded he shall be protector?
Q. ELIZ. It is determined, not concluded[2] yet:
But so it must be, if the king miscarry.[3]

Enter BUCKINGHAM *and* DERBY

25. *at charges*] incur costs for (a looking-glass).
26. *entertain*] take into service.

1. *brook*] bear, endure. (Here, the sense is, "If you cannot endure the King's illness, it will make him worse.")
2. *determined, not concluded*] settled, but not formally recorded.
3. *miscarry*] perish, die.

GREY. Here come the lords of Buckingham and Derby.[4]
BUCK. Good time of day unto your royal grace!
DER. God make your majesty joyful as you have been!
Q. ELIZ. The Countess Richmond,[5] good my Lord of Derby,
To your good prayers will scarcely say amen.
Yet, Derby, notwithstanding she's your wife,
And loves not me, be you, good lord, assured
I hate not you for her proud arrogance.
DER. I do beseech you, either not believe
The envious slanders of her false accusers;
Or, if she be accused in true report,
Bear with her weakness, which, I think, proceeds
From wayward sickness, and no grounded malice.[6]
RIV. Saw you the king to-day, my Lord of Derby?
DER. But now the Duke of Buckingham and I
Are come from visiting his majesty.
Q. ELIZ. What likelihood of his amendment, lords?
BUCK. Madam, good hope; his grace speaks cheerfully.
Q. ELIZ. God grant him health! Did you confer with him?
BUCK. Madam, we did: he desires to make atonement[7]
Betwixt the Duke of Gloucester and your brothers,
And betwixt them and my lord chamberlain;
And sent to warn them to his royal presence.
Q. ELIZ. Would all were well! but that will never be:
I fear our happiness is at the highest.

Enter GLOUCESTER, HASTINGS, *and* DORSET

GLOU. They do me wrong, and I will not endure it:
Who are they that complain unto the king,
That I, forsooth, am stern and love them not?
By holy Paul, they love his grace but lightly
That fill his ears with such dissentious rumours.
Because I cannot flatter and speak fair,
Smile in men's faces, smooth, deceive and cog,[8]

4. *Derby*] In Act III, Sc. ii, and frequently in Act IV, he is called more correctly Lord Stanley. He was Thomas, Lord Stanley, who was created first Earl of Derby by Henry VII, after Richard III's death. The premature designation of Derby is due to Shakespeare's carelessness.
5. *The Countess Richmond*] Margaret, only child of John Beaufort, first Duke of Somerset, and descendant of John of Gaunt, had married Lord Stanley as her third husband. She was mother, by her first husband, Edmund Tudor, Earl of Richmond, of King Henry VII.
6. *grounded malice*] inveterate hatred.
7. *atonement*] reconciliation.
8. *smooth . . . and cog*] cajole . . . and cheat.

Duck with French nods and apish courtesy,
I must be held a rancorous enemy.
Cannot a plain man live and think no harm,
But thus his simple truth must be abused
By silken, sly, insinuating Jacks?[9]

RIV. To whom in all this presence speaks your grace?

GLOU. To thee, that hast nor[10] honesty nor grace.
When have I injured thee? when done thee wrong?
Or thee? or thee? or any of your faction?
A plague upon you all! His royal person—
Whom God preserve better than you would wish!—
Cannot be quiet scarce a breathing-while,
But you must trouble him with lewd[11] complaints.

Q. ELIZ. Brother of Gloucester, you mistake the matter.
The king, of his own royal disposition,
And not provoked by any suitor else;
Aiming, belike, at your interior[12] hatred,
Which in your outward actions shows itself
Against my kindred, brothers, and myself,
Makes him to send; that thereby he may gather
The ground of your ill-will, and to remove it.

GLOU. I cannot tell: the world is grown so bad,
That wrens make prey where eagles dare not perch:
Since every Jack became a gentleman,
There's many a gentle person made a Jack.

Q. ELIZ. Come, come, we know your meaning, brother Gloucester;
You envy my advancement and my friends':
God grant we never may have need of you!

GLOU. Meantime, God grants that we have need of you:
Our brother is imprison'd by your means,
Myself disgraced, and the nobility
Held in contempt; whilst many fair promotions
Are daily given to ennoble those
That scarce, some two days since, were worth a noble.[13]

Q. ELIZ. By Him that raised me to this careful[14] height
From that contented hap which I enjoy'd,
I never did incense his majesty
Against the Duke of Clarence, but have been

9. *Jacks*] contemptuous term for saucy, paltry or silly men.
10. *nor*] neither.
11. *lewd*] vulgar, ignorant.
12. *interior*] inwardly cherished.
13. *a noble*] a pun on the word in the sense of a gold coin, worth about six shillings, eight pence.
14. *careful*] full of care, anxiety.

An earnest advocate to plead for him.
My lord, you do me shameful injury,
Falsely to draw me in these vile suspects.[15]

GLOU. You may deny that you were not the cause
Of my Lord Hastings' late imprisonment.

RIV. She may, my lord, for—

GLOU. She may, Lord Rivers! why, who knows not so?
She may do more, sir, than denying that:
She may help you to many fair preferments;
And then deny her aiding hand therein,
And lay those honours on your high deserts.
What may she not? She may, yea, marry, may she,—

RIV. What, marry, may she?

GLOU. What, marry, may she! marry with a king,
A bachelor, a handsome stripling too:
I wis[16] your grandam had a worser match.

Q. ELIZ. My Lord of Gloucester, I have too long borne
Your blunt upbraidings and your bitter scoffs:
By heaven, I will acquaint his majesty
With those gross taunts I often have endured.
I had rather be a country servant-maid
Than a great queen, with this condition,
To be thus taunted, scorn'd, and baited at:

Enter QUEEN MARGARET,[17] *behind*

Small joy have I in being England's queen.

Q. MAR. And lessen'd be that small, God, I beseech thee!
Thy honour, state and seat is due to me.

GLOU. What! threat you me with telling of the king?
Tell him, and spare not: look, what I have said
I will avouch in presence of the king:
I dare adventure to be sent to the Tower.
'Tis time to speak; my pains[18] are quite forgot.

Q. MAR. Out, devil! I remember them too well:
Thou slewest my husband Henry in the Tower,
And Edward, my poor son, at Tewksbury.

GLOU. Ere you were queen, yea, or your husband king,
I was a pack-horse in his great affairs;

15. *suspects*] suspicions.
16. *I wis*] usually spelled I-wis, meaning surely, certainly.
17. *Queen Margaret*] Margaret of Anjou, widow of Henry VI and mother of Edward Plantagenet (1453–1471), who was killed at the Battle of Tewkesbury by Gloucester and his brothers. She was banished in 1475 and died in France without ever returning to England. Her presence in the play is for dramatic effect and is historically inaccurate.
18. *pains*] labors.

A weeder out of his proud adversaries,
A liberal rewarder of his friends:
To royalise[19] his blood I spilt mine own.
Q. MAR. Yea, and much better blood than his or thine.
GLOU. In all which time you and your husband Grey
Were factious for the house of Lancaster;
And, Rivers, so were you. Was not your husband
In Margaret's battle at Saint Alban's slain?
Let me put in your minds, if you forget,
What you have been ere now, and what you are;
Withal, what I have been, and what I am.
Q. MAR. A murderous villain, and so still thou art.
GLOU. Poor Clarence did forsake his father, Warwick;
Yea, and forswore himself,—which Jesu pardon!—
Q. MAR. Which God revenge!
GLOU. To fight on Edward's party for the crown;
And for his meed,[20] poor lord, he is mew'd up.
I would to God my heart were flint, like Edward's;
Or Edward's soft and pitiful, like mine:
I am too childish-foolish for this world.
Q. MAR. Hie thee to hell for shame, and leave the world,
Thou cacodemon![21] there thy kingdom is.
RIV. My Lord of Gloucester, in those busy days
Which here you urge to prove us enemies,
We follow'd then our lord, our lawful king:
So should we you, if you should be our king.
GLOU. If I should be! I had rather be a pedlar:
Far be it from my heart, the thought of it!
Q. ELIZ. As little joy, my lord, as you suppose
You should enjoy, were you this country's king,
As little joy may you suppose in me,
That I enjoy, being the queen thereof.
Q. MAR. A little joy enjoys the queen thereof;
For I am she, and altogether joyless.
I can no longer hold me patient. [*Advancing.*]
Hear me, you wrangling pirates, that fall out
In sharing that which you have pill'd[22] from me!
Which of you trembles not that looks on me?
If not, that, I being queen, you bow like subjects,
Yet that, by you deposed, you quake like rebels?
O gentle villain, do not turn away!

19. *royalise*] make royal.
20. *meed*] reward.
21. *cacodemon*] evil spirit.
22. *pill'd*] pillaged, plundered.

GLOU. Foul wrinkled witch, what makest[23] thou in my sight?
Q. MAR. But repetition of what thou hast marr'd;
That will I make before I let thee go.
GLOU. Wert thou not banished on pain of death?
Q. MAR. I was; but I do find more pain in banishment,
Than death can yield me here by my abode.
A husband and a son thou owest to me;
And thou a kingdom; all of you allegiance:
The sorrow that I have, by right is yours,
And all the pleasures you usurp are mine.
GLOU. The curse my noble father laid on thee,
When thou didst crown his warlike brows with paper,
And with thy scorns drew'st rivers from his eyes,
And then, to dry them, gavest the duke a clout,[24]
Steep'd in the faultless blood of pretty Rutland,—
His curses, then from bitterness of soul
Denounced against thee, are all fall'n upon thee;
And God, not we, hath plagued[25] thy bloody deed.[26]
Q. ELIZ. So just is God, to right the innocent.
HAST. O, 'twas the foulest deed to slay that babe,[27]
And the most merciless that e'er was heard of!
RIV. Tyrants themselves wept when it was reported.
DOR. No man but prophesied revenge for it.
BUCK. Northumberland, then present, wept to see it.
Q. MAR. What! were you snarling all before I came,
Ready to catch each other by the throat,
And turn you all your hatred now on me?
Did York's dread curse prevail so much with heaven,
That Henry's death, my lovely Edward's death,
Their kingdom's loss, my woful banishment,
Could all but answer for that peevish brat?
Can curses pierce the clouds and enter heaven?
Why, then, give way, dull clouds, to my quick curses!
If not by war, by surfeit die your king,

23. *makest*] doest.
24. *clout*] cloth.
25. *plagued*] punished.
26. *When . . . bloody deed*] In 3 *Hen. VI*, I, iv, York had defeated Henry VI, who named York (rather than his own son Edward) successor to the throne. Queen Margaret, however, continued the fight against the Yorkists and eventually captured York. In the play, after taking him prisoner, Margaret and her followers taunt him and bid him weep, offering him a handkerchief stained with the blood of his youngest son, the Earl of Rutland, who was killed by Lord Clifford in the preceding battle. She then forces him to wear a paper crown and at the end of the scene she and Clifford stab him to death.
27. *babe*] i.e., Rutland. The term was sometimes used to refer to older children.

As ours by murder, to make him a king!
Edward thy son, which now is Prince of Wales,
For Edward my son, which was Prince of Wales,
Die in his youth by like untimely violence!
Thyself a queen, for me that was a queen,
Outlive thy glory, like my wretched self!
Long mayst thou live to wail thy children's loss;
And see another, as I see thee now,
Deck'd in thy rights, as thou art stall'd in mine!
Long die thy happy days before thy death;
And, after many lengthen'd hours of grief,
Die neither mother, wife, nor England's queen!
Rivers and Dorset, you were standers by,
And so wast thou, Lord Hastings, when my son
Was stabb'd with bloody daggers: God, I pray him,
That none of you may live your natural age,
But by some unlook'd accident cut off!

GLOU. Have done thy charm, thou hateful withered hag!

Q. MAR. And leave out thee? stay, dog, for thou shalt hear me.
If heaven have any grievous plague in store
Exceeding those that I can wish upon thee,
O, let them[28] keep it till thy sins be ripe,
And then hurl down their indignation
On thee, the troubler of the poor world's peace!
The worm of conscience still begnaw thy soul!
Thy friends suspect for traitors while thou livest,
And take deep traitors for thy dearest friends!
No sleep close up that deadly eye of thine,
Unless it be whilst some tormenting dream
Affrights thee with a hell of ugly devils!
Thou elvish-mark'd,[29] abortive, rooting hog![30]
Thou that wast seal'd in thy nativity
The slave of nature and the son of hell!
Thou slander of thy mother's heavy womb
Thou loathed issue of thy father's loins!
Thou rag of honour! thou detested—

GLOU. Margaret.

Q. MAR. Richard!

GLOU. Ha!

Q. MAR. I call thee not.

---

28. *them*] heaven; the word has a collective or plural significance.
29. *elvish-mark'd*] the common superstition that persons born with scars or deformities had been marked by wicked fairies or elves.
30. *hog*] Richard's heraldic blazon featured a boar.

GLOU. I cry thee mercy then, for I had thought
That thou hadst call'd me all these bitter names.
Q. MAR. Why, so I did; but look'd for no reply.
O, let me make the period to my curse!
GLOU. 'Tis done by me, and ends in "Margaret."
Q. ELIZ. Thus have you breathed your curse against yourself.
Q. MAR. Poor painted queen, vain flourish of my fortune!
Why strew'st thou sugar on that bottled spider,[31]
Whose deadly web ensnareth thee about?
Fool, fool! thou whet'st a knife to kill thyself.
The time will come that thou shalt wish for me
To help thee curse that poisonous bunch-back'd toad.
HAST. False-boding woman, end thy frantic curse,
Lest to thy harm thou move our patience.
Q. MAR. Foul shame upon you! you have all moved mine.
RIV. Were you well served, you would be taught your duty.
Q. MAR. To serve me well, you all should do me duty,
Teach me to be your queen, and you my subjects:
O, serve me well, and teach yourselves that duty!
DOR. Dispute not with her; she is lunatic.
Q. MAR. Peace, master marquess, you are malapert:[32]
Your fire-new[33] stamp of honour is scarce current.
O, that your young nobility could judge
What 't were to lose it, and be miserable!
They that stand high have many blasts to shake them;
And if they fall, they dash themselves to pieces.
GLOU. Good counsel, marry: learn it, learn it, marquess.
DOR. It toucheth you, my lord, as much as me.
GLOU. Yea, and much more: but I was born so high,
Our aery buildeth in the cedar's top,
And dallies with the wind and scorns the sun.
Q. MAR. And turns the sun to shade; alas! alas!
Witness my son, now in the shade of death;
Whose bright out-shining beams thy cloudy wrath
Hath in eternal darkness folded up.
Your aery buildeth in our aery's nest.
O God, that seest it, do not suffer it;
As it was won with blood, lost be it so!
BUCK. Have done! for shame, if not for charity.
Q. MAR. Urge neither charity nor shame to me:
Uncharitably with me have you dealt,

31. *bottled spider*] an exceptionally large or bottle-shaped spider.
32. *malapert*] pert, forward, saucy.
33. *fire-new*] brand-new.

And shamefully by you my hopes are butcher'd.
My charity is outrage, life my shame;
And in that shame still live my sorrow's rage!
BUCK. Have done, have done.
Q. MAR. O princely Buckingham, I'll kiss thy hand,
In sign of league and amity with thee:
Now fair befall thee[34] and thy noble house!
Thy garments are not spotted with our blood,
Nor thou within the compass of my curse.
BUCK. Nor no one here; for curses never pass
The lips of those that breathe them in the air.
Q. MAR. I'll not believe but they ascend the sky,
And there awake God's gentle-sleeping peace.
O Buckingham, take heed of yonder dog!
Look, when he fawns, he bites; and when he bites,
His venom tooth will rankle to the death:
Have not to do with him, beware of him;
Sin, death, and hell have set their marks on him,
And all their ministers attend on him.
GLOU. What doth she say, my Lord of Buckingham?
BUCK. Nothing that I respect, my gracious lord.
Q. MAR. What, dost thou scorn me for my gentle counsel?
And soothe the devil that I warn thee from?
O, but remember this another day,
When he shall split thy very heart with sorrow,
And say poor Margaret was a prophetess.
Live each of you the subjects to his hate,
And he to yours, and all of you to God's! [*Exit.*]
HAST. My hair doth stand on end to hear her curses.
RIV. And so doth mine: I muse why she's at liberty.
GLOU. I cannot blame her: by God's holy mother,
She hath had too much wrong; and I repent
My part thereof that I have done to her.
Q. ELIZ. I never did her any, to my knowledge.
GLOU. But you have all the vantage of her wrong.
I was too hot to do somebody good,
That is too cold in thinking of it now.
Marry, as for Clarence, he is well repaid;
He is frank'd up[35] to fatting for his pains:
God pardon them that are the cause of it!

34. *fair befall thee*] good fortune attend you!
35. *frank'd up*] cooped up as in a pen or sty, which was commonly called a "frank." The verb is used of animals, especially hogs, being fattened for the butcher.

RIV. A virtuous and a Christian-like conclusion,
To pray for them that have done scathe[36] to us.
GLOU. So do I ever: [*Aside*] being well advised:
For had I cursed now, I had cursed myself.

Enter CATESBY

CATES. Madam, his majesty doth call for you;
And for your grace; and you, my noble lords.
Q. ELIZ. Catesby, we come. Lords, will you go with us?
RIV. Madam, we will attend your grace.
[*Exeunt all but* GLOUCESTER.]
GLOU. I do the wrong, and first begin to brawl.
The secret mischiefs that I set abroach[37]
I lay unto the grievous charge of others.
Clarence, whom I, indeed, have laid in darkness,
I do beweep to many simple gulls;[38]
Namely, to Hastings, Derby, Buckingham;
And say it is the queen and her allies
That stir the king against the duke my brother.
Now, they believe it; and withal whet me
To be revenged on Rivers, Vaughan, Grey:
But then I sigh; and, with a piece of Scripture,
Tell them that God bids us do good for evil:
And thus I clothe my naked villany
With old odd ends[39] stolen out of holy writ;
And seem a saint, when most I play the devil.

Enter two Murderers

But, soft! here come my executioners.
How now, my hardy stout resolved mates!
Are you now going to dispatch this deed?
FIRST MURD. We are, my lord; and come to have the warrant,
That we may be admitted where he is.
GLOU. Well thought upon; I have it here about me.
[*Gives the warrant.*]
When you have done, repair to Crosby Place.
But, sirs, be sudden in the execution,
Withal obdurate, do not hear him plead;
For Clarence is well-spoken, and perhaps
May move your hearts to pity, if you mark him.

36. *scathe*] injury, hurt.
37. *set abroach*] to cause, set into action, agitate.
38. *gulls*] tricks, impositions.
39. *old odd ends*] quoted tags, odds and ends.

FIRST MURD. Tush!
Fear not, my lord, we will not stand to prate;
Talkers are no good doers: be assured
We come to use our hands and not our tongues.
GLOU. Your eyes drop millstones,[40] when fools' eyes drop tears.
I like you, lads: about your business straight.
Go, go, dispatch.
FIRST MURD. We will, my noble lord. [*Exeunt.*]

SCENE IV. *London. The Tower.*

Enter CLARENCE *and* BRAKENBURY

BRAK. Why looks your grace so heavily to-day?
CLAR. O, I have pass'd a miserable night,
So full of ugly sights, of ghastly dreams,
That, as I am a Christian faithful[1] man,
I would not spend another such a night,
Though 't were to buy a world of happy days,
So full of dismal terror was the time!
BRAK. What was your dream? I long to hear you tell it.
CLAR. Methoughts that I had broken from the Tower,
And was embark'd to cross to Burgundy;
And, in my company, my brother Gloucester;
Who from my cabin tempted me to walk
Upon the hatches: thence we look'd toward England,
And cited up a thousand fearful times,
During the wars of York and Lancaster,
That had befall'n us. As we paced along
Upon the giddy footing of the hatches,
Methought that Gloucester stumbled; and, in falling,
Struck me, that thought to stay him, overboard,
Into the tumbling billows of the main.
Lord, Lord! methought, what pain it was to drown!
What dreadful noise of waters in mine ears!
What ugly sights of death within mine eyes!
Methought I saw a thousand fearful wrecks;

40. *Your eyes drop millstones*] an expression very commonly applied to hard-natured persons who were not in the habit of weeping at all.

1. *faithful*] as opposed to "infidel."

Ten thousand men that fishes gnaw'd upon;
Wedges of gold, great anchors, heaps of pearl,
Inestimable stones, unvalued[2] jewels,
All scattered in the bottom of the sea:
Some lay in dead men's skulls; and in those holes
Where eyes did once inhabit, there were crept,
As 't were in scorn of eyes, reflecting gems,
Which woo'd[3] the slimy bottom of the deep,
And mock'd the dead bones that lay scattered by.

BRAK. Had you such leisure in the time of death
To gaze upon the secrets of the deep?

CLAR. Methought I had; and often did I strive
To yield the ghost: but still the envious[4] flood
Kept in my soul, and would not let it forth
To seek the empty, vast and wandering air;
But smothered it within my panting bulk,[5]
Which almost burst to belch it in the sea.

BRAK. Awaked you not with this sore agony?

CLAR. O no, my dream was lengthened after life;
O, then began the tempest to my soul,
Who pass'd, methought, the melancholy flood,
With that grim ferryman which poets write of,[6]
Unto the kingdom of perpetual night.
The first that there did greet my stranger soul,
Was my great father-in-law, renowned Warwick;
Who cried aloud, "What scourge for perjury
Can this dark monarchy afford false Clarence?"
And so he vanish'd: then came wandering by
A shadow like an angel, with bright hair
Dabbled in blood; and he squeak'd out aloud,
"Clarence is come; false, fleeting,[7] perjured Clarence,
That stabb'd me in the field by Tewksbury:[8]
Seize on him, Furies, take him to your torments!"
With that, methoughts, a legion of foul fiends
Environ'd me about, and howled in mine ears
Such hideous cries, that with the very noise
I trembling waked, and for a season after
Could not believe but that I was in hell,

---

2. *unvalued*] invaluable.
3. *woo'd*] ogled.
4. *envious*] cruel, malicious.
5. *bulk*] body, frame, trunk.
6. *Who pass'd . . . poets write of*] a reference to the myth of Charon, the Stygian ferryman.
7. *fleeting*] wavering, inconstant.
8. A *shadow . . . Tewksbury*] the ghost of Edward Plantagenet, Prince of Wales.

Such terrible impression made the dream.
BRAK. No marvel, my lord, though it affrighted you;
I promise you, I am afraid to hear you tell it.
CLAR. O Brakenbury, I have done those things,
Which now bear evidence against my soul,
For Edward's sake; and see how he requites me!
O God! if my deep prayers cannot appease thee,
But thou wilt be avenged on my misdeeds,
Yet execute thy wrath in me alone;
O, spare my guiltless wife[9] and my poor children!
I pray thee, gentle keeper, stay by me;
My soul is heavy, and I fain would sleep.
BRAK. I will, my lord: God give your grace good rest!
[CLARENCE *sleeps.*]
Sorrow breaks seasons and reposing hours,
Makes the night morning and the noon-tide night.
Princes have but their titles for their glories,
An outward honour for an inward toil;
And, for unfelt imagination,
They often feel a world of restless cares:[10]
So that, betwixt their titles and low names,
There's nothing differs but the outward fame.

Enter the two Murderers

FIRST MURD. Ho! who's here?
BRAK. In God's name what are you, and how came you hither?
FIRST MURD. I would speak with Clarence, and I came hither on my legs.
BRAK. Yea, are you so brief?
SEC. MURD. O sir, it is better to be brief than tedious.
Show him our commission; talk no more.
[BRAKENBURY *reads it.*]
BRAK. I am in this commanded to deliver
The noble Duke of Clarence to your hands:
I will not reason what is meant hereby,
Because I will be guiltless of the meaning.
Here are the keys, there sits the duke asleep:
I'll to the king; and signify to him
That thus I have resign'd my charge to you.

9. *guiltless wife*] an historical error. Clarence's wife, Isabella Neville, the elder daughter of the Earl of Warwick, died December 21, 1476, long before Clarence's imprisonment.

10. *for unfelt imagination . . . cares*] In return for imaginary gratification, which does not touch their feeling, they often feel any amount of disturbing cares.

FIRST MURD. Do so, it is a point of wisdom: fare you well.

[*Exit* BRAKENBURY.]

SEC. MURD. What, shall we stab him as he sleeps?

FIRST MURD. No; then he will say 't was done cowardly, when he wakes.

SEC. MURD. When he wakes! why, fool, he shall never wake till the judgement-day.

FIRST MURD. Why, then he will say we stabbed him sleeping.

SEC. MURD. The urging of that word "judgement" hath bred a kind of remorse in me.

FIRST MURD. What, art thou afraid?

SEC. MURD. Not to kill him, having a warrant for it; but to be damned for killing him, from which no warrant can defend us.

FIRST MURD. I thought thou hadst been resolute.

SEC. MURD. So I am, to let him live.

FIRST MURD. Back to the Duke of Gloucester, tell him so.

SEC. MURD. I pray thee, stay a while: I hope my holy humour will change; 't was wont to hold me but while one would tell[11] twenty.

FIRST MURD. How dost thou feel thyself now?

SEC. MURD. Faith, some certain dregs of conscience are yet within me.

FIRST MURD. Remember our reward, when the deed is done.

SEC. MURD. 'Zounds, he dies: I had forgot the reward.

FIRST MURD. Where is thy conscience now?

SEC. MURD. In the Duke of Gloucester's purse.

FIRST MURD. So when he opens his purse to give us our reward, thy conscience flies out.

SEC. MURD. Let it go; there's few or none will entertain it.

FIRST MURD. How if it come to thee again?

SEC. MURD. I'll not meddle with it: it is a dangerous thing: it makes a man a coward: a man cannot steal, but it accuseth him; he cannot swear, but it checks him; he cannot lie with his neighbour's wife, but it detects him: it is a blushing shamefast spirit that mutinies in a man's bosom; it fills one full of obstacles: it made me once restore a purse of gold, that I found; it beggars any man that keeps it: it is turned out of all towns and cities for a dangerous thing; and every man that means to live well endeavours to trust to himself and to live without it.

FIRST MURD. 'Zounds, it is even now at my elbow, persuading me not to kill the duke.

SEC. MURD. Take the devil in thy mind, and believe him[12] not: he would insinuate with thee[13] but to make thee sigh.

---

11. *tell*] count to.
12. *him*] i.e., thy conscience.
13. *insinuate with thee*] beguile thee.

FIRST MURD. Tut, I am strong-framed, he cannot prevail with me, I warrant thee.

SEC. MURD. Spoke like a tall[14] fellow that respects his reputation. Come, shall we to this gear?[15]

FIRST MURD. Take him over the costard[16] with the hilts of thy sword, and then we will chop[17] him in the malmsey-butt[18] in the next room.

SEC. MURD. O excellent device! make a sop of him.

FIRST MURD. Hark! he stirs: shall I strike?

SEC. MURD. No, first let's reason with him.

CLAR. Where art thou, keeper? give me a cup of wine.

SEC. MURD. You shall have wine enough, my lord, anon.

CLAR. In God's name, what art thou?

SEC. MURD. A man, as you are.

CLAR. But not, as I am, royal.

SEC. MURD. Nor you, as we are, loyal.

CLAR. Thy voice is thunder, but thy looks are humble.

SEC. MURD. My voice is now the king's, my looks mine own.

CLAR. How darkly and how deadly dost thou speak!
Your eyes do menace me: why look you pale?
Who sent you hither? Wherefore do you come?

BOTH. To, to, to—

CLAR. To murder me?

BOTH. Ay, ay.

CLAR. You scarcely have the hearts to tell me so,
And therefore cannot have the hearts to do it.
Wherein, my friends, have I offended you?

FIRST MURD. Offended us you have not, but the king.

CLAR. I shall be reconciled to him again.

SEC. MURD. Never, my lord; therefore prepare to die.

CLAR. Are you call'd forth from out a world of men
To slay the innocent? What is my offence?
Where are the evidence that do accuse me?
What lawful quest[19] have given their verdict up
Unto the frowning judge? or who pronounced
The bitter sentence of poor Clarence' death?
Before I be convict by course of law,
To threaten me with death is most unlawful.
I charge you, as you hope to have redemption

14. *tall*] bold, daring; a common usage.
15. *to this gear*] to this business.
16. *Take him over the costard*] hit him over the head.
17. *chop*] to do something with a quick motion.
18. *malmsey-butt*] a large cask of malmsey (a kind of sweet wine).
19. *quest*] inquest or trial by jury; an empanelled jury.

By Christ's dear blood shed for our grievous sins,
That you depart and lay no hands on me:
The deed you undertake is damnable.
FIRST MURD. What we will do, we do upon command.
SEC. MURD. And he that hath commanded is the king.
CLAR. Erroneous vassal! the great King of kings
Hath in the tables of his law commanded
That thou shalt do no murder: and wilt thou then
Spurn at his edict, and fulfil a man's?
Take heed; for he holds vengeance in his hands,
To hurl upon their heads that break his law.
SEC. MURD. And that same vengeance doth he hurl on thee,
For false forswearing, and for murder too:
Thou didst receive the holy sacrament,
To fight in quarrel of the house of Lancaster.
FIRST MURD. And, like a traitor to the name of God,
Didst break that vow; and with thy treacherous blade
Unrip'dst the bowels of thy sovereign's son.
SEC. MURD. Whom thou wert sworn to cherish and defend.
FIRST MURD. How canst thou urge God's dreadful law to us,
When thou hast broke it in so dear degree?
CLAR. Alas! for whose sake did I that ill deed?
For Edward, for my brother, for his sake:
Why, sirs,
He sends ye not to murder me for this;
For in this sin he is as deep as I.
If God will be revenged for this deed,
O, know you yet, he doth it publicly:
Take not the quarrel from his powerful arm;
He needs no indirect nor lawless course
To cut off those that have offended him.
FIRST MURD. Who made thee then a bloody minister,
When gallant-springing[20] brave Plantagenet,
That princely novice, was struck dead by thee?
CLAR. My brother's love, the devil, and my rage.
FIRST MURD. Thy brother's love, our duty, and thy fault,
Provoke us hither now to slaughter thee.
CLAR. Oh, if you love my brother, hate not me;
I am his brother, and I love him well.
If you be hired for meed, go back again,
And I will send you to my brother Gloucester,
Who shall reward you better for my life,
Than Edward will for tidings of my death.

20. *gallant-springing*] like a gallant in the spring of life.

SEC. MURD. You are deceived, your brother Gloucester hates you.
CLAR. O, no, he loves me, and he holds me dear:
Go you to him from me.
BOTH. Ay, so we will.
CLAR. Tell him, when that our princely father York
Bless'd his three sons with his victorious arm,
And charged us from his soul to love each other,
He little thought of this divided friendship:
Bid Gloucester think of this, and he will weep.
FIRST MURD. Ay, millstones;[21] as he lesson'd us to weep.
CLAR. O, do not slander him, for he is kind.
FIRST MURD. Right,
As snow in harvest. Thou deceivest thyself:
'Tis he that sent us hither now to slaughter thee.[22]
CLAR. It cannot be; for when I parted with him,
He hugg'd me in his arms, and swore, with sobs,
That he would labour my delivery.
SEC. MURD. Why, so he doth, now he delivers thee
From this world's thraldom to the joys of heaven.
FIRST MURD. Make peace with God, for you must die, my lord.
CLAR. Hast thou that holy feeling in thy soul,
To counsel me to make my peace with God,
And art thou yet to thy own soul so blind,
That thou wilt war with God by murdering me?
Ah, sirs, consider, he that set you on
To do this deed will hate you for the deed.
SEC. MURD. What shall we do?
CLAR. Relent, and save your souls.
FIRST MURD. Relent! 'tis cowardly and womanish.
CLAR. Not to relent is beastly, savage, devilish.
Which of you, if you were a prince's son,
Being pent from liberty, as I am now,
If two such murderers as yourselves came to you,
Would not entreat for life?
My friend, I spy some pity in thy looks;
O, if thine eye be not a flatterer,
Come thou on my side, and entreat for me,
As you would beg, were you in my distress:
A begging prince what beggar pities not?
SEC. MURD. Look behind you, my lord.

21. *Ay, millstones*] see note 40, Act I, Sc. iii.
22. *'Tis . . . thee*] There is no historical evidence linking Gloucester with the death of Clarence. Sixteenth-century chroniclers do report the rumour that he was drowned in a butt of malmsey.

FIRST MURD. Take that, and that: if all this will not do, [*Stabs him.*]
I'll drown you in the malmsey-butt within. [*Exit, with the body.*]
SEC. MURD. A bloody deed, and desperately dispatch'd!
How fain, like Pilate, would I wash my hands
Of this most grievous guilty murder done!

Re-enter First Murderer

FIRST MURD. How now! what mean'st thou, that thou help'st me not?
By heavens, the duke shall know how slack thou art!
SEC. MURD. I would he knew that I had saved his brother!
Take thou the fee, and tell him what I say;
For I repent me that the duke is slain. [*Exit.*]
FIRST MURD. So do not I: go, coward as thou art.
Now must I hide his body in some hole,
Until the duke take order for his burial:
And when I have my meed, I must away;
For this will out, and here I must not stay. [*Exit.*]

ACT II.

SCENE I. *London. The Palace.*

Flourish. Enter KING EDWARD *sick,* QUEEN ELIZABETH, DORSET, RIVERS, HASTINGS, BUCKINGHAM, GREY, *and others*

K. EDW. Why, so: now have I done a good day's work:
You peers, continue this united league:
I every day expect an embassage
From my Redeemer to redeem me hence;
And now in peace my soul shall part[1] to heaven,
Since I have set my friends at peace on earth.
Rivers and Hastings, take each other's hand;
Dissemble not your hatred, swear your love.
RIV. By heaven, my soul is purged from grudging hate;
And with my hand I seal my true heart's love.
HAST. So thrive I, as I truly swear the like!
K. EDW. Take heed you dally not before your king;

1. *part*] depart.

Lest he that is the supreme King of kings
Confound[2] your hidden falsehood, and award
Either of you to be the other's end.

HAST. So prosper I, as I swear perfect love!

RIV. And I, as I love Hastings with my heart!

K. EDW. Madam, yourself are not exempt in this,
Nor your son Dorset; Buckingham, nor you;
You have been factious one against the other.
Wife, love Lord Hastings, let him kiss your hand;
And what you do, do it unfeignedly.

Q. ELIZ. Here, Hastings; I will never more remember
Our former hatred, so thrive I and mine!

K. EDW. Dorset, embrace him; Hastings, love lord marquess.

DOR. This interchange of love, I here protest,
Upon my part shall be unviolable.

HAST. And so swear I, my lord. [*They embrace.*]

K. EDW. Now, princely Buckingham, seal thou this league
With thy embracements to my wife's allies,
And make me happy in your unity.

BUCK. [*To the* QUEEN] Whenever Buckingham doth turn his hate
On you or yours, but with all duteous love
Doth[3] cherish you and yours, God punish me
With hate in those where I expect most love!
When I have most need to employ a friend,
And most assured that he is a friend,
Deep, hollow, treacherous and full of guile,
Be he unto me! this do I beg of God,
When I am cold in zeal to you or yours. [*They embrace.*]

K. EDW. A pleasing cordial, princely Buckingham,
Is this thy vow unto my sickly heart.
There wanteth now our brother Gloucester here,
To make the perfect period of this peace.

BUCK. And, in good time, here comes the noble duke.

Enter GLOUCESTER

GLOU. Good morrow to my sovereign king and queen;
And, princely peers, a happy time of day!

K. EDW. Happy indeed, as we have spent the day.
Brother, we have done deeds of charity;
Made peace of enmity, fair love of hate,
Between these swelling wrong-incensed peers.

---

2. *Confound*] ruin, destroy.
3. *but . . . Doth*] and doth not.

GLOU. A blessed labour, my most sovereign liege:
Amongst this princely heap,[4] if any here,
By false intelligence, or wrong surmise,
Hold me a foe;
If I unwittingly, or in my rage,
Have aught committed that is hardly borne
By any in this presence, I desire
To reconcile me to his friendly peace:
'Tis death to me to be at enmity;
I hate it, and desire all good men's love.
First, madam, I entreat true peace of you,
Which I will purchase with my duteous service;
Of you, my noble cousin Buckingham,
If ever any grudge were lodged between us;
Of you, Lord Rivers, and, Lord Grey, of you,
That all without desert have frown'd on me;
Dukes, earls, lords, gentlemen; indeed, of all.
I do not know that Englishman alive
With whom my soul is any jot at odds,
More than the infant that is born to-night:
I thank my God for my humility.
Q. ELIZ. A holy day shall this be kept hereafter:
I would to God all strifes were well compounded.
My sovereign liege, I do beseech your majesty
To take our brother Clarence to your grace.
GLOU. Why, madam, have I offer'd love for this
To be so flouted in this royal presence?
Who knows not that the noble duke is dead? [*They all start.*]
You do him injury to scorn his corse.
RIV. Who knows not he is dead! who knows he is?
Q. ELIZ. All-seeing heaven, what a world is this!
BUCK. Look I so pale, Lord Dorset, as the rest?
DOR. Ay, my good lord; and no one in this presence
But his red colour hath forsook his cheeks.
K. EDW. Is Clarence dead? the order was reversed.
GLOU. But he, poor soul, by your first order died,
And that a winged Mercury did bear;
Some tardy cripple bore the countermand,
That came too lag to see him buried.
God grant that some, less noble and less loyal,
Nearer in bloody thoughts, but not in blood,

4. *heap*] throng, company.

Deserve not worse than wretched Clarence did,
And yet go current[5] from suspicion!

Enter DERBY

DER. A boon, my sovereign, for my service done!
K. EDW. I pray thee, peace: my soul is full of sorrow.
DER. I will not rise, unless your highness grant.
K. EDW. Then speak at once what is it thou demand'st.
DER. The forfeit, sovereign, of my servant's life;
Who slew to-day a riotous gentleman
Lately attendant on the Duke of Norfolk.
K. EDW. Have I a tongue to doom my brother's death,
And shall that tongue give pardon to a slave?
My brother slew no man; his fault was thought,
And yet his punishment was cruel death.
Who sued to me for him? who, in my rage,
Kneel'd at my feet and bade me be advised?
Who spake of brotherhood? who spake of love?
Who told me how the poor soul did forsake
The mighty Warwick, and did fight for me?
Who told me, in the field by Tewksbury,
When Oxford had me down, he rescued me,
And said "Dear brother, live, and be a king"?
Who told me, when we both lay in the field
Frozen almost to death, how he did lap me
Even in his own garments, and gave himself,
All thin and naked, to the numb cold night?
All this from my remembrance brutish wrath
Sinfully pluck'd, and not a man of you
Had so much grace to put it in my mind.
But when your carters or your waiting-vassals
Have done a drunken slaughter, and defaced
The precious image of our dear Redeemer,
You straight are on your knees for pardon, pardon;
And I, unjustly too, must grant it you:
But for my brother not a man would speak,
Nor I, ungracious, speak unto myself
For him, poor soul. The proudest of you all
Have been beholding to him in his life;
Yet none of you would once plead for his life.
O God, I fear thy justice will take hold

5. *go current*] go as though perceived to be honest.

On me, and you, and mine, and yours for this!
Come, Hastings, help me to my closet. Oh, poor Clarence!
[*Exeunt some with King and Queen.*]
GLOU. This is the fruit of rashness. Mark'd you not
How that the guilty kindred of the queen
Look'd pale when they did hear of Clarence' death?
O, they did urge it still unto the king!
God will revenge it. But come, let us in,
To comfort Edward with our company.
BUCK. We wait upon your grace. [*Exeunt.*]

SCENE II. *The Palace.*

Enter the DUCHESS OF YORK, *with the two children of* CLARENCE

BOY. Tell me, good grandam,[1] is our father dead?
DUCH. No, boy.
BOY. Why do you wring your hands, and beat your breast,
And cry "O Clarence, my unhappy son"?
GIRL. Why do you look on us, and shake your head,
And call us wretches, orphans, castaways,
If that our noble father be alive?
DUCH. My pretty cousins,[2] you mistake me much.
I do lament the sickness of the king,
As loath to lose him; not your father's death;
It were lost sorrow to wail one that's lost.
BOY. Then, grandam, you conclude that he is dead.
The king my uncle is to blame for this:
God will revenge it; whom I will importune
With daily prayers all to that effect.
GIRL. And so will I.

---

1. *good grandam*] the widow of Richard, Duke of York, who was slain at the battle of Wakefield, 1460, and the mother of Edward IV, Richard III, and Clarence. She survived her husband thirty-five years. Her grandchildren, Clarence's son and daughter, with whom she converses in this scene, were respectively Edward Plantagenet, Earl of Warwick, who was executed by Henry VII on November 21, 1499, and the famous Margaret, Countess of Salisbury, mother of Cardinal Pole; the Countess was beheaded on Tower Hill at Henry VIII's instance on May 27, 1541.
2. *cousins*] This word was used for kinsfolk of any degree.

DUCH. Peace, children, peace! the king doth love you well:
Incapable[3] and shallow innocents,
You cannot guess who caused your father's death.
BOY. Grandam, we can; for my good uncle Gloucester
Told me, the king, provoked by the queen,
Devised impeachments to imprison him:
And when my uncle told me so, he wept,
And hugg'd me in his arm, and kindly kiss'd my cheek;
Bade me rely on him as on my father,
And he would love me dearly as his child.
DUCH. Oh, that deceit should steal such gentle shapes,
And with a virtuous vizard hide foul guile!
He is my son; yea, and therein my shame;
Yet from my dugs[4] he drew not this deceit.
BOY. Think you my uncle did dissemble, grandam?
DUCH. Ay, boy.
BOY. I cannot think it. Hark! what noise is this?

Enter QUEEN ELIZABETH, *with her hair about her ears;* RIVERS *and* DORSET *after her*

Q. ELIZ. Oh, who shall hinder me to wail and weep,
To chide my fortune and torment myself?
I'll join with black despair against my soul,
And to myself become an enemy
DUCH. What means this scene of rude impatience?
Q. ELIZ. To make an act[5] of tragic violence:
Edward, my lord, your son, our king, is dead.
Why grow the branches now the root is wither'd?
Why wither not the leaves the sap being gone?
If you will live, lament; if die, be brief,
That our swift-winged souls may catch the king's,
Or, like obedient subjects, follow him
To his new kingdom of perpetual rest.
DUCH. Ah, so much interest have I in thy sorrow
As I had title in thy noble husband!
I have bewept a worthy husband's death,
And lived by looking on his images:[6]
But now two mirrors of his princely semblance
Are crack'd in pieces by malignant death,

3. *Incapable*] i.e., incapable of understanding.
4. *dugs*] teats.
5. *an act*] in a theatrical sense.
6. *his images*] the children who preserve his likeness.

And I for comfort have but one false glass,
Which grieves me when I see my shame in him.
Thou art a widow; yet thou art a mother,
And hast the comfort of thy children left thee:
But death hath snatch'd my husband from mine arms,
And pluck'd two crutches from my feeble limbs,
Edward and Clarence. O, what cause have I,
Thine being but a moiety of my grief,
To overgo thy plaints[7] and drown thy cries!

BOY. Good aunt, you wept not for our father's death,
How can we aid you with our kindred tears?

GIRL. Our fatherless distress was left unmoan'd;
Your widow-dolour likewise be unwept!

Q. ELIZ. Give me no help in lamentation;
I am not barren to bring forth complaints:
All springs reduce[8] their currents to mine eyes,
That I, being govern'd by the watery moon,
May send forth plenteous tears to drown the world!
Oh for my husband, for my dear lord Edward!

CHIL. Oh for our father, for our dear lord Clarence!

DUCH. Alas for both, both mine, Edward and Clarence!

Q. ELIZ. What stay had I but Edward? and he's gone.

CHIL. What stay had we but Clarence? and he's gone.

DUCH. What stays had I but they? and they are gone.

Q. ELIZ. Was never widow had so dear a loss.

CHIL. Were never orphans had so dear a loss.

DUCH. Was never mother had so dear a loss.
Alas, I am the mother of these moans!
Their woes are parcell'd, mine are general.[9]
She for an Edward weeps, and so do I;
I for a Clarence weep, so doth not she:
These babes for Clarence weep, and so do I;
I for an Edward weep, so do not they:
Alas, you three, on me threefold distress'd
Pour all your tears! I am your sorrow's nurse,
And I will pamper it with lamentations.

DOR. Comfort, dear mother: God is much displeased
That you take with unthankfulness his doing:
In common worldly things, 'tis call'd ungrateful,
With dull unwillingness to repay a debt

7. *overgo thy plaints*] exceed thy lamentations.
8. *reduce*] bring, lead back.
9. *Their woes . . . general*] Their woes are divided up amongst them; each has his own particular woe; my woes cover all theirs.

Which with a bounteous hand was kindly lent;
Much more to be thus opposite with heaven,
For it requires the royal debt it lent you.
RIV. Madam, bethink you, like a careful mother,
Of the young prince your son: send straight for him;
Let him be crown'd; in him your comfort lives:
Drown desperate sorrow in dead Edward's grave,
And plant your joys in living Edward's throne.

Enter GLOUCESTER, BUCKINGHAM, DERBY, HASTINGS, *and* RATCLIFF

GLOU. Madam, have comfort: all of us have cause
To wail the dimming of our shining star;
But none can cure their harms by wailing them.
Madam, my mother, I do cry you mercy;
I did not see your grace: humbly on my knee
I crave your blessing.
DUCH. God bless thee, and put meekness in thy mind,
Love, charity, obedience, and true duty!
GLOU. [*Aside*] Amen; and make me die a good old man!
That is the butt-end of a mother's blessing:
I marvel why her grace did leave it out.
BUCK. You cloudy[10] princes and heart-sorrowing peers,
That bear this mutual heavy load of moan,
Now cheer each other in each other's love:
Though we have spent our harvest of this king,
We are to reap the harvest of his son.
The broken rancour[11] of your high-swoln hearts,
But lately splinter'd,[12] knit and join'd together,
Must gently be preserved, cherish'd, and kept:
Me seemeth good, that, with some little train,
Forthwith from Ludlow[13] the young prince[14] be fetch'd
Hither to London, to be crown'd our king.
RIV. Why with some little train, my Lord of Buckingham?
BUCK. Marry, my lord, lest, by a multitude,
The new-heal'd wound of malice should break out;
Which would be so much the more dangerous,

10. *cloudy*] sullen.
11. *broken rancour*] the rancour that has been broken and destroyed, the cessation of rancour, the reconciliation.
12. *splinter'd*] joined together with splints.
13. *Ludlow*] As Prince of Wales, the young prince, according to established custom, resided at Ludlow Castle on the Welsh border.
14. *the young prince*] the oldest son of Edward IV and Elizabeth Woodville, and soon to be Edward V, king at the age of 13.

By how much the estate[15] is green and yet ungovern'd:
Where every horse bears his commanding rein,
And may direct his course as please himself,
As well the fear of harm as harm apparent,
In my opinion, ought to be prevented.

GLOU. I hope the king made peace with all of us;
And the compact is firm and true in me.

RIV. And so in me; and so, I think, in all:
Yet, since it is but green, it should be put
To no apparent likelihood of breach,
Which haply by much company might be urged:
Therefore I say with noble Buckingham,
That it is meet so few should fetch the prince.

HAST. And so say I.

GLOU. Then be it so; and go we to determine
Who they shall be that straight shall post to Ludlow.
Madam, and you, my mother, will you go
To give your censures[16] in this weighty business?

Q. ELIZ. }
DUCH. } With all our hearts.

[*Exeunt all but* BUCKINGHAM *and* GLOUCESTER.]

BUCK. My lord, whoever journeys to the prince,
For God's sake, let not us two stay behind;
For, by the way, I'll sort occasion,[17]
As index[18] to the story we late talk'd of,
To part the queen's proud kindred from the king.

GLOU. My other self, my counsel's consistory,[19]
My oracle, my prophet!—My dear cousin,
I, like a child, will go by thy direction.
Towards Ludlow then, for we'll not stay behind. [*Exeunt.*]

---

15. *the estate*] the state.
16. *censures*] opinions.
17. *sort occasion*] contrive an opportunity.
18. *index*] prelude, prologue. In early printed books, the index was placed in the preliminary pages.
19. *consistory*] a council or solemn assembly.

SCENE III. *London. A Street.*

Enter two Citizens, *meeting*

FIRST CIT. Neighbour, well met: whither away so fast?
SEC. CIT. I promise you, I scarcely know myself:
Hear you the news abroad?
FIRST CIT. Ay, that the king is dead.
SEC. CIT. Bad news, by 'r lady, seldom comes the better:
I fear, I fear, 'twill prove a troublous world.

Enter another Citizen

THIRD CIT. Neighbours, God speed!
FIRST CIT. Give you good morrow, sir.
THIRD CIT. Doth this news hold of good King Edward's death?
SEC. CIT. Ay, sir, it is too true; God help the while!
THIRD CIT. Then, masters, look to see a troublous world.
FIRST CIT. No, no; by God's good grace his son shall reign.
THIRD CIT. Woe to that land that's govern'd by a child!
SEC. CIT. In him there is a hope of government,
That in his nonage council under him,
And in his full and ripen'd years himself,
No doubt, shall then and till then govern well.
FIRST CIT. So stood the state when Henry the Sixth
Was crown'd in Paris but at nine months old.
THIRD CIT. Stood the state so? No, no, good friends, God wot;
For then this land was famously enrich'd
With politic grave counsel; then the king
Had virtuous uncles to protect his grace.
FIRST CIT. Why, so hath this, both by the father and mother.
THIRD CIT. Better it were they all came by the father,
Or by the father there were none at all;
For emulation now, who shall be nearest,
Will touch us all too near,[1] if God prevent not.
O, full of danger is the Duke of Gloucester!
And the queen's sons and brothers haught[2] and proud:
And were they to be ruled, and not to rule,
This sickly land might solace[3] as before.

1. *touch . . . near*] injure, hurt, hit.
2. *haught*] a common form of "haughty."
3. *solace*] find comfort, *not* give comfort.

FIRST CIT. Come, come, we fear the worst; all shall be well.
THIRD CIT. When clouds appear, wise men put on their cloaks;
When great leaves fall, the winter is at hand;
When the sun sets, who doth not look for night?
Untimely storms make men expect a dearth.
All may be well; but, if God sort[4] it so,
'Tis more than we deserve, or I expect.
SEC. CIT. Truly, the souls of men are full of dread:
Ye cannot reason almost with a man
That looks not heavily and full of fear.
THIRD CIT. Before the times of change, still is it so:
By a divine instinct men's minds mistrust
Ensuing dangers; as, by proof, we see
The waters swell before a boisterous storm.
But leave it all to God. Whither away?
SEC. CIT. Marry, we were sent for to the justices.
THIRD CIT. And so was I: I'll bear you company. [*Exeunt.*]

SCENE IV. *London. The Palace.*

Enter the ARCHBISHOP OF YORK, *the young* DUKE OF YORK, QUEEN ELIZABETH, *and the* DUCHESS OF YORK

ARCH. Last night, I hear, they lay at Northampton;
At Stony-Stratford will they be to-night:
To-morrow, or next day, they will be here.
DUCH. I long with all my heart to see the prince:
I hope he is much grown since last I saw him.
Q. ELIZ. But I hear, no; they say my son of York
Hath almost overta'en him in his growth.
YORK. Ay, mother; but I would not have it so.
DUCH. Why, my young cousin, it is good to grow.
YORK. Grandam, one night, as we did sit at supper,
My uncle Rivers talk'd how I did grow
More than my brother: "Ay," quoth my uncle Gloucester,
"Small herbs have grace, great weeds do grow apace:"
And since, methinks, I would not grow so fast,

4. *sort*] ordain.

Because sweet flowers are slow and weeds make haste.
DUCH. Good faith, good faith, the saying did not hold
In him that did object the same to thee:
He was the wretched'st thing when he was young,
So long a-growing and so leisurely,
That, if this rule were true, he should be gracious.
ARCH. Why, madam, so, no doubt, he is.
DUCH. I hope so too; but yet let mothers doubt.
YORK. Now, by my troth, if I had been remember'd,
I could have given my uncle's grace a flout,
To touch his growth nearer[1] than he touch'd mine.
DUCH. How, my pretty York? I pray thee, let me hear it.
YORK. Marry, they say my uncle grew so fast
That he could gnaw a crust at two hours old:
'Twas full two years ere I could get a tooth.
Grandam, this would have been a biting jest.
DUCH. I pray thee, pretty York, who told thee this?
YORK. Grandam, his nurse.
DUCH. His nurse! why, she was dead ere thou wert born.
YORK. If 'twere not she, I cannot tell who told me.
Q. ELIZ. A parlous boy:[2] go to, you are too shrewd.
ARCH. Good madam, be not angry with the child.
Q. ELIZ. Pitchers have ears.

Enter a Messenger

ARCH. Here comes a messenger. What news?
MESS. Such news, my lord, as grieves me to unfold.
Q. ELIZ. How fares the prince?
MESS. Well, madam, and in health.
DUCH. What is thy news then?
MESS. Lord Rivers and Lord Grey are sent to Pomfret,
With them Sir Thomas Vaughan, prisoners.
DUCH. Who hath committed them?
MESS. The mighty dukes,
Gloucester and Buckingham.
Q. ELIZ. For what offence?
MESS. The sum of all I can, I have disclosed;
Why or for what these nobles were committed
Is all unknown to me, my gracious lady.
Q. ELIZ. Ay me, I see the downfall of our house!
The tiger now hath seized the gentle hind;
Insulting tyranny begins to jet

1. *touch . . . nearer*] hit, in the slang sense of "get at."
2. *parlous boy*] an *enfant terrible*.

Upon the innocent and aweless throne:[3]
Welcome, destruction, death, and massacre!
I see, as in a map, the end of all.

DUCH. Accursed and unquiet wrangling days,
How many of you have mine eyes beheld!
My husband lost his life to get the crown;
And often up and down my sons were toss'd,
For me to joy and weep their gain and loss:
And being seated, and domestic broils
Clean over-blown, themselves, the conquerors,
Make war upon themselves; blood against blood,
Self against self: O, preposterous
And frantic outrage, end thy damned spleen;
Or let me die, to look on death no more!

Q. ELIZ. Come, come, my boy; we will to sanctuary.[4]
Madam, farewell.

DUCH. I'll go along with you.

Q. ELIZ. You have no cause.

ARCH. My gracious lady, go;
And thither bear your treasure and your goods.
For my part, I'll resign unto your grace
The seal[5] I keep: and so betide to me
As well I tender you and all of yours!
Come, I'll conduct you to the sanctuary. [*Exeunt.*]

ACT III.

SCENE I. *London. A Street.*

The trumpets sound. Enter the young PRINCE, *the Dukes of* GLOUCESTER *and* BUCKINGHAM, CARDINAL BOURCHIER, CATESBY, *and others*

BUCK. Welcome, sweet prince, to London, to your chamber.[1]

---

3. *to jet . . . throne*] to encroach upon a throne filled by an innocent child, and one inspiring no fear.
4. *sanctuary*] the precincts of Westminster Abbey, where no arrests of suspected persons were permitted.
5. *The seal*] the Great Seal of England.

---

1. *chamber*] London, the capital city of the kingdom, was formally called "camera regis" (king's chamber).

GLOU. Welcome, dear cousin, my thoughts' sovereign:
The weary way hath made you melancholy.
PRINCE. No, uncle; but our crosses on the way
Have made it tedious, wearisome, and heavy:
I want more uncles here to welcome me.
GLOU. Sweet prince, the untainted virtue of your years
Hath not yet dived into the world's deceit:
Nor more can you distinguish of a man
Than of his outward show; which, God he knows,
Seldom or never jumpeth with the heart.
Those uncles which you want were dangerous;
Your grace attended to their sugar'd words,
But look'd not on the poison of their hearts:
God keep you from them, and from such false friends!
PRINCE. God keep me from false friends! but they were none.
GLOU. My lord, the mayor of London comes to greet you.

Enter the Lord Mayor, *and his train*

MAY. God bless your grace with health and happy days!
PRINCE. I thank you, good my lord; and thank you all.
I thought my mother and my brother York
Would long ere this have met us on the way:
Fie, what a slug is Hastings, that he comes not
To tell us whether they will come or no!

Enter LORD HASTINGS

BUCK. And, in good time here comes the sweating lord.
PRINCE. Welcome, my lord: what, will our mother come?
HAST. On what occasion, God he knows, not I,
The queen your mother and your brother York
Have taken sanctuary: the tender prince
Would fain have come with me to meet your grace,
But by his mother was perforce withheld.
BUCK. Fie, what an indirect and peevish course
Is this of hers! Lord cardinal, will your grace
Persuade the queen to send the Duke of York
Unto his princely brother presently?
If she deny, Lord Hastings, go with him,
And from her jealous arms pluck him perforce.
CARD. My Lord of Buckingham, if my weak oratory
Can from his mother win the Duke of York,
Anon expect him here; but if she be obdurate
To mild entreaties, God in heaven forbid

We should infringe the holy privilege
Of blessed sanctuary! not for all this land
Would I be guilty of so deep a sin.

BUCK. You are too senseless-obstinate,[2] my lord,
Too ceremonious and traditional:
Weigh it but with the grossness of this age,[3]
You break not sanctuary in seizing him.
The benefit thereof is always granted
To those whose dealings have deserved the place,
And those who have the wit to claim the place:
This prince hath neither claim'd it nor deserved it;
And therefore, in mine opinion, cannot have it:
Then, taking him from thence that is not there,
You break no privilege nor charter there.
Oft have I heard of sanctuary men;
But sanctuary children ne'er till now.

CARD. My lord, you shall o'er-rule my mind for once.
Come on, Lord Hastings, will you go with me?

HAST. I go, my lord.

PRINCE. Good lords, make all the speedy haste you may.
[*Exeunt* CARDINAL *and* HASTINGS.]
Say, uncle Gloucester, if our brother come,
Where shall we sojourn till our coronation?

GLOU. Where it seems best unto your royal self.
If I may counsel you, some day or two
Your highness shall repose you at the Tower:
Then where you please, and shall be thought most fit
For your best health and recreation.

PRINCE. I do not like the Tower, of any place.
Did Julius Cæsar build that place, my lord?

BUCK. He did, my gracious lord, begin that place;
Which, since, succeeding ages have re-edified.

PRINCE. Is it upon record, or else reported
Successively from age to age, he built it?

BUCK. Upon record, my gracious lord.

PRINCE. But say, my lord, it were not register'd,
Methinks the truth should live from age to age,
As 'twere retail'd[4] to all posterity,
Even to the general all-ending day.

GLOU. [*Aside*] So wise so young, they say, do never live long.

---

2. *senseless-obstinate*] unreasonable in obstinacy.
3. *Weigh . . . age*] Consider it in the light of the unlicensed temper of the times (which calls for high-handed action).
4. *retail'd*] recounted, rehearsed.

PRINCE. What say you, uncle?
GLOU. I say, without characters,[5] fame lives long.
[*Aside*] Thus, like the formal vice, Iniquity,[6]
I moralize two meanings in one word.
PRINCE. That Julius Cæsar was a famous man;
With what his valour did enrich his wit,
His wit set down to make his valour live:
Death makes no conquest of this conqueror;
For now he lives in fame, though not in life.
I'll tell you what, my cousin Buckingham,—
BUCK. What, my gracious lord?
PRINCE. An if I live until I be a man,
I'll win our ancient right in France again,
Or die a soldier, as I lived a king.
GLOU. [*Aside*] Short summers lightly[7] have a forward spring.

Enter young YORK, HASTINGS, *and the* CARDINAL

BUCK. Now, in good time, here comes the Duke of York.
PRINCE. Richard of York! how fares our loving brother?
YORK. Well, my dread lord; so must I call you now.
PRINCE. Ay, brother, to our grief, as it is yours:
Too late[8] he died that might have kept that title,
Which by his death hath lost much majesty.
GLOU. How fares our cousin, noble Lord of York?
YORK. I thank you, gentle uncle. O, my lord,
You said that idle weeds are fast in growth:
The prince my brother hath outgrown me far.
GLOU. He hath, my lord.
YORK. And therefore is he idle?
GLOU. O, my fair cousin, I must not say so.
YORK. Then he is more beholding to you than I.
GLOU. He may command me as my sovereign;
But you have power in me as in a kinsman.
YORK. I pray you, uncle, give me this dagger.
GLOU. My dagger, little cousin? with all my heart.
PRINCE. A beggar, brother?

5. *without characters*] without the help of letters or inscriptions.
6. *Thus . . . Iniquity*] In the old Morality plays the leading character in attendance on the Devil bore the conventional ("formal") designation of "The Vice," and indulged in persistent word-play. The character was occasionally known by the more specific name of "Iniquity" or "Hypocrisy" or some other sin.
7. *lightly*] commonly; a rare usage deduced from the meaning of "easily" or "readily" which often attaches to the word.
8. *late*] lately, recently.

YORK. Of my kind uncle, that I know will give;
And being but a toy, which is no grief to give.
GLOU. A greater gift than that I'll give my cousin.
YORK. A greater gift! O, that's the sword to it.[9]
GLOU. Ay, gentle cousin, were it light enough.
YORK. O, then, I see, you will part but with light gifts;
In weightier things you'll say a beggar nay.
GLOU. It is too heavy for your grace to wear.
YORK. I weigh it lightly,[10] were it heavier.
GLOU. What, would you have my weapon, little lord?
YORK. I would, that I might thank you as you call me.
GLOU. How?
YORK. Little.
PRINCE. My Lord of York will still be cross[11] in talk:
Uncle, your grace knows how to bear with him.
YORK. You mean, to bear me, not to bear with me:
Uncle, my brother mocks both you and me;
Because that I am little, like an ape,
He thinks that you should bear me on your shoulders.
BUCK. With what a sharp-provided wit he reasons!
To mitigate the scorn he gives his uncle,
He prettily and aptly taunts himself:
So cunning and so young is wonderful.
GLOU. My lord, will 't please you pass along?
Myself and my good cousin Buckingham
Will to your mother, to entreat of her
To meet you at the Tower and welcome you.
YORK. What, will you go unto the Tower, my lord?
PRINCE. My lord protector needs will have it so.
YORK. I shall not sleep in quiet at the Tower.
GLOU. Why, what should you fear?
YORK. Marry, my uncle Clarence' angry ghost:
My grandam told me he was murder'd there.
PRINCE. I fear no uncles dead.
GLOU. Nor none that live, I hope.
PRINCE. An if they live, I hope I need not fear.
But come, my lord; and with a heavy heart,
Thinking on them, go I unto the Tower.
[A *Sennet.*[12] *Exeunt all but* GLOUCESTER, BUCKINGHAM *and* CATESBY.

9. *the sword to it*] The belt, which carried the dagger, bore a sword in addition.
10. *I . . . lightly*] I should mind very little.
11. *cross*] at cross purposes, malapert.
12. A *Sennet*] a flourish on a trumpet, marking the entrance or exit of a procession.

BUCK. Think you, my lord, this little prating York
Was not incensed by his subtle mother
To taunt and scorn you thus opprobriously?
GLOU. No doubt, no doubt: O, 'tis a parlous boy;
Bold, quick, ingenious, forward, capable:
He is all the mother's, from the top to toe.
BUCK. Well, let them rest. Come hither, Catesby.
Thou art sworn as deeply to effect what we intend,
As closely to conceal what we impart:
Thou know'st our reasons urged upon the way;
What think'st thou? is it not an easy matter
To make William Lord Hastings of our mind,
For the instalment of this noble duke
In the seat royal of this famous isle?
CATE. He for his father's sake so loves the prince,
That he will not be won to aught against him.
BUCK. What think'st thou then of Stanley? what will he?
CATE. He will do all in all as Hastings doth.
BUCK. Well, then, no more but this: go, gentle Catesby,
And, as it were far off, sound thou Lord Hastings,
How he doth stand affected[13] to our purpose;
And summon him to-morrow to the Tower,
To sit about the coronation.
If thou dost find him tractable to us,
Encourage him, and show him all our reasons:
If he be leaden, icy-cold, unwilling,
Be thou so too; and so break off your talk,
And give us notice of his inclination:
For we to-morrow hold divided councils,[14]
Wherein thyself shalt highly be employ'd.
GLOU. Commend me to Lord William: tell him, Catesby,
His ancient knot of dangerous adversaries
To-morrow are let blood[15] at Pomfret-castle;
And bid my friend, for joy of this good news,
Give Mistress Shore[16] one gentle kiss the more.
BUCK. Good Catesby, go, effect this business soundly.
CATE. My good lords both, with all the heed I may.
GLOU. Shall we hear from you, Catesby, ere we sleep?
CATE. You shall, my lord.

13. *stand affected*] feel disposed.
14. *divided councils*] two separate councils, one of Gloucester's supporters and the other of the young prince's.
15. *let blood*] killed, executed.
16. *Mistress Shore*] On Edward IV's death, according to Holinshed's *Chronicles*, Hastings made Jane Shore his mistress.

GLOU. At Crosby Place, there shall you find us both.
[*Exit* CATESBY.]
BUCK. Now, my lord, what shall we do, if we perceive
Lord Hastings will not yield to our complots?[17]
GLOU. Chop off his head, man; somewhat we will do:
And, look, when I am king, claim thou of me
The earldom of Hereford, and the moveables[18]
Whereof the king my brother stood possess'd.
BUCK. I'll claim that promise at your grace's hands.
GLOU. And look to have it yielded with all willingness.
Come, let us sup betimes, that afterwards
We may digest our complots in some form. [*Exeunt.*]

SCENE II. *Before Lord Hastings' House.*

Enter a Messenger

MESS. What, ho! my lord
HAST. [*Within*] Who knocks at the door?
MESS. A messenger from the Lord Stanley.

Enter LORD HASTINGS

HAST. What is 't o'clock?
MESS. Upon the stroke of four.
HAST. Cannot thy master sleep these tedious nights?
MESS. So it should seem by that I have to say.
First, he commends him to your noble lordship.
HAST. And then?
MESS. And then he sends you word
He dreamt to-night the boar had razed his helm:[1]
Besides, he says there are two councils held;
And that may be determined at the one
Which may make you and him to rue at the other.
Therefore he sends to know your lordship's pleasure,
If presently you will take horse with him,
And with all speed post with him toward the north,
To shun the danger that his soul divines.

---

17. *complots*] conspiracies.
18. *moveables*] any property, such as furniture, not fixed in place.

---

1. *razed his helm*] tore off his head. The boar refers to Gloucester.

HAST. Go, fellow, go, return unto thy lord;
Bid him not fear the separated councils:
His honour and myself are at the one,
And at the other is my servant Catesby;
Where nothing can proceed that toucheth[2] us,
Whereof I shall not have intelligence.
Tell him his fears are shallow, wanting instance:[3]
And for his dreams, I wonder he is so fond
To trust the mockery of unquiet slumbers:
To fly the boar before the boar pursues,
Were to incense the boar to follow us,
And make pursuit where he did mean no chase.
Go, bid thy master rise and come to me;
And we will both together to the Tower,
Where, he shall see, the boar will use us kindly.
MESS. My gracious lord, I'll tell him what you say. [*Exit.*]

Enter CATESBY

CATE. Many good morrows to my noble lord!
HAST. Good morrow, Catesby; you are early stirring:
What news, what news, in this our tottering state?
CATE. It is a reeling world indeed, my lord;
And I believe 'twill never stand upright
Till Richard wear the garland of the realm.
HAST. How! wear the garland! dost thou mean the crown?
CATE. Ay, my good lord.
HAST. I'll have this crown of mine cut from my shoulders,
Ere I will see the crown so foul misplaced.
But canst thou guess that he doth aim at it?
CATE. Ay, on my life, and hopes to find you forward
Upon his party for the gain thereof:
And thereupon he sends you this good news,
That this same very day your enemies,
The kindred of the queen, must die at Pomfret.
HAST. Indeed, I am no mourner for that news,
Because they have been still[4] mine enemies:
But, that I'll give my voice on Richard's side,
To bar my master's heirs in true descent,
God knows I will not do it, to the death.
CATE. God keep your lordship in that gracious mind!

2. *toucheth*] injureth.
3. *wanting instance*] without example or proof.
4. *still*] always.

HAST. But I shall laugh at this a twelve-month hence,
That they who brought me in my master's hate,
I live to look upon their tragedy.
I tell thee, Catesby,—
CATE. What, my lord?
HAST. Ere a fortnight make me elder,
I'll send some packing that yet think not on it.
CATE. 'Tis a vile thing to die, my gracious lord,
When men are unprepared and look not for it.
HAST. O monstrous, monstrous! and so falls it out
With Rivers, Vaughan, Grey: and so 'twill do
With some men else, who think themselves as safe
As thou and I; who, as thou know'st, are dear
To princely Richard and to Buckingham.
CATE. The princes both make high account of you;
[*Aside*] For they account his head upon the bridge.[5]
HAST. I know they do; and I have well deserved it.

Enter LORD STANLEY

Come on, come on; where is your boar-spear, man?
Fear you the boar, and go so unprovided?
STAN. My lord, good morrow; good morrow, Catesby:
You may jest on, but, by the holy rood,[6]
I do not like these several councils, I.
HAST. My lord,
I hold my life as dear as you do yours;
And never in my life, I do protest,
Was it more precious to me than 'tis now:
Think you, but that I know our state secure,
I would be so triumphant as I am?
STAN. The lords at Pomfret, when they rode from London,
Were jocund and supposed their state was sure,
And they indeed had no cause to mistrust;
But yet, you see, how soon the day o'ercast.
This sudden stab of rancour I misdoubt:
Pray God, I say, I prove a needless coward!
What, shall we toward the Tower? the day is spent.
HAST. Come, come, have with you.[7] Wot[8] you what, my lord?
To-day the lords you talk of are beheaded.

5. *they account . . . bridge*] It was customary to put the heads of those who were executed for high treason on a pole fixed to the roof of a tower on London Bridge.
6. *rood*] the cross (on which Christ died).
7. *have with you*] I will go along with you.
8. *Wot*] know.

STAN. They, for their truth, might better wear their heads,
Than some that have accused them wear their hats.
But come, my lord, let us away.

Enter a Pursuivant[9]

HAST. Go on before; I'll talk with this good fellow.
[*Exeunt* STANLEY *and* CATESBY.]
How now, sirrah! how goes the world with thee?
PURS. The better that your lordship please to ask.
HAST. I tell thee, man, 'tis better with me now,
Than when I met thee last where now we meet:
Then was I going prisoner to the Tower,
By the suggestion of the queen's allies;
But now, I tell thee—keep it to thyself—
This day those enemies are put to death,
And I in better state than e'er I was.
PURS. God hold it,[10] to your honour's good content!
HAST. Gramercy,[11] fellow: there, drink that for me.
[*Throws him his purse.*]
PURS. God save your lordship. [*Exit.*]

Enter a Priest

PRIEST. Well met, my lord; I am glad to see your honour.
HAST. I thank thee, good Sir John,[12] with all my heart.
I am in your debt for your last exercise;[13]
Come the next Sabbath, and I will content you.
[*He whispers in his ear.*]

Enter BUCKINGHAM

BUCK. What, talking with a priest, lord chamberlain?
Your friends at Pomfret, they do need the priest;
Your honour hath no shriving work[14] in hand.
HAST. Good faith, and when I met this holy man,
Those men you talk of came into my mind.
What, go you toward the Tower?
BUCK. I do, my lord; but long I shall not stay:
I shall return before your lordship thence.

9. *Pursuivant*] Properly, an attendant on a herald, an officer of the college of arms, but the word was more often used, as here, for any messenger of a court of justice. It is also found in the general sense of messenger.
10. *God hold it*] God continue your good fortune.
11. *Gramercy*] great thanks.
12. *good Sir John*] "Sir" was a courtesy title given to all clergymen.
13. *exercise*] religious exhortation, sermon.
14. *shriving work*] confession.

HAST. 'Tis like enough, for I stay dinner there.
BUCK. [*Aside*] And supper too, although thou know'st it not.
 Come, will you go?
HAST. I'll wait upon your lordship. [*Exeunt.*]

SCENE III. *Pomfret Castle.*

Enter SIR RICHARD RATCLIFF, *with halberds, carrying* RIVERS, GREY, *and* VAUGHAN *to death*

RAT. Come, bring forth the prisoners.
RIV. Sir Richard Ratcliff, let me tell thee this:
 To-day shalt thou behold a subject die
 For truth, for duty, and for loyalty.
GREY. God keep the prince from all the pack of you!
 A knot you are of damned blood-suckers.
VAUG. You live that shall cry woe for this hereafter.
RAT. Dispatch; the limit of your lives is out.
RIV. O Pomfret, Pomfret! O thou bloody prison,
 Fatal and ominous to noble peers!
 Within the guilty closure[1] of thy walls
 Richard the second here was hack'd to death;
 And, for more slander to thy dismal seat,
 We give thee up our guiltless blood to drink.
GREY. Now Margaret's curse is fall'n upon our heads,
 For standing by when Richard stabb'd her son.
RIV. Then cursed she Hastings, then cursed she Buckingham,
 Then cursed she Richard. O, remember, God,
 To hear her prayers for them, as now for us!
 And for my sister and her princely sons,
 Be satisfied, dear God, with our true blood,
 Which, as thou know'st, unjustly must be spilt.
RAT. Make haste; the hour of death is expiate.[2]
RIV. Come, Grey, come, Vaughan, let us all embrace:
 And take our leave, until we meet in heaven. [*Exeunt.*]

1. *closure*] enclosure, compass.
2. *expiate*] brought to a close, finished.

SCENE IV. *The Tower of London.*

Enter BUCKINGHAM, DERBY, HASTINGS, *the* BISHOP OF ELY, RATCLIFF, LOVEL, *with others, and take their seats at a table*

HAST. My lords, at once: the cause why we are met
Is, to determine of the coronation.
In God's name, speak: when is the royal day?
BUCK. Are all things fitting for that royal time?
DER. It is, and wants but nomination.[1]
ELY. To-morrow then I judge a happy day.
BUCK. Who knows the lord protector's mind herein?
Who is most inward[2] with the noble duke?
ELY. Your grace, we think, should soonest know his mind.
BUCK. Who, I, my lord! We know each other's faces,
But for our hearts, he knows no more of mine
Than I of yours;
Nor I no more of his, than you of mine.
Lord Hastings, you and he are near in love.
HAST. I thank his grace, I know he loves me well;
But, for his purpose in the coronation,
I have not sounded him, nor he deliver'd
His gracious pleasure any way therein.
But you, my noble lords, may name the time;
And in the duke's behalf I'll give my voice,
Which, I presume, he'll take in gentle part.

Enter GLOUCESTER

ELY. Now in good time, here comes the duke himself.
GLOU. My noble lords and cousins all, good morrow.
I have been long a sleeper; but, I hope,
My absence doth neglect no great designs,
Which by my presence might have been concluded.
BUCK. Had not you come upon your cue, my lord,
William Lord Hastings had pronounced your part,—
I mean, your voice,—for crowning of the king.
GLOU. Than my Lord Hastings no man might be bolder;
His lordship knows me well, and loves me well.
HAST. I thank your grace.

1. *nomination*] the naming of the day.
2. *inward*] intimate.

GLOU. My Lord of Ely!
ELY. My lord?
GLOU. When I was last in Holborn,
I saw good strawberries in your garden there:
I do beseech you send for some of them.
ELY. Marry, and will, my lord, with all my heart. [*Exit.*]
GLOU. Cousin of Buckingham, a word with you.
[*Drawing him aside.*]
Catesby hath sounded Hastings in our business,
And finds the testy gentleman so hot,
As he will lose his head ere give consent
His master's son, as worshipful he terms it,
Shall lose the royalty of England's throne.
BUCK. Withdraw you hence, my lord, I'll follow you.
[*Exit* GLOUCESTER, BUCKINGHAM *following.*]
DER. We have not yet set down this day of triumph.
To-morrow, in mine opinion, is too sudden;
For I myself am not so well provided
As else I would be, were the day prolong'd.

Re-enter BISHOP OF ELY

ELY. Where is my lord protector? I have sent for these strawberries.
HAST. His grace looks cheerfully and smooth to-day;
There's some conceit or other likes him[3] well,
When he doth bid good morrow with such a spirit.
I think there's never a man in Christendom
That can less hide his love or hate than he;
For by his face straight shall you know his heart.
DER. What of his heart perceive you in his face
By any likelihood he show'd to-day?
HAST. Marry, that with no man here he is offended;
For, were he, he had shown it in his looks.
DER. I pray God he be not, I say.

Re-enter GLOUCESTER *and* BUCKINGHAM

GLOU. I pray you all, tell me what they deserve
That do conspire my death with devilish plots
Of damned witchcraft, and that have prevail'd
Upon my body with their hellish charms?
HAST. The tender love I bear your grace, my lord,
Makes me most forward in this noble presence

3. *some conceit . . . likes him*] Some thought or other pleases him.

To doom the offenders, whatsoever they be:
I say, my lord, they have deserved death.
GLOU. Then be your eyes the witness of this ill:
See how I am bewitch'd; behold, mine arm
Is like a blasted sapling, withered up:
And this is Edward's wife, that monstrous witch,
Consorted with that harlot strumpet Shore,
That by their witchcraft thus have marked me.
HAST. If they have done this thing, my gracious lord,—
GLOU. If! thou protector of this damned strumpet,
Tellest thou me of "ifs"? Thou art a traitor:
Off with his head! Now, by Saint Paul I swear,
I will not dine until I see the same.
Lovel and Ratcliff, look that it be done:
The rest that love me, rise and follow me.
[*Exeunt all but* HASTINGS, RATCLIFF *and* LOVEL.]
HAST. Woe, woe for England! not a whit for me;
For I, too fond, might have prevented this.
Stanley did dream the boar did raze his helm;
But I disdain'd it, and did scorn to fly:
Three times to-day my foot-cloth horse did stumble,[4]
And startled, when he look'd upon the Tower,
As loath to bear me to the slaughter-house.
O, now I want the priest that spake to me:
I now repent I told the pursuivant,
As 'twere triumphing at mine enemies,
How they at Pomfret bloodily were butcher'd,
And I myself secure in grace and favour.
O Margaret, Margaret, now thy heavy curse
Is lighted on poor Hastings' wretched head!
RAT. Dispatch, my lord; the duke would be at dinner:
Make a short shrift;[5] he longs to see your head.
HAST. O momentary grace of mortal men,
Which we more hunt for than the grace of God!
Who builds his hopes in air of your fair looks,
Lives like a drunken sailor on a mast,
Ready, with every nod, to tumble down
Into the fatal bowels of the deep.
LOV. Come, come, dispatch; 'tis bootless to exclaim.
HAST. O bloody Richard! miserable England!
I prophesy the fearfull'st time to thee

4. *foot-cloth . . . stumble*] horse adorned with a rich cloth reaching nearly to the ground on each side. It was considered an ill omen if one's horse stumbled.
5. *shrift*] confession.

That ever wretched age hath look'd upon.
Come, lead me to the block; bear him my head:
They smile at me that shortly shall be dead. [*Exeunt.*]

SCENE V. *The Tower-Walls.*

Enter GLOUCESTER *and* BUCKINGHAM, *in rotten*[1] *armour, marvellous ill-favoured*

GLOU. Come, cousin, canst thou quake, and change thy colour,
Murder thy breath in middle of a word,
And then begin again, and stop again,
As if thou wert distraught and mad with terror?
BUCK. Tut, I can counterfeit the deep tragedian,
Speak and look back, and pry on every side,
Tremble and start at wagging of a straw,
Intending[2] deep suspicion: ghastly looks
Are at my service, like enforced smiles;
And both are ready in their offices,
At any time, to grace my stratagems.
But what, is Catesby gone?
GLOU. He is; and, see, he brings the mayor along.

Enter the Mayor *and* CATESBY

BUCK. Lord mayor,—
GLOU. Look to the drawbridge there!
BUCK. Hark! a drum.
GLOU. Catesby, o'erlook the walls.
BUCK. Lord mayor, the reason we have sent—
GLOU. Look back, defend thee, here are enemies.
BUCK. God and our innocency defend and guard us!
GLOU. Be patient, they are friends, Ratcliff and Lovel.

Enter LOVEL *and* RATCLIFF, *with* HASTINGS' *head*

LOV. Here is the head of that ignoble traitor,
The dangerous and unsuspected Hastings.
GLOU. So dear I loved the man, that I must weep.
I took him for the plainest harmless creature

1. *rotten*] rusty.
2. *Intending*] pretending.

That breathed upon this earth a Christian;
Made him my book, wherein my soul recorded
The history of all her secret thoughts:
So smooth he daub'd his vice with show of virtue
That, his apparent open guilt omitted,[3]
I mean, his conversation[4] with Shore's wife,
He lived from all attainder of suspect.[5]

BUCK. Well, well, he was the covert'st shelter'd traitor
That ever lived.
Would you imagine, or almost believe,
Were 't not that, by great preservation,
We live to tell it you, the subtle traitor
This day had plotted, in the council-house
To murder me and my good Lord of Gloucester?

MAY. What, had he so?

GLOU. What, think you we are Turks or infidels?
Or that we would, against the form of law,
Proceed thus rashly to the villain's death,
But that the extreme peril of the case,
The peace of England and our persons' safety,
Enforced us to this execution?

MAY. Now, fair befall you![6] he deserved his death;
And you, my good lords both, have well proceeded,
To warn false traitors from the like attempts.
I never look'd for better at his hands,
After he once fell in with Mistress Shore.

GLOU. Yet had not we determined he should die,
Until your lordship came to see his death;
Which now the loving haste of these our friends,
Somewhat against our meaning, have prevented:
Because, my lord, we would have had you heard
The traitor speak and timorously confess
The manner and the purpose of his treason;
That you might well have signified the same
Unto the citizens, who haply may
Misconstrue us in him and wail his death.

MAY. But, my good lord, your grace's word shall serve,
As well as I had seen and heard him speak:
And doubt you not, right noble princes both,
But I'll acquaint our duteous citizens

3. *apparent . . . omitted*] manifest . . . excepted.
4. *conversation*] criminal conversation.
5. *from all attainder of suspect*] free from all taint of suspicion.
6. *fair befall you!*] Good fortune attend you!

With all your just proceedings in this cause.
GLOU. And to that end we wish'd your lordship here,
To avoid the carping censures of the world.
BUCK. But since you come too late of our intents,[7]
Yet witness what you hear we did intend:
And so, my good lord mayor, we bid farewell. [*Exit* Mayor.]
GLOU. Go, after, after, cousin Buckingham.
The mayor towards Guildhall hies him in all post:
There, at your meet'st advantage[8] of the time,
Infer[9] the bastardy of Edward's children:
Tell them how Edward put to death a citizen,
Only for saying he would make his son
Heir to the crown, meaning indeed his house,
Which, by the sign thereof, was termed so.[10]
Moreover, urge his hateful luxury
And bestial appetite in change of lust;[11]
Which stretched to their servants, daughters, wives,
Even where his lustful eye or savage heart,
Without control, listed to make his prey.
Nay, for a need, thus far come near my person:
Tell them, when that my mother went with child
Of that unsatiate Edward, noble York,
My princely father, then had wars in France;
And, by just computation of the time,
Found that the issue was not his begot;
Which well appeared in his lineaments,
Being nothing like the noble duke my father:
But touch this sparingly, as 'twere far off;
Because you know, my lord, my mother lives.
BUCK. Fear not, my lord, I'll play the orator,
As if the golden fee for which I plead
Were for myself: and so, my lord, adieu.
GLOU. If you thrive well, bring them to Baynard's Castle;[12]

---

7. *too late of our intents*] too late for our plans or purposes.
8. *meet'st advantage*] fittest opportunity.
9. *Infer*] allege, suggest.
10. *a citizen . . . termed so*] The historian Edward Hall (c. 1498–1547) describes the execution by Edward IV's order, on the grounds given in these lines, of a citizen named Burdet, "who dwelt in Cheap Side, *at the signe of the Croune*, . . . over against Soper Lane."
11. *in change of lust*] driven by a constant desire for new mistresses.
12. *Baynard's Castle*] a palatial residence in the city of London, on the north bank of the Thames, not far from the south side of St. Paul's Cathedral. It had been recently occupied by Gloucester's father, Richard, Duke of York.

Where you shall find me well accompanied
With reverend fathers and well-learned bishops.
BUCK. I go; and towards three or four o'clock
Look for the news that the Guildhall affords. [*Exit.*]
GLOU. Go, Lovel, with all speed to Doctor Shaw;
[*To Cate.*] Go thou to Friar Penker;[13] bid them both
Meet me within this hour at Baynard's Castle.
[*Exeunt all but* GLOUCESTER.]
Now will I in, to take some privy order,
To draw the brats of Clarence out of sight;
And to give notice, that no manner of person
At any time have recourse unto the princes. [*Exit.*]

SCENE VI. *The Same. A Street.*

Enter a Scrivener, *with a paper in his hand*

SCRIV. This is the indictment of the good Lord Hastings;
Which in a set hand fairly is engross'd,
That it may be this day read o'er in Paul's.
And mark how well the sequel hangs together:
Eleven hours I spent to write it over,
For yesternight by Catesby was it brought me;
The precedent[1] was full as long a-doing:
And yet within these five hours lived Lord Hastings,
Untainted, unexamined, free, at liberty.
Here's a good world the while! Why, who's so gross,
That seeth not this palpable device?
Yet who's so blind, but says he sees it not?
Bad is the world; and all will come to nought,
When such bad dealing must be seen in thought.[2] [*Exit.*]

13. *Doctor Shaw . . . Friar Penker*] well-known preachers of the day. Doctor Shaw was brother of the Lord Mayor.

1. *precedent*] first draft.
2. *in thought*] in silence, unvoiced.

SCENE VII. *Baynard's Castle.*

Enter GLOUCESTER *and* BUCKINGHAM, *at several doors*

GLOU. How now, my lord, what say the citizens?
BUCK. Now, by the holy mother of our Lord,
The citizens are mum, and speak not a word.
GLOU. Touch'd you the bastardy of Edward's children?
BUCK. I did; with his contract with Lady Lucy,
And his contract by deputy in France;[1]
The insatiate greediness of his desires,
And his enforcement of the city wives;
His tyranny for trifles; his own bastardy,
As being got, your father then in France,
And his resemblance, being not like the duke:
Withal I did infer your lineaments,
Being the right idea of your father,
Both in your form and nobleness of mind;
Laid open all your victories in Scotland,
Your discipline in war, wisdom in peace,
Your bounty, virtue, fair humility;
Indeed left nothing fitting for the purpose
Untouch'd or slightly handled in discourse:
And when mine oratory grew to an end,
I bid them that did love their country's good
Cry "God save Richard, England's royal king!"
GLOU. Ah! and did they so?
BUCK. No, so God help me, they spake not a word;
But, like dumb statuës[2] or breathing stones,
Gazed each on other, and look'd deadly pale.
Which when I saw, I reprehended them;
And ask'd the mayor what meant this wilful silence:
His answer was, the people were not wont
To be spoke to but by the recorder.
Then he was urged to tell my tale again:
"Thus saith the duke, thus hath the duke inferr'd;"

1. *contract . . . France*] It was said that Edward was contracted to marry a woman named Elizabeth Lucy before his marriage to Lady Elizabeth Grey; a proposal that Edward IV should marry Lady Bona, the sister of King Louis XI of France, was made by the Earl of Warwick, acting as the king's deputy, but did not get beyond the stage of discussion.
2. *statuës*] This word is always a trisyllable in Shakespeare, and is often written "statuas."

But nothing spake in warrant from himself.
When he had done, some followers of mine own
At the lower end of the hall hurl'd up their caps,
And some ten voices cried "God save King Richard!"
And thus I took the vantage of those few,
"Thanks, gentle citizens and friends!" quoth I,
"This general applause and loving shout
Argues your wisdoms and your love to Richard;"
And even here brake off, and came away.

GLOU. What tongueless blocks were they! would they not speak?

BUCK. No, by my troth, my lord.

GLOU. Will not the mayor then and his brethren come?

BUCK. The mayor is here at hand: intend[3] some fear;
Be not you spoke with, but by mighty suit:
And look you get a prayer-book in your hand,
And stand betwixt two churchmen, good my lord;
For on that ground I'll build a holy descant:[4]
And be not easily won to our request;
Play the maid's part, still answer nay, and take it.

GLOU. I go; and if you plead as well for them
As I can say nay to thee for myself,
No doubt we'll bring it to a happy issue.

BUCK. Go, go up to the leads;[5] the lord mayor knocks.
[*Exit* GLOUCESTER.]

Enter the Mayor *and* Citizens

Welcome, my lord: I dance attendance here;
I think the duke will not be spoke withal.

Enter CATESBY

Here comes his servant: how now, Catesby,
What says he?

CATE. My lord, he doth entreat your grace
To visit him to-morrow or next day:
He is within, with two right reverend fathers,
Divinely bent to meditation;
And in no worldly suit would he be moved,
To draw him from his holy exercise.

BUCK. Return, good Catesby, to thy lord again;

3. *intend*] pretend.
4. *ground . . . descant*] "Ground" is the core melody to which "descant" is added as an accompaniment, usually in a higher voice.
5. *the leads*] the roof, the topmost part of the building, which was covered with sheets of lead.

Tell him, myself, the mayor and citizens,
In deep designs and matters of great moment,
No less importing than our general good,
Are come to have some conference with his grace.
CATE. I'll tell him what you say, my lord. [*Exit.*]
BUCK. Ah, ha, my lord, this prince is not an Edward!
He is not lolling on a lewd day-bed,
But on his knees at meditation;
Not dallying with a brace of courtezans,
But meditating with two deep divines;
Not sleeping, to engross[6] his idle body,
But praying, to enrich his watchful soul:
Happy were England, would this gracious prince
Take on himself the sovereignty thereof:
But, sure, I fear, we shall ne'er win him to it.
MAY. Marry, God forbid his grace should say us nay!
BUCK. I fear he will.

Re-enter CATESBY

How now, Catesby, what says your lord?
CATE. My lord,
He wonders to what end you have assembled
Such troops of citizens to speak with him,
His grace not being warn'd thereof before:
My lord, he fears you mean no good to him.
BUCK. Sorry I am my noble cousin should
Suspect me, that I mean no good to him:
By heaven, I come in perfect love to him;
And so once more return and tell his grace. [*Exit* CATESBY.]
When holy and devout religious men
Are at their beads, 'tis hard to draw them thence,
So sweet is zealous contemplation.

Enter GLOUCESTER *aloft, between two* Bishops. CATESBY *returns*

MAY. See, where he stands between two clergymen!
BUCK. Two props of virtue for a Christian prince,
To stay him from the fall of vanity:
And, see, a book of prayer in his hand,
True ornaments to know a holy man.
Famous Plantagenet, most gracious prince,
Lend favourable ears to our request;
And pardon us the interruption
Of thy devotion and right Christian zeal.

6. *engross*] make gross, fatten.

GLOU. My lord, there needs no such apology:
I rather do beseech you pardon me,
Who, earnest in the service of my God,
Neglect the visitation of my friends.
But, leaving this, what is your grace's pleasure?
BUCK. Even that, I hope, which pleaseth God above,
And all good men of this ungovern'd isle.
GLOU. I do suspect I have done some offence
That seems disgracious in the city's eyes,
And that you come to reprehend my ignorance.
BUCK. You have, my lord: would it might please your grace,
At our entreaties, to amend that fault!
GLOU. Else wherefore breathe I in a Christian land?
BUCK. Then know, it is your fault that you resign
The supreme seat, the throne majestical,
The scepter'd office of your ancestors,
Your state of fortune and your due of birth,
The lineal glory of your royal house,
To the corruption of a blemish'd stock:
Whilst, in the mildness of your sleepy thoughts,
Which here we waken to our country's good,
This noble isle doth want her proper limbs;
Her face defaced with scars of infamy,
Her royal stock graft with ignoble plants,
And almost shoulder'd in[7] the swallowing gulf
Of blind forgetfulness and dark oblivion.
Which to recure,[8] we heartily solicit
Your gracious self to take on you the charge
And kingly government of this your land;
Not as protector, steward, substitute,
Or lowly factor for another's gain;
But as successively,[9] from blood to blood,
Your right of birth, your empery,[10] your own.
For this, consorted with the citizens,
Your very worshipful and loving friends,
And by their vehement instigation,
In this just suit come I to move your grace.
GLOU. I know not whether to depart in silence,
Or bitterly to speak in your reproof,
Best fitteth my degree or your condition:

7. *shoulder'd in*] jostled into.
8. *recure*] cure.
9. *successively*] in due succession.
10. *empery*] dominion.

If not to answer, you might haply think
Tongue-tied ambition, not replying, yielded
To bear the golden yoke of sovereignty,
Which fondly you would here impose on me;
If to reprove you for this suit of yours
So season'd with your faithful love to me,
Then, on the other side, I check'd my friends.
Therefore, to speak, and to avoid the first,
And then, in speaking, not to incur the last,
Definitively thus I answer you.
Your love deserves my thanks, but my desert
Unmeritable shuns your high request.
First, if all obstacles were cut away
And that my path were even to the crown,
As my right revenue and due by birth;
Yet so much is my poverty of spirit,
So mighty and so many my defects,
As I had rather hide me from my greatness,
Being a bark[11] to brook no mighty sea,
Than in my greatness covet to be hid,
And in the vapour of my glory smother'd.
But, God be thanked, there's no need of me,
And much I need to help you,[12] if need were;
The royal tree hath left us royal fruit,
Which, mellow'd by the stealing hours of time,
Will well become the seat of majesty,
And make, no doubt, us happy by his reign.
On him I lay what you would lay on me,
The right and fortune of his happy stars;
Which God defend that I should wring from him!

BUCK. My lord, this argues conscience in your grace;
But the respects thereof are nice[13] and trivial,
All circumstances well considered.
You say that Edward is your brother's son:
So say we too, but not by Edward's wife;
For first he was contract[14] to Lady Lucy—
Your mother lives a witness to that vow—
And afterward by substitute betroth'd
To Bona, sister to the King of France.
These both put by, a poor petitioner,

11. *bark*] a boat propelled by oars or sails.
12. *need*] lack (the capacity to help you).
13. *nice*] punctilious, fanciful.
14. *contract*] betrothed.

A care-crazed mother of a many children,
A beauty-waning and distressed widow,
Even in the afternoon of her best days,
Made prize and purchase of his lustful eye,
Seduced the pitch[15] and height of all his thoughts
To base declension and loathed bigamy:[16]
By her, in his unlawful bed, he got[17]
This Edward, whom our manners term the prince.
More bitterly could I expostulate,
Save that, for reverence to some alive,
I give a sparing limit to my tongue.
Then, good my lord, take to your royal self
This proffer'd benefit of dignity;
If not to bless us and the land withal,
Yet to draw forth your noble ancestry
From the corruption of abusing times,
Unto a lineal true-derived course.

MAY. Do, good my lord, your citizens entreat you.

BUCK. Refuse not, mighty lord, this proffer'd love.

CATE. O, make them joyful, grant their lawful suit!

GLOU. Alas, why would you heap these cares on me?
I am unfit for state and majesty:
I do beseech you, take it not amiss;
I cannot nor I will not yield to you.

BUCK. If you refuse it,—as, in love and zeal,
Loath to depose the child, your brother's son;
As well we know your tenderness of heart
And gentle, kind, effeminate remorse,[18]
Which we have noted in you to your kin,
And egally[19] indeed to all estates,—
Yet whether you accept our suit or no,
Your brother's son shall never reign our king;
But we will plant some other in the throne,
To the disgrace and downfall of your house:
And in this resolution here we leave you.
Come, citizens: 'zounds![20] I'll entreat no more.

---

15. *pitch*] a common term in falconry for the hawk's highest flight.
16. *bigamy*] According to canon law in Edward IV's time, marriage with a widow constituted bigamy.
17. *got*] begot, sired.
18. *remorse*] sense of pity.
19. *egally*] equally.
20. *'zounds!*] an oath contracted from "God's wounds!", a reference to the wounds Christ received at his trial and on the Cross.

GLOU. O, do not swear, my lord of Buckingham.
[*Exit* BUCKINGHAM *with the* Citizens.]
CATE. Call them again, my lord, and accept their suit:
ANOTHER. Do, good my lord, lest all the land do rue it.
GLOU. Would you enforce me to a world of care?
Well, call them again. I am not made of stones,
But penetrable to your kind entreats,
Albeit against my conscience and my soul.

Re-enter BUCKINGHAM *and the rest*

Cousin of Buckingham, and you sage, grave men,
Since you will buckle fortune on my back,
To bear her burthen, whether I will or no,
I must have patience to endure the load:
But if black scandal or foul-faced reproach
Attend the sequel of your imposition,
Your mere enforcement shall acquittance[21] me
From all the impure blots and stains thereof;
For God he knows, and you may partly see,
How far I am from the desire thereof.
MAY. God bless your grace! we see it, and will say it.
GLOU. In saying so, you shall but say the truth.
BUCK. Then I salute you with this kingly title:
Long live Richard, England's royal king!
MAY. AND CIT. Amen.
BUCK. To-morrow will it please you to be crown'd?
GLOU. Even when you please, since you will have it so.
BUCK. To-morrow then we will attend your grace:
And so most joyfully we take our leave.
GLOU. Come, let us to our holy task again.
Farewell, good cousin; farewell, gentle friends. [*Exeunt.*]

21. *acquittance*] acquit.

ACT IV.

SCENE I. *Before the Tower.*

Enter, on one side, QUEEN ELIZABETH, DUCHESS OF YORK, *and* MARQUESS OF DORSET; *on the other,* ANNE, DUCHESS OF GLOUCESTER, *leading* LADY MARGARET PLANTAGENET, CLARENCE'S *young daughter*

DUCH. Who meets us here? my niece[1] Plantagenet
Led in the hand of her kind aunt Gloucester?[2]
Now, for my life, she's wandering to the Tower,
On pure heart's love to greet the tender princes.
Daughter, well met.
ANNE. God give your graces both
A happy and a joyful time of day!
Q. ELIZ. As much to you, good sister! Whither away?
ANNE. No farther than the Tower, and, as I guess,
Upon the like devotion as yourselves,
To gratulate the gentle princes there.
Q. ELIZ. Kind sister, thanks: we'll enter all together.

Enter BRAKENBURY

And, in good time, here the lieutenant comes.
Master lieutenant, pray you, by your leave,
How doth the prince, and my young son of York?
BRAK. Right well, dear madam. By your patience,
I may not suffer you to visit them;
The king hath straitly charged the contrary.
Q. ELIZ. The king! why, who's that?
BRAK. I cry you mercy: I mean the lord protector.
Q. ELIZ. The Lord protect him from that kingly title!
Hath he set bounds betwixt their love and me?
I am their mother; who should keep me from them?
DUCH. I am their father's mother; I will see them.
ANNE. Their aunt I am in law,[3] in love their mother:

---

1. *niece*] granddaughter.
2. *aunt Gloucester*] Anne, widow, or rather affianced bride, of Prince Edward, Henry VI's son and heir, was solicited in marriage by Gloucester while acting as chief mourner at Henry VI's funeral and is now married to him. Lady Margaret Plantagenet, whom she holds by the hand, was daughter of her sister, the late Duchess of Clarence.
3. *in law*] by marriage.

Then bring me to their sights; I'll bear thy blame,
And take thy office from thee, on my peril.
BRAK. No, madam, no; I may not leave it[4] so:
I am bound by oath, and therefore pardon me. [*Exit.*]

Enter LORD STANLEY

STAN. Let me but meet you, ladies, one hour hence,
And I'll salute your grace of York as mother,
And reverend looker on, of two fair queens.
[*To Anne.*] Come, madam, you must straight to Westminster,
There to be crowned Richard's royal queen.
Q. ELIZ. O, cut my lace in sunder, that my pent heart
May have some scope to beat, or else I swoon
With this dead-killing news!
ANNE. Despiteful tidings! O unpleasing news!
DOR. Be of good cheer: mother, how fares your grace?
Q. ELIZ. O Dorset, speak not to me, get thee hence!
Death and destruction dog thee at the heels;
Thy mother's name is ominous to children.
If thou wilt outstrip death, go cross the seas,
And live with Richmond,[5] from the reach of hell:
Go, hie thee, hie thee from this slaughter-house,
Lest thou increase the number of the dead;
And make me die the thrall of Margaret's curse,
Nor mother, wife, nor England's counted queen.
STAN. Full of wise care is this your counsel, madam.
Take all the swift advantage of the hours;
You shall have letters from me to my son
To meet you on the way, and welcome you.
Be not ta'en tardy by unwise delay.
DUCH. O ill-dispersing wind of misery!
O my accursed womb, the bed of death!
A cockatrice[6] hast thou hatch'd to the world,
Whose unavoided eye is murderous.
STAN. Come, madam, come; I in all haste was sent.
ANNE. And I in all unwillingness will go.
I would to God that the inclusive verge
Of golden metal that must round my brow

---

4. *leave it*] part from my office, infringe my duty.
5. *cross . . . Richmond*] Henry Tudor, Earl of Richmond (later Henry VII) and head of the House of Lancaster after Henry VI's death, was in Brittany at the time.
6. *cockatrice*] a fabulous serpent, also known as the basilisk, whose glance was deadly.

Were red-hot steel,[7] to sear me to the brain!
Anointed let me be with deadly venom,
And die, ere men can say, God save the queen!

Q. ELIZ. Go, go, poor soul, I envy not thy glory;
To feed my humour, wish thyself no harm.

ANNE. No! why? When he that is my husband now
Came to me, as I follow'd Henry's corse,
When scarce the blood was well wash'd from his hands
Which issued from my other angel husband,
And that dead saint which then I weeping follow'd;
O, when, I say, I look'd on Richard's face,
This was my wish: "Be thou," quoth I, "accursed,
For making me, so young, so old a widow!
And, when thou wed'st, let sorrow haunt thy bed;
And be thy wife — if any be so mad —
As miserable by the death of thee
As thou hast made me by my dear lord's death!"
Lo, ere I can repeat this curse again,
Even in so short a space, my woman's heart
Grossly grew captive to his honey words,
And proved the subject of my own soul's curse,
Which ever since hath kept my eyes from rest;
For never yet one hour in his bed
Have I enjoy'd the golden dew of sleep,
But have been waked by his timorous dreams.
Besides, he hates me for my father Warwick;
And will, no doubt, shortly be rid of me.

Q. ELIZ. Poor heart, adieu! I pity thy complaining.

ANNE. No more than from my soul I mourn for yours.

DOR. Farewell, thou woful welcomer of glory!

ANNE. Adieu, poor soul, that takest thy leave of it!

DUCH. [*To* DORSET] Go thou to Richmond, and good fortune guide thee!
[*To* ANNE] Go thou to Richard, and good angels guard thee!
[*To* QUEEN ELIZ.] Go thou to sanctuary, and good thoughts possess thee!
I to my grave, where peace and rest lie with me!
Eighty odd years of sorrow have I seen,
And each hour's joy wreck'd with a week of teen.[8]

Q. ELIZ. Stay, yet look back with me unto the Tower.

---

7. *red-hot steel*] Regicides or conspirators against the lives of kings were often punished in the middle ages by setting on their brows a crown of iron heated red-hot.

8. *teen*] grief.

Pity, you ancient stones, those tender babes
Whom envy hath immured within your walls!
Rough cradle for such little pretty ones!
Rude ragged nurse, old sullen playfellow
For tender princes, use my babies well!
So foolish sorrow bids your stones farewell. [*Exeunt.*]

SCENE II. *London. The Palace.*

Sennet. Enter RICHARD, *in pomp, crowned;* BUCKINGHAM, CATESBY, *a* Page, *and others*

K. RICH. Stand all apart. Cousin of Buckingham!
BUCK. My gracious sovereign?
K. RICH. Give me thy hand. [*Here he ascendeth the throne.*] Thus high, by thy advice
And thy assistance, is king Richard seated:
But shall we wear these honours for a day?
Or shall they last, and we rejoice in them?
BUCK. Still live they, and for ever may they last!
K. RICH. O Buckingham, now do I play the touch,[1]
To try if thou be current gold indeed:
Young Edward lives: think now what I would say.
BUCK. Say on, my loving lord.
K. RICH. Why, Buckingham, I say, I would be king.
BUCK. Why, so you are, my thrice renowned liege.
K. RICH. Ha! am I king? 'tis so: but Edward lives.
BUCK. True, noble prince.
K. RICH. O bitter consequence,
That Edward still should live true noble prince!
Cousin, thou wert not wont to be so dull:
Shall I be plain? I wish the bastards dead;
And I would have it suddenly perform'd.
What sayest thou? speak suddenly; be brief.
BUCK. Your grace may do your pleasure.
K. RICH. Tut, tut, thou art all ice, thy kindness freezeth:
Say, have I thy consent that they shall die?
BUCK. Give me some breath, some little pause, my lord,
Before I positively speak herein:

1. *play the touch*] make play with the touchstone, or true test (of metals).

I will resolve[2] your grace immediately. [*Exit.*]
CATE. [*Aside to a stander by*] The king is angry: see, he bites the lip.
K. RICH. I will converse with iron-witted[3] fools
And unrespective[4] boys: none are for me
That look into me with considerate eyes:
High-reaching Buckingham grows circumspect.
Boy!
PAGE. My lord?
K. RICH. Know'st thou not any whom corrupting gold
Would tempt unto a close exploit of death?
PAGE. My lord, I know a discontented gentleman,
Whose humble means match not his haughty mind:
Gold were as good as twenty orators,
And will, no doubt, tempt him to any thing.
K. RICH. What is his name?
PAGE. His name, my lord, is Tyrrel.
K. RICH. I partly know the man: go, call him hither. [*Exit* Page.]
The deep-revolving witty[5] Buckingham
No more shall be the neighbour to my counsel:
Hath he so long held out with me untired,
And stops he now for breath?

Enter STANLEY

How now! what news with you?
STAN. My lord, I hear the Marquis Dorset's fled
To Richmond, in those parts beyond the seas
Where he abides. [*Stands apart.*]
K. RICH. Catesby!
CATE. My lord?
K. RICH. Rumour it abroad
That Anne, my wife, is sick and like to die:
I will take order[6] for her keeping close.
Inquire me out some mean-born gentleman,
Whom I will marry straight to Clarence' daughter:
The boy is foolish, and I fear not him.
Look, how thou dream'st! I say again, give out
That Anne my wife is sick, and like to die:
About it; for it stands me much upon,[7]

---

2. *resolve*] definitely answer, satisfy.
3. *iron-witted*] dull-witted, wooden-headed.
4. *unrespective*] careless, thoughtless.
5. *witty*] knowing, clever.
6. *take order*] take measures, arrange.
7. *it stands me much upon*] It is a matter of importance for me.

To stop all hopes whose growth may damage me.
[*Exit* CATESBY.]
I must be married to my brother's daughter,[8]
Or else my kingdom stands on brittle glass.
Murder her brothers, and then marry her!
Uncertain way of gain! But I am in
So far in blood that sin will pluck on[9] sin:
Tear-falling pity dwells not in this eye.

Re-enter Page, *with* TYRREL

Is thy name Tyrrel?
TYR. James Tyrrel, and your most obedient subject.
K. RICH. Art thou, indeed?
TYR. Prove me, my gracious sovereign.
K. RICH. Darest thou resolve to kill a friend of mine?
TYR. Ay, my lord;
But I had rather kill two enemies.
K. RICH. Why, there thou hast it: two deep enemies,
Foes to my rest and my sweet sleep's disturbers
Are they that I would have thee deal upon:[10]
Tyrrel, I mean those bastards in the Tower.
TYR. Let me have open means to come to them,
And soon I'll rid you from the fear of them.
K. RICH. Thou sing'st sweet music. Hark, come hither, Tyrrel:
Go, by this token: rise, and lend thine ear: [*Whispers.*]
There is no more but so: say it is done,
And I will love thee, and prefer thee too.
TYR. 'Tis done, my gracious lord.
K. RICH. Shall we hear from thee, Tyrrel, ere we sleep?
TYR. Ye shall, my lord. [*Exit.*]

Re-enter BUCKINGHAM

BUCK. My lord, I have consider'd in my mind
The late demand that you did sound me in.
K. RICH. Well, let that pass. Dorset is fled to Richmond.
BUCK. I hear that news, my lord.
K. RICH. Stanley, he is your wife's son:[11] well, look to it.
BUCK. My lord, I claim your gift, my due by promise,
For which your honour and your faith is pawn'd;

---

8. *my brother's daughter*] Edward IV's eldest daughter Elizabeth, who happily escaped marriage with her uncle and became the wife of his successor Henry VII.
9. *pluck on*] excite, cause.
10. *deal upon*] deal with.
11. *Stanley . . . son*] Stanley was married to Margaret Beaufort, the widow of Edmund Tudor, Richmond's father.

The earldom of Hereford and the moveables
The which you promised I should possess.
K. RICH. Stanley, look to your wife: if she convey
Letters to Richmond, you shall answer it.
BUCK. What says your highness to my just demand?
K. RICH. As I remember, Henry the Sixth
Did prophesy that Richmond should be king,
When Richmond was a little peevish boy.
A king, perhaps, perhaps, —
BUCK. My lord!
K. RICH. How chance the prophet could not at that time
Have told me, I being by, that I should kill him?
BUCK. My lord, your promise for the earldom, —
K. RICH. Richmond! When last I was at Exeter,
The mayor in courtesy show'd me the castle,
And call'd it Rougemont: at which name I started,
Because a bard of Ireland told me once,
I should not live long after I saw Richmond.
BUCK. My lord!
K. RICH. Ay, what's o'clock?
BUCK. I am thus bold to put your grace in mind
Of what you promised me.
K. RICH. Well, but what's o'clock?
BUCK. Upon the stroke of ten.
K. RICH. Well, let it strike.
BUCK. Why let it strike?
K. RICH. Because that, like a Jack,[12] thou keep'st the stroke
Betwixt thy begging and my meditation.
I am not in the giving vein to-day.
BUCK. Why, then resolve me whether you will or no.
K. RICH. Tut, tut,
Thou troublest me; I am not in the vein.
[*Exeunt all but* BUCKINGHAM.]
BUCK. Is it even so? rewards he my true service
With such deep contempt? made I him king for this?
O, let me think on Hastings, and be gone
To Brecknock,[13] while my fearful[14] head is on! [*Exit.*]

12. *a Jack*] a small mechanical figure that struck the hour on the bell of a clock.
13. *Brecknock*] Brecknock Castle, in South Wales, was one of the Duke of Buckingham's residences.
14. *fearful*] full of fear.

SCENE III. *The Same.*

Enter TYRREL

TYR. The tyrannous and bloody deed is done,
The most arch[1] act of piteous massacre
That ever yet this land was guilty of.
Dighton and Forrest, whom I did suborn
To do this ruthless piece of butchery,
Although they were flesh'd[2] villains, bloody dogs,
Melting with tenderness and kind compassion
Wept like two children in their deaths' sad stories.
"Lo, thus," quoth Dighton, "lay those tender babes:"
"Thus, thus," quoth Forrest, "girdling one another
Within their innocent alabaster arms:
Their lips were four red roses on a stalk,
Which in their summer beauty kiss'd each other.
A book of prayers on their pillow lay;
Which once," quoth Forrest, "almost changed my mind;
But O! the devil"—there the villain stopp'd;
Whilst Dighton thus told on: "We smothered
The most replenished[3] sweet work of nature
That from the prime creation e'er she framed."
Thus both are gone with conscience and remorse;
They could not speak; and so I left them both,
To bring this tidings to the bloody king.
And here he comes.

Enter KING RICHARD

All hail, my sovereign liege!
K. RICH. Kind Tyrrel, am I happy in thy news?
TYR. If to have done the thing you gave in charge
Beget your happiness, be happy then,
For it is done, my lord.
K. RICH. But didst thou see them dead?
TYR. I did, my lord.
K. RICH. And buried, gentle Tyrrel?

1. *arch*] consummate, notable.
2. *flesh'd*] inured to bloodshed.
3. *replenished*] complete, perfect.

TYR. The chaplain of the Tower hath buried them;
But how or in what place I do not know.
K. RICH. Come to me, Tyrrel, soon at after supper,[4]
And thou shalt tell the process of their death.
Meantime, but think how I may do thee good,
And be inheritor of thy desire.
Farewell till soon. [*Exit* TYRREL.]
The son of Clarence have I pent up close;
His daughter meanly have I match'd in marriage;[5]
The sons of Edward sleep in Abraham's bosom,
And Anne my wife hath bid the world good night.
Now, for I know the Breton Richmond aims
At young Elizabeth, my brother's daughter,
And, by that knot, looks proudly o'er the crown,
To her I go, a jolly thriving wooer.

Enter CATESBY

CATE. My lord!
K. RICH. Good news or bad, that thou comest in so bluntly?
CATE. Bad news, my lord: Ely[6] is fled to Richmond;
And Buckingham, back'd with the hardy Welshmen,
Is in the field, and still his power increaseth.
K. RICH. Ely with Richmond troubles me more near
Than Buckingham and his rash-levied army.
Come, I have heard that fearful commenting
Is leaden servitor to dull delay;
Delay leads impotent and snail-paced beggary:[7]
Then fiery expedition[8] be my wing,
Jove's Mercury,[9] and herald for a king!
Come, muster men: my counsel is my shield;
We must be brief when traitors brave the field.[10] [*Exeunt.*]

4. *soon at after supper*] about the time when supper is over.
5. *His . . . marriage*] Clarence's daughter Margaret was married to Sir Richard Pole, who was of somewhat better birth than the text indicates. Contrary to the statement of the text, the union took place about 1491, some years after Richard's death, by direction of Henry VII.
6. *Ely*] John Morton, Bishop of Ely, afterwards Archbishop of Canterbury, by the appointment of Henry VII.
7. *fearful . . . beggary*] timorous reflection serves the slow purpose of sluggish procrastination; procrastination superinduces feeble and creeping beggary.
8. *fiery expedition*] rapidity of fire or lightning.
9. *Mercury*] the swift messenger of Jove.
10. *brave the field*] vauntingly challenge (us) to the battlefield.

SCENE IV. *Before the Palace.*

Enter QUEEN MARGARET

Q. MAR. So, now prosperity begins to mellow
And drop into the rotten mouth of death.
Here in these confines slily have I lurk'd,
To watch the waning of mine adversaries.
A dire induction[1] am I witness to,
And will to France, hoping the consequence
Will prove as bitter, black, and tragical.
Withdraw thee, wretched Margaret: who comes here?

Enter QUEEN ELIZABETH *and the* DUCHESS OF YORK

Q. ELIZ. Ah, my young princes! ah, my tender babes!
My unblown flowers, new-appearing sweets!
If yet your gentle souls fly in the air,
And be not fix'd in doom perpetual,
Hover about me with your airy wings,
And hear your mother's lamentation!
Q. MAR. Hover about her; say, that right for right
Hath dimm'd your infant morn to aged night.[2]
DUCH. So many miseries have crazed my voice,
That my woe-wearied tongue is mute and dumb.
Edward Plantagenet, why art thou dead?
Q. MAR. Plantagenet doth quit[3] Plantagenet,
Edward for Edward pays a dying debt.
Q. ELIZ. Wilt thou, O God, fly from such gentle lambs,
And throw them in the entrails of the wolf?
When didst thou sleep when such a deed was done?
Q. MAR. When holy Harry died, and my sweet son.
DUCH. Blind sight, dead life, poor mortal living ghost,
Woe's scene, world's shame, grave's due by life usurp'd,
Brief abstract and record of tedious days,

---

1. *induction*] preparation, prelude.
2. *right for right . . . night*] Supreme right, justice answering the claims of justice, has dimmed or blotted out the bright dawn of your infant's life and put in its place the darkness of death, which commonly awaits old age. The losses which Queen Margaret has suffered cause her to regard Queen Elizabeth's bereavement as just retribution for the removal of her own kindred.
3. *quit*] requite.

Rest thy unrest on England's lawful earth, [*Sitting down.*]
Unlawfully made drunk with innocents' blood!
Q. ELIZ. O, that thou wouldst as well afford a grave
As thou canst yield a melancholy seat!
Then would I hide my bones, not rest them here.
O, who hath any cause to mourn but I? [*Sitting down by her.*]
Q. MAR. If ancient sorrow[4] be most reverend,
Give mine the benefit of seniory,[5]
And let my woes frown on the upper hand.
If sorrow can admit society, [*Sitting down with them.*]
Tell o'er your woes again by viewing mine:
I had an Edward, till a Richard kill'd him;
I had a Harry, till a Richard kill'd him:
Thou hadst an Edward, till a Richard kill'd him;
Thou hadst a Richard, till a Richard kill'd him.
DUCH. I had a Richard too, and thou didst kill him;
I had a Rutland too, thou holp'st to kill him.
Q. MAR. Thou hadst a Clarence too, and Richard kill'd him.
From forth the kennel of thy womb hath crept
A hell-hound that doth hunt us all to death:
That dog, that had his teeth[6] before his eyes,
To worry lambs and lap their gentle blood,
That foul defacer of God's handiwork,
That excellent grand tyrant of the earth,
That reigns in galled eyes of weeping souls,
Thy womb let loose, to chase us to our graves.
O upright, just, and true-disposing God,
How do I thank thee, that this carnal[7] cur
Preys on the issue of his mother's body,
And makes her pew-fellow[8] with others' moan!
DUCH. O Harry's wife, triumph not in my woes!
God witness with me, I have wept for thine.
Q. MAR. Bear with me; I am hungry for revenge,
And now I cloy me with beholding it.
Thy Edward he is dead, that stabb'd my Edward;
Thy other Edward dead, to quit my Edward;
Young York he is but boot,[9] because both they

4. *ancient sorrow*] sorrow of age.
5. *seniory*] seniority.
6. *dog . . . teeth*] Richard was reported to have been born with teeth.
7. *carnal*] flesh-consuming, cannibal.
8. *pew-fellow*] companion, comrade, partner.
9. *boot*] a mere trifle (an extra bit of merchandise thrown in by a vendor to entice potential buyers).

Match not the high perfection of my loss:
Thy Clarence he is dead that kill'd my Edward;
And the beholders of this tragic play,
The adulterate[10] Hastings, Rivers, Vaughan, Grey,
Untimely smother'd in their dusky graves.
Richard yet lives, hell's black intelligencer,[11]
Only reserved their[12] factor,[13] to buy souls
And send them thither: but at hand, at hand,
Ensues his piteous and unpitied end:
Earth gapes, hell burns, fiends roar, saints pray,
To have him suddenly convey'd away.
Cancel his bond of life, dear God, I pray,
That I may live to say, The dog is dead!

Q. ELIZ. O, thou didst prophesy the time would come
That I should wish for thee to help me curse
That bottled spider, that foul bunch-back'd toad!

Q. MAR. I call'd thee then vain flourish of my fortune;
I call'd thee then poor shadow, painted queen;
The presentation of but what I was;
The flattering index[14] of a direful pageant;
One heaved a-high, to be hurl'd down below;
A mother only mock'd with two sweet babes;
A dream of what thou wert, a breath, a bubble,
A sign of dignity, a garish flag
To be the aim of every dangerous shot;
A queen in jest, only to fill the scene.
Where is thy husband now? where be thy brothers?
Where are thy children? wherein dost thou joy?
Who sues to thee, and cries "God save the queen"?
Where be the bending peers that flattered thee?
Where be the thronging troops that followed thee?
Decline all this,[15] and see what now thou art:
For happy wife, a most distressed widow;
For joyful mother, one that wails the name;
For queen, a very caitiff[16] crown'd with care;
For one being sued to, one that humbly sues;
For one that scorn'd at me, now scorn'd of me;

---

10. *adulterate*] adulterous.
11. *intelligencer*] agent, emissary, informer.
12. *their*] i.e., hell's (treated as a plural because it signifies a community of evil spirits).
13. *factor*] agent (of hell).
14. *index*] prelude.
15. *Decline all this*] Go through all this (as through the declension of a verb or noun in a grammar book).
16. *caitiff*] wretch, slave.

For one being fear'd of all, now fearing one;
For one commanding all, obey'd of none.
Thus hath the course of justice wheel'd about,
And left thee but a very prey to time;
Having no more but thought of what thou wert,
To torture thee the more, being what thou art.
Thou didst usurp my place, and dost thou not
Usurp the just proportion of my sorrow?
Now thy proud neck bears half my burthen'd yoke;
From which even here I slip my weary neck,
And leave the burthen of it all on thee.
Farewell, York's wife, and queen of sad mischance:
These English woes will make me smile in France.

Q. ELIZ. O thou well skill'd in curses, stay awhile,
And teach me how to curse mine enemies!

Q. MAR. Forbear to sleep the nights, and fast the days;
Compare dead happiness with living woe;
Think that thy babes were fairer than they were,
And he that slew them fouler than he is:
Bettering thy loss[17] makes the bad causer worse:
Revolving this will teach thee how to curse.

Q. ELIZ. My words are dull; O, quicken them with thine!

Q. MAR. Thy woes will make them sharp and pierce like mine. [*Exit.*]

DUCH. Why should calamity be full of words?

Q. ELIZ. Windy attorneys to their client woes,
Airy succeeders of intestate joys,[18]
Poor breathing orators of miseries!
Let them have scope: though what they do impart
Help not at all, yet do they ease the heart.

DUCH. If so, then be not tongue-tied: go with me,
And in the breath of bitter words let's smother
My damned son, which thy two sweet sons smother'd.
I hear his drum: be copious in exclaims.

Enter KING RICHARD, *marching, with drums and trumpets*

K. RICH. Who intercepts my expedition?

DUCH. O, she that might have intercepted thee,
By strangling thee in her accursed womb,
From all the slaughters, wretch, that thou hast done!

Q. ELIZ. Hidest thou that forehead with a golden crown,

17. *Bettering thy loss*] exaggeration of thy loss.
18. *Airy succeeders of intestate joys*] breath-born heirs or inheritors of poor joys, which (with nothing to bequeath) have made no will.

Where should be graven, if that right were right,
The slaughter of the prince that owed[19] that crown,
And the dire death of my two sons and brothers?
Tell me, thou villain slave, where are my children?

DUCH. Thou toad, thou toad, where is thy brother Clarence?
And little Ned Plantagenet, his son?

Q. ELIZ. Where is kind Hastings, Rivers, Vaughan, Grey?

K. RICH. A flourish, trumpets! strike alarum, drums!
Let not the heavens hear these tell-tale women
Rail on the Lord's anointed: strike, I say! [*Flourish. Alarums.*]
Either be patient, and entreat[20] me fair,
Or with the clamorous report of war
Thus will I drown your exclamations.

DUCH. Art thou my son?

K. RICH. Ay, I thank God, my father, and yourself.

DUCH. Then patiently hear my impatience.

K. RICH. Madam, I have a touch of your condition,[21]
Which cannot brook the accent of reproof.

DUCH. O, let me speak!

K. RICH. Do then; but I'll not hear.

DUCH. I will be mild and gentle in my speech.

K. RICH. And brief, good mother; for I am in haste.

DUCH. Art thou so hasty? I have stay'd for thee,
God knows, in anguish, pain and agony.

K. RICH. And came I not at last to comfort you?

DUCH. No, by the holy rood, thou know'st it well,
Thou camest on earth to make the earth my hell.
A grievous burthen was thy birth to me;
Tetchy[22] and wayward was thy infancy;
Thy school-days frightful,[23] desperate, wild, and furious,
Thy prime of manhood daring, bold, and venturous,
Thy age confirm'd,[24] proud, subtle, bloody, treacherous;
More mild, but yet more harmful, kind in hatred:
What comfortable hour canst thou name,
That ever graced me in thy company?

K. RICH. Faith, none, but Humphrey Hour, that call'd your grace

19. *owed*] owned.
20. *entreat*] treat, use.
21. *a touch of your condition*] a dash of your temperament.
22. *Tetchy*] fretful, peevish.
23. *frightful*] causing fright.
24. *Thy age confirm'd*] thy ripened age.

To breakfast once forth of[25] my company.[26]
If I be so disgracious in your sight,
Let me march on, and not offend your grace.
Strike up the drum.

DUCH. I prithee, hear me speak.

K. RICH. You speak too bitterly.

DUCH. Hear me a word;
For I shall never speak to thee again.

K. RICH. So.

DUCH. Either thou wilt die, by God's just ordinance,
Ere from this war thou turn a conqueror,
Or I with grief and extreme age shall perish
And never look upon thy face again.
Therefore take with thee my most heavy curse;
Which, in the day of battle, tire thee more
Than all the complete armour that thou wear'st!
My prayers on the adverse party fight;
And there the little souls of Edward's children
Whisper the spirits of thine enemies,
And promise them success and victory.
Bloody thou art, bloody will be thy end;
Shame serves thy life and doth thy death attend. [*Exit.*]

Q. ELIZ. Though far more cause, yet much less spirit to curse
Abides in me; I say amen to all.

K. RICH. Stay, madam; I must speak a word with you.

Q. ELIZ. I have no moe sons of the royal blood
For thee to murder: for my daughters, Richard,
They shall be praying nuns, not weeping queens;
And therefore level not to hit their lives.

K. RICH. You have a daughter call'd Elizabeth,
Virtuous and fair, royal and gracious.

Q. ELIZ. And must she die for this? O, let her live,
And I'll corrupt her manners, stain her beauty;
Slander myself as false to Edward's bed;
Throw over her the veil of infamy:
So she may live unscarr'd of bleeding slaughter,
I will confess she was not Edward's daughter.

---

25. *forth of*] away from.
26. *Humphrey Hour . . . company*] The reference is probably to the hour when the Duchess gave birth to Richard, and to the first meal which she took after her delivery. According to homely wit, after delivery the mother traditionally breakfasted apart from the child whom she had hitherto fed in her womb along with herself. "To dine with the Duke of Humphrey," meant to go hungry, to go without one's dinner.

K. RICH. Wrong not her birth, she is of royal blood.
Q. ELIZ. To save her life, I'll say she is not so.
K. RICH. Her life is only safest in her birth.
Q. ELIZ. And only in that safety died her brothers.
K. RICH. Lo, at their births good stars were opposite.[27]
Q. ELIZ. No, to their lives bad friends were contrary.
K. RICH. All unavoided[28] is the doom of destiny.
Q. ELIZ. True, when avoided grace makes destiny:
My babes were destined to a fairer death,
If grace had bless'd thee with a fairer life.
K. RICH. You speak as if that I had slain my cousins.
Q. ELIZ. Cousins, indeed; and by their uncle cozen'd
Of comfort, kingdom, kindred, freedom, life.
Whose hand soever lanced their tender hearts,
Thy head, all indirectly,[29] gave direction:
No doubt the murderous knife was dull and blunt,
Till it was whetted on thy stone-hard heart,
To revel in the entrails of my lambs.
But that still use[30] of grief makes wild grief tame,
My tongue should to thy ears not name my boys,
Till that my nails were anchor'd in thine eyes;
And I, in such a desperate bay of death,
Like a poor bark, of sails and tackling reft,
Rush all to pieces on thy rocky bosom.
K. RICH. Madam, so thrive I in my enterprise,
And dangerous success of bloody wars,
As I intend more good to you and yours,
Than ever you or yours were by me wrong'd!
Q. ELIZ. What good is cover'd with the face of heaven,
To be discover'd, that can do me good?
K. RICH. The advancement of your children, gentle lady.
Q. ELIZ. Up to some scaffold, there to lose their heads?
K. RICH. No, to the dignity and height of honour,
The high imperial type[31] of this earth's glory.
Q. ELIZ. Flatter my sorrows with report of it;
Tell me what state, what dignity, what honour,
Canst thou demise to any child of mine?
K. RICH. Even all I have; yea, and myself and all,

27. *opposite*] hostile, in opposition; an astrological term.
28. *unavoided*] unavoidable.
29. *indirectly*] wickedly, disingenuously.
30. *still use*] continual habit.
31. *type*] symbol, emblem, crown.

Will I withal endow a child of thine;
So in the Lethe[32] of thy angry soul
Thou drown the sad remembrance of those wrongs,
Which thou supposest I have done to thee.
Q. ELIZ. Be brief, lest that the process of thy kindness
Last longer telling than thy kindness' date.
K. RICH. Then know, that from my soul I love thy daughter.
Q. ELIZ. My daughter's mother thinks it with her soul.
K. RICH. What do you think?
Q. ELIZ. That thou dost love my daughter from[33] thy soul:
So from thy soul's love didst thou love her brothers;
And from my heart's love I do thank thee for it.
K. RICH. Be not so hasty to confound my meaning:
I mean, that with my soul I love thy daughter,
And mean to make her queen of England.
Q. ELIZ. Say then, who dost thou mean shall be her king?
K. RICH. Even he that makes her queen: who should be else?
Q. ELIZ. What, thou?
K. RICH. I, even I: what think you of it, madam?
Q. ELIZ. How canst thou woo her?
K. RICH. That would I learn of you,
As one that are best acquainted with her humour.
Q. ELIZ. And wilt thou learn of me?
K. RICH. Madam, with all my heart.
Q. ELIZ. Send to her, by the man that slew her brothers,
A pair of bleeding hearts; thereon engrave
Edward and York; then haply she will weep:
Therefore present to her,—as sometime Margaret
Did to thy father, steep'd in Rutland's blood,—
A handkerchief; which, say to her, did drain
The purple sap from her sweet brother's body,
And bid her dry her weeping eyes therewith.
If this inducement force her not to love,
Send her a story of thy noble acts;
Tell her thou madest away her uncle Clarence,
Her uncle Rivers; yea, and, for her sake,
Madest quick conveyance with her good aunt Anne.
K. RICH. Come, come, you mock me; this is not the way
To win your daughter.
Q. ELIZ. There is no other way;

---

32. *Lethe*] in classical mythology, the river of forgetfulness.
33. *from*] here meaning "away from," as opposed to "from the depths of," which is Richard's use of the preposition.

Unless thou couldst put on some other shape,
And not be Richard that hath done all this.
K. RICH. Say that I did all this for love of her.
Q. ELIZ. Nay, then indeed she cannot choose but hate thee,
Having bought love with such a bloody spoil.
K. RICH. Look, what is done cannot be now amended:
Men shall deal unadvisedly sometimes,
Which after-hours give leisure to repent.
If I did take the kingdom from your sons,
To make amends, I'll give it to your daughter.
If I have kill'd the issue of your womb,
To quicken your increase, I will beget
Mine issue of your blood upon your daughter:
A grandam's name is little less in love
Than is the doting title of a mother;
They are as children but one step below,
Even of your mettle, of your very blood;
Of all one pain, save for a night of groans
Endured of her, for whom you bid like sorrow.[34]
Your children were vexation to your youth,
But mine shall be a comfort to your age.
The loss you have is but a son being king,
And by that loss your daughter is made queen.
I cannot make you what amends I would,
Therefore accept such kindness as I can.
Dorset your son, that with a fearful soul
Leads discontented steps in foreign soil,
This fair alliance quickly shall call home
To high promotions and great dignity:
The king, that calls your beauteous daughter wife,
Familiarly shall call thy Dorset brother;
Again shall you be mother to a king,
And all the ruins of distressful times
Repair'd with double riches of content.
What! we have many goodly days to see:
The liquid drops of tears that you have shed
Shall come again, transform'd to orient pearl,
Advantaging[35] their loan with interest
Of ten times double gain of happiness.
Go then, my mother, to thy daughter go;
Make bold her bashful years with your experience;
Prepare her ears to hear a wooer's tale;

34. *Endured . . . sorrow*] endured by her for whom you suffered like grief.
35. *Advantaging*] increasing.

Put in her tender heart the aspiring flame
Of golden sovereignty; acquaint the princess
With the sweet silent hours of marriage joys:
And when this arm of mine hath chastised
The petty rebel, dull-brain'd Buckingham,
Bound with triumphant garlands will I come,
And lead thy daughter to a conqueror's bed;
To whom I will retail my conquest won,
And she shall be sole victress, Cæsar's Cæsar.

Q. ELIZ. What were I best to say? her father's brother
Would be her lord? or shall I say, her uncle?
Or, he that slew her brothers and her uncles?
Under what title shall I woo for thee,
That God, the law, my honour and her love,
Can make seem pleasing to her tender years?

K. RICH. Infer fair England's peace by this alliance.

Q. ELIZ. Which she shall purchase with still lasting war.

K. RICH. Say that the king, which may command, entreats.

Q. ELIZ. That at her hands which the king's King forbids.

K. RICH. Say, she shall be a high and mighty queen.

Q. ELIZ. To wail the title, as her mother doth.

K. RICH. Say, I will love her everlastingly.

Q. ELIZ. But how long shall that title "ever" last?

K. RICH. Sweetly in force unto her fair life's end.

Q. ELIZ. But how long fairly shall her sweet life last?

K. RICH. So long as heaven and nature lengthens it.

Q. ELIZ. So long as hell and Richard likes of it.

K. RICH. Say, I, her sovereign, am her subject love.

Q. ELIZ. But she, your subject, loathes such sovereignty.

K. RICH. Be eloquent in my behalf to her.

Q. ELIZ. An honest tale speeds best being plainly told.

K. RICH. Then in plain terms tell her my loving tale.

Q. ELIZ. Plain and not honest is too harsh a style.

K. RICH. Your reasons are too shallow and too quick.

Q. ELIZ. O no, my reasons are too deep and dead;[36]
Too deep and dead, poor infants, in their grave.

K. RICH. Harp not on that string, madam; that is past.

Q. ELIZ. Harp on it still shall I till heart-strings break.

K. RICH. Now, by my George,[37] my garter, and my crown,—

Q. ELIZ. Profaned, dishonour'd, and the third usurp'd.

---

36. *quick . . . dead*] Richard uses "quick" in its ordinary sense of "rapid," "nimble." Queen Elizabeth quibblingly takes it in the sense of "alive," of which "dead" is the negative.
37. *George*] a jewel in the shape of a figure of England's patron saint, which formed part of the insignia of the Order of the Garter.

K. RICH. I swear—
Q. ELIZ. By nothing; for this is no oath:
The George, profaned, hath lost his holy honour;
The garter, blemish'd, pawn'd his knightly virtue;
The crown, usurp'd, disgraced his kingly glory.
If something thou wilt swear to be believed,
Swear then by something that thou hast not wrong'd.
K. RICH. Now, by the world—
Q. ELIZ. 'Tis full of thy foul wrongs.
K. RICH. My father's death—
Q. ELIZ. Thy life hath that dishonour'd.
K. RICH. Then, by myself—
Q. ELIZ. Thyself thyself misusest.
K. RICH. Why then, by God—
Q. ELIZ. God's wrong is most of all.
If thou hadst fear'd to break an oath by Him,
The unity the king thy brother made
Had not been broken, nor my brother slain:
If thou hadst fear'd to break an oath by Him,
The imperial metal, circling now thy brow,
Had graced the tender temples of my child,
And both the princes had been breathing here,
Which now, two tender playfellows for dust,
Thy broken faith hath made a prey for worms.
What canst thou swear by now?
K. RICH. The time to come.
Q. ELIZ. That thou hast wronged in the time o'erpast;
For I myself have many tears to wash
Hereafter time, for time past wrong'd by thee.
The children live, whose parents thou hast slaughter'd,
Ungovern'd youth, to wail it in their age;
The parents live, whose children thou hast butcher'd,
Old withered plants, to wail it with their age.
Swear not by time to come; for that thou hast
Misused ere used, by time misused o'erpast.[38]
K. RICH. As I intend to prosper and repent,
So thrive I in my dangerous attempt
Of hostile arms! myself myself confound!
Heaven and fortune bar me happy hours!
Day, yield me not thy light; nor, night, thy rest!
Be opposite all planets of good luck
To my proceedings, if, with pure heart's love,

38. *for that . . . o'erpast*] for thou hast misused the future before it was at your disposal, by virtue of the misuse to which you have put the time that is over and past.

Immaculate devotion, holy thoughts,
I tender not thy beauteous princely daughter!
In her consists my happiness and thine;
Without her, follows to this land and me,
To thee, herself, and many a Christian soul,
Death, desolation, ruin and decay:
It cannot be avoided but by this;
It will not be avoided but by this.
Therefore, good mother,—I must call you so—
Be the attorney of my love to her:
Plead what I will be, not what I have been;
Not my deserts, but what I will deserve:
Urge the necessity and state of times,
And be not peevish-fond[39] in great designs.
Q. ELIZ. Shall I be tempted of the devil thus?
K. RICH. Ay, if the devil tempt thee to do good.
Q. ELIZ. Shall I forget myself to be myself?
K. RICH. Ay, if yourself's remembrance wrong yourself.
Q. ELIZ. But thou didst kill my children.
K. RICH. But in your daughter's womb I bury them:
Where in that nest of spicery[40] they shall breed
Selves of themselves, to your recomforture.[41]
Q. ELIZ. Shall I go win my daughter to thy will?
K. RICH. And be a happy mother by the deed.
Q. ELIZ. I go. Write to me very shortly,
And you shall understand from me her mind.
K. RICH. Bear her my true love's kiss; and so, farewell.
[*Exit* QUEEN ELIZABETH.]
Relenting fool, and shallow, changing woman!

Enter RATCLIFF; CATESBY *following*

How now! what news?
RAT. My gracious sovereign, on the western coast
Rideth a puissant[42] navy; to the shore
Throng many doubtful hollow-hearted friends,
Unarm'd, and unresolved to beat them back:
'Tis thought that Richmond is their admiral;

39. *peevish-fond*] perversely stupid.
40. *nest of spicery*] an allusion to the fable of the phœnix, which was consumed every thousand years on a funeral pyre of spices on which the bird was at the same time reincarnated.
41. *recomforture*] comfort, consolation.
42. *puissant*] mighty, powerful.

And there they hull,[43] expecting but the aid
Of Buckingham to welcome them ashore.
K. RICH. Some light-foot friend post to the Duke of Norfolk:
Ratcliff, thyself, or Catesby; where is he?
CATE. Here, my lord.
K. RICH. Fly to the duke. [*To* RATCLIFF] Post thou to Salisbury:
When thou comest thither, — [*To* CATESBY] Dull unmindful villain,
Why stand'st thou still, and go'st not to the duke?
CATE. First, mighty sovereign, let me know your mind,
What from your grace I shall deliver to him.
K. RICH. O, true, good Catesby: bid him levy[44] straight
The greatest strength and power he can make,
And meet me presently[45] at Salisbury.
CATE. I go. [*Exit.*]
RAT. What is't your highness' pleasure I shall do
At Salisbury?
K. RICH. Why, what wouldst thou do there before I go?
RAT. Your highness told me I should post before.
K. RICH. My mind is changed, sir, my mind is changed.

Enter LORD STANLEY

How now, what news with you?
STAN. None good, my lord, to please you with the hearing;
Nor none so bad, but it may well be told.
K. RICH. Hoyday,[46] a riddle! neither good nor bad!
Why dost thou run so many mile about,
When thou mayst tell thy tale a nearer way?
Once more, what news?
STAN. Richmond is on the seas.
K. RICH. There let him sink, and be the seas on him!
White-liver'd runagate,[47] what doth he there?
STAN. I know not, mighty sovereign, but by guess.
K. RICH. Well, sir, as you guess, as you guess?
STAN. Stirr'd up by Dorset, Buckingham, and Ely,
He makes for England, there to claim the crown.
K. RICH. Is the chair empty? is the sword unsway'd?
Is the king dead? the empire unpossess'd?
What heir of York is there alive but we?
And who is England's king but great York's heir?

---

43. *hull*] to float, drift with sails furled.
44. *levy*] raise (an army).
45. *presently*] immediately.
46. *Hoyday*] an exclamation of contemptuous surprise.
47. *White-liver'd runagate*] cowardly runaway.

Then, tell me, what doth he upon the sea?
STAN. Unless for that, my liege, I cannot guess.
K. RICH. Unless for that he comes to be your liege,
You cannot guess wherefore the Welshman[48] comes.
Thou wilt revolt and fly to him, I fear.
STAN. No, mighty liege; therefore mistrust me not.
K. RICH. Where is thy power then to beat him back?
Where are thy tenants and thy followers?
Are they not now upon the western shore,
Safe-conducting the rebels from their ships?
STAN. No, my good lord, my friends are in the north.
K. RICH. Cold friends to Richard: what do they in the north,
When they should serve their sovereign in the west?
STAN. They have not been commanded, mighty sovereign:
Please it your majesty to give me leave,
I'll muster up my friends, and meet your grace
Where and what time your majesty shall please.
K. RICH. Ay, ay, thou wouldst be gone to join with Richmond:
I will not trust you, sir.
STAN. Most mighty sovereign,
You have no cause to hold my friendship doubtful:
I never was nor never will be false.
K. RICH. Well,
Go muster men; but, hear you, leave behind
Your son, George Stanley: look your faith be firm,
Or else his head's assurance is but frail.
STAN. So deal with him as I prove true to you. [*Exit.*]

Enter a Messenger

MESS. My gracious sovereign, now in Devonshire,
As I by friends am well advertised,[49]
Sir Edward Courtney, and the haughty prelate
Bishop of Exeter, his brother there,[50]
With many moe confederates, are in arms.

Enter another Messenger

SEC. MESS. My liege, in Kent, the Guildfords are in arms;

---

48. *the Welshman*] i.e., Richmond. Richmond's grandfather was Owen Tudor, who married the widow of Henry V, Catharine of France. Richmond was descended on the maternal side through the Beaufords to John of Gaunt (son of Edward III) and Catherine Swynford, from which connection he derived his claim to the throne.

49. *advertised*] informed, notified. The accents fall on the second and fourth syllables.

50. *brother there*] Peter Courtney, the Bishop of Exeter, was cousin, *not* brother, of Sir Edward Courtney.

And every hour more competitors[51]
Flock to their aid, and still their power increaseth.

Enter another Messenger

THIRD MESS. My lord, the army of the Duke of Buckingham—
K. RICH. Out on you, owls! nothing but songs of death?
[*He striketh him.*]
Take that, until thou bring me better news.
THIRD MESS. The news I have to tell your majesty
Is, that by sudden floods and fall of waters,
Buckingham's army is dispersed and scatter'd;
And he himself wander'd away alone,
No man knows whither.
K. RICH. I cry thee mercy:
There is my purse to cure that blow of thine.
Hath any well-advised friend proclaim'd
Reward to him that brings the traitor in?
THIRD MESS. Such proclamation hath been made, my liege.

Enter another Messenger

FOURTH MESS. Sir Thomas Lovel and Lord Marquess Dorset,
'Tis said, my liege, in Yorkshire are in arms.
Yet this good comfort bring I to your grace,
The Breton navy is dispersed by tempest:
Richmond, in Dorsetshire, sent out a boat
Unto the shore, to ask those on the banks
If they were his assistants, yea or no;
Who answer'd him, they came from Buckingham
Upon his party:[52] he, mistrusting them,
Hoised sail and made away for Brittany.
K. RICH. March on, march on, since we are up in arms;
If not to fight with foreign enemies,
Yet to beat down these rebels here at home.

Re-enter CATESBY

CATE. My liege, the Duke of Buckingham is taken;
That is the best news: that the Earl of Richmond
Is with a mighty power landed at Milford,
Is colder tidings, yet they must be told.
K. RICH. Away towards Salisbury! while we reason here,

51. *competitors*] confederates, associates.
52. *Upon his party*] to join his party, to take his side.

A royal battle might be won and lost:
Some one take order[53] Buckingham be brought
To Salisbury; the rest march on with me. [*Flourish. Exeunt.*]

SCENE V. *Lord Derby's House.*

Enter DERBY *and* SIR CHRISTOPHER URSWICK[1]

DER. Sir Christopher, tell Richmond this from me:
That in the sty of this most bloody boar
My son George Stanley is frank'd up[2] in hold:
If I revolt, off goes young George's head;
The fear of that withholds my present aid.
But, tell me, where is princely Richmond now?
CHRIS. At Pembroke, or at Ha'rford-west,[3] in Wales.
DER. What men of name resort to him?
CHRIS. Sir Walter Herbert, a renowned soldier;
Sir Gilbert Talbot, Sir William Stanley;
Oxford, redoubted Pembroke, Sir James Blunt,
And Rice ap Thomas, with a valiant crew,
And many moe of noble fame and worth:
And towards London they do bend their course,
If by the way they be not fought withal.
DER. Return unto thy lord; commend me to him:
Tell him the queen hath heartily consented
He shall espouse Elizabeth her daughter.
These letters will resolve[4] him of my mind.
Farewell. [*Exeunt.*]

53. *take order*] take measures, arrange.

1. *Sir Christopher Urswick*] a priest in the service of the Countess of Richmond, and employed by her in confidential communication with her son.
2. *frank'd up*] cooped up, confined.
3. *Ha'rford-west*] Haverfordwest, on the coast of Pembrokeshire.
4. *resolve*] inform, satisfy.

ACT V.

SCENE I. *Salisbury. An open place.*

Enter the Sheriff, *and* BUCKINGHAM, *with halberds, led to execution*

BUCK. Will not King Richard let me speak with him?
SHER. No, my good lord; therefore be patient.
BUCK. Hastings, and Edward's children, Rivers, Grey,
Holy King Henry, and thy fair son Edward,
Vaughan, and all that have miscarried
By underhand corrupted foul injustice,
If that your moody discontented souls
Do through the clouds behold this present hour,
Even for revenge mock my destruction!
This is All-Souls' day,[1] fellows, is it not?
SHER. It is, my lord.
BUCK. Why, then All-Souls' day is my body's doomsday.
This is the day that, in King Edward's time,
I wish'd might fall on me when I was found
False to his children or his wife's allies;
This is the day wherein I wish'd to fall
By the false faith of him I trusted most;
This, this All-Souls' day to my fearful soul
Is the determined respite of my wrongs:[2]
That high All-seer that I dallied with
Hath turn'd my feigned prayer on my head,
And given in earnest what I begg'd in jest.
Thus doth he force the swords of wicked men
To turn their own points on their masters' bosoms:
Now Margaret's curse is fallen upon my head;
"When he," quoth she, "shall split thy heart with sorrow,
Remember Margaret was a prophetess."
Come, sirs, convey me to the block of shame;
Wrong hath but wrong, and blame the due of blame. [*Exeunt.*]

---

1. *All-Souls' day*] November 2 was the festival day appointed by the Roman Catholic Church in honor of the souls of all the dead, and was believed to be a time when spirits communicated with the living.
2. *determined . . . wrongs*] the term or close of the period to which the punishment of my offences was postponed.

SCENE II. *The Camp near Tamworth.*

Enter RICHMOND, OXFORD, BLUNT, HERBERT, *and others, with drum and colours*

RICHM. Fellows in arms, and my most loving friends,
Bruised underneath the yoke of tyranny,
Thus far into the bowels of the land
Have we march'd on without impediment;
And here receive we from our father Stanley
Lines of fair comfort and encouragement.
The wretched, bloody, and usurping boar,
That spoil'd your summer fields and fruitful vines,
Swills your warm blood like wash,[1] and makes his trough
In your embowell'd[2] bosoms, this foul swine
Lies[3] now even in the centre of this isle,
Near to the town of Leicester, as we learn:
From Tamworth thither is but one day's march.
In God's name, cheerly on, courageous friends,
To reap the harvest of perpetual peace
By this one bloody trial of sharp war.
OXF. Every man's conscience is a thousand swords,
To fight against that bloody homicide.
HERB. I doubt not but his friends will fly to us.
BLUNT. He hath no friends but who are friends for fear,
Which in his greatest need will shrink from him.
RICHM. All for our vantage. Then, in God's name, march:
True hope is swift, and flies with swallow's wings;
Kings it makes gods, and meaner creatures kings. [*Exeunt.*]

1. *Swills . . . like wash*] drinks . . . as a boar sucks up hogwash.
2. *embowell'd*] ripped up, disembowelled.
3. *Lies*] sojourns.

SCENE III. *Bosworth Field.*

Enter KING RICHARD *in arms with* NORFOLK, *the* EARL OF SURREY, *and others*

K. RICH. Here pitch our tents, even here in Bosworth field.
My Lord of Surrey, why look you so sad?
SUR. My heart is ten times lighter than my looks.
K. RICH. My Lord of Norfolk, —
NOR. Here, most gracious liege.
K. RICH. Norfolk, we must have knocks; ha! must we not?
NOR. We must both give and take, my gracious lord.
K. RICH. Up with my tent there! here will I lie to-night:
But where to-morrow? Well, all's one for that.
Who hath descried the number of the foe?
NOR. Six or seven thousand is their utmost power.
K. RICH. Why, our battalion trebles that account:
Besides, the king's name is a tower of strength,
Which they upon the adverse party want.[1]
Up with my tent there! Valiant gentlemen,
Let us survey the vantage of the field;
Call for some men of sound direction:[2]
Let's want no discipline, make no delay;
For, lords, to-morrow is a busy day. [*Exeunt.*]

Enter, on the other side of the field, RICHMOND, SIR WILLIAM BRANDON, OXFORD, *and others. Some of the* Soldiers *pitch Richmond's tent*

RICHM. The weary sun hath made a golden set,
And by the bright track of his fiery car
Gives signal of a goodly day to-morrow.
Sir William Brandon, you shall bear my standard.
Give me some ink and paper in my tent:
I'll draw the form and model of our battle,
Limit each leader to his several charge,
And part in just proportion our small strength.
My Lord of Oxford, you, Sir William Brandon,
And you, Sir Walter Herbert, stay with me.
The Earl of Pembroke keeps[3] his regiment:

1. *want*] lack.
2. *sound direction*] sound judgment, tried skill in leadership.
3. *keeps*] stays with.

Good Captain Blunt, bear my good-night to him,
And by the second hour in the morning
Desire the earl to see me in my tent:
Yet one thing more, good Blunt, before thou go'st,
Where is Lord Stanley quarter'd, dost thou know?
BLUNT. Unless I have mista'en his colours much,
Which well I am assured I have not done,
His regiment lies half a mile at least
South from the mighty power of the king.
RICHM. If without peril it be possible,
Good Captain Blunt, bear my good-night to him,
And give him from me this most needful scroll.
BLUNT. Upon my life, my lord, I'll undertake it;
And so, God give you quiet rest to-night!
RICHM. Good night, good Captain Blunt. Come, gentlemen,
Let us consult upon to-morrow's business:
In to our tent! the air is raw and cold.
[*They withdraw into the tent.*]

Enter, to his tent, KING RICHARD, NORFOLK, RATCLIFF, CATESBY, *and others*

K. RICH. What is't o'clock?
CATE. It's supper-time, my lord;
It's nine o'clock.
K. RICH. I will not sup to-night.
Give me some ink and paper.
What, is my beaver[4] easier[5] than it was!
And all my armour laid into my tent?
CATE. It is, my liege; and all things are in readiness.
K. RICH. Good Norfolk, hie thee to thy charge;
Use careful watch, choose trusty sentinels.
NOR. I go, my lord.
K. RICH. Stir with the lark to-morrow, gentle Norfolk. [*Exit.*]
NOR. I warrant you, my lord.
K. RICH. Catesby!
CATE. My lord?
K. RICH. Send out a pursuivant at arms
To Stanley's regiment; bid him bring his power
Before sunrising, lest his son George fall
Into the blind cave of eternal night. [*Exit* CATESBY.]
Fill me a bowl of wine. Give me a watch.[6]

4. *beaver*] properly the part of the helmet that could be drawn up and down over the face, but often used for the helmet itself.
5. *easier*] more loosely fitting.
6. *watch*] watchlight, candle.

Saddle white Surrey[7] for the field to-morrow.
Look that my staves[8] be sound, and not too heavy.
Ratcliff!

RAT. My lord?

K. RICH. Saw'st thou the melancholy Lord Northumberland?

RAT. Thomas the Earl of Surrey, and himself,
Much about cock-shut time,[9] from troop to troop
Went through the army, cheering up the soldiers.

K. RICH. So, I am satisfied. Give me a bowl of wine:
I have not that alacrity of spirit,
Nor cheer of mind, that I was wont to have.
Set it down. Is ink and paper ready?

RAT. It is, my lord.

K. RICH. Bid my guard watch. Leave me. Ratcliff,
About the mid of night come to my tent,
And help to arm me. Leave me, I say.

[*Exeunt* RATCLIFF *and the other attendants.*]

Enter DERBY *to* RICHMOND *in his tent, Lords and others attending*

DER. Fortune and victory sit on thy helm!

RICHM. All comfort that the dark night can afford
Be to thy person, noble father-in-law!
Tell me, how fares our loving mother?

DER. I, by attorney,[10] bless thee from thy mother,
Who prays continually for Richmond's good:
So much for that. The silent hours steal on,
And flaky darkness[11] breaks within the east.
In brief, for so the season bids us be,
Prepare thy battle early in the morning,
And put thy fortune to the arbitrement[12]
Of bloody strokes and mortal-staring[13] war.
I, as I may—that which I would I cannot,—
With best advantage will deceive the time,
And aid thee in this doubtful shock of arms:
But on thy side I may not be too forward,
Lest, being seen, thy brother, tender George,
Be executed in his father's sight.

---

7. *white Surrey*] According to historical sources, Richard was "mounted on a great white courser." The horse's name was presumably Shakespeare's invention.
8. *staves*] the wooden shafts of the lances.
9. *cock-shut time*] twilight.
10. *by attorney*] by deputy, messenger.
11. *flaky darkness*] darkness streaked with light.
12. *arbitrement*] decision.
13. *mortal-staring*] looking with deadly glance.

Farewell: the leisure[14] and the fearful time
Cuts off the ceremonious vows of love,
And ample interchange of sweet discourse,
Which so long sunder'd friends should dwell upon:
God give us leisure for these rites of love!
Once more, adieu: be valiant, and speed well!

RICHM. Good lords, conduct him to his regiment:
I'll strive, with troubled thoughts, to take a nap,
Lest leaden slumber peise[15] me down to-morrow,
When I should mount with wings of victory:
Once more, good night, kind lords and gentlemen.

[*Exeunt all but* RICHMOND.]

O Thou, whose captain I account myself,
Look on my forces with a gracious eye;
Put in their hands thy bruising irons of wrath,
That they may crush down with a heavy fall
The usurping helmets of our adversaries!
Make us thy ministers of chastisement,
That we may praise thee in the victory!
To thee I do commend my watchful soul,
Ere I let fall the windows of mine eyes:
Sleeping and waking, O, defend me still! [*Sleeps.*]

Enter the Ghost of PRINCE EDWARD, *son to* HENRY THE SIXTH

GHOST. [*To* RICHARD] Let me sit heavy on thy soul to-morrow!
Think, how thou stab'dst me in my prime of youth
At Tewksbury: despair, therefore, and die!
[*To* RICHMOND] Be cheerful, Richmond; for the wronged souls
Of butcher'd princes fight in thy behalf:
King Henry's issue, Richmond, comforts thee.

Enter the Ghost of HENRY THE SIXTH

GHOST. [*To* RICHARD] When I was mortal, my anointed body
By thee was punched full of deadly holes:
Think on the Tower and me: despair, and die!
Harry the Sixth bids thee despair and die!
[*To* RICHMOND] Virtuous and holy, be thou conqueror!
Harry, that prophesied thou shouldst be king,
Doth comfort thee in thy sleep: live, and flourish!

Enter the Ghost of CLARENCE

GHOST. [*To* RICHARD] Let me sit heavy on thy soul to-morrow!

14. *leisure*] time at our free disposal.
15. *peise*] weigh.

I, that was wash'd to death with fulsome wine,[16]
Poor Clarence, by thy guile betray'd to death.
To-morrow in the battle think on me,
And fall thy edgeless sword: despair, and die!
[*To* RICHMOND] Thou offspring of the house of Lancaster,
The wronged heirs of York do pray for thee:
Good angels guard thy battle! live, and flourish!

Enter the Ghosts of RIVERS, GREY, *and* VAUGHAN

GHOST OF R. [*To* RICHARD] Let me sit heavy on thy soul to-morrow,
Rivers, that died at Pomfret! despair, and die!
GHOST OF G. [*To* RICHARD] Think upon Grey, and let thy soul despair!
GHOST OF V. [*To* RICHARD] Think upon Vaughan, and, with guilty fear,
Let fall thy lance: despair, and die!
ALL. [*To* RICHMOND] Awake, and think our wrongs in Richard's bosom
Will conquer him! awake, and win the day!

Enter the Ghost of HASTINGS

GHOST. [*To* RICHARD] Bloody and guilty, guiltily awake,
And in a bloody battle end thy days!
Think on Lord Hastings: despair, and die!
[*To* RICHMOND] Quiet untroubled soul, awake, awake!
Arm, fight, and conquer, for fair England's sake!

Enter the Ghosts of the two young Princes

GHOSTS. [*To* RICHARD] Dream on thy cousins smothered in the Tower:
Let us be lead within thy bosom, Richard,
And weigh thee down to ruin, shame, and death!
Thy nephews' souls bid thee despair and die!
[*To* RICHMOND] Sleep, Richmond, sleep in peace, and wake in joy;
Good angels guard thee from the boar's annoy![17]
Live, and beget a happy race of kings!
Edward's unhappy sons do bid thee flourish.

Enter the Ghost of LADY ANNE *his wife*

GHOST. [*To* RICHARD] Richard, thy wife, that wretched Anne thy wife,
That never slept a quiet hour with thee,
Now fills thy sleep with perturbations:
To-morrow in the battle think on me,
And fall thy edgeless sword: despair, and die!
[*To* RICHMOND] Thou quiet soul, sleep thou a quiet sleep:

16. *fulsome wine*] abundance or surfeit of wine.
17. *boar's annoy*] injury from the boar, i.e. Richard.

Dream of success and happy victory!
Thy adversary's wife doth pray for thee.

Enter the Ghost of BUCKINGHAM

GHOST. [*To* RICHARD] The first was I that help'd thee to the crown;
The last was I that felt thy tyranny:
O, in the battle think on Buckingham,
And die in terror of thy guiltiness!
Dream on, dream on, of bloody deeds and death:
Fainting, despair; despairing, yield thy breath!
[*To* RICHMOND] I died for hope[18] ere I could lend thee aid:
But cheer thy heart, and be thou not dismay'd:
God and good angels fight on Richmond's side;
And Richard falls in height of all his pride.
[*The Ghosts vanish.* KING RICHARD *starts out of his dream.*]

K. RICH. Give me another horse: bind up my wounds.
Have mercy, Jesu! — Soft! I did but dream.
O coward conscience, how dost thou afflict me!
The lights burn blue.[19] It is now dead midnight.
Cold fearful drops stand on my trembling flesh.
What do I fear? myself? there's none else by:
Richard loves Richard; that is, I am I.
Is there a murderer here? No. Yes, I am:
Then fly. What, from myself? Great reason why:
Lest I revenge. What, myself upon myself?
Alack, I love myself. Wherefore? for any good
That I myself have done unto myself?
O, no! alas, I rather hate myself
For hateful deeds committed by myself!
I am a villain: yet I lie, I am not.
Fool, of thyself speak well: fool, do not flatter.
My conscience hath a thousand several tongues,
And every tongue brings in a several tale,
And every tale condemns me for a villain.
Perjury, perjury, in the high'st degree;
Murder, stern murder, in the direst degree;
All several sins, all used in each degree,
Throng to the bar,[20] crying all "Guilty! guilty!"
I shall despair. There is no creature loves me;
And if I die, no soul will pity me:
Nay, wherefore should they, since that I myself

---

18. *for hope*] for lack of hope, in despair.
19. *lights burn blue*] thought to be the usual effect of ghostly apparitions.
20. *bar*] the railing at which prisoners stand when on trial.

Find in myself no pity to myself?
Methought the souls of all that I had murder'd
Came to my tent, and every one did threat
To-morrow's vengeance on the head of Richard.

Enter RATCLIFF

RAT. My lord!
K. RICH. 'Zounds! who is there?
RAT. Ratcliff, my lord; 'tis I. The early village-cock
Hath twice done salutation to the morn;
Your friends are up, and buckle on their armour.
K. RICH. O Ratcliff, I have dream'd a fearful dream!
What thinkest thou, will our friends prove all true?
RAT. No doubt, my lord.
K. RICH. O Ratcliff, I fear, I fear,—
RAT. Nay, good my lord, be not afraid of shadows.
K. RICH. By the apostle Paul, shadows to-night
Have struck more terror to the soul of Richard,
Than can the substance of ten thousand soldiers
Armed in proof,[21] and led by shallow Richmond.
It is not yet near day. Come, go with me;
Under our tents I'll play the eaves-dropper,
To see if any mean to shrink from me. [*Exeunt.*]

Enter the Lords *to* RICHMOND, *sitting in his tent*

LORDS. Good morrow, Richmond!
RICHM. Cry mercy, lords and watchful gentlemen,
That you have ta'en a tardy sluggard here.
LORDS. How have you slept, my lord?
RICHM. The sweetest sleep, and fairest-boding dreams
That ever enter'd in a drowsy head,
Have I since your departure had, my lords.
Methought their souls, whose bodies Richard murder'd,
Came to my tent, and cried on[22] victory:
I promise you, my soul is very jocund
In the remembrance of so fair a dream.
How far into the morning is it, lords?
LORDS. Upon the stroke of four.
RICHM. Why, then 'tis time to arm and give direction.

---

21. *Armed in proof*] equipped in proved, tested armour.
22. *cried on*] called out.

His oration to his soldiers

More than I have said, loving countrymen,
The leisure and enforcement of the time
Forbids to dwell upon: yet remember this,
God and our good cause fight upon our side;
The prayers of holy saints and wronged souls,
Like high-rear'd bulwarks, stand before our faces.
Richard except, those whom we fight against
Had rather have us win than him they follow:
For what is he they follow? truly, gentlemen,
A bloody tyrant and a homicide;
One raised in blood, and one in blood establish'd;
One that made means to come by what he hath,
And slaughter'd those that were the means to help him;
A base foul stone, made precious by the foil
Of England's chair, where he is falsely set;[23]
One that hath ever been God's enemy:
Then, if you fight against God's enemy,
God will in justice ward you as his soldiers;
If you do sweat to put a tyrant down,
You sleep in peace, the tyrant being slain;
If you do fight against your country's foes,
Your country's fat[24] shall pay your pains the hire;
If you do fight in safeguard of your wives,
Your wives shall welcome home the conquerors;
If you do free your children from the sword,
Your children's children quit[25] it in your age.
Then, in the name of God and all these rights,
Advance your standards, draw your willing swords.
For me, the ransom of my bold attempt[26]
Shall be this cold corpse on the earth's cold face;
But if I thrive, the gain of my attempt
The least of you shall share his part thereof.
Sound drums and trumpets boldly and cheerfully;
God and Saint George! Richmond and victory! [*Exeunt.*]

Re-enter KING RICHARD, RATCLIFF, *Attendants and Forces*

K. RICH. What said Northumberland as touching Richmond?

23. *chair . . . set*] throne . . . set, as in a jewel.
24. *fat*] wealth.
25. *quit*] requite.
26. *the ransom . . . attempt*] the fine due from me in requital of my boldness.

RAT. That he was never trained up in arms.
K. RICH. He said the truth: and what said Surrey, then?
RAT. He smiled and said "The better for our purpose."
K. RICH. He was in the right; and so indeed it is.
[*The clock striketh.*]
Tell the clock there. Give me a calendar.
Who saw the sun to-day?
RAT. Not I, my lord.
K. RICH. Then he disdains to shine; for by the book[27]
He should have braved[28] the east an hour ago:
A black day will it be to somebody.
Ratcliff!
RAT. My lord?
K. RICH. The sun will not be seen to-day;
The sky doth frown and lour upon our army.
I would these dewy tears were from the ground.
Not shine to-day! Why, what is that to me
More than to Richmond? for the selfsame heaven
That frowns on me looks sadly upon him.

Re-enter NORFOLK

NOR. Arm, arm, my lord; the foe vaunts in the field.
K. RICH. Come, bustle, bustle. Caparison my horse.
Call up Lord Stanley, bid him bring his power:
I will lead forth my soldiers to the plain,
And thus my battle shall be ordered:
My foreward[29] shall be drawn out all in length,
Consisting equally of horse and foot;
Our archers shall be placed in the midst:
John Duke of Norfolk, Thomas Earl of Surrey,
Shall have the leading of this foot and horse.
They thus directed, we will follow
In the main battle, whose puissance[30] on either side
Shall be well winged with our chiefest horse.
This, and Saint George to boot![31] What think'st thou, Norfolk?
NOR. A good direction, warlike sovereign.
This found I on my tent this morning.

27. *book*] almanac.
28. *braved*] made splendid, glorified.
29. *foreward*] vanguard.
30. *puissance*] armed force.
31. *This, and Saint George to boot!*] this order of battle and the favour of our patron saint in addition!

[*He sheweth him a paper.*]

K. RICH. [*Reads*] "Jockey of Norfolk, be not so bold,
For Dickon[32] thy master is bought and sold."
A thing devised by the enemy.
Go, gentlemen, every man unto his charge:
Let not our babbling dreams affright our souls:
Conscience is but a word that cowards use,
Devised at first to keep the strong in awe:
Our strong arms be our conscience, swords our law.
March on, join bravely, let us to't pell-mell;
If not to heaven, then hand in hand to hell.

His oration to his Army

What shall I say more than I have inferr'd?[33]
Remember whom you are to cope withal;
A sort[34] of vagabonds, rascals, and runaways,
A scum of Bretons, and base lackey peasants,
Whom their o'er-cloyed country vomits forth
To desperate ventures and assured destruction.
You sleeping safe, they bring to you unrest;
You having lands and blest with beauteous wives,
They would restrain[35] the one, distain the other.
And who doth lead them but a paltry fellow,
Long kept in Bretagne at our mother's cost?[36]
A milk-sop, one that never in his life
Felt so much cold as over shoes in snow?
Let's whip these stragglers o'er the seas again,
Lash hence these overweening rags of France,
These famish'd beggars, weary of their lives,
Who, but for dreaming on this fond exploit,
For want of means, poor rats, had hang'd themselves:
If we be conquer'd, let men conquer us,
And not these bastard Bretons, whom our fathers

32. *Dickon*] a colloquial form of Richard. "Bought and sold" means "betrayed."
33. *inferr'd*] alleged.
34. *sort*] set, company.
35. *restrain*] put restraint on, withhold from lawful owners.
36. *our mother's*] Shakespeare is following Richard's speech as it appears in the *second* edition of Holinshed's *Chronicle*, where Richmond is said to have been "brought up by *my moothers* meanes . . . in the court of Francis, Duke of Britaine." Hall's *Chronicle* and the *first* edition of Holinshed read *brother's* for *mother's*. There is little doubt that *brother's* is the right reading. Richard's brother, King Edward IV, had arranged with the Duke of Brittany for Richmond to reside at his court.

Have in their own land beaten, bobb'd,[37] and thump'd,
And in record left them the heirs of shame.
Shall these enjoy our lands? lie with our wives?
Ravish our daughters? [*Drum afar off.*] Hark! I hear their drum.
Fight, gentlemen of England! fight, bold yeomen!
Draw, archers, draw your arrows to the head!
Spur your proud horses hard, and ride in blood;
Amaze the welkin[38] with your broken staves!

Enter a Messenger

What says Lord Stanley? will he bring his power?[39]
MESS. My lord, he doth deny to come.
K. RICH. Off with his son George's head!
NOR. My lord, the enemy is past the marsh:
After the battle let George Stanley die.
K. RICH. A thousand hearts are great within my bosom:
Advance our standards, set upon our foes;
Our ancient word of courage, fair Saint George,
Inspire us with the spleen of fiery dragons!
Upon them! Victory sits on our helms. [*Exeunt.*]

SCENE IV. *Another Part of the Field.*

Alarum: excursions. Enter NORFOLK *and forces fighting; to him* CATESBY

CATE. Rescue, my Lord of Norfolk, rescue, rescue!
The king enacts more wonders than a man,
Daring an opposite[1] to every danger:
His horse is slain, and all on foot he fights,
Seeking for Richmond in the throat of death.
Rescue, fair lord, or else the day is lost!

Alarums. Enter KING RICHARD

K. RICH. A horse! a horse! my kingdom for a horse!
CATE. Withdraw, my lord; I'll help you to a horse.
K. RICH. Slave, I have set my life upon a cast,

37. *bobb'd*] buffeted.
38. *the welkin*] the skies.
39. *power*] force, army.

1. *Daring an opposite*] venturing to oppose himself.

And I will stand the hazard of the die.
I think there be six Richmonds in the field;
Five have I slain to-day instead of him.
A horse! a horse! my kingdom for a horse! [*Exeunt.*]

SCENE V. *Another Part of the Field.*

Alarum. Enter RICHARD *and* RICHMOND; *they fight.* RICHARD *is slain. Retreat and flourish. Re-enter* RICHMOND, DERBY *bearing the crown, with divers other Lords*

RICHM. God and your arms be praised, victorious friends!
The day is ours; the bloody dog is dead.
DER. Courageous Richmond, well hast thou acquit thee.
Lo, here, this long usurped royalty
From the dead temples of this bloody wretch
Have I pluck'd off, to grace thy brows withal:
Wear it, enjoy it, and make much of it.
RICHM. Great God of heaven, say amen to all!
But, tell me, is young George Stanley living?
DER. He is, my lord, and safe in Leicester town;
Whither, if it please you, we may now withdraw us.
RICHM. What men of name are slain on either side?
DER. John Duke of Norfolk, Walter Lord Ferrers, Sir Robert Brakenbury, and Sir William Brandon.
RICH. Inter their bodies as becomes their births:
Proclaim a pardon to the soldiers fled,
That in submission will return to us:
And then, as we have ta'en the sacrament,
We will unite the white rose and the red.
Smile heaven upon this fair conjunction,
That long have frown'd upon their enmity!
What traitor hears me, and says not amen?
England hath long been mad, and scarr'd herself;
The brother blindly shed the brother's blood,
The father rashly slaughter'd his own son,
The son, compell'd, been butcher to the sire:
All this divided York and Lancaster,
Divided in their dire division,
O, now let Richmond and Elizabeth,

The true succeeders of each royal house,
By God's fair ordinance conjoin together!
And let their heirs, God, if thy will be so,
Enrich the time to come with smooth-faced peace,
With smiling plenty and fair prosperous days!
Abate the edge[1] of traitors, gracious Lord,
That would reduce[2] these bloody days again,
And make poor England weep in streams of blood!
Let them not live to taste this land's increase,
That would with treason wound this fair land's peace!
Now civil wounds are stopp'd, peace lives again:
That she may long live here, God say amen! [*Exeunt.*]

---

1. *Abate the edge*] dull the force or spirit.
2. *reduce*] bring back.